Deborah,
Live your
every single
XOXO "Mia Kay"

MW01591834

Marry Me For Money

MIA
KAYLA

Marry Me for Money
Copyright © 2014 by Mia Kayla
All rights reserved.

No part of this book may be reproduced or transmitted in any form or by any means, electronic or mechanical, including photocopying, recording, or by any information storage and retrieval system without the written permission of the author, except for the use of brief quotations in a book review

This book is a work of fiction. Names, characters, places, and incidents either are products of the author's imagination or are used fictitiously. Any resemblance to actual persons, living or dead, events, or locales is entirely coincidental.

Cover Designer
Sarah Hansen, Okay Creations

Copy Editor
Jovana Shirley, Unforeseen Editing

Content Editor and Proof Editor
Kayla Robichaux and Becky Johnson, Hot Tree Editing

Interior Design and Formatting
Christine Borgford, Perfectly Publishable

Dedication

To Marvin, my very own happily-ever-after. You're my book boyfriend come to life and I can't wait to see how our story unfolds.

Prologue

THE WOMAN WAS beautiful. She looked like a super-model ready to walk the runway. The blackest of black eyelashes swept upward, accenting the depths of her emerald eyes. Curls of mahogany sat on top of her head while the apple of her cheeks were highlighted with a slight pink as if the sun had kissed her.

I should have been excited. I should have been anxious.

But as my heartbeat thrashed in my ears, all I felt was dread.

I sat on the stool, staring at the girl in the mirror. I wondered who this girl was. I wondered where the old girl had gone and how I could get her back. The problem was I couldn't. The lie was so deep, the charade so long that there was nowhere else to go, but to move forward.

It was an out-of-body experience as the chaos of the circus around me was happening. I hardly noticed the woman in front of me as she swished her little brush of pink gloss on my pouty lips.

Everybody was getting ready for the big day.

My big day.

Four photographers were scattered around the room, catching every moment and every detail from the shoes to the invitation to the flowers.

Orchids.

Orchids didn't give off a scent like every other flower. Too much water would drown them. Not enough sunlight would kill them. They were useless and high maintenance.

So, when the florist had asked me what kind of flowers I would like for my bouquet, I'd said, "Orchids."

It was the flower I despised the most. It wasn't because of its lack of beauty or its uselessness, but I didn't want anything that I would pick for my real day.

The photographers moved to the king-sized bed, and they snapped pictures of the regal designer wedding gown. This was another thing I never would have picked for myself. I remembered my last fitting. I had barely squeezed into the strapless couture dress. I would never choose a dress that I couldn't walk, dance, or eat in. I hated it, and that was the reason I'd picked it.

My stomach growled from starvation. I had no appetite the night before, and today Kendy, my maid of honor, wouldn't allow me to eat. It was so unlike her. I guessed it was for my benefit because I could barely fit into my dress. Either way, my stomach was eating itself because it had nothing else to feed off of.

The time went by slowly as if it were dragging on purpose to punish me for living the biggest lie of my life. Everyone always said their wedding day had flown by. This day was killing me, killing me softly and slowly.

All I wanted was for it to be over, but the day had just begun.

I took a deep breath and closed my eyes. *If I can only get through this day…this one day…*

I just needed to get through today.

Chapter One

FOUR MONTHS EARLIER

FINANCIAL STATE BANK stood in the heart of the financial district in downtown Chicago. Directly in front of my new office building, I peered up at the magnificent architectural masterpiece of glass windows encompassing all seventy-five floors and smiled the biggest smile ever. This was exactly where I wanted to be. All those late nights spent studying in the library and working random jobs to pay for school had gotten me to this point and in front of this big, bad bank.

I took the deepest breath of my life, made my way through the revolving doors, and stopped at the security desk. I took in my surroundings. Men and women, all dressed in their pressed dark suits, emerged through the revolving doors, most with a Starbucks coffee in hand. I straightened my skirt, pulled at my navy suit jacket, and exhaled a sigh of relief.

I made it. I'm meant to be here. Finally, somewhere I fit right in.

"YOU'LL HAVE A lot of team meetings next week to discuss the pipeline and also online training. I'll put everything in your calendar, so you'll know." Renee, my new manager, stepped from the elevator and I followed behind her.

Low cubicles spanned the length of the office area. It was already eight fifteen in the morning, and everyone was busy at their desks, typing away on their computers. I made a mental note to make it to work earlier. I wanted to be one of the first people in the office, not the trailing last that shouted slacker. I had never been one, and I wasn't going to start now.

A grin was fixed on my face, and I could feel my cheeks hurting already.

"This place is intense, but you'll like it here. We work hard, and you young people play hard," Renee said.

My smile widened and inside I was singing at the top of my lungs.

"I'm excited," I told her, not like she couldn't already tell.

Everyone's eyes followed me as I walked behind Renee. I met their stares and smiled slightly toward them, but I kept my ear-to-ear cheeky grin to myself. I didn't want to scare people away.

Renee introduced me to the group—my team. "Everyone, this is Bethany Casse, our new underwriter. She's a fresh graduate from Indiana State University."

One by one, my team stood from the seats in their cubicles to introduce themselves. I shook each person's hand firmly and learned that my team consisted of bankers on the sales team and another underwriter, like myself. Where the bankers were in the business to wine and dine and get more clients, underwriters were in the business to assess the risk of the deals the bankers made.

"Welcome, Beth." Jim, the head banker on my team, shook my hand before immediately turning to Renee. "Renee, are you available tomorrow? Plack Industries has a request on the table."

He'd barely taken notice of me, and my smile faltered as he moved past me into Renee's line of sight.

Renee straightened her back to stand a little taller and her gaze flicked upward. "Thanks for letting me know in advance," she said, sarcasm etched in her tone. "No, I'm not available. I already committed to going with another banker on a client call tomorrow."

He scratched his head. I noticed his receding reddish-brown hair matched the light freckles on his face.

"I need an underwriter there. This deal needs to move quickly," he prompted, placing his hand on his hip.

Renee crossed her arms over her chest. I could see annoyance written all over her face.

"Well then, take Beth. Plack Industries is in her portfolio now. She's the underwriter on that account."

I shifted from one foot to the other, glancing back and forth between them.

Jim offered me a fake small smile before turning back to Renee. "Plack Industries is one of my biggest clients. I want you there. I need someone experienced."

"Beth's new, but she can handle it. She interned here before. She knows our systems and how to draw up a credit workup."

It surprised me when Renee rolled her eyes in front of him, and suddenly, I wanted to hide from the tension emanating in the room.

"Renee," Jim pleaded.

Renee ignored his plea and pivoted to a sweet-looking brunette typing away on her computer. "Caroline, show Beth where the file room is. Beth, study Plack Industries and their latest financial statements, and come up with your questions for the company tomorrow. If you need help, ask Caroline. I'd like to see the proposal on my desk in two days."

My face must have registered shock because a moment later, Renee placed her hand on my shoulder.

"Beth, don't worry. You will do fine." Her eyes softened before she marched straight past Jim.

He stomped back to his desk, muttering something under his breath.

I blinked a couple of times, looking toward Renee's retreating back. I was surprised that I was being thrown into work after being here for less than twenty minutes. All the while, I was also making lists in my head of what I needed to do before tomorrow's meeting.

"Hi, neighbor. I'm Caroline."

I turned to the young woman sitting right next to my new desk.

Her smile was brief but genuine. "Jim can be a prick. He'll always try to do the deal. Your job is to make sure that we don't lose money while he's doing it. I'll brief you during lunch. So, you're a fresh grad, huh?"

I studied her cute bob cut to her petite frame to her natural pouty lips. "Yeah, this is my first job out of college," I said, glad that my neighbor exuded friendliness.

What nobody here knew was that although this was my first job out of college, I'd started working when I was thirteen. I'd had random jobs, like babysitting, bagging groceries, and waitressing. Working had never been an option. It had been a necessity.

As I sat at my desk, I realized that all those late-night vanilla lattes, study groups, and staying in while everyone else had partied had led me to this point. My hand brushed against my nameplate.

BETHANY CASSE

UNDERWRITER

And I smiled again.

SITTING AT A table in the cafeteria during my lunch hour with Caroline, I watched the women in their hip-hugging suits and high heels, carrying their designer bags, saunter past us. Chicago was a fast-paced city—well, fast-paced compared to where I'd come from.

Caroline continued to talk about her family and her college boyfriend, whom she had been dating for years. I kept silent, listening and smiling, as she continued. Midway through my turkey sandwich, I was chewing a mouthful of food when a tall male knocked on our table, breaking our conversation and causing me to look up.

"Hey, Caroline. I'm glad you're showing Miss New Girl around." He turned to me and waved.

When our eyes caught, I noticed that his eyes were the lightest shade of blue.

"Hi, I'm Brian," he said, sporting a boyish grin. "I hope Caroline is being nice to you."

The specimen in front of me was all-American. He looked like a spokesmodel for the bank with his broad shoulders filling out his gray pinstriped professional suit.

"Hi," I said, cheeks full of food. I put down my sandwich and wiped the crumbs from my fingers. "I'm Beth."

I swallowed the remnants of my lunch before taking his hand. His hand lingered on mine a second longer than comfortable, and when he released me, I picked up my drink and took a sip, giving my hands something else to do.

"I hope you'll like it here, Beth," he said. "And you tell me if Caroline is being mean to you. I know her boss." He winked.

The color of his eyes reminded me of a clear summer sky, light with flecks of different shades of blue reflected in his irises.

"You should join us, Brian," Caroline said, bringing me back to reality. She kicked out the chair next to her, offering the empty seat between us. He looked behind him toward a group of guys congregated at another table.

"Ladies, I totally would, but I've made plans already," he said as our eyes caught. "I'll definitely take you up on that offer soon. Nice meeting you, Beth." He gave me a small smile before he turned away.

I watched as he continued to walk through the cafeteria until he sat by the other men.

"Holy hotness. Wow, right?" Caroline said, all wide-eyed.

I shrugged shyly and peered at him through my lashes.

"He's not only good-looking, but he's really smart. Brian started when I did, but he's moved up the chain, and management likes him. He went to the University of Wisconsin and I want to say that he even got a scholarship for football." She beamed dreamily in his direction and then shook herself out of her reverie. "If I wasn't almost engaged, I would have to hit on that fine masterpiece."

I cast her a look, and at that, we both laughed.

THAT EVENING, BACK in my one-bedroom apartment, I glanced at the neutral walls surrounding me before ducking my head back into my papers. Plack Industries' financial statements covered most of my plush couch. For the last two hours, my determination to be well prepared for tomorrow's client call had kept me seated Indian style on the couch, staring at the numbers in front of me and writing notes.

The phone ringing forced me up, and I rubbed my numb bottom as I reached for the phone.

"Beth Boo, I miss you!" Kendy said, her squeaky voice echoing through the receiver.

An instant smile appeared on my face. Her voice reminded me of home.

We had practically grown up in the same house, and this was the only time we had ever really been apart. Kendy was my cousin, my best friend, and the sister I never had. Now, she was one of the few family members I had left.

"I miss you, too, Kendy." I took the phone to the couch and plopped down before moving the financial statements from the seat to the floor.

"So, tell me everything. How was your first day at work? Do you like it? Are you busy? Do you have a nice desk? Oh, are there any cute boys?" she rambled on.

My heart ached from just thinking of the distance between us, and I pulled the phone closer as I felt myself loosen at the sound of her voice.

"Hello? Anybody there? Am I talking to myself here? If so, that's rude," Kendy said.

I shook my head, but of course, she couldn't see me. "Kendy, life does not revolve around men. I just got to Chicago this past weekend. They have me so involved in work already, and that's all I want to be involved with right now."

"Come on, give me some juice, Beth! I have to live vicariously through you. Tell me your life is more exciting than being a registered nurse at Bowlesville Hospital where no one dies or gets sick. I just sit there, waiting for the next big emergency, because helping old people pee all the time sucks."

I let out a carefree laugh. "I didn't say there wasn't any eye candy at work," I said, trying to tame her curiosity.

"That's it? Eye candy? You're single. You're hot. You have this amazing job. You're a triple threat. You are the perfect package. Girlfriend, get out there, and put yourself on the market. Date, Bethany Marie. Date a lot. Have fun, girlfriend. You deserve it."

"I will. Don't worry. I have a plan for these things. Right now, I have to concentrate on my job." I yawned and glanced at the clock. Remembering my early customer call the next day, I clutched the phone closer to my ear. "Kendy," I exhaled.

"Yeah?"

"I wouldn't be here if it wasn't for you," I said, thanking the heavens above that I had her.

"Pfft, girlfriend. You got that high-paying job all by yourself. Helping you get that apartment was no big deal."

I huffed, thinking of all the ways I could thank my

cousin for cosigning my lease. "Still, I owe you," I said.

"You owe me nothing. We're family. It's not your fault things are the way they are. Shoot, I'm just proud you made your way out of here. And you know what?" she said slowly, making sure I was taking her words in. "Nana would be proud of you, too."

I bit my cheek to stop the emotions running through me at the mention of my dead grandmother. There was silence on the phone, but it was a comfortable silence that we always had around each other, a silence shared among best friends. I knew what she was thinking because I was thinking the same thing. We missed Nana.

My eyes moved to the financial statements on the floor, triggering memories from the past.

I peeked up from my high school calculus book and sat up on my bed when I heard the door open. "Hey, Nana," I said, noting the bouquet of red roses in her hands.

"You know he's going to keep coming here every day until you answer his calls."

I sighed as I swung my feet over the bed and reached for the flowers. I put them on the wooden desk that already had three-dozen roses in separate vases.

"I don't know what to tell him. He's never gonna let me go. I just know it. And I hate seeing him cry," I said, dropping my butt on the edge of the bed.

I felt the bed indent as she sat next to me.

"Honey, you're the only one I know who can make the captain of the football team cry."

"Seriously, I don't know what to do. That's why I've been avoiding him like the plague." I lifted my head to meet her eyes.

When she raised an eyebrow and cast me one of her looks, I let out a low laugh.

"Bethany Marie, you know darn well what to do. You do the right thing. There are always two roads to take in life, two choices you can make. In the end, you do the right thing because that's how I raised you. If you don't want to be with him, you let him go. You break up with him—properly." She shook her head slowly. "What's going on between you two anyway?" she asked, concern etched on her face.

I looked into my grandmother's eyes. They were dull from age, yet they were still full of life. Her forehead creased with worry. I wanted to take my finger and even out the wrinkles. I normally didn't tell her many of my problems because she had a lifetime of worry, and I didn't want to add to that. I leaned into her, resting my head on her shoulder. Ever since I was younger, her closeness had always provided me with comfort.

"It's not like he did anything wrong. I swear, sometimes, I wish he had, so I would have a good enough reason to break up with him," I whispered.

I thought of the week that had just passed. Jason had followed me around school like a lost little puppy dog. I'd known he could sense that something was wrong between us. I'd thought if I just cut him off cold, he would get pissed-off and leave me, but he'd just tried harder to figure out what was bothering me and why I was distancing myself.

I pulled at my ponytail. "We're just going in different directions. We're graduating in two weeks. Two weeks! I don't want to spend the summer with him, knowing that I'll be leaving for college at the end of it while he'll just stay here."

She placed her hand on my lap, placating me. "He loves you. You know that, right?"

"Nana, I know that. That's why it is that much harder to leave him. It's not like I don't care for him. I do," I said, looking up at her. "But he was born, raised, and will probably die in Bowlesville, and that's not the life I want to live. If he had it his *way, he'd be working at the local factory, and I'd be barefoot and pregnant in his kitchen. I didn't work through high school and study my butt off to end up here, just raising kids. I want out, Nana. I want the bright city lights. I want corporate America. Eventually, I want those four kids with the big house and white picket fence, but I don't want it anytime soon," I said, determination set in my face. "Jason doesn't want those things. He's content here in Bowlesville," I said, releasing a breath. "And I'm just not."*

"I want you out of here as much as you do. That's why I've been pushing school on you so much. I can't help but feel bad for the boy though," she said, lifting herself from the bed. "You need to do the right thing and break up with that boy if you don't want to be with him anymore."

I looked up at her expectant eyes and nodded slowly.

Her eyes crinkled as a small smile appeared. "Graduation is in two weeks," she said, her voice softening. "Where did the time go?" She reached for a strand of dark brown hair that had escaped from my ponytail, and she tucked it behind my ear. "I'm so very proud of you, baby girl," she said, resting her hand on the side of my face. "I'm very proud of the young lady you've become and the woman you are going to be."

Leaning into her hand, I reveled in the softness even though her skin was folded in wrinkles from many years of working at the Laundromat. "Thanks, Nana." I rested my hand on top of hers. "I do my best to make you proud of me," I said, meeting the eyes of the woman who had raised me since I was six.

Bringing myself back to the present, I shook my head and glanced at the ticking clock beside me, mentally counting the hours of sleep that I had left.

"I have to go and get some sleep, so I am recharged for my meeting tomorrow. You'll visit me soon, right?

You promised," I whined. Being in this new city and not knowing a single soul made me nervous and lonely all at once.

"Girlfriend, you're the first person I'm seeing once they grant me some vacation over here."

"Okay," I said, releasing a breath. "And, Kendy, I know I've said this before, but—"

"You don't have to say it," she said, cutting me off. "We haven't heard from her. Don't you worry though. If she does ask about you, I'll never tell her where you went."

I calmed at her reassurance. "Thanks. I don't want anything to do with that woman."

I glanced at the pile of mail held together by a single half-inch rubber band. The letters never ceased to keep on coming. They reminded me of my past and prevented me from moving forward. I'd have to deal with the mail eventually.

I shook my head to focus.

This is my fresh start, and I will not let that woman ruin it.

SITTING AT THE country club's restaurant, I felt the fluttering in my stomach from nervousness. According to Caroline, the owners of the companies needing loans were middle-aged men, who I would soon learn I had nothing in common with.

Mr. Jack Plack, CEO of Plack Industries, sat back while drinking his coffee. I watched the steam rise from his cup. Behind him, through the floor-to-ceiling windows, I could see golfers teeing off.

"I'm estimating ten million to renovate and expand

our oldest plant. We want to make Bowlesville the pilot plant with new state-of-the-art equipment, and eventually, we want to roll this out throughout the nation," Mr. Plack noted.

Sitting a little taller, I tried to look confident as I grabbed a pen to take notes in my portfolio. I glanced at Jim, my banker, as I listened attentively, and stopped myself from chewing the top of the pen in my hand.

Last night, I'd instantly recognized the name of our client. Plack's logo covered all of my moving boxes. They were a household name, big on packaging materials and distribution. It amazed me how the father of the person in front of me had started the company from scratch before it had grown into a multimillion-dollar corporation.

Mr. Plack took a sip of his coffee. "What do you need from us to get this moving?"

I moved to his line of sight, ready to fire off my questions. "Do you have your second-quarter numbers with you? It looks like first quarter indicated a ten percent drop in sales from the previous year?"

"Yes, I do. We lost a client, but we have gained a few more to make up for that decline." He shuffled through his papers, and as he handed me the financials, he spotted someone behind me.

"Kent!" he yelled over my shoulder.

When I twisted my head to see whom his attention was directed to, I almost had to hold my chin up to prevent my jaw from dropping to the ground. Over six feet of tall, dark, and handsome filled my eyes. I swore, he walked straight off the cover of *GQ* magazine. His eyes were the deepest golden brown, reminding me of chestnuts, which complemented his wavy dark brown hair that didn't have a strand out of place.

When his eyes caught mine, I felt my cheeks warm because he'd caught me staring, and I immediately looked between Mr. Plack and Jim to avert my eyes. When I glanced up again, he was standing by our table.

"Kent, have lunch with us. We're discussing business." Mr. Plack gestured for him to sit down.

"Dad, all work and no play…" He laughed. "You should enjoy the weather and get out on the course."

Mr. Plack stirred uncomfortably in his seat. "I'm booked with meetings all day. Come on, you should join us, son."

I couldn't help myself and stole another glance. When Kent caught my stare, I saw a small dimple emerge, and my temperature rose ten degrees. I wiped my hands on my skirt and looked to the bread to prevent myself from gawking any further.

"Well, I haven't eaten, so maybe I will join you," he replied.

Guys usually didn't make me nervous, but I felt uneasy under his gaze, and fidgeted in my seat.

"Okay, good," Mr. Plack said, sounding relieved.

"Dad, I'm just sitting for lunch," he said, matter-of-factly. "I'm on my way to see Mother."

Mr. Plack motioned for the waitress. She brought in an extra chair and positioned it right beside me.

"Jim, this is my son, Kent. Bethany, Kent."

Jim shook Kent's hand first as I wiped my hands on my skirt again before I stood and took his. His piercing eyes surveyed me, and I pulled my hand back and quickly sat down.

"Please, don't let me interrupt your business meeting," Kent said, taking a seat next to me. He selected a piece of bread and popped it into his mouth.

I watched him as he chewed. I lowered my head into my financial statements as I told myself not to gawk, but I couldn't help it. I wasn't used to seeing super fine men sauntering around in my small town of Bowlesville. Then again, I was no longer in my hometown.

"So, Kent, are you in the business of packaging and distribution with your father? Learning the ropes?" Jim reached for a piece of bread and swirled it in the olive oil.

"No, I don't do anything actually. I don't work." Kent shrugged.

Jim was taken aback, and the whole table was silent for what seemed like forever even though it was only a couple of seconds. I peered up from my financials and studied Kent's beautiful face. I was slightly disappointed. In the few seconds of silence, I mentally noted that his attractiveness had died down multiple notches because of his lack of ambition. The fact that he'd admitted it made him look like a spoiled brat. *Bummer that the looker in front of me has brawn but no brains.*

"Yes, all my son does is plays golf all day, goes to the beach, shops, gallivants with his women, and spends money that his grandfather and I have worked so hard to earn," Mr. Plack said, sounding aggravated and not in the least bit amused.

At the tension in his voice, my head dipped lower into the financial statements as this was a conversation meant between two people and not for the whole table to hear.

"Not interested in succeeding your father in the business?" Jim pressed.

I wanted to kick Jim for prying any further and causing more awkwardness at the table.

"No, not at all—not even with my Ivy League college

degree."

My head perked up, and I caught Kent staring at me while chewing yet another piece of bread. Jim changed the subject by talking about the basketball playoffs, and I was happy that the conversation was steering into a normal, comfortable zone.

"Hey, sugar?" Kent asked.

"Huh?" My heartbeat doubled in my chest, and I blatantly stared at him, oblivious to the playoff talk around me.

"Can you please pass me the sugar?"

I blinked a couple of times before realizing what he just said. "Oh. Okay. Sorry," I grabbed the sugar near me and passed it to him.

"So, what do you do for the bank?" he asked, spooning the sugar into his coffee.

I peered at him from under my eyelashes. "I'm an underwriter."

"Interesting," he noted.

"It is interesting. As an underwriter, we basically look at the company's credit and the needs of the company, and based on their performance, we see if they can service the loan. If not, we build parameters around the loan to ensure that the client can repay us." I noticed an increased pitch in my tone, and I pressed my hands on my lap to stop my fidgeting.

He smiled at me, and I immediately warmed.

"You know, you're cute when you blush," he whispered, leaning toward me.

That flush on my face started to burn up. I looked to the others and was glad they were engrossed in deep conversation about the Chicago Bulls, so they were oblivious to the comment he'd just made. The feeling of shyness dissipated as irritation inside me began to rise. I found myself annoyed that he had been trying to embarrass me and get a reaction out of me in front of my colleague and customer. I didn't care that he looked like a model from *GQ.*

I glared at him, and the corners of his mouth lifted at the evil look I was giving him. The silence grew, and we were interrupted by our lunch being served. When the waitress dropped off our plates at our table, I noticed she was trying to catch Kent's attention. I wondered if he was oblivious to her attention or if he got this everywhere and just didn't care. When she put his plate down, her arm brushed against his and when he finally lifted his eyes to meet hers, her cheeks flushed pink.

Seeing this small interaction, I realized he must have this effect on all women. I suddenly wished my face hadn't given me away and that his good looks hadn't made me blush like a little schoolgirl. I mentally noted not to do it again.

Staring at my grilled chicken sandwich, I couldn't eat. I loved food, yet sitting next to this man made me self-conscious. Aggravation was seeping into my skin because I couldn't enjoy my sandwich in peace. Instead of grabbing the sandwich with both hands and stuffing my face like I normally would, I took my knife and fork and poked at the sandwich.

"So, continue and tell me more about the expansion of the Bowlesville plant," Jim added before chewing a French fry.

Mr. Plack took a sip of water. "Yes, we will also be expanding our product line, so we will need more storage space. Bowlesville will be our test factory, and eventually, we want to renovate the rest of our distribution centers to mirror it. Jim, have you been to our Bowlesville plant? You would be able to see that it is in need of expansion."

"No, not yet. Hey, Beth, isn't that where you're from?" Jim glanced my way, and everyone else's eyes also shifted in my direction.

I widened my eyes before taking a big gulp of water. "Yes, I'm originally from Bowlesville. It's a small town with lots of manufacturing companies, but Plack Industries is the biggest one," I lifted my glass to my lips and kept drinking, hoping they'd continue on to the next subject.

"Have you ever been to the plant? I'd love to give you a tour sometime when you're available," Kent said.

It took all my energy to keep my face steady as I placed my glass back on the table.

"When would you like to go?" he asked.

Mr. Plack studied his son with an amused look on his face. "You haven't been to the Bowlesville plant in years." He paused, assessing his son, and then he turned to Jim and me. "Are you available next week for Kent to take you on a tour of our Bowlesville facility? I'll be out of town, visiting our plant in California, so I won't be able to make it."

From what I knew, Kent was not involved in the company. Why he would want to take us on a tour, I had no idea.

As the waitress started to clear out our plates, Jim reached for his phone. "I will have to check my schedule, but I'm pretty booked next week. I'm sure if Beth is available, she can go."

My mouth dropped at Jim's comment, and I composed myself before he could catch me giving him a dirty look. I cleared my throat and tried to sound confident as

I said, "I'll check my schedule at the office, but I do believe Renee said I will be busy with meetings." My hands were clenched under the table, my fingers digging ridges against the inside of my palms.

"Why don't you check now? Don't you have access through your smartphone?" Kent tried to suppress laughter as his dimple flashed on his cheek.

I had a sudden urge to kick him under the table to erase that smug look off his face. Before I gave him the satisfaction of my face turning redder than it already was, I picked up my phone, gritted my teeth and mustered up a smile. "Let's see."

Everyone stared at me as I fidgeted with my phone. It took all the control I had not to call Jim every expletive in the book. I didn't care that Plack Industries was his biggest client in his portfolio.

"I'm free next Wednesday and Friday," I said, steadying my voice.

I told the truth. I could have lied, but I hadn't. Jim could have easily checked my calendar at the office since he had access.

"Friday it is then," Kent said, casting me a satisfied look. He winked in my direction when no one was looking and it took all my energy not to flip him the finger.

"Fine. Since that is settled, I need to get back to the office." Mr. Plack stood up, and everyone else followed.

Finally, we exchanged our good-byes, and as I turned to face Kent, he slowly shook my hand, holding it a little longer than I wanted.

"Hope you don't mind, but I will be picking you up at your office. It's quite a drive to Bowlesville," he said.

FRIDAY MORNING, I jumped as the phone rang, and I stared at it like it was on fire. Caroline gave me the most perplexed look over her desk, and I returned an awkward smile before picking up the phone.

"Hi, Financial State. This is Beth," I said in my usual cheery voice.

"I'm downstairs in the black Bentley. Meet me on Kennedy Street," Kent said.

No, *Hello, how are you, good morning to you?*

I replied with, "Sounds good."

On my way out, Jim stopped me, moving into my direct path to the elevators. "Hey, real quick, Beth. Not sure what is going on with Kent, but Mr. Plack is pretty happy that his son is visiting the plant. He thinks this might spark Kent's interest about the business. I'd join you, but I already had a meeting planned. Thanks for taking one for the team," he said, giving me a pat on my shoulder.

"Sure," I said before walking toward the elevators and rolling my eyes behind his back.

I was irritated that I'd been put in this situation and was further annoyed that this felt like a first date. I told myself to be nice as the elevator descended. The trip to Bowlesville would take the whole day, and it was pointless to be aggravated. I tried to look at the bright side.

Today, my eyes would get a break from staring at financial statements, annual reports, and the computer screen. I decided that was something to be happy about.

I stepped out on Kennedy Street and surveyed several men looking at the sleek, newly waxed black Bentley while women gawked at the Calvin Klein model sitting behind the wheel. Kent quickly stepped out of the driver's side and opened my door.

The new-car smell filled my nose as I plopped myself down on the black leather seat of his fancy ride. He sat down, all alpha-male like, and placed one hand on the wheel. I noticed his pale yellow polo shirt had a small Burberry logo on his chest, the Burberry pattern peeking out slightly from underneath his collar.

For a brief moment, I felt like an actress in a movie as I sat there in my suit next to a model-looking male in an expensive automobile. In this movie, we were on our first date, heading out for a long drive down the Pacific Coast Highway. I couldn't help but smile at my own imagination.

"Ready to go?" he asked, flashing a dimple on his cheek.

If this were a date, I would reach for his hand and hold it while he drove off, but obviously, it wasn't.

"Yeah. Thanks for driving."

I looked at his dark brown locks above his handsome face. There wasn't a strand out of place. It really wasn't fair.

"Let's grab breakfast in an hour."

He smiled lightly at me, and I naturally smiled back.

My mind wandered, and I was vaguely curious why he'd really invited me on this trip. Maybe he was interested in me. I wasn't sure how I felt about that. Although he was obscenely good-looking, lazy and spoiled were definitely not my type.

We were stopped at a red light when he turned and looked directly into my eyes. He was so close that I could smell mint on his lips. I stared, motionless, as I was mesmerized by his long lashes that women everywhere would die for. When he leaned in even closer, I held my breath at his proximity.

"Listen," he said, lowering his head toward me, "you're not my type."

I didn't know what I looked like at that moment, but I knew how I felt. As heat rose to my ears, I wanted to crawl into a dark hole and hide. It was like that moment when you were walking down the street, staring at a handsome man who had waved at you, and you waved back because you thought he had been checking you out, but really, he'd been waving at the attractive girl behind you. Well, that was how I felt—but worse. I could have walked away from that guy on the street, but this guy was driving me to his father's company about three hours away. So, not only was I unable to walk away from this situation, I was going to have to sit here and feel mortified for the next few hours.

Oh. My. Word.

I composed myself and mustered all I had inside. "You're not my type either. You're just my driver." It was the truth. I faced forward as humiliation seeped further into my skin. "Go. It's a green light," I said as the stoplight changed.

I cleared my throat and sat straighter on my seat. "Mr. Plack, this is not a date. You invited me to visit your facility. I'm here strictly on business—to find out more about your operations and to report your needs back to the bank," I said, trying to sound professional.

"Miss Casse, my facility?"

He suppressed his laughter, and in return, I turned beet red—again. At that moment, I hated him. I hated his pretty face, his stupid fancy car, and his ability to embarrass me so easily. Most of all, I hated that I had to sit in this car with him for the next three hours.

"Sorry, but the only facility I have is attached. As for my needs, the bank doesn't have to know them. I have to remind you that we are going to my father's company, not mine."

"I'm sorry," I said, narrowing my eyes at him. "What's your reason for inviting me to your father's company again? You're obviously not interested in it," I snapped.

He lifted one eyebrow quizzically, and I stared at him again. I always wondered how someone could pull one eyebrow up while refraining the other one from coming up as well.

"Honestly, I was bored, and I thought, you know… maybe I'd get lucky." He shrugged and faced the road. A small dimple emerged on his cheek as if his honesty shouldn't affect me.

I couldn't prevent my mouth from falling. *The nerve of this guy!* I'd never, ever met a male of this breed before, and I could feel myself getting warmer and warmer from irritation. I squeezed my hands together on my lap, resisting the urge to flip off this infuriating man in front of me. I bit my tongue before I said something I would regret and faced forward.

He shifted toward me as one side of his mouth lifted. "What?" he smirked.

And then, I couldn't hold it in any longer. "I can't believe you just said that. Who says those things? You can't say stuff like that! You can think them, but you can't say those things out loud. I mean, who does that?" I said, fisting my hands on my lap. "What type of girl gives it up that easily?"

"You'd be surprised," he said. "You asked, and I answered. I was just being honest."

I glared at him, stunned that he had the audacity to be so blunt. "There's such a thing called tact. Ever heard of it?" I had the sudden urge to punch something, and normally, I didn't have a violent tendency in my body.

"Listen, you're a pretty girl, but you're not my type. I didn't mean to invite you to Bowlesville. I just mentioned it. I never thought my father would insist on me going. I want nothing to do with his business. Like I said, I was just bored."

He was way out of line, and I wanted to turn around and go back to the office. I should have demanded that he take me back, but then I wouldn't have anything to report to Jim or my manager. I needed this job. I'd wanted this job, and I'd worked hard as hell to get it. For the sake of having something to report to the team, I decided I could bite my tongue and suffer through his presence for one day. *It's just one day.*

"Good to know we are on the same page," I said.

I faced the road in front of me as I promised myself I would ignore him the rest of the way. In the silence, Kent turned on the radio. I peered out the window as we hit the outskirts of the city while I realized that this was going to be a very trying day.

"WE'RE HERE. LET'S have breakfast."

I felt Kent nudge me, and when I opened my eyes, his annoyingly perfect face was in my view. I didn't realize I'd fallen asleep. I touched my shoulder, glad that I didn't have the regular drool pool next to me. I yawned, stretched my arms toward the sky, and released a sound as if a wolf were slowly dying. Kent studied me. Amusement appeared on his face, but I didn't care.

As I wobbled out of the car, I took in my surroundings. The sign read *Benny's Diner*. We were still two hours away from the plant, but I already felt at home. We were definitely in hick town, and the only reason I knew this was because I'd come from hick town. The Bentley proved to be the fanciest car in the lot, surrounded by worn-down pickup trucks and rusted vans.

Kent held the restaurant door open. "After you."

I stepped inside. A redhead named Dilly greeted us and sat us at a booth. I surveyed the people around us. Two busy servers were hustling through the quaint, bare-walled restaurant. The aroma of greasy bacon filled my nose, and my stomach growled in response.

"The grits and pancakes are good here. That's why I like this place. I remember coming here when I was younger," Kent said, staring at me expectedly.

I wasn't sure what he wanted me to say. Still offended by our earlier conversation, I remained silent and flipped through the menu.

"Okay, I know we got off to a bad start. I don't know much about the company, but I know that the operations manager is around today, so he can answer all your questions."

I regarded him for a few seconds and shrugged. "I've decided I'm not talking to you. I feel a headache coming on and I'm pretty sure it's triggered every time you open your mouth." Looking at the menu in front of me, I concentrated on what I was going to order.

A low laugh left his lips. "You're very entertaining when you're upset," he said.

I could feel the calmness that had lingered from my nap slowly disappear. The fact that he found me comical started to get under my skin. I decided to turn the rudeness up a notch. "Listen, buddy, you're not going to get lucky today with this chick, so quit pretending to be nice because I know you're not the kind and considerate type." I rolled my eyes at him and dropped my head back into the menu. With my fingers, I rubbed at my temple trying to ward off the oncoming headache.

After a beat, he said, "Don't worry. Like I said, you're not my type."

I shot him a look, and the side of his mouth lifted.

"I call a truce. Sorry for being honest."

"I just met you. I don't care who you are, what you do, or what your type is," I said, leaning in and trying to keep my tone down. "You want honesty? You're self-centered and arrogant. You assume any breathing being with tits wants to sleep with you when in reality, they don't. Guys who look like you are always so pigheaded, and that proves to me that you can judge a book by its cover."

Kent's laughter rolled throughout the restaurant. I scanned the room and noticed everyone's eyes had turned to our table.

Picking up my glass, I pretended to drink water. "I don't know what's so funny. Keep it down." I looked to my menu as my ears warmed, embarrassed by the attention he was causing.

"Beth, I knew this trip would be very interesting. I love your candor."

This guy definitely had a screw loose, and I was now worried about my safety. I still had to sit in the car with this guy for a couple of hours, and then I would have to do it again on our way back.

The waitress broke the moment by taking our order, and my silence continued. He was still observing me, and he laughed when I shot him a mean-girl look.

"So, Beth, what's your deal?" Kent asked as the waitress came back and placed our food in front of us.

The aroma of eggs, bacon and pancakes made my mouth water. "My deal? I have no deal," I said, pulling my eyebrows together. I picked up my fork and jammed a piece of egg into my mouth.

"No, tell me what you're about."

"We're not friends, so I'm not sharing my life story with you. Plus, I'm pretty sure I don't even like you," I snapped.

He laughed, but I ignored him as I chowed down on a big piece of pancake. When the maple syrup touched my lips, I sighed inwardly. The syrupy liquid coated my tongue and slid down my throat, the tastiness satisfying the hunger pangs in my belly.

"Delicious, right?" he asked, raising an eyebrow with a slight smile.

"Maybe," I said, my mouth still full of food. I scrunched my face, still trying to stay mad, even though the meal was beginning to lighten my mood.

"You know," he said, "you really shouldn't talk with your mouth full."

I opened my mouth wide to show him the eggs mixed with bacon and pancakes. I didn't care that I was acting juvenile. It wasn't like I was trying to impress him. He made a face, feigning disgust, and a small laugh escaped

29

his lips.

"So, back to my question, tell me about yourself, Bethany Casse. Tell me the stuff that I can't find on paper."

"I don't have any secrets." I chomped on a piece of bacon.

"Come on, tell me. The good girls always have secrets."

When he smiled, I purposely distorted my face even more. My rudeness wasn't bothering him. If anything, he was more entertained at my annoyance, so I decided to turn the table on him.

"What's your deal?" I asked, pointing my knife in his direction. "Tell me your deal," I said, narrowing my eyes at him.

"I thought my deal was pretty obvious. My deal is, I do what I want to, whenever I want to, and with whomever I want to. I, Miss Bethany Casse, have a very good deal."

"Must be nice," I blurted.

"Yes, it is," he said, leaning back against the booth.

"Rich people work, too. Ever heard of Bill Gates? I mean, your dad works hard to sustain his company. Don't you have ambitions? What do you want to do when you grow up?" I couldn't help but be curious about the entitled male in front of me.

"I want to do what I'm doing now—absolutely nothing and everything. I'm one of the very few people who can say I have the luxury of doing that. I'm not trying to be conceited, but it's just the truth."

He took a sip of water. "I have an allowance from my trust fund, so I will never have to work. And at the age of twenty-five, I will be entitled to the whole trust. Anyone with this option would do the same. Wouldn't you?"

"No. I wouldn't. I'd choose normalcy. I'd choose be- ing productive and contributing to society by going to work," I said, making a face.

Both of his dimples emerged. "Did you just stick your tongue out at me?"

"No," I lied, pretending that it just hadn't happened. "So, what makes you happy? Don't you want more from life?"

I wanted to kill the curious cat, but the more he spoke, the more I wanted to know. His answers had annoyed me, but even more than that, my uncontrollable inquisi- tiveness irritated me.

"What makes me content is the here and now. I'm content with sitting here with you and eating this pan- cake because I want to. If I weren't, I'd get up and leave. I rarely have to do what I don't want to do. If I get bored, I plan a vacation…or go to Bowlesville," he said with a smirk.

"I'm sorry, but what about company succession? Is there an uncle or someone else?"

I thought of Jack Plack, a father who had worked so hard to grow and sustain a company that had been passed down from his father. He'd seemed excited that his son was visiting the plant today, and I couldn't help but sympathize with him and his hope for the future of his company.

"No, it's only me. My father was the only son, and so am I."

"What if he forces you into taking over the company? I can't imagine he would want someone else to run it. It's been in your family for generations."

He glanced at the glass of water he was holding as his eyebrows pulled in slightly. "I hate to give him false hope by coming here, but I've been honest with him." His voice was quiet, melancholy.

For a short second, I sensed sadness in his tone, but then it was gone.

"He's tried to force me into it, and he has tried to cut me off before. That lasted all but two days. My mother wouldn't have it," he said. "That is one woman I would do anything for. To her, I can do no wrong."

I pictured his plastic stay-at-home mother, who had given her little boy every little thing he wanted whenever he wanted. Just as my upbringing had shaped me, his upbringing had most likely shaped him into his spoiled self today.

The check came and Kent reached for it before I could pick it up.

"Here, let me get that. This is a business expense," I said, snatching the check from his hands.

I drew my wallet from my purse and grabbed the only credit card I had—the Financial State corporate card. For me, cash was king. I always paid cash, and I despised credit cards, but this time, it was a justified expense.

WHITE FREIGHTLINER TRUCKS covered with *Plack Industries* surrounded the plant as we pulled in. The massive factory split into two portions. Grayish-white siding spanned the exterior of the manufacturing facility toward the rear of the building while red brick covered the office area in the front.

As we were seated in the reception area, an older man wearing a white coat with the Plack Industries logo approached to greet us. "Hey, Kent," he said, as his eyes lit up. "It's so great to see you. I haven't seen you since you were twelve."

The older male proceeded to lean in for a hug, but Kent stepped back and confidently shook his hand.

I introduced myself immediately, "Hi, I'm Bethany Casse from Financial State."

The corner of his eyes wrinkled as he shook my hand firmly. "Nice to meet you. I'm Jared, head of operations. Let's take a tour of our facility. Shall we?"

"That would be great," I replied, ready to ask questions about the expansion.

He led us through the building to where the offices ended and the manufacturing plant began. Kent trailed behind me.

The factory tour lasted no more than forty-five minutes. During the tour, my eyes had flickered behind me toward Kent. I'd caught interest in his eyes as Jared talked of the day-to-day operations, but as soon as Kent had noticed me staring, I swore, he'd feigned boredom.

Before I knew it, we were already walking out of the factory.

As we left the building, my phone rang while we proceeded toward the car. My heart picked up speed as I saw Pete Carlson's name come up before I answered the call.

"Beth, you're late again," he said.

I forgot. Crap.

I looked toward Kent. "Hey, just one minute. I need to take this."

When Kent stepped into the car, I placed the phone back on my ear and leaned against the car door. "Hey, Pete. How are you?" I pulled at the strands of dark brown hair over my shoulder with my free hand to try to calm myself.

"Beth, I can't make any more excuses for you. I have to run a business here."

"I know. I'm so sorry. I had to move, and then I started a new job. It totally slipped my mind. Can I find out from Kendy when she's off next, and I'll have her drop off the money?" I said, talking faster than normal.

"No, Beth, I can't cut you any more slack. Either come in and pay the interest today, or I'm selling your stuff. Like I said, I gotta run a business here. I have bills to pay, too."

I fisted the top of my hair to try to steady myself. "I'll have the money for you. Promise me, you won't sell her stuff." I glanced toward Kent sitting in the car and gave him a nervous smile.

"Today, Beth. You have till the end of the day."

My heart started to pound in my ears, and the beginning of a full-on panic attack was about to overtake my body. I felt the hot sweats creeping up my neck. There was no other option. I had to make it to Pete's today. I needed to take action.

Think, think, think.

Okay, Beth, be nice.

I stepped into the car and turned toward Kent. "I'm starving. Do you want to try this great burrito place? They're famous for their guacamole."

A small smile crossed his face. "I saw what you ate for brunch. You're hungry again?"

I guessed he was most likely surprised at how much food this girl could put down.

"Yeah, really hungry," I said, grabbing my stomach. "Hear that? It's growling." I gave him the puppy-dog face I usually saved for when I wanted something from Kendy. In desperation, I turned up the cuteness a tad bit more as I gave him a forced sad smile.

He laughed once. "Sure. Where to?" he asked, placing both hands on the steering wheel.

DOWNTOWN AREAS WERE normally full of beautiful fountains, lush gardens, delicious restaurants, and cute one-of-a-kind boutiques. That was not downtown Bowlesville. As we drove, we passed by vacant and no-name storefronts, mostly discount stores or resale clothes shops.

"Appealing area we have here." Kent's face turned serious.

He glanced around to the people at the bus stop. They were gawking back at us, most likely because of the car they'd only seen in the movies or in magazines.

"It's just a few more blocks that way." I pointed as Kent continued to drive.

I placed both hands in my lap to stop the bouncing of my knees, and I tried to take deep breaths to calm the rushed beating in my chest.

"I'm not sure this is such a good idea. Why don't we pick up something on the way? I need to get gas anyway."

"No, you'll love this joint. You'll probably never come back to Bowlesville. The food at this place is awesome. One bite of their Burrito Bomb, and I swear, you'll forget your name. It's just that good." I gave him my sweetest smile. "Unless you're scared," I sassed. I crossed my fingers on my lap, hoping he'd take me to my destination.

He shook his head. "I was in college wrestling, and I am a black belt. I don't do scared, but I'd rather not put myself in situations I can avoid," he said, scanning the vicinity around us.

We arrived at Tasty Tacos. I stepped out of the car and followed Kent into the restaurant. I doubted this was a good idea, but I had no other choice. I had to get to Pete's before he sold everything that mattered.

The waitress led us to a table in the corner. I scooted into the red booth, feeling the coldness of the leather hit the back of my legs. When she dropped the menu in front of us, I ordered right away. "Can I have one steak taco and a Coke? Thanks." I closed my menu and handed it to the waitress.

"I thought you were hungry," Kent said, his face perplexed.

"I meant a steak taco meal. Can I have the meal please?" I said, turning back to the waitress.

Food was the last thing on my mind, but I had to make this believable. My heart beat loudly in my chest as I stared at my destination through the restaurant's floor to ceiling windows behind Kent.

"So, Bowlesville. You grew up here," Kent stated, breaking through my thoughts and forcing me to make eye contact.

I crossed my arms in front of me and leaned into the table. "Yeah. So?" I wasn't in the mood for a snarky comment about my hometown, especially when I had a mission to accomplish.

His eyes widened in amusement. "Easy there, I was just asking. You must be one of those people who gets cranky when she doesn't eat."

I softened my face. "Yeah, I grew up here. Actually, my house is ten minutes away."

"It's amazing that you turned out okay," he said, observing our surroundings.

My annoyed face was back. "Just so you know, not all of us were brought up with a silver spoon in our mouths. Bowlesville is fine. It's not so much where I came from. It's the drive that gets people to where they're at," I said, tapping my foot against the floor. My eyes flickered back to my destination behind Kent.

He laughed. "Okay, okay," he said, raising both hands in surrender.

When the waitress dropped our food on the table, my stomach grumbled at the scent of grease and spices, but I was in no mood to eat.

Kent took a bite of his burrito and paused to praise me. "You're right. This is good stuff. You and I have a knack for picking great places to eat," he said before taking another bite.

"I told you." I ate a chunk of the greasy taco in front of me.

Nowhere near hungry, it took everything I had to force the food down and keep my knees from shaking. There was a disconnect between my stomach and my brain. My stomach wanted to enjoy the meal from one of my favorite places in my hometown, but my brain had me thinking of my purpose, which made me queasy.

My mission had me standing right before the check came. "Excuse me for a second. I have to go to the restroom."

I rose to my feet, left the table, and jolted toward the door. I squinted through the glass window of the restaurant, and my eyes zoned in on the pink neon lights flashing brightly in front of me. My brisk walk turned into a full-on sprint to Pete's Pawn across the street. When I entered the shop, Pete stood at attention from behind the bulletproof glass.

"Pete, I'm so sorry," I said, trying to catch my breath. "I had so much going on. I'm in the process of moving." I reached in my purse and handed him the pawn slip and payment. "Here, this should take care of it until next month." I released a silent sigh of relief as soon as the money left my hands, knowing my payment was up to date.

"I feel for you. I do. You know how many sob stories come in here, month after month, with excuses on why they can't pay for their stuff? I'm sorry, Beth, but if I cut slack for one, I'll have to do it for all." He took my money through the window and placed it in the register. "Beth, you can pick up what you can afford. If you just want the jewelry, you can pay for that, and I'll just sell the rest of it. It's just junk—old movies, electronics, and—"

"No, I want it all," I said, stopping him mid-sentence. I felt a tightness in my chest at the thought of losing all of Nana's belongings.

It was all I had left of Nana, and I'd promised myself that I would buy it all back, every last piece. It was everything she'd used, everything she'd touched, everything she'd worn. I would buy it all back even if I had to get another job to do it.

"When your mom pawned all this stuff, I told her she could pick up the pieces one at a time. Just because I gave her a loan on all of the items doesn't mean it has to be paid off all at once. I lent her money on each individual item."

"She's not my mom," I said, cringing at the term.

I didn't want to see sympathy in his eyes, but it was there.

"I'm just saying, Beth. If you want the jewelry, you can just pay for that in full and take that home, so you don't have to pay interest on everything every month. If you don't need the rest, which is just junk, I can sell it."

I twisted as I heard the door open.

"Nice place you've got here."

My stomach dropped, and I could feel the blood draining from my face. If I could have shriveled up and died, I would have.

Damn it.

It was Kent.

Chapter Three

"HEY, WELCOME TO Pete's. Whatever you're looking for, we have it." Pete exited from behind the bulletproof glass and strolled to the front of the store.

I watched as he eyed Kent. Kent's aura, from his clothes to his demeanor, reeked of wealth.

"What are you doing here?" I said under my breath, tugging on Kent's sleeve. I clenched my jaw as he walked further into the shop.

"I'm in the market for a new watch," he said, peering at Pete's display cases of pawned watches.

The glint from his gold Rolex flashed in my eyes, and annoyance started to rise within me. "Yeah, right." I didn't even wait for a reaction.

I pivoted and stormed out the door. I heard the door fly open and felt his presence right behind me.

"I saw you running across the street and into a pawn shop of all places." He laughed. "It's always the so-called good girls," he said, amusement in his tone. "So, what's your habit? Do tell. Is it gambling, drugs, or drinking a little too much perhaps? Hey, slow down, will you?"

I heard his footsteps hit the gravel, briskly trailing behind me to meet my pace.

"So, what's the truth? What habit does Beth need to support that forced her to pawn all her stuff?"

I wheeled around so quickly that he knocked into me and shoved his chest with both hands. "You want to know the truth?" I yelled. "The truth is that the stuff in there belonged to my Nana," I said, pointing to the pawn-shop behind me. "That's all I have left from my dead grandmother and I pay every month on that stuff because I can't bear to lose it. I've never done drugs, I'm not a drunk, and I've been to a casino once. So, no, I wasn't the one who pawned that stuff. I didn't pawn any of it. I'm just trying to save it."

I shook my head. "I don't know why I'm even telling you this. I don't owe you anything. My business is my business, and you need to stay out of it. Do you understand?" I glared at him and did not relent.

A look of shock crept up his face, followed by sympathy. "I'm sorry. I didn't mean to—"

I held up my hands to stop him from speaking further.

He wore the exact same face that had met me day in and day out in Bowlesville. It was so familiar. It was the face of every person in my small town who had known my mother was a drunk and hung out every night at the local bar. It had been written on Pete's face earlier. It was that look of pity for the girl who had endured a messed-up childhood. It was the same look that I'd been trying to leave behind when I moved to Chicago. And now, my problems were following me straight into my new city, my new life, and it just pissed me off.

I straightened out my skirt and stomped toward the car.

"Beth, I'm sorry."

"I don't want to hear it." I crossed my arms in front of me as I stopped in front of his car. "I want to go back to Chicago," I commanded.

41

AN AWKWARD SILENCE filled the air, but I embraced it. It was either that or answer questions I didn't want to answer.

Twenty minutes into the ride, he asked if I'd like to turn on the radio.

I shrugged and looked out to the wide-open fields of land to my right. As the quiet grew, I felt him stealing glances in my direction, but I continued to stare out the window. I wasn't in the mood to converse. All I wanted to do was crawl into bed and pretend today didn't happen.

After thirty more minutes, he spoke. "I don't like to fail, and I wouldn't know the first thing about running a company," he said quietly.

His words had me turning slowly in his direction. It was the first time I looked at him since we'd gotten into the car. He stared straight out at the open road ahead of him. I should have left it at that, but it was the only thing that came out of his mouth that had broken his confident, arrogant facade. I should have kept my mouth shut, but curiosity won out.

"Why are you telling me this?" I asked softly.

He shrugged. "Honestly?" he asked, meeting my eyes. "It's only fair, one for one. Also, I have selfish reasons. Looks are deceiving, and I want to know the whole story about why a sweet-looking girl was at a pawn shop today."

"How do you know you're going to fail when you haven't even tried?" I asked.

He shook his head as a melancholy smile crept up his face. "That's not how it works. I asked you first."

I didn't want to continue, but he was curious about me, like I was about him. I wanted to know more. With his jaw-dropping good looks and all the money in the world, he strutted around as if he were king of the universe. In reality, he was a total walking contradiction. Inside, he was rattled with insecurity, and it shocked me.

I let out a long sigh and rubbed the back of my neck. "Jamie, my mother, pawned all my grandmother's stuff, and I want to get them back."

"Why would your mother pawn your grandmother's things?"

I laughed at his perplexed look.

"She's a deadbeat, Kent."

He still looked confused.

"She left me when I was six, and I stayed with my grandmother ever since. I'd rather not talk about it, but if you must know, my mother is the one with the habit. Drinking, gambling, and putting herself into debt is more of her thing." I looked out the window, so I wouldn't see the familiar look in his eyes. "Once Nana passed away, my mother pawned Nana's stuff for her habits," I said, my voice lowering. The heartbroken ache in the middle of my chest was back at the thought of Nana.

"I'm sorry," he said, his words laced with sympathy.

"Stop right there. I don't want your pity. She's dead. I loved Nana. I want her stuff back. That's it." My heart constricted, and I didn't want to talk about it anymore. I wasn't going to cry, especially not in front of someone I barely knew. But as hard as I tried, I couldn't hide the hurt on my face.

After a while, he broke the silence. "Besides running the company, I'm slightly afraid of clowns." He made a face, trying to break my mood.

43

I tucked an escaping strand of hair behind my ear and shot him a bemused look. "So, you don't want a clown for your birthday?"

"My mother once got me a clown to surprise me for my birthday. I'll never forget that day. As soon as I saw him, I punched him in the face and ran." He let out a low laugh as a dimple emerged on his cheek.

"I guess the surprise was on him," I said.

THE REST OF the ride back to Chicago was relaxing. It was as if a layer of Kent's facade had peeled off, and the more he talked, the more I became at ease.

"So, I've been kind of wondering about something. You're not gay, are you?" I asked.

His laughter was contagious. Instead of feeling stupid for asking such a question, I laughed along with him.

"No, I like women, and only women."

I briefly thought of his earlier comment about me not being his type.

As if he'd read my mind, he said, "I only date women who do not want a relationship, so it's mutual. I don't like complications, and I don't like to play games. My type would be the type who doesn't expect more."

"Don't worry. I'm not offended that I'm not your type. Trust me when I say, you're not my type either. I'd rather have a boyfriend who works for a living, who is not so spoiled, who is good-looking but not so into his looks, and who is a nice guy overall."

He let out a carefree laugh. "You'd think I would be offended at what you just said, insinuating that I'm not those things. I'm not though because you are being honest. So, who is the lucky guy?"

"No lucky guy. I had a boyfriend in high school, but we broke up."

"What happened?"

"You know, same old story. Fell in love with my high school boyfriend, lost my V-card at prom, and broke up before we went off to college." I laughed, thinking of the memory. "Basically, I grew up, and he didn't. He wanted to stay in Bowlesville, and I had other plans. He thought my life revolved around him, but my life began when Financial State called to offer me the position."

"You lost your virginity at prom?" he asked.

"I figured you would pick that after all I said. Yeah, in the back of his pickup truck. How romantic." I sighed, fluttering my eyelashes.

He laughed and continued to tell me about his first time and how he'd had no idea what he was doing. By the end of his story, we were both in tears. Our conversation flowed so effortlessly that when I glanced up, we were on the outskirts of the city as the sun was setting in front of us.

"That's the most I've laughed in a while." He pulled up in front of my apartment and shifted the gear to park. "I have this great idea," he said, searching my face as I reached for the door handle. "I think we should be friends."

My eyes were cautious. "Okay..." I said, sounding unsure.

He continued, "We know quite a few things about each other, so it only makes sense."

"Friends?" I tested out the word mentally. *What does it take to be friends with a multimillionaire who is conceited yet insecure, rude yet honest, and last but not least, an admitted*

45

man-whore?

"Just friends, and nothing more," he said, waiting for my reply.

"I guess I don't have any new friends in Chicago, so okay." I shrugged, pretending to concede.

He shook his head in amusement. "Have a good evening, Beth."

"You, too," I said, stepping out of the car.

As he drove off, I wondered what a friendship with Kent entailed.

THE WEEKEND FLEW by and before I knew it, I was back to work on Monday. I glanced at the time on my computer, and it was already eleven thirty. On cue, my stomach grumbled. My phone rang, outdoing my loud stomach.

"Hello? Financial State. This is Beth."

"Beth, I'm calling in my friendship card. It's Kent. I'm bored. I'm downtown by your office, and I need someone to go shopping with me."

I was surprised he'd called so soon. It must be nice to be wealthy. Without a full-time job, he was able to go shopping in the middle of the weekday.

"You can't pick out your own clothes? Don't rich people have personal shoppers or something?" I asked teasingly.

"Come on, I want someone to come with me. Let's go. Meet me at *Barney's* in ten minutes."

"Fine, but you're buying me lunch."

"Just hurry up," he said before dropping the call.

I grabbed my wallet, logged off my computer, and

headed out the door.

Lifting my head, I felt the sun's warmth on my skin as I took my time strolling down the street. The streets were full of working professionals, all in suits, hustling to lunch or heading back to work.

I was used to the quiet of my home town but now, walking down the street on my lunch hour, I realized I didn't miss home, I only missed Kendy. I embraced the noise and hustle of Chicago because it meant that my old life was behind me.

Strolling into *Barney's*, I immediately spotted Kent with his Ray-Ban sunglasses sitting on top of his head. I laughed quietly as I witnessed the pretty brunette sales-clerk pulling down her shirt and pushing up her bra to reveal more cleavage. Kent was oblivious as he searched through the pile of polo shirts. As I walked toward him, I saw two other women scoping out the handsome man in front of them with his tight crisp polo accenting his broad shoulders before slimming inwardly toward his pelvis. They were laughing and whispering to each other, like little schoolgirls. I observed as they secretly gawked at him.

"Hey." I sauntered toward him and touched the po-los in front of him.

"Pink or red?" He held up two shirts, wanting my opinion.

"Uh, neither. One, only certain guys can pull off pink, and you can't. Two, I don't like red unless it's Christmas."

"Okay, no red." He picked up the pink shirt. "I'm not one of those guys who can pull off pink? Interesting. I thought I was."

I looked from the pink shirt to his perfectly placed hair and to the Hugo Boss polo he was wearing. "Never

47

mind. Pink suits you. I mean, you are metrosexual."

"I'll take this one." He handed the pink shirt to the saleslady.

As he glided farther down the aisle to a pile of shorts, I followed behind him as I noticed the two women from before were roaming around to the other side, staying in his plain view. I found it humorous that they were both vying for his attention. I raised my eyebrows toward them, and once they caught my stare, they looked away. I bet they thought I was his girlfriend.

"So, friend, where are we going for lunch?" I asked loudly, emphasizing the word *friend*, as I gave him a brotherly shove on his shoulder.

He regarded me and furrowed his eyebrows, most likely at the increase in my tone. "Anywhere you want." He lifted up two pairs of khaki shorts. "Which one?"

"I like the ones you're wearing now." I laughed because the shorts in his hands matched exactly to what he was currently wearing.

"Funny girl. No, it's different." He held both shorts against his own. "There is a difference in the material. See?"

I compared the three pairs of shorts. One was a tad bit lighter, but I could only tell the contrast between them by looking closely.

"Seriously, Kent?" I gave him the most incredulous look as I stepped up to him and took hold of the shorts. "They're the same. Khaki is khaki. It might be different material than yours, but the color is very similar to the ones you're wearing. Also, I think the two you picked up are the same shorts. There is no difference in color here."

Smiling, he grabbed the shorts from me. "No attention to detail, Beth." He handed them to the saleslady.

"I'll take both," he said, amusement in his tone.

"You know you just bought two of the same thing. You probably have two more of those pink shirts at home, too."

He shrugged.

"You do, don't you?" I wondered what his closet looked like, and I had no doubt that this well-dressed, metrosexual male had more clothes than most of the women in this store. I glanced at my watch, noting the time. "Although I love being your personal shopper, I have to go back to work. My lunch break is almost over."

"I already have a personal shopper, who works at Neiman Marcus. I made the mistake of sleeping with her, and it didn't work out too well."

He turned to the register before seeing the appalled look I was giving him.

"Wait, let me pay first, and I'll walk you back. I told you I'd get lunch," he said, placing his black AmEx on top of the counter.

I waited outside the store, leaning against the red brick building. I lifted my head again to enjoy the sunshine one last time before I had to step back into the office.

Kent strolled his way toward me, holding the bag of purchases in his one hand. "Not bad, Miss Beth—one shirt, two pairs of shorts, and a phone number."

"You got Miss Pretty Brunette's phone number?" I asked. My eyes widened in shock.

I didn't know why I was surprised. She had practically stripped in front of him.

"Yes, I did. Do you wish it were you?" He took my arm and linked it through his.

"No, I prefer to avoid sexually transmitted diseases, thank you very much."

49

I stuck my tongue out at him, and his dimple appeared. We strolled down the street, comfortably connected by our arms. I found it odd that just a few days ago I hated this spoiled brat next to me and now, we were friends. There was a part of him, maybe his honest humor, that reminded me of Kendy.

"My mother enjoys shopping as much as I do, and I have to admit, I love spoiling her," he said, breaking me from my thoughts.

His eyes lit up as he spoke of his mother, and part of me was curious to meet her.

"I should take you shopping sometime," he added.

"Uh, no." I rolled my eyes at him. "That's not going to happen. Friends just don't take friends on shopping sprees. It's not normal." I wondered if it was typical for the elite to take turns splurging on each other. "You get this friendship," I motioned between us with one hand, "for free." My eyes moved to the time shown on a nearby clock tower. "But you can buy me lunch. I'll let you do that. Really, I have to go though. I don't have time to eat out, so I'll have to eat at my desk."

I hurried and tugged him forward. We ended up in line at a taco place. Kent motioned for me to order first.

"I'll have two tacos, a nacho supreme, and a side of rice. Oh, and please give me a glass of horchata," I looked at Kent and back at the cashier, "and a churro for later. All to go, please." I wrinkled my nose at his amused smile.

"You know, it's cheaper to buy you clothes than to support your food habit," he said while turning to pay.

"Shut up," I whined.

So what if I have a healthy-eating habit? I wasn't the typical girl who counted calories and watched what she ate. If I wanted a cupcake, hell yeah, I'd have that cupcake without even thinking twice. Where other people my age could throw back beers, I could eat and loved doing it.

"If I didn't see you eat before, then I wouldn't believe you could finish it all. With all you eat, it's amazing you are not obese. Tell me, Beth, where does it go?"

"I just have a fast metabolism." I replied.

After the cashier called out our number, we grabbed our food and strolled our way back to Financial State.

"Next week is restaurant week. I've scheduled us lunch on Monday, Wednesday, and Friday. I had to book these things early as reservations fill up quickly," he said, squinting at his calendar on his phone.

"And when were you going to ask me?" I took the bag full of food from his hands. "Thanks for assuming that I had no plans."

"Well, you don't. You can't possibly. You don't know many people here yet, and I only wanted to go with you because you can eat. You eat like a horse actually." He laughed at his own joke that he thought was funny. "Plus, I know you can't turn down three good meals."

He looked to me, and I shrugged.

"Yeah, I guess you're right. Food is my weakness." I gave him a quick smile, a half hug, and walked inside the bank.

OUT THE DOOR of Financial State, I began strolling home after work when I felt a tap on my shoulder. I pulled one earbud from my ear and wheeled around to see all-American Brian Benson standing behind me.

"Hey, where you headed?" he asked.

There was something about a man in a suit. He looked

professional and adorable all at the same time. I blushed at my inward thought.

"Nowhere special. Just going home."

"I'm walking you home. You might get lost." He reached for my laptop bag and carried it over his shoulder.

"I live four blocks away from here. I think I'll manage."

He had the most boyish grin on his face, and I didn't want to tell him no. There was no wonder this man was in sales. I'm sure it was hard for his own customers to tell him no especially with a convincing face like his.

"Well, I've heard it's quite dangerous here in Chicago. As a man of honor, I have to make sure you're safe," he said, placing his free hand on his heart.

"Okay." I nodded and crossed the street while he followed.

"So, where were you today for lunch? Caroline was terribly disappointed that you didn't show up."

"I went shopping with a friend. Totally my fault that I didn't even tell Caroline."

I mentally kicked myself. I'd been having lunch with Caroline almost every day, and I'd forgotten to tell her about my surprise shopping date. Brian had joined us a couple of times when he wasn't on a customer lunch.

"I'm just playin'. Caroline went on a customer call. I, on the other hand, was waiting for you all alone at our lunchroom table." He frowned slightly and looked to the ground, feigning sadness.

I had an urge to take my finger and lift his pouty lip. He was truly adorable—an all-American man package wrapped up in a suit. It wasn't that he was just good eye candy, but the fact that he was such a motivated go-getter added to his appeal. Management loved him and not because he brownnosed with the bigwigs. It was because he worked hard, loved his job, and had fun doing it.

But we worked together, and although this flirting back and forth was fun, work was the single most important thing for me. What I didn't want to do was mix business with boys.

"Brian, listen—" I stopped. *What if he is like this toward everyone?* I didn't want to assume he was interested.

"I'm listening," he said, waiting for me to speak.

"Brian, well, um…we're friends, right?" I lifted my eyebrows to make sure he knew what I was trying to say.

He lifted his eyebrows to mimic mine. "Friends? Sure, unless you want to be 'friends-friends'"—he made air quotes, "which is all right with me."

I laughed at him and his boyish grin. Just so I was clear, I took the more formal and direct approach. "Brian, we work together, and I don't date coworkers."

He took his thumb and forefinger and ran them against his chin. We were stopped at a light as the bluest of blue eyes squinted down at me. I felt the first of the butterflies fluttering in my stomach as he stared at me intensely.

"What?" I laughed at his look of concentration.

"I'm debating if I should quit."

I hit him on the shoulder. "You're so crazy." The crosswalk sign turned to walk so I continued to cross the street.

"So, if you don't date coworkers, how about a drink after work?" he asked, catching up to me. "Next weekend. As friends."

I couldn't hide the incredulous look I gave him.

He continued, "It's Tim's retirement party. A bunch of people from work will be going. Caroline might even go."

We were stopped in front of my apartment as I stared at his charming face. His eyes were the deepest set of crystal blue.

"Come on, Beth, I can't attack you in front of all those people. It will be fun."

I grabbed my laptop bag from him. "Fine, I'll go, but strictly as friends."

He smiled again, and my breath caught. I waved to him before I stepped inside my apartment as I secretly wished he wasn't off-limits.

SATURDAY AFTERNOON, THE aroma of fresh basil and tomatoes filled my one-bedroom apartment. I was multi-tasking—cooking dinner and watching reruns of my favorite reality TV show. Slowly lifting the wooden spoon from the saucepan, I tasted my concoction. The loud banging from the door caused me to drop the spoon, spilling hot spaghetti sauce on my leg before it hit the floor.

"Open up! I know you're in there."

I froze, no longer concerned with my burned leg. My heart pounded loudly in my ears as my pulse accelerated.

"Open the door. Now! I know you're in there, and I'm not leaving till you open up."

My hands started to sweat and my eyes scanned the room as though someone would miraculously appear to save me.

The banging on the door continued, and I knew my neighbors down the hall could hear all of this. I took quick deep breaths through my mouth and out my nose, to try and calm myself.

"Open up now!"

Maybe he has me mistaken for someone else.

"I hear the TV. Open up the door."

Crap. I closed my eyes tightly and tried to think of what to do.

Embarrassment gave out over fear. Before his abrasiveness caused me more embarrassment on my floor— where I'd wanted a new start, where I had been living for less than a month, and where all these people did not know about all the havoc in my life—I decided to open the door. And as soon as I did, I regretted it.

Every muscle in my body tensed as a tall, burly man with a goatee stood in front of me. The only barrier between us was the chain lock that I was peering over. He was wearing a T-shirt and jeans, and I wouldn't be surprised if he'd come straight over from the county jail. He'd come here to do damage. I was sure of it.

I gave him my meanest face and mustered all I had inside as I said, "What do you want?" My voice was firm and powerful, opposite of what I was truly feeling—ultimate fear.

"You're gonna let me in, and I'm gonna tell you what I want."

My heartbeat resonated in my ears. *Haven't I seen this scenario in movies?* This was the part where the serial killer cut up his victim before putting her in the fridge or scattering the body all over the city. "No way. You're not coming in here."

Mr. Goatee pushed at the door, the chain now taut. "Don't tempt me to use force."

"Stop," I said, my voice wavering. I used my foot to prevent the door from opening farther. "Tell me what you want."

"Open the damn door, woman!"

Mr. Goatee shoved the door, and I jumped back.

He shifted toward me and I flinched. "I'm here to collect a debt."

Shit. The mob.

My clammy hands pushed at the door with all my might, but Mr. Goatee placed his steel-toed boot in the crack to stop it.

"You're pissing me off, lady," he said, his eyes hard. "Give me the car, and I'll leave you alone."

I took in his words and took a step back. "What car?" I asked, peering up at him and noting all the tattoos that lined his neck.

"The Chevy. You haven't paid on it in six months," he said, leaning toward me.

"Wait a minute," I said, realization setting in. I placed my palm against my forehead. "Shit," I muttered.

"You bought a car six months ago, brand new, and you haven't paid on it."

"Hold on." I left the door and snatched my mace out of my laptop bag.

Unchaining the door, I stepped to the side and let him in. I held the mace in full view and tilted my head back to take in all of the six-foot, large and in charge, scary guy. If he hurt me, I'd mace him in the face and scream till my lungs fell out. It wouldn't even matter anyway because I was sure Mr. Goatee could break my neck in one swift move, if he wanted to.

"Where are the keys to the car?" he pressed, stepping closer.

"I don't have them. It was never my car. I cosigned with my mom—I mean, Jamie," I stuttered. "I don't have the car. It's back in Bowlesville."

"Don't lie to me," he said, aggressively inching forward.

I backed away until I felt the wall against me, until I couldn't move any further, stuck in between the slab of concrete behind me and the massive male in front of me. "Stop. Don't move an inch, or I swear to God, I'll mace this whole can into your face," I hated how everything came down to this whenever Jamie brought me into her drama.

"I told you, I swear, I don't have it. Do you think I need a car in downtown Chicago? I walk everywhere. I work four blocks away. I have no need for a car here. I co-signed with my deadbeat mom because she didn't have good credit to get a car on her own," I said, my voice firm and shoulders tense. "Now, leave. Look for that car in Bowlesville, and I hope you get it."

His eyes narrowed, studying me. I steadied myself against the door as I tried to calm my already shot nerves.

"If you're lying, I'll be back," he said as he peered down at me.

My eyes locked with his. I didn't break eye contact so he knew I was telling the truth. "You won't because I'm not."

When he left, my legs gave out underneath me. I slumped against the door, slid to the floor, and released the breath that I'd been holding. I felt tired all of a sudden, the rush of adrenaline no longer present.

"Crap. My spaghetti." I got up and jolted to the stove.

My sauce was burned. My eyes focused on the dark crusted sauce at the bottom of my pan and at that moment, I wanted to cry. I flipped off the stove and placed both hands at the edge of the counter, head hanging low.

Why is my drama from Bowlesville leaking into my new

life in Chicago?

I stood there for a minute before grabbing my cell phone. I called Kendy first, but her phone went straight to voice mail. I huffed with frustration. I needed someone to vent to, and I needed to be out of my apartment—now.

When Caroline's phone also went straight to voice mail, I left a message. "Caroline, it's Beth. Wondering what you are doing tonight. Want to go out with the new girl for a drink? Call me back, and let me know."

I didn't want to call Brian and lead him on any further, so I called Kent.

He answered on the first ring.

"Hey, I'm calling in my friendship card," I said, staring at my failed spaghetti on the stove. The smell of burned sauce filled my nose. "What are you doing tonight? I can't stay here."

Somehow, I could feel his slight smile through the phone.

"I'm sure you called everyone down your short list. What? They didn't answer?" he asked.

I laughed. "Actually, yes, no one answered. Anyway, do you want to hang out tonight or not?" I instantly wished I hadn't called but there was no way I could just hang up on him now.

"Sure, Beth." He paused before he continued, "I'm going clubbing tonight. Small-town girl, you think you can handle that?"

"Listen, buddy, you don't know me or what I've been through. I'm sure I can handle going out with you."

"I'll pick you up at eleven," he said.

"See you then," I said, before hanging up the phone

I shuffled to the bathroom to get myself ready to hit the club.

Chapter Four

PUNCTUAL, KENT HAD picked me up exactly at eleven. I'd settled on wearing a jean skirt and a black halter-top and felt satisfied with the only fancy outfit I had in my closet besides my suits.

"I don't get it," Kent said, his face perplexed as he drove through traffic in downtown Chicago.

"I told you, she's a deadbeat mother. She left me with Nana when I was six and ran away with one of her boyfriends. She came back when I was eighteen. I thought she wanted a new start, but her habits hadn't changed."

I glanced in the visor's mirror and applied a thick coat of mascara.

He shook his head. "I still don't get it. Why would a mother do that to her own child?"

"Because she's selfish. She needed a car, but her credit was shot, so she asked me to cosign. I wanted to show her that I trusted her and that I forgave her for leaving me the first time." I applied a dab of blush on my cheeks. "Boy, was I wrong. She filled out credit card applications with my social security number and info, and then she racked up my debt. By the time I found out because creditors were calling me, I was in college." I turned to him and blotted powder on my shiny nose.

His eyebrows scrunched together in confusion as he

glanced at the road ahead of him.

"I tried to contest it, but the creditors wouldn't believe me. I didn't have enough money to hire a lawyer, so I've been paying the minimum on her debt ever since. Honestly, I never want to see that witch even if it's in court."

"Your mother is dysfunctional," he said with a scowl on his face. "How much debt are we talking about here?"

I glanced in his direction when we stopped at a red light. "I don't know. Sixty, maybe eighty grand now, including that damn car." I shook my head. "Can we not talk about this? I just want to have fun tonight. Please?" I begged him with my eyes, wanting to forget what had happened earlier along with all the drama my mother constantly brought into my life.

He regarded me, squeezed my hand and gave me a small smile. "Okay," he said, as he pressed on the gas to bring us to our destination.

Cars were lined up and double-parked in front of the warehouse. I could hear the bass echoing from inside the building. Red brick spanned the entire warehouse while people lined the exterior, waiting to get inside. I leaned into my window, my nose almost pressing against the glass, as I took the scene in. There was a massive amount of people congregating outside. The glint from a girl's sequin dress caught my eye and I noticed most of the women were dressed in similar clothing.

"I'm going to give you my valet ticket. I have a spare. You'll probably leave before me. I'll have someone take me home. Don't worry, you'll be okay," he said, making me turn in his direction.

"I'm not a little girl anymore." I pursed my lips and gave him my sexiest look. "I'm going to give out my digits tonight, and in a couple of days, I'll be on a date."

He let out a carefree deep-belly laugh. "Oh, this should be interesting."

I reached for the door and stepped out of the car. Kent walked over to meet me and gestured for me to take his elbow. I linked my arm through his as he handed the valet guy his keys. When Kent handed me the valet ticket, I placed it in my purse and tucked it away for safe keeping. I surveyed the area as men eyed his car while women eyed me. I assumed the women were most likely comparing the plain Jane to the Greek god. The women outside were half-naked, competing over who had the shortest skirt and tightest outfit. They were all made up from head to toe, all in tall thin heels and designer clothing.

I felt like we were on the set of *The Bold and the Beautiful* and I was definitely underdressed.

As we drifted on the outskirts of the line that never seemed to end, two tall bouncers stood at attention, checking IDs. When we glided to the front, outside the roped area, I noticed dirty looks being thrown our way because we were bypassing the line.

Kent nodded to the guard standing on duty. "Busy night, Chris?"

"Yep, I'll be here till six in the morning." Chris unhooked the velvet rope to let us in. With my free hand, I straightened out my jean skirt.

Relaxing his arm, Kent released me and placed his hand on the small of my back. He pushed me forward and trailed right behind me. The warm air stuck to my skin as the damp sweat of the herd on the crowded dance floor filled the air. Trance music pounded in my ears, and my eyes blurred. I tried to focus past the laser lights shining everywhere. I'd never been to a place like this before. This was a real club. I'd only ever really been to Bowlesville's small-town bars.

Two hands on my shoulders pushed me through the crowd. Kent leaned in to shout in my ear, "Keep moving forward!"

I had to strain my ears to hear him over the deafening music. All around me, bodies were clasped tightly together, entranced by the sound of the music. Kent inched toward the front of me, taking my wrist, to force us through the crowds. Even though I was rocking three-inch heels, I felt tiny while gliding through the sea of people. We made our way toward the back of the club to another roped area guarded by a good-looking tattooed bodyguard. I had to tilt my head upward to look at him.

He nodded toward Kent and let us in. The music in the new room was more techno. The pounding of the bass echoed in my ears as I trailed behind Kent. Pop music was my usual sound of choice, so I wasn't accustomed to the noise around me.

He released my wrist and motioned me toward the bar. "You okay?" he asked.

I gave him my winning smile. "Yep, just ready to have some fun."

"What do you want to drink?" he asked, his eyes scanning the area.

"Gin and tonic," I replied, noticing that this new area was not as loud as the first area we walked through.

His eyes searched the vicinity, as if he was looking for someone. Kent raised his hand to the bartender and ordered our first round. When our drinks came, Kent handed me mine. "Don't drink anything that's not from me, okay?" His dimple flashed as he took a sip from his glass.

When Kent lifted his eyes, I shifted to look in the

direction of his attention. A tall, broad male headed our way.

Yes, we are definitely in the land of the bold and the beautiful. I was amazed that they were all in one place. There must have been a prescreening before people were let into this area. I knew I'd gotten a pass because I came in with a Greek god.

As he approached the bar, Kent introduced us. "Beth, this is Luke. Luke, Beth."

Luke took my hand and gave me a once-over.

Where Kent was a Greek god, Luke was the spitting image of a Ken doll with his blond hair accenting his green eyes. He was built perfectly and evenly tanned. A couple of the top buttons on his shirt were undone, and I couldn't prevent my eyes from going to his chest.

"What are you drinking?" Luke leaned into the counter and motioned to the bartender.

"I'm fine right now. Thank you," I replied politely, pulling at the strands of my long dark hair.

He twisted to face the redhead on his other side and started chatting her up. I was momentarily offended that I'd either bored him or I wasn't hot enough to further more conversation.

Everywhere around me, beautiful women were drinking their cocktails, dancing with each other, or draping themselves across equally beautiful men. The smell of money filled the air. Normality had welcomed me in the first room we'd come in. That was where I belonged, not in this room. I was used to line-dancing in plaid shirts and jeans, so all this glitz and glam reminded me that I was far, far away from Bowlesville. My confidence from earlier in the car faded.

I'll definitely be leaving early tonight, so I shouldn't have too much to drink.

I turned when I felt Kent nudge me with his elbow. "You sure you're okay?" he asked as he leaned over. "Get any numbers yet?" he teased.

I automatically smiled at him. "No, not yet. You have to pace these things."

Before he got a chance to respond, female hands wrapped around him from behind.

My eyes widened at the voluptuous and very attractive blonde woman flush against Kent. A white halter-top dress hugged her hips and dipped low to accentuate her breasts. Individual curls flowed down her back.

Kent turned to her with a devilish glint in his eye. "Helen," he murmured.

Her blue eyes met his and then mine. Slowly, her eyes swallowed me in, studying me. "Does she want to join us?" she asked, her eyes alight.

It was warm in the room, but at her words, I got goose bumps.

"No, she's not into that." Kent whispered something into her ear and patted her backside.

She glanced at me once more, shrugged, and strutted away.

"She's pretty," I said, not knowing what else to say. "And very blunt, too. Don't let me stop you from having your fun." I regretted saying it once it had left my mouth. I already felt uncomfortable, and if he left, I wouldn't know anyone in this exclusive club of the beautiful and wealthy. I reached in my purse and squeezed the valet ticket, relieved it was still there.

"I've had her already. I don't have the same girl twice."

"Ugh, gross," I said, surprised by his honesty. "Why

not? Is it because you have a little black book, and you want to make sure you have as many names in there as possible? " I couldn't hide the repulsion in my voice.

"Because I don't want to lead her on." He shrugged his shoulders. "One time is casual. More than that leads to expectations."

I screwed my face, disgusted.

He leaned in a little closer. "Don't look at me like that."

I furrowed my eyebrows, crossed my arms, and shot him a look.

"What? Let me ask you something. Do you think a woman who has sex with a man she just met at a club for the first time wants a serious relationship? Well, do you?"

He looked to me for an answer, and I gave him none.

"Well, the answer is no. She's here for the same thing I'm here for—a little release. If she does want something more than that, then she needs to change her approach because no man will ever take a woman who gives it up that easily seriously."

I had nothing to say to that, so I set my empty glass on the bar, and motioned to the bartender. "I'm buying the next round. What are you having?"

He shook his head, as a dimple flashed on his cheek. "I like how you change the subject when I'm right," Kent said. "I'll have a shot of Crown."

I held up two fingers to the bartender and she placed both shots in front of us. I ordered a glass of Coke as the chaser.

He had been right. I had no right to judge him. The situation would only be wrong if we were dating, but we weren't, so really, he could do as he pleased.

I raised my glass up to him, and he mirrored my

actions before we both threw back the shots of Crown. The burn touched my tongue and slid down my throat. I closed my eyes and chugged my Coke back to minimize the scorch. When I opened them, Kent was staring at me with a smug smile.

I widened my eyes. "Yes?"

"Interesting. I never would have coined you as someone who could handle her liquor."

"I said I wasn't a drunk. I never said that I didn't drink. Kendy introduced me to wine coolers at fifteen."

When he raised two more fingers to the bartender, I pulled down his arm.

"Uh, no. Let's not push our luck, okay? Plus, I still have to drive home," I said.

He tossed money to the bartender as she placed two more shots of Crown in front of us.

"To friendship," he said, lifting up his shot glass.

I reached for my drink and lightly tapped my glass against his, and we swallowed the shot together.

"Ugh," I said, making a face. This time, I had nothing to wash the shot down with, and I coughed a little, which made Kent laugh.

"Hey, I'll be back in one second," he said, glancing at someone behind me.

When Kent left my side, I already felt the hard liquor coursing through my body. I stepped toward the barrier between where the pretty-people room ended and where the common folk began. Trance music dragged me closer and closer to the other room. I glanced up at the bouncer who was guarding the roped area separating the rooms. When he sidestepped to let me pass, I wondered if I could get back in again later.

Music filled my ears, and my body started to move

to the rhythm. I made my way toward the exterior of the dance circle. Scantily clad bodies moved and swayed against each other. When I felt small hands on my hips, I rotated and noticed a tall, lanky boy dancing to the music behind me. His grip was not overly aggressive, his nearness not as close, so I didn't resist. I turned around and placed my hands in the air while his hands remained on my hips. I closed my eyes and danced to the trance beat, swaying my hips from side to side.

I didn't know how long I'd been dancing there when I sensed someone different behind me. I twisted to see a broader male moving to the music. He was more aggressive as I felt his body flush against mine. I advanced closer to the lankier guy in front of me to give the guy behind me a hint, but he just inched forward.

Now sandwiched in the middle of the two men, I tightened up and froze on the dance floor. When I tried to disentangle myself, the lankier guy leaned in for a kiss. I turned my head, and he grazed my cheek. My pulse quickened as I used both hands to shove him away, but he didn't budge.

The more I tried to disengage myself, the more they pressed me in between them. The guy behind me planted his hands on my behind and slowly down to where my short skirt ended and my bare legs began.

"Hey," I said, jabbing him with my elbow. My eyes skittered over the area. I thought of screaming, but wondered if anyone would hear me above the deafening music. *Probably not.*

I used both hands to shove the guy in front of me, but he gripped my upper arms with force.

He smiled, and when I looked into his eyes, they were dilated, and they slightly rolled to the back of his head.

Realization that he was high on something set in, and my adrenaline spiked.

Fight or flight rang in my head, and right before I decided I would bite down on his hand and draw blood, I noticed Kent plowing toward us. There was a tightness around his eyes that frightened me.

He stopped right in front of us. "Get off of her," he said slowly, not shouting but firm and loud enough for both of them to hear. His chestnut eyes were dark with intensity as he flexed his fingers at his side.

The lankier guy moved away from me while Mr. Brawny grabbed my backside one more time before placing himself in front of Kent, challenging him. He was broader than Kent and slightly taller. Kent was over six feet, so this guy looked massive.

"What are you going to do about it, pretty boy?" he snapped, giving Kent a slight push on his chest.

When I looked at Kent, shivers ran down my spine.

Kent let out a slight smile that was eerily disconnected, not meeting his eyes. "I'm going to break your arm for violating a woman."

Before I could even blink, the broader guy swung at Kent, but he moved, avoiding the impact. Kent grabbed the guy's arm, twisted it, and brought the broader male to his knees. The harder Kent twisted, the louder the guy moaned in pain. The high-pitched cry of pain didn't sound as if it could come from a male that immense. Kent showed no mercy as he had the other guy immobilized.

I knew Kent had meant it when he said he would break the guy's arm, and I was scared. "Stop, Kent." I inched closer as he tightened his grip and maneuvered the guy's arm.

"Didn't your mother ever teach you some manners

about how to treat a woman?" he said slowly, twisting the male's arm to an uncomfortable angle.

"Kent!" I yelled louder, looking at his face.

I knew he hadn't heard me. He seemed so focused, so intent. The hair stood at attention at the nape of my neck as I knew what was going to happen next.

"Apparently not, but I will."

I grabbed his arm, tugging it toward me. "Kent, he's had enough."

"Oh, I don't think he has," he said, maintaining his grip on the immense male in front of him.

"No, stop!" I yelled, lunging toward him. I hugged his arm, yanking it toward me. "Please stop," I begged.

Kent angled his head to look at me, finally seeing me and realizing I was there. Slowly, he released the guy and stepped away. He ran one hand through his dark brown hair as he released a heavy sigh.

Two bouncers moved through the spectators who had already surrounded us. Before they could reach Kent, I stepped in front of them.

"That guy assaulted me." I pointed to the man lying on the ground, clutching his arm. "My friend here taught him a lesson," I said, linking my arm through Kent's.

The bouncers picked the man up from the floor, forcing him forward through the crowd.

Kent took hold of my wrist and dragged me toward the other room. Tension was in the air and I released the breath I'd been holding because the near event had been averted.

"Where did you learn how to do that?" I asked, trying to regain my composure while processing what had just happened.

"Black belt in karate," he said, glancing behind me

and toward the brawny guy being led out.

We drifted past the roped-off area and back into the pretty-people room. After Kent plopped me down on a stool by the bar, he motioned toward the bartender and asked for a glass of water.

"Drink this," Kent ordered, placing the water in front of me.

"Thanks," I replied.

"Are you okay?" His eyes quickly inspected me from head to toe before meeting my eyes.

I nodded my head but didn't speak. I was afraid that my voice would quiver as my pulse lowered to its regular pace. He observed me while I drank my water.

"Beth, pick yourself a nice guy, okay? Don't pick up a guy at a club. Club guys are not good for girls like you. Understand?"

I was surprised at his sentiment, and I nodded again. "I was only dancing. Plus, you're a club guy."

"Exactly." His tone was serious, matching his eyes. My insides warmed at Kent's protectiveness.

Luke walked up behind Kent, tapped him on his shoulder, and whispered something in his ear.

Kent's demeanor changed as a slow smile crept up his face. "Beth, I'll be back." He pointed one finger at Luke. "You—watch this girl and make sure she drinks. Understood?" He turned to leave and passed through another roped-off area toward the back. I focused on his retreating back until I couldn't see his figure any longer.

I took a swig of my water as Luke observed me, quietly studying me like I was some sort of animal he'd never seen before.

"How do you know Kent?"

"He's my friend." I continued to drink my water.

Luke laughed once. "Yeah, right. Kent doesn't have any friends—well, me maybe, but no female friends, that's for sure." He raised two fingers to the bartender in front of us and pointed to his glass.

"So, what happened out there? I only saw Kent gripping that guy in a death hold," he asked, leaning against the bar.

"Those guys were getting frisky, too frisky, and then...I don't know. Kent came out of nowhere and helped me out." I took another drink.

Luke examined me from head to chest with another bewildered look on his face. He was silent, studying me once again. To ease the awkwardness, I glanced to my side at the couple groping each other.

Silence was broken when the bartender placed two drinks in front of us.

"No, that's okay," I said, pushing the glass toward Luke.

He tossed money on the counter and inched the glass back in my direction. "Well, Kent told me to have you drink. You heard him."

"I'm sure he didn't mean whatever is in that glass," I said, eyeing the deep gold liquid in front of me.

"Come on, I bought you a drink." He lifted his glass toward me and nodded to my drink on the bar.

"Fine." I reached for the glass, feeling the coldness. It was a hard contrast to my warm hands. I lifted the glass and wrinkled my nose at the potent smell. "What is this anyway?" I took a sip and made a face. Whatever it was, it was strong enough to kill the germs on my kitchen counter.

"Keep drinking. It's good."

I shook my head as I took another chug. The liquid

coated my throat and hit my stomach with a burn. I felt queasy. I lowered my head and closed my eyes as I felt the burn deep within my belly. "Crap, that stuff was strong."

"Don't throw up. That's one sure way to get us kicked out of this place."

He caressed my neck and massaged it with one hand. His touch gave me goose bumps and not the good kind.

I lifted my head and moved slightly away. "I don't even know how I'm going to drive home."

He leaned in and ran a finger on my outer thigh. Bile rose in my throat, and I flinched at his touch.

"I can take you home," he said, edging closer toward me.

The scent of liquor on his breath mixed with the smell of the expensive cologne he was wearing. Everything about him repulsed me.

I pushed myself off the bar stool in one swift movement and moved away. I was tired of being fondled today.

"No flippin' chance, loser." I said, narrowing my eyes at him. I stomped toward the roped area where Kent had entered.

A stoic bouncer stood there. I tried to stand straight, but failed and stumbled slightly. I was queasy from the drink Luke had given me, and all I needed was to get home. "I'm here to see Kent," I said.

The bouncer nodded and moved to let me pass.

Darkness engulfed the room. The only sources of light came from tea lights on the tables. The music pounded in my ears, but as I skimmed the room, I saw no one was dancing. People were sitting and drinking at the tables.

I moved past a girl straddling a guy on the couch. His hands were up her skirt. I scurried to the next table and watched a group of three crowd around a mirror sprinkled with a powder-like substance. I'd seen enough movies to know what they were doing.

I walked faster and scanned the room for Kent. I wanted to tell him that I was leaving. The faster I moved, the more I felt like falling. Taking off my heels, I stepped barefoot on the cold, hard floor. My eyes searched the room and I finally felt my shoulders relax as I spotted Kent in the corner.

I was relieved that he wasn't snorting something. His head was rested back against the couch, his lips slightly parted. When I approached closer, I noticed his breathing was accelerated. I would have thought he was sleeping, but his eyes were shut tight in concentration. His breathing became erratic, and that was when I looked below.

I stopped dead in my tracks as I saw red high heels sticking out from under the table. The last thing I saw was his pants dropped to the floor before I gasped and wheeled around to run out of the room. Panic began to rise as I discovered that I was totally out of my element. I wasn't familiar with the surroundings nor did I know my new friend as well as I thought I had.

I swayed, feeling unsteady, and then stopped to place my heels back on. I had to grip the table closest to me for support. I rushed myself out of the dark room and into the pretty-people room. I took one last glance behind me and realized that I was way out of my league. I didn't belong with this group of people—not that I would ever want to be a part of this group anyways.

When I crossed from the pretty-people room into the normal clubbing room, loud music filled my ears. I wobbled as my vision doubled. I stumbled into a girl, and she pushed me off of her.

"Sorry," I said, trying to regain my footing.

I raced toward the front, and when I finally made it outside, I gasped for air, blowing a series of short breaths to keep myself steady. I had to concentrate hard on not throwing up on the valet guy in front of me as I handed him my ticket. I fished in my purse for a dollar and pulled out a twenty. I pushed it back into my purse and yanked out a ten. Clutching my stomach with both hands, all of a sudden, I felt faint. I gave him the ten, and he reluctantly handed me the keys.

"It's right there on the corner, unless you want me to drive it up." He pointed at the end of the street where the black Bentley was sitting under a lamppost.

I shook my head, unable to voice an answer.

I held my mouth and rushed toward the Bentley down the street. When I pressed the unlock button, the Bentley's lights flashed. Falling to my knees, I gripped the door handle and threw up all over the exterior of Kent's shiny black car. I wiped my mouth with the back of my hand, stepped into the car, and locked myself inside. After reclining the passenger seat all the way back, I passed out.

Chapter Five

MY HEAD WAS pounding, and the light was shining too brightly in the room. I flipped over, placed the pillow over my eyes, and inhaled the scent of freshly laundered sheets. The smell of the detergent was one I was not familiar with. I opened one eye and took a peek from under the pillow to take in my surroundings.

Immediately, I jumped up to a sitting position, causing my head to spin from the abrupt movement. Glancing under the thick duvet, I saw I was only wearing my underwear and a man's T-shirt. My heart pounded in my chest as I remembered the last person I had seen was Luke.

In a king-sized bed, fluffy down pillows surrounded me. In front of me was a massive flat screen TV, and at the foot of the bed was a low white couch. One wall was floor-to-ceiling windows while the other was painted a neutral beige. I deciphered that I was in a hotel room.

I could feel the heat building up behind my eyes, tears threatening to spill over. I placed my hands over my face. I was on the verge of crying. I was not this kind of girl. I never drank myself to the point of oblivion where I couldn't remember what had happened the night before. I cocked my head up as I heard the door open, and when I peered up from my hands, I gave the look of death.

I was surprised to see Kent.

He studied me and scanned the room. Raising one eyebrow, he paced around and stopped in front of me. "Is something wrong? Is someone here?" he asked, his face concerned as he peered over the side of the bed.

I could feel the color draining from my face, and I pulled the covers up to my chin. "No," I snapped, narrowing my eyes at him. "How did I get here? Why am I only in a T-shirt? What happened last night? Why am I here in this hotel room with you?"

His eyes filled with confusion. "I brought you here. I changed you last night because your clothes were covered in vomit. I have no idea what happened. I found you passed out in my car. This is not a hotel room. This is my condo," he said in one breath.

He walked toward me, his arms cautious and careful at his sides. "Why are you so mad? Actually, I think a thank-you is in order. Also, I'd like to thank you for leaving vomit that has now hardened on the exterior of my brand-new car."

"Did we sleep together?" I asked, barely audible. I couldn't even hear my own voice. I was afraid of his answer, but I needed to know. Panic began to rise within me, and I held my breath.

He paused to take in what I'd said. "Oh..." His widened as he registered my question. "Like I told you, you're not my type. When will you believe that I only want a friendship with you?"

I released a long sigh of relief that was loud enough for him to hear. "I feel dumb now." I realized I had spoken that thought out loud. Like a small child, I rubbed my eyes with both palms.

"It's fine. I understand how you jumped to that

conclusion, but I was a perfect gentleman last night. Even if I'd wanted to, I was pretty messed-up myself."

"My head hurts," I whined. I dropped back down and closed my eyes. My head was pounding so loudly that I thought it would explode all over the soft down pillow behind me.

"What the hell did you take?" he asked before walking out of the room. "Hold on, let me get you some Advil."

A few seconds later, he was above me with a glass of water in one hand and Advil in the other. His brown hair was in disarray. He wore bed head well, and I swore, he could have modeled for toothpaste.

"How do you manage to still look cute in the morning?" I said, squinting up at him.

He laughed. "I think you're still drunk. Take this," he said, putting the glass on the side table next to me and handing me the Advil.

I pushed myself up, resting on my elbows against the satin sheets under me. "I saw you last night with the girl wearing the red heels."

"Red heels?" His eyes widened in awareness. "Oh, you did now, did you?" His dimple was apparent on his cheek. "She was a present from Luke."

"Okay, gross." I rolled my eyes, took a sip of water, and swallowed the Advil.

"You're the one who brought it up," he said. He moved to assist me, grabbing my glass and setting it on the side table again.

"Luke bought me another drink, and it put me over the edge. He gave me some strong stuff." My throat felt dry, like sandpaper. "How do you know him anyway?"

"He's an old friend from high school." He frowned slightly as his eyebrows pulled in as though he was deep

77

in thought.

My eyes moved to the alarm clock beside me. It was almost two in the afternoon. "Crap, it's Sunday. I should go." I pushed my legs over the bed and froze. My head was still pounding, like someone was playing the drums in my brain. It took all my strength to just stand upright.

"You can stay as long as you want. You don't look well," he stated as he gripped my elbow to assist me.

"No, really, I have to go. I have to meet someone."

"A date? With the guy at the bar last night?" he asked, surprised.

"Oh yeah, a date with both of those guys who basically assaulted me on the dance floor. Actually, I have a date with the guy with one arm. You took the other arm off, remember?" I looked at him like he was crazy. "No, dummy, I'm meeting my friend Caroline."

"Interesting," he said, slightly smiling at my comment. "I was serious when I said, don't pick up guys from a club. You don't want to catch anything. Plus, a good girl like you can do better than that."

"Are you talking from experience?" I asked. "Too much information. I'd rather not know."

He sat at the foot of the bed, resting his elbows on his knees. "For your information, I get tested twice a year, and I always use protection," he said, amused by my comment.

"Good to know, but it doesn't matter because we're not sleeping together." I bent down and reached for my jean skirt lying on the floor. "Turn around."

He turned to face the TV as I slipped on my vomit-crusted skirt. My body ached and the first thing I needed to do when I got back to my apartment was take a hot shower.

"Also, I've decided that we can't be friends anymore," I said.

His one eyebrow shot up at my words. "Okay…" he said slowly, turning to face me. "Why not? Did I do something to offend you?"

"No. I just realized that I don't know you very well, and your type of people are just way out of my league. I don't do drugs or casual sex, and I don't want to be around that. It makes me feel…" I paused to search for a word. "Uncomfortable." I pulled my hair into a bun on the top of my head and stepped in front of him to grab my heels.

"Beth," he said, as he stood from the bed, "let me remind you that you invited yourself to my little outing. I asked you before if you could handle it, and you said you could."

He offered me his hand, and I gripped it for support while I hopped on one leg to put on my heel.

"When you refer to my type of people, you're stereotyping. One, the only person I knew from that place last night was Luke. Two, everyone has casual sex—okay, everyone but you has casual sex. Three, I don't do drugs," he said as he released me. His eyebrows pulled in. "Plus, I knew you were with me, and I felt responsible for you." He looked surprised by his own comment.

"Why?" I asked, pausing to assess him.

He laughed. "Now that I think about it, I could sort of tell you weren't used to that environment. I've seen a lot of things happen, and I didn't want anything to happen to you." His eyebrows pulled together. "When I left you with Luke, I thought you'd be okay. I didn't think he'd get you piss-ass drunk."

I softened at his comment. "Oh."

He straightened his shoulders. "Did I make you take any drugs last night?"

"Is this a trick question?" I asked, confused.

"Don't overthink. Answer the question."

My eyes were cautious as I wondered where this conversation was heading. "No," I replied.

"Did I try to make a pass at you or coerce you into doing anything against your will?"

"Uh...no?" I said, lifting my eyebrows.

"Yes, that's right. I told you specifically not to take drinks from anyone but me, and I remember a particular instance when I almost took someone's arm off because he was being disrespectful. Also, I was very considerate when I let you spend the night. I even changed you out of your vomit-covered clothes before I left you to sleep in my guest room."

I opened my mouth to speak but Kent raised one finger to indicate he was not done. "If that is not a definition of friendship, I don't know what is."

"Why?" I asked.

"Why what?"

"Why do you want to be friends?"

"What an odd question." His eyebrows drew in. "I don't know," he said, studying my face. "Because you make me laugh, and I guess I like that you love to eat and don't care." He seemed finally satisfied by his own answer.

I thought of all he'd said, and the fact that he hadn't tried anything on me when I was passed out had to count for something. I gave him a small smile. "Okay, fine. We're friends who eat together."

I made my way to the side mirror and the image of my hideous face stopped me dead in my tracks. My eyes were smeared with eyeliner. My cheeks were red from leftover blush. My lipstick went beyond my lips to the corners of my mouth and up toward my nose.

"Uh…okay, if we're friends, you have to always tell me the truth. Why didn't you tell me I look like death right now?"

"I always tell you the truth, Beth." He walked behind me, so I could see both of our reflections in the mirror. "You look like death right now." He framed my shoulders with his hands. "And smell like vomit."

At that, we both laughed.

Looking at his reflection again, I thought to myself, *It's not fair that he looks like a model in the morning, even while hungover.*

THE NEXT WEEK was restaurant week with Kent. There were over three hundred restaurants participating with prix fixe menus. It took forever and a half to decide together on where we wanted to go. We compromised by trying both of our top five picks. On multiple days, we went to lunch and dinner. I'm certain I gained over five pounds getting my eat on.

Before I knew it, the workweek was over, Friday night had come, and I was out at the bar with my coworkers. It was a different environment, seeing everyone out of the corporate element. Jim was by the bar, laughing like I'd never seen him laugh before. He was wearing jeans and a Northwestern alumni T-shirt, looking younger and more relaxed.

Sitting on a bar stool next to Caroline, I watched as she wrapped her arms around her tall, lanky boyfriend,

Jeff. They couldn't keep their hands off of each other, and I wondered if they remembered that I was right beside them.

I jumped when I felt a hand on the small of my back. When I turned, Brian was behind me with a beer in his other hand.

"Hey," he said, leaning into me.

I moved from his touch, hoping Caroline hadn't seen it.

"Brian, finally, you're here. Beth over here has been waiting for you." Caroline giggled before tilting her beer bottle all the way back.

I gave her my evil eye before taking a sip of my drink.

"Beth, I'm so kidding." She hiccupped. "What number is this one?" she asked, turning to her boyfriend and lifting her bottle.

"Caroline, don't you know? Beth doesn't date coworkers, so there is no way she could have been waiting for me." Brian gave me a wink, breaking the awkwardness.

I silently thanked him and awarded him with a small smile.

"I'm going to order the next round. What are you guys drinking?" he asked.

After we gave him our requests, Brian headed toward the bar, and I watched his broad shoulders move under his fitted T-shirt.

"Beth, look at all that hotness! If you only gave in a little…" She hiccupped. "Quit being so uptight, and live the life. Plus, you two would make the cutest couple."

Before I had a chance to snap at her for teasing me one too many times, Jeff grabbed her beer bottle.

"You're cut off," he said before giving her a kiss on the lips.

"Aw, why?" she whined, trying to reach for the bottle. She slumped against his arms when he tipped her drink all the way back.

"Because you had too much to drink, that's why, and when you have too much to drink, you have no filter."

I lifted my beer bottle to tap against Jeff's in thanks. "Yeah, you're a mean drunk, Caroline."

She looked me deep in the eyes with her sad Caroline pout, jutting out her lip. "I'm sorry, Beth. I was just telling you how it is." Her arms draped around my neck, and the next minute, she started crying, confirming that she was officially drunk.

I wrapped my arms around her lower back. "It's okay, Caroline. I forgive you. Plus, you're my one and only girlfriend in Chicago, so I'm not left with much of a choice." I said, patting her back and giving Jeff a small smirk.

When her sobs accelerated, Jeff gathered her from my arms. "Okay, babe, this is our cue to go home."

I gave him a hug as he held her by the waist, and I watched them move toward Brian, who was surrounded by a bunch of bankers. Leaning against the bar, he was in conversation with the others, making them laugh. He was probably telling them some joke. I'd only seen Brian in the office, and he seemed very professional. I hadn't been out on a customer call with him, but I'd heard customers loved him because he was easy to talk to, and he made everyone in a room feel at ease.

I watched Caroline tiptoe to give him a hug, and then Brian reached for Jeff's hand to signal good-bye. When Brian's eyes caught mine, I looked to my beer bottle and tipped it back. When I glanced back up, he was making his way toward me.

"So, you having fun?" he asked.

83

"Yeah. Everyone at the bank is pretty cool." I took another swig of my beer.

"How many is that now?" he asked.

"I'm not sure—three or four maybe." Suddenly feeling shy, I looked at the beer bottle in my hand.

"Just so you know, I hate when she teases you and me. It makes me uncomfortable. It's not like I don't think you're cute. It's because we work together," I said, looking up into his clear baby-blue eyes. The way our eyes caught stir butterflies in my belly that I hadn't felt in a long time.

He chuckled lightly and lifted a finger. "Waitress, another Corona, please," he said, speaking over the noise. "You're more honest when there is liquor in you. Let's see how far this can go?" He squared his shoulders to face me directly. "So, Beth, what's the worst that can happen if we start dating while we work together? Making out on the copier?" He gave me his boyish grin. "You think too much. Just live in the moment. Who knows? I could be your future husband, and you're turning me away. How are we going to have our six kids in uptown Manhattan?"

I blushed at his comment. It really took all my power not to gravitate toward this perfect man in front of me. After all, I was only human, and he was the ideal male that I was sure everyone pictured in their storybooks. He was good-looking and hardworking, and he was able to provide for a family in the future.

"Uptown Manhattan?" I asked, breaking into my own thoughts.

"Yeah, I'm trying to get placed as a corporate banker there. I had a couple of leads, but that's a tough position to score."

The waitress approached with our beers, and I tipped

mine back as he talked about New York and how he always wanted to live there but life had just landed him in Chicago. I asked him about his family to deter the questions from myself and because I was generally interested.

Both of his parents were working professionals. He had grown up in the Midwest with three sisters who had loved to dress him up as a child. His face lit up as he talked about them, and I laughed as he reminisced about his childhood.

My mind drifted to Kendy. I missed her so much that my heart ached. Talking to her every day hadn't been enough. I missed the physical Kendy—the person I could tell my deepest darkest secrets to, the person who I didn't have to pretend with, and the person who knew everything about me, including my past and what I wanted for my future.

As I guzzled my drink, I felt the cold beer move down the back of my throat. My body began to warm as my mind began to haze over. I didn't know how long we had been sitting at our table, but when I glanced up, all of our coworkers were long gone. Listening to the bar music, I was sure I had a goofy, drunk smile all over my face. Brian was so animated when he was drunk that I laughed even louder.

A cheeky grin hit my face when the music changed to "SexyBack" by Justin Timberlake. It brought back memories from the good old days.

"Come on, let's dance." I grabbed Brian's hand and pulled him toward the dance floor.

After tossing his beer back, he took my hand. "Just so you know, this white boy *can* dance," he said, pointing to himself.

"Sure!" I yelled over the music. "And just so you

know, this girl was on the pom team in high school," I said, bobbing my head to the sounds.

His hands moved to my hips as we made our way to the dance floor. Turning to face him, I bounced slowly to the beat and nodded my head to the music. We both started swaying to the bass echoing through the bar. I felt tingling sensations where his hands met my body. Inching closer to me, he started to let loose. Brian could dance. I put my arms on his shoulders and shifted toward him, swaying my head from side to side as our bodies moved in unison to the music.

When he looked at me under hooded eyes and dropped his head, I held my breath. He brushed his lips against mine, soft as a whisper and just barely touching, as if his lips were asking for permission. I let his lips linger a little longer than what I should have allowed. I wanted to blame it on the alcohol, but every part of me wanted to kiss him back, especially with his hands all over me, causing my insides to heat up to immeasurable temperatures.

My no-business-and-boys rule rang in my head, and I slowly backed away.

Brian eyes peered down at me. "What?" A smile slowly crept across his face.

Before I crossed the line any further, I shook my head, pivoted, and headed toward the bar. "I need another drink," I said, trying to calm my raging hormones.

He followed me and ordered us both drinks. We sat on the bar stools, silently watching the crowd moving to the beat of the music on the dance floor.

When I finished my drink, I stood. "It's late. I think I should go." I just needed to distance myself, especially with this much liquor in me. I couldn't think straight, and I didn't want the night to progress into something I would regret later.

"Hey, I'll walk you home."

"No, it's fine. It's only a couple of blocks. Plus, I have this," I said, taking out my mace from my back pocket. "See?"

"That thing is not going to save you against a six-hundred-pound ogre. I'm taking you home." He grabbed my hand and pulled me out of the bar.

A little past one in the morning, we walked in silence back to my apartment. Downtown Chicago was vacant, except for a group of drunken partygoers lingering at a bar down the street. Our hands were linked together, and I knew I should pull away, but I didn't. When we were in front of my apartment, I reached up to give him a hug. When I released him, he dropped his head and kissed me. This time, my self-control was shot. I let him do it—again.

His lips were soft and gentle. He tasted of hard liquor and beer. I was buzzed, but his mouth moving against mine awakened all my senses. My whole body leaned into him, wanting more, even though I shouldn't because I was breaking my own rule. But it felt so good. I hadn't been kissed in such a long time. Pushing through the haze of liquor, I painfully pulled away from him and took a deep breath.

I shook my head slowly. "I'm sorry. I shouldn't have let you do that," I said, my voice not very convincing. "Listen, Brian, we work together."

"So?" he said, coming down for another kiss.

I pulled farther away from him but was still locked in his embrace. "Sorry, I shouldn't lead you on like this. Seriously, I don't want to complicate things at work," I said, finally finding my voice.

"It won't," he said, his arms still wrapped around my

lower back.

"I've worked very hard to get this job. I don't date coworkers because I don't want to be the talk of Financial State." I finally pulled away from our entanglement, instantly regretting my temporary lapse of weakness from his irresistible lips.

"Okay, what are you doing next weekend?" Brian asked as a half-smile appeared on his face.

"Did you not just hear what I said?"

"Yeah, we can hang out though, right? Just as friends."

"I think you used that one before, and that went all so well," I said sarcastically, shaking my head.

His eyes met mine, his blue to my emerald, and I stood there under the lamppost, admiring how the light accented all his boyish features.

"Okay," he said, finally taking a step back. "I'll see you at work then."

I paused and studied his smiling face, while a car horn blared in the background. "See you at work," I said as I reached for the door.

He pushed against the door, keeping it closed and blocking my path. "Just as friends." He pointed to his cheek, gesturing for me to kiss him.

I looked at him, shook my head, and tiptoed to plant one on his cheek, taking in the musky scent of his cologne. He put his hand on the spot I'd just kissed and sighed heavily.

"Bye, Brian." I laughed once as I headed into my apartment. *What am I going to do with this boy?*

Chapter Six

IT READ 6:30 on my computer monitor. Everyone had left work for the evening, but I wanted to get this credit workup done and ready for tomorrow's team discussion. The sound of shuffled footsteps caused me to glance up from my screen, and I locked eyes with Brian as he strolled toward my desk.

"Hey, I figured you were still here." He peered over my cubicle, leaning his arms against the ledge wearing a serious face that was unlike Brian. "Uh...I wanted to ask you to dinner," he continued as he rubbed the back of his neck.

I started shutting down my computer, already mentally exhausted from the day, and my stomach growled at the thought of food. "Sure. Where are we going?" I reached for my wallet, stuffed it into my laptop bag, and turned off my computer monitor.

Brian's eyes dropped to his shoes and up again to meet my eyes. I quirked an eyebrow, wondering what he was up to.

"Not today. I wanted to ask you to dinner this weekend." He fiddled with his hands. "As in a dinner date."

I took his words in and could not help but feel flattered. This usually confident banker was nervous for once, and it was because of me. "Brian, I thought we discussed this. We can't go there."

"I know what you said, Beth, but I've been thinking. I know it matters to you, but it doesn't matter to me. Plus," Brian looked nervously to the floor again, "I like you, and I'd like to take you on a date." He lifted his eyes to mine.

I couldn't help the smile on my face, which I felt gave him courage as his eyes lit up. "I don't want you to think that I'm the kind of guy who makes out with girls at the bar," he said. "I mean, I used to be that guy who made out with every girl at the bar, but you're not that type of girl. You're a dinner-and-movie kind of girl." Determination was set in his face as he stood straighter. He didn't break eye contact. "Listen, one date. That's it. No commitment. If you're embarrassed or don't want to be teased, no one in the office has to know. Like I said, I'm into you. I want to take this one girl who is funny, smart, motivated, and unbelievably cute out for a nice dinner. Come on," he said, giving me puppy-dog eyes.

Looking into the deepest pair of blue eyes, I knew I could fall for this guy if I let myself. Kendy's voice rang in my head. *Maybe I should live a little. Have fun and date.* It wasn't like we reported to the same boss.

"I don't know," I said, doubt in my voice.

"One date. Come on. We do have fun together, Beth, and it's free dinner on me. How can you turn that down? I'll pick a good restaurant, I promise," Brian said, lifting two fingers in a Boy Scout oath.

"Fine," I said, exasperated but still smiling.

His boyish, relaxed demeanor was back at my answer. "See? I knew my persistence and stalkerish tendencies would win out." He winked.

When he turned to leave, I smiled and put my fingers on my lips, thinking of the other night. Even though I didn't want to admit it, I was excited about our date.

I grabbed my stuff and pulled out my cell phone. I knew it was too late to back out of my date. I'd already accepted going with Brian. I was excited, and I wanted someone to share in my excitement. I didn't know if it was a good idea, but either way, I was jumping up and down inside. I hadn't been on a date in quite a while.

The phone call went directly into voice mail.

"Hey, this is Kendy. Leave a message."

"Kendy, where are you?" I huffed. "I've been calling you for days. Miss you, babe. Call me back." I frowned, dropped the call, and stared at my phone. *Where is she?*

I'd always shared my giddiness with her. We had been talking about boys since we were in sixth grade. Also, I wanted her advice. It frustrated me that our calls were becoming less and less frequent. I knew part of the reason was due to her work schedule. Either way, it was at times like this I missed her the most.

INSTEAD OF WALKING directly home, I drifted toward Trump Tower and headed past security. Before I knew it, I was knocking at his door. I paused a little bit before knocking again. I was about to turn around when a pretty redhead wrapped in a navy silk robe opened the door. I looked at the numbers on the door and felt my cheeks warm. I was definitely at the right place.

"Hi, um...is Kent here?" I asked shyly, squeezing my hands together.

"Oh, yes, come in. He's in the shower." She pulled the door wide open to let me enter.

I stepped in and stood by the door as she shut it

behind me. I felt the warmth creep up from my neck to the apple of my cheeks as I shifted from one foot to another. My eyes scanned the area in his condo but Kent was nowhere to be seen.

"Have a seat. I'll let him know that you're here."

I stuck out my hand awkwardly and introduced myself. "Hi, I'm Beth, Kent's friend," I said, drawing out the last word. I didn't want her to think I was another one of his girls, especially when they were obviously more than friends.

She chuckled and shook my hand. "I'm Anne. Let me tell him you're here." She glided into his room and shut the door behind her, leaving me standing there, wishing I wasn't.

I sat down on the edge of the couch and contemplated leaving, but at this point, it was too late. He would already know I was here. When she returned, she was wearing skinny jeans, accentuating her height, and a tank top, showing off her perfect figure. Kent, wearing only a towel, followed right behind her. I caught sight of the well-defined lines of his eight-pack slightly glistening, not fully dry from his shower, and I dropped my eyes to the floor.

"Hi, Beth," Kent said, using another towel to dry his hair.

I glanced up and concentrated only on his face. "Hey," I said with a small wave before quickly dropping my hand to my lap.

A dimple emerged on his cheek, and I felt the warmth move from my face to my ears.

He turned to the redhead beside him. "Do you need money for a cab home?" he asked softly, walking her to the door.

Looking at my flip-flops, I felt as if I was intruding on something intimate. At that moment, I wanted to leave.

"No, I think I can manage. I'd tell you to call me, but I know you won't."

I glanced up to see a sad smile on her face, making me feel sorry for her. She tiptoed and kissed Kent on the lips before he led her out and shut the door behind her.

"I'm sorry. I know I should have called. I mean, it's seven. I didn't think you'd have company—obviously. Either way, I should have called." I shook my head and stood up to leave.

"It's fine. You didn't interrupt anything. We were done anyway," he said, readjusting his towel.

My eyes moved to where his hands were—right by his happy trail.

"Seriously, can you please put on some clothes?" I angled my head to the floor, embarrassed that he'd caught me staring.

"Stay right there. Let me change," he said. "Don't leave," he commanded before heading to his bedroom.

I sat back on the couch and ran my hands against the black leather, feeling the cool material under my fingertips. Turning to the right, I looked outside through the floor-to-ceiling windows to the amazing view of the city below.

"So, Beth, did you need something?" he asked, pulling a gray shirt over his semi-wet hair.

My eyes moved to his chisled hard-tone abs again and I shook my head to focus. I thought back to why I'd come here. "I'm sorry for barging in. Next time, I'll call. I called Kendy first, but she didn't pick up. I needed girlie advice." I smiled.

He sat right beside me on the couch. "Girlie advice?"

"Why are you smiling like a cheeseball?" I asked.

"Because you're smiling like a cheeseball," he said, motioning with his hands for me to continue. "Go on."

"I have a date," I said, eyes wide. "But with a coworker," I added, overly frowning. I explained the situation with Brian and me—how I thought he exuded perfection but how working together complicated things.

Kent rested his ankle on his knee as he listened intently. He did not speak until I was finished talking.

"You're interested in him, right?"

"Yeah, but we work together. If it didn't work out, I'd still have to see him day in and day out. Plus, I'd be the gossip of Financial State," I said.

I'd moved here to escape the gossip, the snickers, the looks of sympathy from the people of Bowlesville, and I didn't want that to happen here—in my new home in a new city.

"Women are so confusing." He shook his head. "From the way you described him, he seems like a nice guy."

"Oh my gosh, he's perfect," I squealed. "He's smart, nice, and successful. He's funny and super cute. He has the nicest eyes," I said, bouncing up and down slightly on the couch. "Seriously, he's happily ever after material."

"Well then, that's settled. What's the problem? Go out with what's-his-name, have fun, and see where it leads." Kent shrugged.

"Okay," I said, clasping my hands together. All I needed was for someone to tell me that besides my doubts, everything would turn out okay. I always had Kendy for that, depending on her for advice when I needed it. I was surprised that Kent was beginning to take her place.

Before I could take it back, I jumped on Kent and wrapped my arms around his neck, giving him a hug.

"I'm so excited. He's über cute," I said. I felt my ears warm when I realized I was practically on his lap and I backed away, embarrassed.

Kent's smile matched my own.

"Just invite me to the wedding," he said. "Since I won't have a wedding of my own, you can have me stand up on your side."

"Deal." I nodded.

"Glad that's decided." He stood and walked into the kitchen. "I'm hungry. Did you eat?" he asked, opening the fridge.

On cue, my stomach grumbled. "No, but really, I should get going, I have a big day at work tomorrow," I said, getting up. I reached my arms above my head in a satisfying stretch.

"I'm an excellent cook," he said, poking his head in the fridge.

"You cook?" I laughed, thinking of his no-job lazy ways.

Kent glanced back at me and feigned insult. "Yes, I cook, and I'm quite good at it. I went to culinary school for fun a while back. Just stay. I promise to serve an excellent meal."

My eyebrows shot up to the ceiling, but he couldn't see because his head was back in the fridge. Every day, he surprised me with his unexpected behavior. I wondered what else he did in his free time. Must be nice to take classes just for fun, because he was most likely bored. When he took out steaks from the freezer, my mouth watered.

"Okay, I'll stay," I said, knowing my fridge at home was practically empty.

RAYS OF SUNLIGHT warmed my face as I stepped out of Financial State. Done with work and out on time for once, everything was absolutely perfect. I was going on my first date with Brian this weekend. He was the ideal male: cute, smart, and doting. I had the perfect job, a place that appreciated all my hard work yet challenged me every day. Kendy was not here with me, but I realized I had a good friend in Kent.

A grin was on my face as I rode the happy train, walking home from work.

And then, I spotted her.

My stomach dropped as tension rose to my shoulders.

It was my mother.

Jamie stood there in front of my apartment, wearing jean capris too tight for her figure and a red tank top that revealed her heart tattoo right above her breast. Her stringy highlighted blonde hair flowed down her back as she smoked her cigarette. Jesse was standing beside her, and I cringed. I didn't know why Jamie still associated herself with that overweight, tattooed, balding, cheating alcoholic.

I couldn't believe they were here, but in the back of my mind, I wondered what had taken them so long to find me. I was sure Kendy hadn't told them where I was, but I had known it was just a matter of time.

I walked toward them and blocked their path to my door. "What are you doing here?" I snapped, already knowing why they had come.

"Baby, I've missed you." She reached for me and tried to envelop me in a hug.

When I avoided her embrace, her eyes flashed with hurt as it had many times before, only I'd stopped believing her after the second time she'd hurt me.

"How did you find me?" I shook my head and crossed my arms in front of me. "Never mind. Leave me alone."

The alcoholic said, "Beth, long time no see. We've missed you."

"Sure," I said, glaring at both of them.

I pushed open the door to my apartment complex, and they walked behind me, going past security. I debated telling security they were trespassers and didn't live here, but I didn't want to start a scene. Eventually, they would come back. They already knew where to find me.

When someone stepped off the elevator, I stormed in while Jamie and Jesse followed me.

I flipped around to face them. "Why are you here? Oh, wait, I know. Maybe I should ask, how much do you need this time, Jamie?" I glowered at both of them. "I don't have anything. You took everything I had and then some."

The elevator opened on my floor, and I stomped out, anger resonating with every step. I slipped my key in and opened the door to my apartment, and once again, they trailed behind me. If we were going to yell, I didn't want the whole world to know my business involving my deadbeat mother.

"You clean up well, Beth," she said softly, reaching out for a lock of my hair.

I reeled back, away from her grasp. After throwing my laptop bag on the floor and my keys on the kitchen island, I stared them both down.

"Tell me what you want," I scowled, crossing my arms in front of me. I was tired of playing this game of figuring out why they were really here. It could only be for one reason.

"Jesse owes some people money," she mumbled, finally letting out the truth. "And now, he's in trouble. I promise, honey, I'll pay you back. I promise."

I glowered at her. Her hands trembled at her sides, revealing her fear—maybe for his safety from the thugs he owed or maybe for her own safety from him.

"Not my problem." I lifted my chin in defiance and glared at the two losers in front of me.

"Don't talk to your mom like that. She's asking you a question," Jesse said.

"She's not my mom," I countered. "She stopped being my mom when she left me and took me to the bank. She only came back to steal from me and she's back again. What a surprise!" I spat.

"I said, don't talk to your mom like that." He inched forward, step-by-step.

I stood my ground and didn't break eye contact. "I don't have any money. Everything I earn at this job is used to pay for the debt that Jamie put me in and for my own bills. I'm left with nothing, and I have nothing. There's no money to give you. Sorry," I said unapologetically.

He laughed with no humor. "No money? I doubt that's true." His eyes glanced around my apartment and then back to me to do a once-over.

Jamie stopped him from inching forward more and gripped his forearm. "Beth, all we need is five thousand dollars. That's all we need. I swear, I'll pay you back, and we'll leave you alone. I swear it."

Her eyes begged me to give her what she needed.

I'd been here before. Many years ago, she'd needed my help, and I—being the stupid one—had lent her the little money I'd made from my side jobs in addition to cosigning on that car loan when I'd only been beginning to build my credit. I'd wanted to help her because I loved her, because she was my mother, and because I'd thought she loved me, too.

Now, looking into her emerald eyes that were so much like my own, I felt nothing. There was nothing left for me to give to this woman who had left me—not once but twice. It'd left me devastated, wondering why I wasn't good enough. I had nothing else to give her, and if I had, I wouldn't because I refused to be burned again.

"I don't have any money. I don't have it!" I shouted. "Now, leave!" I yelled, pointing toward the door.

Jesse shrugged Jamie off, changed his stance, and moved forward. "Listen, you will give us the money we need, and you'll give it to us now. You got away with talking to your mother like that, but you will not talk to me that way," he said, pointing a finger at me.

He stopped inches from my face, and I could smell the cigarette smoke on his breath.

"You understand?"

I automatically flinched and cowered. I'd seen him hit Jamie before. Although I'd shown no fear earlier, his proximity scared me. I doubted he would restrain from hitting me if he felt the urge to.

I heard a knocking on the door before Kent entered my apartment, holding a bag of Greek Island Gyros.

"Hey, Beth."

All of us turned.

His eyes first showed confusion, taking the scene in. Once he saw my face, his demeanor changed.

"What's going on here? Who are these people?" he asked protectively.

He dropped the food on the island and stalked in my direction before stopping in between Jesse and me. "Is there a problem here?" There was a seriousness in Kent's eyes, I'd recognized. It's the same look he had when he confronted the man at the club.

"Hi, I'm Jamie, Beth's mom." She flattened her hair, smiled sweetly, and offered her hand to Kent.

Kent stared at her outstretched hand and inspected the both of them. "What's going on here?"

Embarrassed, Jamie dropped her hand and her eyes focused on my carpet.

"We just wanted to visit Beth. Plus, she owes us some money, and we are here to collect," Jesse said, taking a step forward and sizing up Kent.

At Jesse's words, I snapped. "I don't owe you anything, you liar!" I tiptoed and peered over Kent's shoulder and glared at Jesse.

His jaw tightened, but I didn't care. My confidence had emerged as soon as Kent walked through that door.

I couldn't hold it in any longer. Letting it all out, I screamed at the top of my lungs, "I owe you *nothing*! I. Don't. Have. Anything! It wasn't enough for you to use my name and rack up debt on credit cards I didn't even know about. You had to take everything of Nana's, too, and pawn it. Those things were hers, not yours!" I was fuming. My fists were clenched to my side, and my face burned red from anger.

"I've never asked you for anything. I raised myself and worked to pay for everything on my own, and now, I'm paying your debt! And you still want more? What else do you want? Blood? I have nothing left to give!" I screamed. "Nothing!"

"How much do you need?" Kent asked, shooting

them a deadpan look.

"Five grand," Jesse replied.

Reaching into his back pocket, Kent pulled out his check book.

I pulled his wrist back. "No."

"Beth, it's only money," Kent said.

His brown eyes filled with sympathy, and all of a sudden, I wanted to cry.

"No, Kent. Please, don't. This is my problem, not yours," I pleaded, peering up at him.

"I'm sure he can afford it." Jesse smirked.

With all self-control lost, I grabbed my hair and stomped my feet like a three-year-old. "This is bullshit! This will never end. They are always going to want more. It's never going to be enough. It might not be next week or next month, but they will come back. I hate this. I hate this! I'm so tired of this crap."

I pulled on my shirt, frustrated, wanting to rip it into shreds. "I told you, I have nothing left. Nothing. Left. I just want you to leave me alone. Leave. Leave! LEAVE! Get the hell out of my apartment! Get! Out!" I yelled as I fisted my hands at my side.

Kent filled out the check and handed it over to Jesse. "You have your money. Now, go." His expressionless face remained as he looked at Jamie and Jesse. "That is the last thing you will ever receive from Beth or me. Unless she reaches out to you first, you will never call or see her ever again. Do you understand?" His silence required a response. "Do you understand?" Kent repeated, enunciating each word as if he were speaking to toddlers.

"Sure thing." Jesse nodded as he smiled victoriously. He grabbed Jamie by the elbow and led her toward the door.

"One more thing," Kent said.

Jesse peered over his shoulder to look back.

"If you ever contact Beth again, I will make sure you go to jail for a very long time for fraud and identity theft. I'm sure the judge would not agree with you using Beth's social security number without her knowledge and forging her signature on credit cards that weren't hers."

When Kent locked the door behind them, I wrapped my arms around myself and stared at the direction where Jesse and Jamie had just left. They'd come back, I was sure of it. Despite Kent's warnings, I know I'd see them again.

"I wanted to start over and forget the past," I said, my voice toneless. All of a sudden, the fight left me. I felt tired. "Whatever I do, I can never win. The past is always coming back to haunt me," I whispered mostly to myself.

His warm arms enveloped around me while my arms remained wrapped around myself.

"I told you not to do it, Kent. It's not your problem. It's mine."

"It's only money, Beth, and it's unsettling to see you this way."

His arms tightened further, and the tension that I'd been holding in released as I reveled in his comfort. My shoulders went limp while I rested my head on his chest and listened to his heart beating.

"I was devastated after hearing that Nana had died," I said softly. "When I rushed home from college to bury her, everything was gone. Everything, Kent," I whispered. "She'd pawned all of Nana's stuff, and at that moment, I knew I hated her. I hated her for what she had done to me, but most of all, I hated her for doing that to Nana. Jamie couldn't even respect the mother who had loved her and had forgiven her time and time again." I leaned into him, the tears threatening to spill over, as my voice shook while I spoke, "She was dead. Dead. And Jamie couldn't even let her leave in peace."

He placed his chin on top of my head and exhaled. He pulled me closer, caging me in with his arms. Silence ensued, and I was comforted by our breathing, by the rhymatic compressions of his chest and by the quietness.

"Everything will be okay. I'm here. We're friends, right?" The continuous motions of Kent rubbing my back continued to calm me. "Well, friends help each other."

I exhaled a heavy sigh. "Kent, friends don't just give friends five grand. I can't pay you back anytime soon. It's not the end. I know they'll come back."

"What you don't know about me is that I have ex-cellent lawyers, and if they come back, I'll go through with what I told them. The five grand…well, let's just say that's an advance. You can come clean my condo every week," he said, trying to break my mood.

I closed my eyes and listened to his breathing while feeling the expansion of his chest against my cheek. Exhausted, I had no energy to even laugh.

Chapter Seven

THE WEEKEND FINALLY came. I tried the best I could to put my deadbeat mother in the back of my mind, so I could prepare for my date with Brian. I would not let that woman damper my mood.

Turning up the music, I pulled out my blow-dryer to straighten my hair. I hadn't had a date in a long time, especially one with someone I really liked. As giddy as a little girl, butterflies fluttered in my stomach, and a smile was fixed on my face while I combed my hair.

Dancing around the bathroom in my robe, I pulled out my makeup bag from under the sink. I looked in the mirror and brushed on my foundation. After an unusually long makeup ritual, I tried on everything in my closet. I decided on a cute floral skirt, a tank top, and a cardigan. Summery and sweet, I looked down at my outfit, feeling content.

The phone rang, and I answered it to tell the doorman to let Brian up. I ran to the bathroom to check my makeup one last time before I heard a knock on the door. I took a deep breath and straightened out my skirt before I opened it.

"Hey, sexy," he said, giving me his winning smile.

I blushed at his endearment. "Hey yourself." I stepped aside to let him in.

He pulled a bouquet of roses from behind his back, and I flashed a cheeky grin.

"Thanks," I said, grabbing the bouquet. "I'm going to put these in water, and then we can go." I should have toned down my excitement but I couldn't help it.

As I filled the vase, I gave him a once-over. The slew of butterflies fluttered in my stomach as my eyes took him in. Freshly shaved, he wore jeans and a blue button-up.

"Where are we going tonight?" I asked, suddenly analyzing if I was overdressed.

"I'm going to show you what Chicago is all about," he replied.

I grabbed my purse and walked toward him. "Okay then, let's get this party started."

He didn't hesitate to hold my hand while leading me out the door, and I let him.

THE AWNING SAID Café Iberico. Latin music filled the air as the waitress recited the specials and put the menus on the table. I scanned the restaurant, bouncing my knees to the rhythm of the Latin beats. Tea lights covered the tables, contributing to the romantic ambience.

"I'll order, if that's okay? Don't worry, I'll make sure you are fully stuffed," Brian said.

After he placed our order and the waitress took our menus away, a nervous silence built between us.

"What? Do I have something on my face?" I asked, suddenly self-conscious from the look he was giving me. "Why are you staring at me?"

"Did you put on extra makeup for our date tonight?" Brian asked, lifting his chin.

"No!" I said, feeling my cheeks warm. I didn't want to make him think that I was trying too hard to impress him, even though I was. Maybe my thirty minute make-up session was a bit too much, when usually it only took me ten minutes to get ready.

He smiled at my discomfort, which made me laugh.

"Maybe," I replied.

"Well, you don't need anything extra. You're beautiful just the way you are," Brian said, leaning back against his chair to assess me.

"Whoa, that's a line if I've ever heard one."

"It's not a line. It's the truth. Baby, I've got lines, but I haven't used one on you yet."

I felt myself tighten as I became nervous from his charm. I looked toward the couple having dinner next to us and tucked a strand of hair behind my ear.

"So, Beth, tell me, what's a nice girl like you doing without a boyfriend?"

"So upfront with the questions. This is definitely not cafeteria talk. I can ask you the same thing. Why no girlfriend? I'm sure it's not because there aren't any takers."

"You first." He leaned in, resting his elbows on the table.

"I had my first and only boyfriend in high school, but we grew apart. I-I mean, we wanted different things, so we broke up."

He tapped his fingers lightly on his chin. "Sounds like you are a heartbreaker, Bethany Casse," he remarked.

"Hardly. I'm totally not." I paused, thinking of what had gotten me here. "He thought my life began and ended with him. My life began when I got that call from Financial State, telling me I'd gotten the job," I said, my eyes lighting up.

I remembered that day so clearly. I'd screamed so hard from excitement that the neighbors heard.

"Where it ends, I don't know. I just know I'm having fun since it began." And I was. Since I'd moved to Chicago, everything was finally falling into place.

"And the night has only begun," Brian said, smiling devilishly at me.

WHEN DINNER WAS over, I patted my stomach when Brian wasn't looking.

"So, you ready to go?" he asked as he took the receipt and placed it in his wallet.

"Can we sit here for a second?" I totally hadn't indulged like I usually would. I'd wanted to pace myself, and I hadn't wanted to eat more than my date, making me think I was more nervous than I'd led myself to believe.

"So, now, it's my turn. Did you think that just because the food came, I'd forget to grill you about your past love life?" Underneath the table, I rubbed my belly that was pushing against the elastic band of my skirt as I eyed the leftover steak on his plate. I should have foregone the sexy and worn a looser skirt.

"Well, okay then, shoot. What do you wanna know?" Brian asked, leaning back on his chair.

"So, why no girlfriend?" A little silent burp escaped my lips. I doubted he'd heard it because he continued to answer my question.

"I moved here two years ago from Wisconsin. Like you, I was busy and stuff. No time for a girlfriend."

"Come on, busy with what? Work? If a man wanted to make time, he would," I said.

"You're right. I just didn't want one. I had a long-term girlfriend in high school and a short-term girl in college. That was real short because she'd slept with my frat brother."

My eyes widened at his revelation. "She cheated on you?" I leaned in, wanting more details and wondering why anyone in her right mind would turn away such long-term material.

"Yep, she played me like the player she was." He laughed it off. "It's fine. We were young. Plus, I did some playin' in my day, too."

"I'm shocked. That totally doesn't sound like you."

"You are only a cheater if you are in a serious relationship. I wasn't," Brian said. "I'm not *that* guy." He smirked. "When I moved here, I didn't have time. I worked a lot in the beginning. Financial State doesn't mess around. Plus, I wasn't looking for something serious."

"Oh," I said as my voice dropped.

"What?"

"Nothing," I replied.

"Was not," he pointed out. "Past tense. I wasn't looking for something serious back then."

His smile made my heart rate speed up, and I nervously played with the edge of my napkin.

"I haven't been on a date like this in a while. If you haven't noticed, I like you. I think I told you that already. You're not like every other girl I've met down here. That's probably because you're not originally from here." He laughed, but then his voice became serious. "You remind me of home, Beth. You're funny and real."

At his admission, I thought I saw him blush slightly, but he immediately shrugged it off and grabbed my hand.

"Come on. Let's go to our next destination."

We made our way down to Michigan Avenue. People bustled around us, but I didn't care. It wasn't the silence like home that made me fond of Chicago. It was the lights, tall buildings, and the cars whizzing by and honking their horns. It was the noise and everything opposite of my hometown that made me love Chicago.

As we walked, Brian talked about his family. I laughed at his stories as he held my hand. I could imagine every grade-school girl having a crush on this humorous blue-eyed, blond boy, who later turned into a high school star quarterback. I couldn't hide my small sense of pride from him holding my hand when he had so many admirers at work.

"Sorry. Sometimes, I talk too much. How about you? Tell me about your family."

I froze at his question. "Nothing to tell." A nervous laugh escaped my lips.

"Come on," he pressed, peering down at me. "I want to know more about Bowlesville and you. Tell me about your folks. Tell me about your childhood and high school." He squeezed my hand as we walked. "Not fair. You know all about me."

"Life in Bowlesville is not very exciting. Only child. Typical childhood. My father died a while back," I said, glancing down at my shoes.

"Oh, I'm sorry," Brian said as we stopped at a crosswalk.

"No, it's okay. It happened a long time ago."

My dad was dead to me, given I didn't know who my father was.

I'd told Brian the truth, my truth. I released my hand from his to pick up a can from the ground, and I tossed it into the garbage.

"How about your mom?"

"She's back in Bowlesville. You know, doing the same thing she's always done."

I touched my half-ponytail nervously, speeding up to cross the street. I didn't want to taint our perfect night with reliving my past, especially when everything he'd told me about his childhood had been straight from an episode of *Leave it to Beaver*. I finally relaxed when we were in front of my apartment. I didn't want him asking me anything more about my past.

"So, what are you doing next weekend?" he asked. He lifted my chin to meet his eyes. "Actually, next weekend is too far away. What are you doing tomorrow?"

I suddenly felt shy as I peered up at him. "Are you trying to ask me on a second date?" I asked.

"Maybe," Brian replied, lightly brushing my bangs away with his finger.

"Well, you're not playing this game very well. First, you have to wait a couple of days before you call, making me wonder, and then you can ask me out. Hello? I know you've done this before," I said teasingly.

"Why play games when I already know what I want?" he said, still smiling his boyish smile.

I blushed at his comment. I remembered I'd told Kent that I would have brunch with him. "Uh…well, I'm hanging out with Kent tomorrow afternoon, but tomorrow night, I'm free."

"Kent? From Plack Industries?" His smile faltered. "So, you and Kent are just friends, right?"

"Yeah, we're just friends," I said, reassuring him. "Trust me, he's not into monogamous relationships. He's far from it. He sleeps with everyone who's breathing." I laughed.

"It's strange though," Brian shrugged, "for a guy to hang out with a girl as much as he does with you and not want more than friendship."

"We're just friends. Really!" I exclaimed.

He wasn't convinced as he raised his eyebrows in question.

"I've seen him with other girls—*seen* him be with other girls."

I made a face at the memory, and he laughed.

"That's some kind of weird relationship you have there," he said, amused at my discomfort.

"Oh no, I accidentally caught him. It's not like he let me watch." I shook my head as I felt my face flare up. "I don't know why we are talking about this. Kent is a friend," I said in finality. "Plus, I don't know many people here in Chicago, and I like hanging out with him." I started to sound defensive, and I was sure he could see that I was getting frustrated.

He lifted my chin to face him, meeting my eyes. "I believe you. Only friends. That's the end of that conversation."

"Okay," I said softly. I turned and made my way toward my door.

"Hey, I'm sorry. I believe you're just friends," Brian said, tugging on my arm.

"No, it's not that. I have to get up early on Sunday for brunch."

"Okay. Well, uh…I had a great time tonight, Beth."

It was that awkward moment after the first date—when I didn't know if we should kiss or not. It wasn't like we hadn't kissed before. If anything, his tongue had definitely been shoved down my throat on that bar's dance floor. This was a formal date though, and it felt different.

We looked at each other, and in that nanosecond, I wondered who would make the first move.

Overthinking this made me smile and then laugh. I tiptoed and pecked him on the lips. I'd had the perfect date, and he deserved a first-date kiss. I felt his smile on my lips before I pulled away.

"Beth, girls don't usually make me nervous, but you do." He pulled at my waist, bringing me closer toward him. Looking down at me, he placed his lips lightly on mine.

His lips moved against mine, slow and deliberate. He tasted of wholesome, good-boy sweetness. It wasn't the drunken sloppy kiss that had happened at the bar. When he finally pulled away, I was breathless, and it looked like he was, too, which gave me pure satisfaction.

"Thanks for a wonderful night," Brian said, releasing me.

I stumbled back, still high on that kiss. When I regained my footing, I waved to him as he held the door open for me. I thought my heart skipped a beat as I rode up the elevator. I touched my lips where he had just kissed as I leaned against the wall of the elevator for support.

When I entered my apartment, my phone started buzzing in my purse. I reached in to pick it up.

"Hey, just wanted to see that you got inside safely," Brian said.

"I did." I was smiling like a giddy little schoolgirl, and I was glad he couldn't see how cheesy I truly looked.

"I'll see you tomorrow, Beth. Good night."

"Good night."

I hung up the phone and started doing the happy dance before jumping up and down twice.

Life in Chicago so far was all I'd imagined and hoped it would be.

───────

I WAS UP, bright and early the next morning for brunch. "Hey, you," I sang in my cheery singsong voice as I approached Kent, waiting outside my apartment.

I linked arms with him as he led us to our destination.

"Shh," he whispered, wearing sunglasses even though there was no sun in sight.

I had a feeling he'd had a long night. He walked slower than usual and his eyebrows pulled together as though he was in deep concentration but most likely it was because his head hurt from the light.

"Okay, so where are we going?" I yelled obnoxiously as we walked.

"Please, Beth, have mercy." He pulled me in the other direction, and we started heading toward the lake.

"I'm sorry. That was mean. You could have canceled. I would have understood. Long night?" I asked, immediately feeling bad. It wasn't like I'd never had a hangover before.

He stopped at the corner and raised his hand to hail down a cab. "Was it ever. I woke up with a woman lying next to me. That never happens. I was so wasted that I didn't have time to show her out," he whispered, his voice hoarse.

I rolled my eyes, but he didn't see as he opened a cab door. I scooted inside and Kent stepped in behind me.

"The Bongo Room," Kent told the cab driver.

"The Bongo Room sounds more like a club than a breakfast place," I said.

"Trust me, it's good food. I know you'll appreciate that." He leaned his head back against the headrest, closing his eyes.

I decided I'd give him some peace and quiet until we reached the restaurant. I thought back to the night before with Brian. I had hoped he would have called me to say good morning. I forgot that only boyfriends did that, not someone I had only been on one date with.

When I looked over at Kent, he was staring at me.

"What?" I asked.

"You have this ridiculous grin on your face. Did you get laid last night?" he asked, still leaning his head against the seat.

My eyes flipped to the cab driver who had his eyes focused on the road. Kent had no regard for who was or wasn't listening. He didn't get embarrassed easily—or more likely, he just didn't care.

"No," I said, glancing back to him. "It was the first date. Hello? Girls don't give it up on the first date," I whispered.

"Clara from last night would beg to differ," he said.

"Okay, too much information, buddy," I said, making a face at his comment. *How the heck did I become good friends with a man-whore?*

"I don't want to know about your hooker last night. Let me rephrase what I said earlier. This girl," I pointed to myself, "does not sleep with guys on the first date."

We reached the Bongo Room before the conversation could continue any further. He paid and grabbed my wrist to pull me out of the cab.

I tugged myself from his grasp. "Why do you do that? I can walk on my own, you know."

Kent shrugged and held the door open for me.

My stomach grumbled as we entered the restaurant. The sweet smell of maple syrup and the greasy scent of eggs and bacon filled my nose. We were seated immediately even though there was a very long wait at the front of the restaurant. I had to wonder if Kent had slept with the greeter or if his dad was one of the investors at this establishment.

After the waitress took our orders, he placed his sunglasses on the table and his head in his hands.

"Are you okay?" I asked. "Maybe you should drink some water."

"No, it's okay. I just need coffee. I'll feel better after coffee." Kent lowered his head and ran his hands back and forth through his hair. "Tell me about your date."

I instantly smiled, but he couldn't see. "You don't want to know about my date."

"I do. I like hearing your happy, happy stories. It's entertaining. Go on, do tell." He lifted his head from the table. "Where did you guys go?"

I started retelling the events from the night before— the flowers, the dinner, the walk home. A dimple emerged on his face as I talked and swooned about my date with Brian, recalling every tiny detail. Kent let out a low laugh when I told him how I'd held back on eating, not wanting to scarf down more than my date.

"I like seeing you happy," he said when I finally finished.

His comment was so unexpected. It surprised me. "Why?" I asked.

He raised an eyebrow and cast me a look. "Can't a friend be happy for another friend? It's a natural reaction."

"Well, let's be real here. You're not a very nice person."

He laughed in amusement.

"Kent Plack, you don't care about anyone but your-self," I said teasingly. "Who else do you like seeing hap-py?" I prompted.

"What kind of question is that?"

"Who?" I raised my eyebrows, waiting for his reply.

"My mother."

"Who else?"

There was a slight hesitation, and I started laughing.

He paused, raising his eyes to the ceiling. "Fine. I don't care about many people, okay?"

I shrugged. "Okay."

The waitress came to pour our coffee. Her eyes flicked to Kent's as the dark liquid filled his mug. He didn't no-tice that she was checking him out. Maybe if he wasn't hungover, he would look up to see that she was attractive in a simple, non-trying way—or maybe, that was why he didn't notice her. The girls I'd seen him with were the flashy porn-star type. I watched him pour creamer into his cup as a whiff of fresh-brewed coffee moved my way.

He sipped his drink in silence, and I bit my tongue to prevent myself from yapping about my date again. I would let the caffeine settle in his veins before I went all jolly on him when he wasn't feeling well.

The waitress dropped off our plates in front of us. Again, I noticed her eyes travel from his face to his arms before finally resting on his chest. She seemed shy as she didn't try to get his attention like other women I'd seen him interact with. When our eyes caught, she turned and walked away to serve another table.

Kent leaned back and closed his eyes. His head tilted to the side, and I wondered why he'd come. He could have canceled, and I would have understood the need to stay locked up in small quarters with all the curtains drawn, head under a pillow, and earplugs in his ears.

Hungover. Been there. Done that. Not the best feeling in the world.

"I have to admit this is the best pancake in the world," I said after a while. I savored the banana-caramel pancake melting in my mouth and sighed inwardly.

His head perked up, and he finally reached for his fork to take a bite of his food. "I've realized your peppy mood improves even more when you're fed," he said, studying me. "Usually, men are like that."

"The way to this girl's heart is through her belly." I cut a piece of pancake and jammed it into my mouth for an exaggerated effect.

He laughed. "Okay, back to your date. If you like him so much, why didn't you let him spend the night?"

I shook my head as I continued to chew my food.

"What's the point of prolonging the inevitable?" Kent asked before lifting a forkful of egg into his mouth.

"What if I'm not into him, and I don't want to date any further?" I prompted. "And I have to clarify, that is not the case."

"It's only sex. If you don't like him, then you don't have to see him again."

"Kent, if you had ever been in love, you would know that sex is not just sex. With the physical comes the emotional."

"Never been, and never will be," he concluded.

"Plus, I'm waiting for romance," I said. "I want him to cook me dinner at his place, a candlelit dinner for two. I just want the night to be perfect before our first time together." I knew I totally sounded like a chick, but I didn't care.

He lowered his fork, shook his head, and stared at me

in disbelief. "You know that only happens in the movies, right?" he said with a dubious look on his face.

"So?" I replied.

He flashed me an amused look.

"I'm a good girl. I play by the rules. I just want the movie version. Is that too much to ask for? Other girls get the movie version. Don't I deserve romance, dinner, and candlelight? Don't I deserve the movies?"

He regarded me with a slight smile and nodded slowly. "Beth, if anyone deserves the movie ending, it's you."

Chapter Eight

THE WORKWEEK HAD come and gone, and the weekend had approached quickly. Before I'd known it, Saturday's morning sunshine and Kendy's call had woken me up from my deep sleep.

"Oh, Kendy, the first date was perfect, and the second date was even more perfect than the first," I squealed. "He's seriously the greatest guy, all in a blue-eyed, blond man package," I said. "When are you coming down here? I want to show you Chicago. I want you to meet him, and I want you to finally meet Kent."

I heard her huff on the phone, and I could picture the crinkle in her nose on her annoyed face. "So, how is your new best friend?" she asked, jealously etched in her voice. "Is he still spoiled and having a hard time keeping his pants up?"

I silently laughed at the intonation of her voice. I could tell she was envious of my friendship with Kent. "Seriously, he's not that bad. He's still spoiled, and yes, he has a hard time keeping his pants up, but to be honest, he's the closest thing I have to you here in Chicago," I said, every inch of me missing my best friend and her sassy self.

"Blah. I don't know," she blurted.

"Promise you, he's not bad news. And I'm still the

good girl who you know and love," I assured her. "When are you coming to visit?"

I crossed my fingers, hoping she would say soon. We hadn't seen each other since I moved, and I missed her physical being, her Kendy-like hugs, and her goofy self.

"I wish I could. They have me working crazy hours over here. I can never get a break. We're short-staffed, and until they start filling positions, it will never let up. Ugh, that reminds me. My break has been over for fifteen minutes. I have to go, babe."

I held the phone closer to my ear, not wanting to drop our call. "I miss you, Kendy. Don't make it too long before you call me again, okay?" I sighed into the phone, wishing she was right next to me.

She used to call me every day, but now, because of her nursing hours, I was lucky if she called me twice a week. I was beginning to resent her job, and I knew that was stupid.

As soon as I hung up, the phone rang again, and my first mistake was not checking the caller ID. The second mistake was picking up. I should have dropped the call as the person started speaking, but I fielded these all the time.

"Yes, I know. I know that it's past due. When was my last payment? No, there's no need to send it to the collection agency." *Like collections didn't already know me by my first name.* "Will you take payment over the phone? Can I just pay the minimum balance for now?" I leaned over the side of my bed to reach for my purse on the floor. Pulling out my wallet, I recited my debit card number.

"There really is no time off for you guys? Nothing. Thanks again." *Jerk.* I hung up the phone and got out of bed. *A call from a creditor. What a way to start the morning.*

I'd avoided this long enough. Trudging toward the kitchen, I picked up the pile of letters. It was my personal hate mail. Most of them were tinted pink, which indicated past due. I sifted through each and every piece. Just in my hand, there were over ten bills. It was the first of the month, and in two weeks, more would come on the fifteenth. My cycle every day was to come home, get mail, and put mail—mostly bills—in a pile to be sorted later.

I huffed and blew my bangs out of my face. Better start now as I didn't want to spend my whole Saturday paying bills.

FINISHED, I PLOPPED on the couch and rewarded myself with some trashy reality TV when my phone rang. It was Kent.

"Hi," I said, my eyes still glued on the screen.

"I'm bored. I'm coming over."

I loved this stuff, even though people thought it was just garbage television. Reality TV was where I got the good, the raw, and the drama.

"My trainer canceled today. I was supposed to go with Luke on his boat, but he canceled, so I'm coming over."

"Sure." I chuckled, giggling at the show holding my attention.

"Hello? Did you hear a word I said?"

"Oh, sorry. Oh, my goodness! This show is flipping crazy funny. Have you ever watched *Keeping up with the Kardashians*? Right now, Kim and Kourtney are fighting, and they are totally getting into it. You'd love this stuff." I stopped because I realized what I'd said. He would never watch *Keeping up with the Kardashians*.

"So, what happened?" I asked, still laughing at the TV. I turned the volume down, so I could concentrate on our conversation.

"I'm coming over," he uttered.

"Oh." I looked down at my puppy pajama pants, and my hand immediately flew to the bun on the crown of my head. "Warning, I look like crap, and my apartment is a disaster."

"That's fine. I don't care. I'll pick up lunch."

As Kent hung up, I shrugged and remained sprawled on the couch.

THIRTY MINUTES LATER, Kent knocked on my door, and I let him in. Dressed down in cargo pants and a navy T-shirt that said *Princeton*, he placed our lunch on the counter and smiled.

"Salad." He lifted the clear container filled with greens.

I automatically made a face. "Lettuce is only for turtles. You know I don't like salad," I whined.

"Salad is good for you. You're not overweight, but you should stop eating grease and eat healthy once in a while. Cute pants," he said, glancing at the white puppies printed on my cotton pink pants.

"Shut up." I snatched the salad container out of his hands and prepared our lunch on the island.

Kent strolled around my apartment. "Glad you cleaned up." He said, eyeing the blanket that I threw over the mess of *People*, *OK*, and *US Weekly* magazines on the floor.

I shrugged, continuing to set up our lunch on the island.

He glided over next to the TV, and he looked at multiple framed pictures on the wall—me by myself in front of my dorm room, me with Kendy and my aunt, and me and Nana. I emptied the salad into bowls and sat down on the stool.

"You're an attractive woman," he said, still examining the pictures, particularly the single one of me alone.

"Yeah, right," I said. "Ha-ha," I mocked.

"I can see why you don't think so."

"I don't think so because I'm not conceited." I stuck my tongue out at him and his dimple appeared.

"Well, take me for instance. I'm smart, an exceptional athlete, and obscenely good-looking. And I know this to be true," he boasted.

"You forgot conceited," I said, stuffing my mouth with a forkful of salad.

"My parents have told me this all my life. You, on the other hand, have never been told these things." He moved to the island, taking the stool next to me.

"Oh no, that's where you're wrong," I said, my mouth full of food. "I've been told that I'm sexy and hot, especially when my ex-boyfriend was banging me in the back of his car." I laughed and half-snorted as a piece of lettuce fell out of my mouth.

"You're crazy," he said, shaking his head.

"You are so beautiful to me. Oh, can't you see?" I said in my sing-song voice, wiggling my eyebrows.

"Okay, let's talk about something else. I know I'm hot. Now, your turn."

I turned, directly facing him. "Why are you so conceited?" I said, pointing my fork in his direction. "Maybe your parents should have toned it down instead of telling you that you were king of the world, master of the universe."

The smile he had a moment earlier slowly left his face. "It's just how they see me. I don't want to disappoint them, so I try my hardest not to."

I sensed his mood shift.

I'd meant my question to be funny, but all of a sudden, his chestnut eyes showed a vulnerability I'd never seen before. He lowered his head into his salad, and I was taken aback, shocked at the walking contradiction in front of me. On the outside, he seemed confident when inside, he was rattled with insecurity.

"Is that why you don't want to work with your father?" I asked. "Because you're afraid you'd disappoint them?"

He shrugged and furrowed his eyebrows as he stared at the salad in front of him.

"It's not that you don't *want* to work for your father. It's just that you're afraid because you might not live up to his expectations? Is that it?" I studied his profile from his eyebrows pulled into a V to his chestnut eyes and then to his downward turned lips.

I had a sudden urge to console him.

When he didn't answer, I placed my hand on his shoulder. "He'll love you anyway. He's your dad, and during the brief moment when I met him, I know it wouldn't matter to him."

The same pride I'd seen in Mr. Plack's face—the way he had lit up when he first saw Kent at the golf club, naturally excited to see him—had mimicked Nana's face every time she had seen me. There was unconditional love there. I knew it and recognized it because I'd felt it every day with my Nana.

I met his line of sight. "How could you not succeed, Mr. Princeton? All you need to do is try."

He shook his head to break himself out of his trance. "I'm always a little too honest with you." He met my eyes. "How did this conversation end up here? Let's eat, shall we?" he said, changing the subject.

I studied his face, but then I let it go. Sometimes, well, most of the time, I would rather not talk about my family.

"I love how you change the subject when we were just getting serious." I maneuvered to the fridge. "Okay, what do you want to drink? We have water, juice, and milk. Oh, I think I still have one can of pop here somewhere."

I had my head in the fridge when I heard boisterous, uninhibited laughter coming from behind me. I turned to see he was standing right next to my laundry basket that I left next to the kitchen island. At that moment, I wanted to die.

"Wow, I've seen a lot of things before, but I don't think I've ever seen anything this big." He pinched my overly large flowery pink-and-green underwear with his fingers on each side of the cotton. His eyes squinted, and both dimples appeared on his face as pretended to examine what he had hold of.

"Kent, drop my granny panties, right now!" I yelled, my ears warming from embarrassment. I bolted toward him and snatched them from his hands.

"Granny panties?" He held his stomach as his laughter echoed through the whole apartment. "Oh. My. God. Granny panties."

"You're mean. I only use them when I don't have any clean underwear or when I'm on my period."

His laughter halted as he blinked. He looked at my

underwear and then to his hands, making a face.

"They're clean, dummy." I dropped the panties into the basket and walked it back into my room.

WE ATE, WE lounged, and I introduced him to every reality TV show there was. Before I knew it, I glanced up and realized the sun was setting. I didn't realize so much time had passed until my stomach grumbled, reminding me of dinnertime.

"What do you want for dinner? I'll order," I said, grabbing the phone next to me. "Pizza?"

"Sure. Pepperoni and sausage," he said.

I walked to the kitchen, snatched my many coupons that were held together by magnets on the fridge, and picked up the phone to place the order.

When the pizza arrived, Kent tipped the delivery boy and walked comfortably to the kitchen island. He reached in the cabinets to look for plates and unloaded the food from the box.

"Can you bring the food in here? I'm being lazy." I was flipping through the channels, still in the same position, while lying on the couch.

He brought the food over, placed it on the low glass table in front of the couch, and sat on the floor in front of me. "Who's this actor?" he asked, nodding toward the TV.

"Channing Tatum. He's in a new movie coming out on Friday," I answered.

"I've never seen any of his movies," he mumbled between chews. "Aren't you going to eat your pizza?" he said, eyeing my food in front of him.

"I'll eat it in a bit." I stretched my legs on the couch and rubbed my eyes with the back of my hands. Tiredness filtered through my body as I thought of the night before. "I had a late night last night. Brian has been working crazy hours, and we finally had a chance to go on another date."

"Oh, yeah? How was your date? Are the flowers from him?"

"Yeah, he buys me flowers on every date," I swooned, glancing at the dozen red roses sitting on my counter.

"Flowers die. He should buy you diamonds. Diamonds last forever."

My mouth dropped at his comment. "You don't buy your dates diamonds, do you?" I asked, plopping my head on my hand as my elbow rested on the cushion.

He shook his head. "I don't go on dates, Beth. My father stopped buying my mother flowers years ago. He buys her jewelry instead." He laughed. "Anyway, keep going. Your date?" he prompted.

"My date was great as always," I said, all giddy. I moved to a sitting position, tucked my feet under my bottom, and hugged the couch pillow close to my chest. My eyes were glued on the TV, but my thoughts were brought back to the most wonderful date I'd had the night before.

At this, Kent spun around. "Great?" he asked. "So, was last night Brian's lucky night?"

"That's none of your business." I squirmed and pulled the pillow closer to my chest. My eyes moved from him back to the TV.

"You like him?" he asked, a smirk on his face.

"Yes, I really do." I sighed, smiling at the TV like an idiot.

"I like seeing you like this. So, tell me the details." He

glanced up at me from his sitting position on the floor.

"What details?"

"Was he good?" Kent's face showed amusement.

He was making me uncomfortable, and he took pleasure in every minute of it.

"There are no details to tell. This is getting weird," I dismissed. I shifted, pulled my knees up to my chest, and placed the pillow on top of my knees.

"So, did he give you one of the best mind-blowing orgasms you've ever had? Is that why you like him?" He put down his pizza and shifted to face me, still sitting on the floor. "Come on, I know this is what girls talk about. I'm interested to know." He smirked, totally delighting in my unease.

"Gross. No. I'm not talking to you about this stuff," I said, wrinkling my nose and fidgeting in my seat.

"Why not? I tell you everything. Okay, so is that no, he didn't move your universe? Or yes, he did?" he asked.

"No, I'm not telling you. Okay? Drop it."

"Come on, tell me, Beth. Just tell me yes or no. Yes? Or no?" he pressed as both dimples emerged.

"Yes or no to what?"

"Did he give you the best mind-shattering orgasm you've ever had in your life? Yes or no?" he asked.

I knew he enjoyed my uneasiness.

"No."

"No? That's disappointing. Well, I guess he didn't know what he was doing then," Kent said.

"I mean, no, I'm not telling you," I said, giving him a look.

"Why not? Yes or no?" He got up and sat on the couch to face me. "Yes or no, Beth? It's an easy answer." His eyes lit in mischief. "Yes or no?" he enunciated each and every word.

Annoyed he wouldn't relent, it just slipped out. "We haven't had sex yet, and I've never had one. I've never had an orgasm before, okay?"

Kent's eyes widened, and his mouth fell open. I'd never seen him shocked, and he was shocked beyond belief.

"Never?" he whispered, stunned. He blinked a couple of times in my direction.

"No, never. Okay? Drop it," I commanded.

He plucked the pillow from my hands and inched closer. "Never?" he repeated, his eyes still wide. You would have thought I just told him there were aliens that were planning to seize the planet by the look on his face.

I seized the pillow back. "Never, ever...okay? This is weird. Stop it."

I turned my head to watch TV, my face burning, but he moved in my direct line of sight.

"I don't understand. You had a boyfriend before. You've never orgasmed with a guy or never even given yourself one?" he continued.

"Seriously, Kent. Never, okay? Never, ever, ever, ever has any man given me an orgasm, and neither have I, for that matter," I said, exasperated.

"That's crazy. I mean, why have sex then? What's the point?"

"I like sex. For your information, it still feels good." I covered my face and shook my head from discomfort. "Weird. Weird. Weird. I'm not comfortable with this conversation. Please drop it." I felt the deep flush across my cheeks spread throughout my body. My palms began to sweat at this uncomfortable conversation.

The shock on his face changed to amusement. "Yes,

it might feel good, but it's like running a race and having no medal at the end or going to dinner and not having dessert. What's the point? And that's why you just like it. You'd love it if you'd had an orgasm before," he said. "Even with my one-night stands, I always leave the girls satisfied every time," he boasted.

"Yeah right, unless they are faking it," I said incredulously.

"They're not, trust me. I just know what I'm doing, unlike the men you have been with," he uttered with confidence.

"Man. Singular." I looked at him, annoyed. "My boyfriend from high school was inexperienced. Plus, he was only concerned about getting himself off. Maybe he didn't know what he was looking for or how to find it," I said even though I wasn't sure what *it* was.

"It's not rocket science," Kent said, smiling.

He scanned my body, and I pulled the pillow closer to myself.

"I'm sure I can find it for you," he said, giving me the most devilish look.

"Gross! This is not some sort of challenge, weirdo." I got up, grabbed his arm, and dragged him toward the door. "This conversation has ended, and so has this night. Thanks for hanging out with me."

"I'm kidding, Beth," he said, laughing as I pushed him out the door. "I'm just kidding. I'm teasing," he continued.

"I don't care. I'm tired, and I want you out. Out. Out. Out." I pushed at his back with both hands.

As I started to shut my door, he caught it with his hand and peered in.

"You know, I can find it." He winked.

"Ew," I said, scrunching my nose. A look of repulsion crossed my face.

As I closed the door, I heard laughter emanating down the hallway.

***

IT WAS SIX thirty in the evening when I looked up from my computer. The office was silent as everyone else had left for the day. My brain was fried, working on the same proposal for the last four hours, and I still had so much more to do before tomorrow's meeting.

I couldn't work anymore in the office, so I packed up my laptop and headed out the door. For a change of scenery, I decided to go to the local bookstore and finish my proposal. Walking down the street, I felt my bag vibrate. I rested the laptop bag against my hip and searched for my phone, which was annoyingly at the bottom of my bag.

"Hey, it's me. What are you doing?" Kent asked.

"I'm on my way home to change and go to the bookstore. I have tons of work to do," I huffed. "I have a meeting tomorrow, and I need to get this proposal done."

"Okay, I'll meet you there in thirty minutes. Barnes and Nobles?" Kent asked. "Where's Mr. Perfect?"

"Mr. Perfect is out tonight with clients—again," I sighed.

One of the things I adored about Brian was his motivation, his drive for greatness at work. But his hardworking self, was putting a damper on our dating life.

"I'll see you in a bit," he said before dropping the line.

"Alright, see you soon," I replied.

131

THIRTY MINUTES LATER, sitting at the coffee shop of the bookstore in jeans and my Bowlesville High School T-shirt, my eyes were glued to the computer screen when I felt a tug on my high ponytail.

"Sandwich?" Kent offered, plopping down on the chair in front of me and dropping it on the table.

I gave him my biggest smile. "And that, sir, is why we're friends," I said, pointing to the sandwich wrapped in plastic wrap.

"From the beginning, I knew this was the key to your friendship. You ate that pancake at that diner as if you hadn't eaten for days."

"Shut up, and give me my food," I sassed.

"You're welcome." He pushed the sandwich toward me and took another one out of the brown paper bag. "I hope they are paying you overtime."

I made a face. "Yeah, right. I'm salaried, not hourly, and boy, they've been working me to the bone." I took a bite of my sandwich and sighed. "What?" I asked, noticing his expression as I took an overly large bite of my sandwich.

"You know, you make strange sounds when you eat," he said, a dimple emerging on his cheek.

"Because it's mmm-mmm good." A piece of turkey almost fell out of my mouth, but I saved it with my tongue. "So, Mr. I Don't Have a Job But I Have All the Money in the World to Do What I Want, what did you do today?"

He held up one finger as he finished chewing his food. "Well, I got up whenever I wanted, which was ten thirty, and then I went out for breakfast, went shopping, talked to my mother, went to the gym for a couple of hours, got a massage, and relaxed a little at home before I came here."

"Must be nice."

"It is," he said without reservation.

"Well, sorry, some of us have to work for a living," I said before taking another overly large bite of my sandwich. "And now, I have to get some work done. Do you want to grab a book or a magazine or something?" I asked, dropping my food and adjusting my laptop in front of me.

He positioned his chair to sit right beside me. "I'm interested. What are you working on?" His eyes observed my screen as I began to type on my computer.

"We have this new client. They want us to fund a buyout of their competitor," I said, looking at the numbers on my computer.

"Well, what's the cash flow of the company? And how much debt can the company handle?" he asked, scanning my screen in front of us.

I shot him a shocked look. "I thought your major was business management?"

"It was. I minored in finance. Beth, I went to Princeton. You know that, right? I'm not dumb," he said, sounding offended.

"No, I never said that. It's just that you surprise me," I said, turning toward him. "Tell me again why you don't want to run Plack Industries. You're a smart guy. It's already a successful business. It would take a dummy to run it into the ground, and you just said you're not dumb."

"Let's not start now, Dad," Kent said, slightly moving away.

I didn't know why I'd pushed him, why I'd wanted to motivate him to run his father's company, to take over.

Maybe a big part of me knew his potential for greatness.

I rested my hand on his arm. "I'm not your dad, Kent, but I see you surprising him, too."

"I'm content just the way I am."

"I know, but why be content when you can be happy? And why be mediocre when you can be great?" I said, raising my voice. "Don't you want to be like me and conquer the world?" I said, exaggerating with my hands, making that dimple reappear again.

He shrugged. "Why change something that is working just fine? Like I said, I'm fine just the way I am."

My phone started ringing, which broke up our conversation. I glanced at the number on my phone and a radiant smile crossed my face "Hi," I said. "You got out early from your client call? I'm at Barnes and Nobles. Kent is here with me. He came earlier."

"Oh. So, he just wanted to hang out?" Brian asked.

I furrowed my brow at his tone.

"I don't know. He wanted to come. He even brought me food. Okay, so you're coming here soon?"

"Yeah. It won't be soon enough. I'll be there."

Kent looked at me as I hung up.

My cheeks were hurting from the smile on my face. "You're finally going to meet him! I talk about you all the time."

"Do you now?" he asked, raising one eyebrow. "So, what do you tell him about me?"

"I tell him that you are a spoiled brat who doesn't like to work." I took out my makeup bag and started applying mascara.

He watched me as I started on my makeup routine.

"What?" I asked, noting the amused look on his face. "It's still the beginning. I want to look cute."

134

"Women," he muttered, shaking his head.

TEN MINUTES LATER, I felt strong hands on both of my shoulders. I glanced up at a blond-haired looker in a navy suit and blue shirt that brought out his eyes.

"Hey," I said, smiling up at Brian.

He leaned down to give me a kiss on the lips. It lingered longer than normal, sending the butterflies in my belly in a frenzy. I was the first to break away.

Kent smiled up from his *Time* magazine, and then he stood and offered his hand. "Kent Plack. You must be Brian."

"Hey, buddy," Brian said, taking his hand with a firm grip. "Yeah, Beth talks about you all the time."

"And you, too. The perfect guy," Kent said, making my face flush.

I gave Kent the evil eye as he sat down, before turning to Brian. "So, how was your client call?"

Brian pulled out a chair and sat with his elbows on his knees. "It's a tough sell. There are a lot of other banks calling on Taper Corp," he said, cranking his neck from side to side. "But if I win this one, that will make my quota for the year, and my year-end bonus will be nice and fat. And the perfect guy might get the perfect girl something nice for Christmas," he said.

"Taper Corp?" Kent asked.

"Yeah. Do you know about the company?" Brian asked.

"Somewhat. I've heard of them."

"They're expanding internationally, and they are outgrowing their current bank," Brian said, holding my

135

hand atop the table. "I'm going to have to work hard to win this deal. I want this one," he said, looking at me.

"You'll win it." I said, confident that my man would land the deal. I rubbed the top of his hand with my thumb as our eyes locked.

I glanced at Kent when he moved to stand and crumpled the sandwich paper bag in his hands. "I should go. I have another engagement tonight."

I stood up and gave him a half-hug. "Thanks for the sandwich and for keeping me company," I said, pulling back and giving him my cheesiest smile.

Kent shook his head in amusement. "Bye, Beth."

As soon as Kent was out of sight, Brian turned to me with a sly smile. "So, that's Kent, huh?"

"The one and only," I replied, glancing back to Kent's retreating back.

"You never said he was very good-looking."

I shrugged, trying to play it off. "Eh, he's okay."

"Beth, I don't usually say this, but that is one fine-looking man. I'm sure you noticed those two girls ogling him during our conversation."

"Maybe they were ogling you," I said, inching my way toward him. I placed my hand on his lap. "I ogle you all the time."

"That's all that matters," he said, placing his hand on top of mine. "Just friends, right?"

"For the millionth time, yes! Kent and I are just friends."

"All right. So, what are we doing now?" Brian asked, changing the subject at my tone.

"Working."

"Sounds like a plan. Can I work on you at your place?" Brian said, leaning into me.

"No, like, really working. I have to get this proposal ready for my meeting tomorrow," I said, moving toward my computer.

Brian reached over and squeezed my knee.

I laughed. "No, really, I have to finish this," I said, pushing his hand off my leg. "You're too much of a distraction. I think you'd better go."

"And here I wanted to enjoy the view all night," he said, leaning over to give me another kiss before standing up to leave.

When I looked at the clock, it was nearly eight. That gave me one more hour before the bookstore closed. *Time to get working.* I placed both hands on my forehead and focused on the screen.

SITTING AT MY desk the next day, I had a small smug smile on my face because I was satisfied with our team meeting. My boss's boss had been impressed by my recommended frame of the deal. I'd laid out a reasonable structure, benefiting the client but also protecting the bank from losses, should any occur.

When my phone rang, I knew who it would be.

"Hey, Kent," I said in my cheery voice. "What's for lunch today? Oh, Caroline wants to join us. Is that okay?"

"Beth, can you meet me after work? I can't do lunch today."

I sat up straighter in my chair at the tone of his voice, which was hoarse and low.

"Are you okay?" I asked.

"Yeah, rough night. Please. Jimmy's Tap after work," he prompted.

"Are you sure you're okay?"

"Yeah, just meet me after work at Jimmy's," he said.

"I'll be there," I replied.

I dropped the phone and stared blankly at the receiver, sensing something was definitely wrong.

Throughout the day, my mind drifted to Kent. I truly hoped he had been just hungover, but the sadness in his voice concerned me.

Right before the end of the day, my manager stopped by my desk. "Hey, great job today. Everyone was impressed by the newbie. You were quite prepared, and I have to commend you for that," Renee said, resting against my cubicle. "You know of our expansion out on the East and West Coasts? We're trying to spread out our talent from here. Brian already got offered a position on the East Coast. I know you just moved here, but I'd like you to consider moving out west to be on my team."

My insides were singing at her high praise, and to even be considered for a spot in the expansion meant that I was on management's radar as a good employee. "Thanks Renee. That means a lot. I'll definitely take it into consideration, but I'm happy here so far."

When Renee left, my thoughts shifted to Brian

I turned to Caroline. "Hey, when did Brian get offered New York?"

She peered at me from her screen and stopped typing. "I don't know. Two weeks ago maybe. Didn't he mention it to you?" she asked before dropping her head back to her computer.

"No," I replied.

"He's not one to brag. Plus, I heard he didn't take it."

"Oh...he didn't?" I released the breath I'd been holding in. We weren't serious yet but I had hopes that we would slowly get there.

"Hey, I heard about your deal today. Good job. Way to impress the bigwigs," she said, giving me a thumbs-up over her cubicle.

The smile slowly crept back up my face, and I put thoughts of Brian behind me.

Chapter Nine

I STEPPED INTO Jimmy's Bar Tap, still high from Caroline's and Renee's praises. Walking into the bar, my mood immediately dampened when I saw Kent slouched over the counter, looking at the wine glass in his hand.

As I approached the bar, he peered up from his spot, his eyes showing defeat.

I immediately rushed to his side and wrapped my arms around him. "Oh my God, Kent, what's wrong?"

He shook his head and exhaled a low sigh. "It's over."

I had to listen carefully because his voice was barely audible. "You're scaring me. What happened? Tell me what happened," I pressed.

"It was always just Dad, but now it's my mom. I don't know, Beth. I don't know how this happened," he said, his voice toneless.

My hug automatically tightened around his waist at the sound of him mentioning his parents. I didn't say a word.

When I released him, he placed his head in his hands. "The trust agreement was just lying out on his desk as if he wanted me to see it. It's been in the trust documents all along," he said, his voice breaking. "I mean, I can't do it. I can't live the life they want me to live. It's not me." He dropped his head against the bar.

Through all his rambling, I couldn't comprehend any of his words. "What happened?" I asked, rubbing his shoulder. "You can tell me."

"The trust set forth by Grandfather stipulates everything...just everything. Married..." He let out a low breath and lifted his head from the bar. "Do you understand? I'm not entitled to anything. It's over. I'm not entitled to the money until I am married." He rubbed both hands down his face in frustration.

"I don't understand," I whispered.

"The trust stipulates that by the age of twenty-five," his voice was coming out in hushed broken huffs, "I need to be married or else the money in my trust will go to... Plack's designated charities."

Immediately, I froze. Out of everything, I didn't expect those words to leave his mouth. I could understand his parents taking away his trust fund to force him into running the business since he was the only heir. I could even see his parents taking it away because of his partying ways since they shouldn't have to fund his outrageous habit. But I never expected this. *Why?*

Reading my mind, he continued, "I know they want me to be happy and to settle down. They want me to have a family. My grandparents were married for fifty years before they passed away, and my parents are going on thirty years. It's over."

"I don't get it, Kent. Why not add in running the company? I mean, that's what your dad has always wanted."

"I don't know. Grandfather should have added that in there, too. Maybe he assumed that I would naturally take that course, but he also knew that I wasn't the type to settle down." He sighed heavily, hanging his head in defeat.

He tugged at his hair in frustration. "I don't know what to do, Beth. I've played the conversations my parents and I have had over and over in my head. My mom has told me that they just want to make sure I'm okay. When they are six feet under the ground, they want to ensure that I'm taken care of and that I have a family of my own who loves me, so I'm not alone. There are not a lot of us, and one thing that has always been number one is family. Even though I'm mad, I can't begrudge them for looking out for my best interest. But what they don't understand is that it's not me. It's just not me, Beth. I can never, ever be the person they want me to be."

"It's okay, Kent. Everything will be okay," I said, rubbing my hands up and down his back to console him. "Do they know that you've seen the trust agreement? Do they know that you know about this stipulation?"

"I have no idea." He shook his head. "Beth, I'm with different women every week. I party with Luke every other night. Does that sound like someone who can take care of a family? Does it? I don't know how to take care of anyone, except for myself, nor do I want to. I don't know what to do." He placed his head back down in his arms on top of the bar.

"It's okay, Kent. Everything is going to be okay, I promise." I wrapped my arms around his waist again and placed my head on his back as he continued to face the bar. "I wish I could help you," I whispered. "It'll be okay. Everything will be fine."

He sat in silence as I kept my head on his back, rubbing my hands up and down his arms.

After a few minutes of silence, his head shot up to turn and look at me. With wide eyes, he squared his shoulders, faced my direction and placed both hands on

142

my shoulders. "Beth…" he whispered. "Beth, you're a genius. You can help me." He stared at me like I was the air he needed to breathe.

My eyes now mimicked his, wide and questioning.

"Marry me, Beth."

I slowly took in what he'd said, considering his words, the words that had left his mouth. My lips turned from a smirk to a full-on smile. He was still holding my shoulders when I started giggling. Then, it transformed to full-blown howling laughter.

Kent's hands left my shoulders, and I used my hand to wipe my eyes.

"I'm glad you are laughing at my misfortune," he said.

"I'm laughing because you are freaking hilarious, seriously hilarious," I said, while my one hand clutched my stomach in uncontained laughter.

"I'm serious, Beth. You said you wanted to help me. This is how you can help."

"No." My laughter was dying down, but a smile still remained on my face.

"Beth, this is life and death for me. This is perfect. You are my best friend. I can't do this with anyone else. Anyone else is going to want more than I can give. This would strictly be on paper, nothing else. We can have rules. You can even dictate the rules. It's perfect," he said as he leaned toward me.

"Perfect, except for the fact that we're not in love. You're crazy. I'm not marrying you."

"Listen, Beth…" He paused. "We can make this work." He paused again and furrowed his brow in concentration. "I'll make you a deal. You marry me on paper alone, and once I have access to my trust fund, I will pay off your debts." Both dimples emerged on his cheeks as if a light bulb had gone off in his head.

Before I had time to muster up a response, he continued, "Consider it a pact. You will marry me, so I can access my trust fund, and in return, I will pay off all your debts. I can clear your debts, Beth...all of it." He smirked. "Marry me for money."

I was stunned into silence, and he took it as an opportunity to continue.

"You can start with a clean slate. I know your debt is the only thing standing in between content Beth and truly happy Beth. When you are out of debt, you could start over. You could be successful at your great job and marry what's-his-name. You could have the life you have always dreamed of. Marry me, Bethany Casse."

I remained silent while contemplating it. I was seriously thinking of taking him up on his offer. Starting a new life without debt enticed me. The deal of a lifetime was being handed to me on a silver platter. Instantly, I felt guilty for even entertaining the idea.

"I don't know, Kent. How would it even work?"

His lips turned upward. "It would work. I will make it work. Marry me, and we can live our lives as we do now. We just have to make everyone else believe we are together. I can be discreet, and no one at work knows you are dating what's-his-name, right?"

"Kent, his name is Brian. You met him yesterday," I said, rolling my eyes.

"Do this, and I can get you out of debt. Then, you can live your happily ever after with Brian. Say you'll marry me, Beth." Getting off his bar stool, he bent down on one knee.

I immediately pulled him up. "Stop it. Get up." I

scanned the area to see if anyone was staring at us and gave him a deadpan look. "I don't know. It's the ultimate lie. I'm the worst liar, and I don't have a poker face."

"Think of it as acting—just in front of my parents. After a month, we can get a divorce, and you get your money. Then, everything will be as it was. Think about it. I can picture it." He looked past the bar, raising his hand in exaggeration. "I'd be dating a successful, beautiful woman who my parents adore and we'd get married in an extravagant ceremony. One month down the line, I'd have an affair with a busty blonde. It would be typical. No one would be surprised. We'd both leave the situation the same—you, an angel, and me, the spoiled playboy. The only difference is that I'll have access to my trust fund, and you'll be out of debt. It's win-win." He smirked. He pinched both of my cheeks as if I were a small child. "Come on."

I tried to stop my grin at seeing his goofy face. "Fine."

"Say it again," he said, pinching my cheeks harder.

"Ouch. Okay, fine," I said. "Fine, I'll marry you."

He lifted me into a big bear hug, my feet dangling midair. "Thanks, Beth. You won't regret it. I'll forever be indebted to you."

He swung me around and around, and I couldn't stop laughing.

"Put me down, Kent. I'm getting dizzy."

FOR THE NEXT hour, we talked logistics and made rules for our upcoming arrangement.

I still doubted my ability to pull this off. My head was a jumbled mess as we hashed out everything while jotting notes on multiple napkins. According to Kent, we needed to play lovey-dovey. We had to make it look real, believable.

"It's not official until we do an oath."

"What?" he asked, looking confused. "Beth, why do you have to be so silly? We've already agreed. We're just fine-tuning the details."

"Nope. It's not valid until we do an oath."

"Fine, Beth. Whatever you want," Kent said, waiting for direction.

I raised my right hand and made him raise his. "Okay, I want you to say, 'I do,' after each statement. Got it?"

Kent shook his head in amusement, but he still complied as he motioned with his hand for me to begin.

"Do you, Kent Plack, promise to live your life and let me live mine as we do now?"

"I do."

"Do you promise to divorce me after one month and give me two hundred and fifty thousand dollars to pay off my debts in return for marrying you?"

"I do."

"Do you promise not to kiss me or touch me in ways other than how friends touch?" I asked, raising my eyebrows.

He laughed. "I do."

"Above all, Kent, do you promise not to let this ever alter our friendship?"

"I do."

"I now pronounce us officially boyfriend and girlfriend. You may now kiss your soon-to-be pretend fiancée," I said, offering my hand.

He leaned over and kissed the top of my hand.

"I'm gonna be out of debt. I'm gonna be out of debt,"

I said in my singsong voice while doing a little shake at my own tune.

"I'm marrying a crazy person." Kent laughed. "Tomorrow, we'll have our first date at my parents' house in Barrington."

I stopped dancing as the cheery smile I had slowly left my face. "Okay," I replied.

FROM THE CITY, the drive to Barrington took forty-five minutes. Beads of sweat dampened my hands as I played pretend conversations with his parents in my head. I imagined telling them how much I was in love with their son. My stomach felt queasy with nervousness because I had no idea how I was going to pull this off. They were definitely going to see right through me, and the last thing I wanted to do was manipulate people. I sighed outwardly and looked out the window.

"We'll be okay. You can do this. It will be fine, and when it's over, you will be out of debt," Kent said, keeping his eyes on the road.

I said nothing in return as I stared blankly at the cars ahead of us.

Before I knew it, we were driving past the security post and into his parents' gated community. I wiped my palms on my jeans and let out a long sigh as I glanced at Kent. Eyes still on the road, he was quiet, and I wondered if he was having second thoughts about lying to his parents.

We turned on Plack Street, and I took in the palatial white brick mansion that spanned half a block in front of me. He stopped adjacent to the round driveway in front of the house and turned off the engine.

Facing me, he said, "Beth, just follow my lead. We have to make my parents believe that I've fallen madly in love with you, so play up the romance. Pretend to love me, okay?"

"Okay," I said in a small voice, I almost couldn't hear. I pressed my hands together on my lap and stared at him, my eyes wide. Not knowing what else to do, I waited for directions.

"Hold on," Kent said.

He exited the car, swaggered over to the passenger side, and opened my door. I raised my eyebrows at him.

"I'd better start acting like a gentleman toward my future wife," he said, lifting my hand to assist me from the car.

I couldn't even laugh at his attempt to be funny as there was really nothing funny about this situation.

"It's showtime," Kent said as he took my hand. He entwined his fingers through mine, pulling me toward the house.

I looked down to our hands and wiggled my fingers. Holding hands with Kent for the first time felt strange, foreign. We'd only linked arms before. Even at the club, he'd grabbed my wrist, not my hand, to lead me through the crowd. The action was so intimate that it felt awkward, and I knew he felt the same because he flexed his fingers and rewrapped them around mine.

He pulled me forward. "Come on, let's go."

I froze in front of the door and jerked us both to a stop.

"You can do this. Come on, Beth. Just take my lead."

Kent punched in a code and walked into the house. "Beth, come on. You have to pretend to like me. Stop looking like you've eaten something awful. Giggle like girls do when they are holding hands with the man they love. I'm not sure where my parents are, but you have to look happy. You need to laugh or flirt or something," he whispered into my ear. "Come on."

I looked at him and raised my eyebrows "Hee, hee, hee, hee," I said, emphasizing every word. Maybe my goofiness would calm my nerves.

"Better," he said, giving me a slight smile. His eyes searched the room for his parents as he shifted from one foot to the other.

"Okay, now, it's your turn," I said, turning to face him. "Come on, do it. It's your turn to laugh like you're holding hands with the woman you love," I said, mimicking his words, fluttering my eyelashes. "Come on." I poked his side with my free hand and laughed.

"Ha, ha, ha, ha." Both dimples emerged on his cheeks as he turned his head to face me.

"Hee, hee, hee, hee," I returned. "Now, you have to slap your side like this." I slapped my hip with the hand he wasn't holding while I accentuated the exaggerated giggles.

Kent shook his head as his chest rose and fell with genuine laughter. My laughter stopped when Kent's mother and father stepped into the foyer. His mom's face lit up as she watched the both of us interact while his father's face was unreadable.

Kent's laughter died down, but a small smile still remained as my reaction turned serious. I felt my heartbeat in my ears, and I was barely moving. I realized I'd stepped slightly behind Kent to hide. He jerked our entwined hands to pull me forward, so we were in line.

"Dad, you know Beth. Mother, this is Beth, my

girlfriend. We were in the area."

"Beth, it's always good to see you," Mr. Plack said, focusing intently on our linked hands.

I pushed a smile on my face, so forced it was almost to the point of pain.

Mrs. Plack walked toward us slowly as if she were approaching a frightened animal. She must have sensed my shyness.

"Hi, I'm Karen," she said, offering her hand.

"Beth," I said so softly that I doubted she'd heard me. I extended my hand to greet her.

Her eyes crinkled when she placed her soft-as-silk hand into mine. "Nice to meet you, Beth."

Karen Plack was not as I'd originally expected. She wasn't blonde, and she was nowhere near plastic-looking. Her hair was the darkest shade of brown, and her eyes matched Kent's chestnut ones. She had the warmest smile, and I instantly felt my face relax.

She embraced Kent tightly, pulling him into a half-hug, as he still held my hand. "Are you staying for dinner?"

"Of course," he replied, basking in her embrace.

"Perfect." Mrs. Plack released him and clasped her hands together. "We're having chicken tonight. I hope you like chicken," she said, turning to me.

"Mom, Beth doesn't discriminate against food. I still haven't heard of anything she doesn't like to eat," Kent said.

I nudged him with my elbow before I remembered that his parents were still there and froze. Mrs. Plack cast me a look of uncontainable joy, and I wondered if Kent had ever brought anyone home. I was pretty certain she had never seen a woman do anything but fawn all over him, much less elbow him in the ribs.

"Well, I'll have to put two extra servings of broccoli in the pot. Jack, will you please come assist me? Let's get dinner ready." Mrs. Plack tugged her husband's arm and pulled him toward the kitchen. She glanced back at us one last time with a glint of happiness in her eyes.

"See? That wasn't bad, except for your sweaty palms. Do I make you nervous?" he joked.

I turned to face him as I released our joined hands and smacked him on the shoulder. "Yeah, you wish. Your parents make me nervous. Plus, it wasn't bad because I was mute the whole time. Wait till I start talking and stuttering. I always raise my eyebrows when I lie, too. It's a good tell that I'm lying." I crossed my arms in front of me, staring into the space where his parents had walked through.

"Come on, let's go watch TV before dinner."

"Okay," I replied.

He grabbed my hand and led me down the hall. I surveyed the staircase filled with family photos along the wall.

"We do need nicknames. Buttercup, okay? Princess doesn't seem fitting as you are not very high maintenance. Honey? Since you love food, a food-related nickname might be more appropriate."

I watched him trying to suppress a smile at his not-so-funny joke.

"Listen here, quit making fun of me and my love of food."

"Okay, I'll try to control myself with the teasing," he said as he pulled me down to the couch to sit next to him. He grabbed the remote. "What do you want to watch?"

"It doesn't matter. I can't think of anything other than

having dinner with your parents."

"Don't stress too much. Just answer their questions, and like I said, I'll take the lead."

He turned the channel to CNN, and we watched TV for a while. When he excused himself to use the bathroom, I took the remote and continued flipping through the channels.

Besides his parents, I wondered if I could pull this off in front of Kendy and her mom, my Aunt Diane. Kendy would have to know the truth. She was the one who knew me the best, and she would be able to tell that I was lying. I decided that the next time I talked to her, I'd tell her the truth. I'd need someone to confide in to keep my sanity. I wondered what would happen with Brian. Kent's proposal had been so sudden, so unexpected that I'd said yes before even thinking it through. Now that I'd made this commitment, I worried about how I would tell Brian. The TV channels continued to change as my mind was a jumbled mess.

Getting restless, I stood from the couch to look for Kent. I couldn't sit motionless while my mind moved a mile a minute. I walked through the halls until I heard Kent and his dad talking. I couldn't help myself from listening as I stood against the wall right by the door.

"Dad, I like her."

"Kent, all I'm saying is to tread carefully."

Suddenly, I felt disappointed at Kent's father trying to convince him not to date me.

Kent started to speak, but his father stopped him. "Wait, and hear me out first. We love you, Kent. You are our only son, and because of that, we only have your best interests in mind. That being said, I want you to meet the perfect girl, and I want you to have what your mother and I have. Beth seems like an exceptional young lady. I'm glad we've met her and you haven't brought the girls you usually date home. I don't want your mother meeting those girls."

Listening in on their conversation, I was glad that I was wrong at my initial assumption. Mr. Plack was looking out for me.

"Dad…"

"Wait, I'm not finished. You haven't taken anyone home before so I'm assuming you guys are exclusive?" Mr. Plack asked.

I found myself leaning in closer and waiting for Kent's answer.

"We're exclusive."

"I just wanted to make sure because I know how you are Kent. You're spoiled. It's the truth. The uglier truth is that it's our fault that you are spoiled. In hindsight, maybe we shouldn't have given you everything you wanted, but as parents, we wanted to. Parents are inclined to give their children the world." Jack laughed without humor. "But you are the way you are because we handed everything over to you on a silver platter. You're a taker, Kent. But don't let your selfish nature promise that girl a relationship you're not intending to give. Beth's a good girl so don't toy with her emotions or play her, son. That's not you."

"Dad, she makes me laugh, and I enjoy her company. When I'm with Beth, it's effortless, and I don't have to try. I'm just spending more time with her, and we'll see how things go."

"I like the sound of that," Mr. Plack said.

I made my way back to the family room before I got caught. My ears had overstayed their welcome.

A little while later, as I continued flipping through the channels while sitting on the couch, Kent stepped back into the room.

"Dinner is finally served. Sorry that I took a while. My father stopped me to give me a lecture."

"Yeah, I overheard. I'm sorry," I whispered.

His eyebrows shot up. "Oh, really?"

"Shut up. I went looking for you, and I couldn't help myself. The conversation was getting juicy."

He looked behind him to make sure no one was listening. "I've surprised him by bringing a good girl home. He knows my ways, but I was very convincing."

"Yes, I heard that part, too. I'm impressed. You're a good liar," I said, giving him a thumbs-up.

"Liar? I'm not a liar." He reached for my hand and pulled me to stand. "Let's go. I'm starving. Plus, I have to get you home early. You have work tomorrow."

Will I ever get used to him holding my hand?

I expected dinner to turn into a disaster, but it didn't. We talked about Plack Industries. Naturally interested, I asked a lot of questions about the expansion in Bowlesville and overseas. When business talk turned boring, Mrs. Plack discussed her latest charity work at St. Jude's Hospital. We didn't once mention Kent's relationship with me. During dinner, I felt more comfortable. I was able to eat my whole meal and then some.

When it was time to leave, Mrs. Plack encased me in a long bear hug. I imagined this woman consoling Kent when he was younger—wiping every tear, kissing every wound, and hugging him when he was distraught. I could see why Kent loved his mother and why he put her on a pedestal. This woman exuded kindness and selflessness. I basked in her warmth, and I had to admit that I was envious of their relationship. I hadn't had these motherly hugs while growing up, and I wished I had. I squeezed her back while thinking of and missing my Nana.

"Hey now," Kent said, maneuvering between us so that his mom had to release me. "It's my turn. I'm getting jealous over here." He enveloped her in a long embrace and smooched her on her cheek.

Mrs. Plack erupted into warm laughter when Kent wouldn't release her.

Mr. Plack took my hand and shook it. "I hope we see you again soon, Beth." He turned to give Kent a stern look. "Kent, make sure you drive safely and get this lovely lady home in one piece."

ON THE DRIVE to the city, we both stayed silent. Already on the highway and almost home, I yawned and glanced at Kent. He seemed to be in deep thought.

"Hey, what are you thinking about?" I asked, snapping my fingers in front of him.

"Nothing. Everything. I don't know." He paused. "My mom likes you," he whispered.

"Obviously, she was won over by my sheer awesomeness," I said, trying to break his mood.

It worked. "Awesomeness? I don't even think that's a word." He laughed once.

"Yes, it is." I smirked. "If you look that word up in the dictionary, you'll see my picture."

A dimple emerged on his cheek, but then his face turned serious. "I can't bear to hurt her," he said, no longer smiling. "My father and I might not see eye to eye on a lot of things, but we both would move heaven and earth

MIA KAYLA

for that woman." He sighed. "She likes you, Beth, and the more time she spends with you, I don't doubt she will fall in love with you. In the end, she'll be hurt, and I'll be the one who hurt her." A brief expression of pain passed over his face.

"We don't have to do this," I said, touching his arm. "It was your idea."

He shook his head to compose himself and the vulnerable state he had shown a moment earlier was gone. "I don't want to hurt her, but I'll do what I need to," he said, his voice resolute.

With that, our conversation ended.

AFTER WORK THE next evening, I strolled straight into Kent's condo, dropped my laptop bag on the hardwood floor, and slumped against his kitchen counter.

"Bad day?" Kent asked. He seated himself at the kitchen table and scanned a *Time* magazine.

The clock on the wall read five thirty, but he was already in his PJs.

"I didn't tell him," I huffed and blew my bangs out of my eyes.

"Tell who?" he asked, still scanning the magazine.

"I didn't tell Brian, the guy I'm dating. I didn't tell him about our deal. Ugh," I said, disgusted with myself. I'd meant to tell him during our lunch hour, but everything I'd mustered up in my mind that I wanted to say sounded ridiculous.

"Well, if you are so upset, then just tell him," Kent said.

He still hadn't glanced up at me, which was starting

156

to irk me.

"I can't," I whined, moving away from the counter and shifting in Kent's line of sight to get his attention.

"Honestly, I don't see what's so difficult. You're upset because you haven't told him about our arrangement, so tell him, and then you will no longer be upset. The end." Kent flipped a page in the magazine and I narrowed my eyes at him as he still hadn't glanced up.

"You don't understand. He doesn't know about my debt. I have to tell him about that first before I can tell him about our deal." I rubbed at my brow, trying to ward off an oncoming headache.

"Well, tell him then," Kent continued.

I gave him the evil stare. "Stop saying that, will you? I can't tell him, so will you quit repeating yourself? It's really starting to piss me off. I don't know why I came here. You're not being a supportive friend right now!" I yelled.

It was moments like this when I truly longed for female friends. Where males saw everything in black or white, females knew that it wasn't that simple. Sometimes, decisions were in the gray.

He put down the magazine and walked toward the counter. "Okay, what's the problem? I'm listening."

"Well, thanks. I thought you were already listening." I rolled my eyes and jutted out my lip in a full on Bethany pout. "The problem is, I can't tell him about our deal because I'll have to explain my debt situation. It will screw everything up."

I looked to him for advice, and he offered none.

"You can't? Or you won't?" Kent asked.

"I won't."

"Women are so complicated. That's why I don't date," he said, shaking his head. "Well then, I can't help you, and you won't help yourself, so nothing's resolved."

He shrugged, turned, and walked back to the kitchen table, causing my blood to boil.

"You are so annoying." I stomped toward him. "You don't understand because you have never been in a relationship before. I can't tell him about my debt. It's too much baggage. That's like basically telling him that I have a kid. Do you get it?" Exasperated, I raised my hand at him.

He lifted one eyebrow. "You don't have a kid. It's debt, and it's your debt, not his. He's not going to pay for it. I don't see what the big deal is, Beth."

"Okay, let's see here. I can just imagine how it would go down. 'Hey, Brian, I have to tell you something. I know you have the perfect parents and the perfect life. But I had a mother who drank herself into oblivion, dated every loser on the block, and put me into debt—a lot of debt. Now, I know you still want to date me because that's just so attractive,'" I said sarcastically.

I shook my head. "You don't understand. When you are dating someone, it's fake in the beginning. It's the getting-to-know-each-other phase where everything is perfect. You are perfect, he is perfect, everything is absolutely effing perfect. Then, the woman brings out her true side, and the guy brings out his I'm-not-going-to-romance-you-as-much-as-I-did-in-the-beginning side. Eventually, things progress, and you think, 'Oh, I know you have flaws, but I still love you, and although you have flaws, I want to keep this relationship going.'

"So, no, I can't just throw him this curve ball in the beginning. It would ruin things. And I don't want to date around. What's the point? Every girl dates around to find that perfect guy but I've already found him," I said, rambling on without taking a breath.

"I just don't want to ruin things. His birthday is in a few weeks, and I want to be around to spend it with him," I said sadly. "I've worked so hard to get where I am, and I just want that happy ending."

Kent's eyes softened, taking my words in. He finally stood, moved toward me, and placed his hand on my shoulder. "Beth, once this is all over, your debt will be gone, and you will get your happy ending with Brian. Don't worry, okay?"

I shrugged and gave him a small smile. "I hope so."

"I promise, you will," he replied.

Chapter Ten

I GLANCED AT the clock on the lower right side of my work computer screen. It was five and time to go. Determined to tell Brian the truth, I'd told him to meet me at my desk after work, so we could walk to my apartment together.

"Hey you, ready to go?" Brian dropped his laptop bag at the foot of my chair. "I'm hungry. Let's grab some dinner."

"Two seconds. Let me shut my computer down." I shifted to power off my computer and turned to Caroline shuffling back to her desk.

She had just come back from a customer call.

"Hey, how was your call?" I put my laptop into my bag as she flashed me a smile.

"Boring as always, but I did hear some gossip." Her eyes widened as she placed her hands on her hips. "Bethany Casse, have you been holding out on us?" she asked. "Are you dating the hot Kent Plack of Plack Industries?"

Her eyes lit up with excitement while I rapidly blinked at her, not believing what had just left her mouth. My head flipped to Brian to see his cheerful mood drop. His mouth was set in a straight line.

"Uh…no…I don't know. Where did you hear that?" I

said, pulling at the strands of brown hair on my shoulder.

I felt myself get warm all over. Beads of sweat formed at the back of my neck as the shock of an upcoming train wreck hit me full force. It wasn't supposed to come out like this. He was supposed to hear it from me.

Brian grabbed his bag and turned to stomp toward the door and I followed right behind him.

"What's his problem?" Caroline asked, glancing in Brian's direction.

"Customer deal gone bad," I said over my shoulder, moving faster to catch him. "See you tomorrow, Caroline."

He faced the elevator, waiting for it to open, as my eyes studied the back of his striped shirt, noticing the thin vertical white lines contrasting with the blue. I squeezed my palms together, cutting off the circulation, as I waited for him to speak.

"I've been played before. Honestly, I've done some of the playing, but I didn't see the signs on this one," he said, still facing the elevator.

"It's not like that. I promise you, it's not what it looks like."

I reached for his arm, but he shrugged it off.

"If you'll just let me, I can tell you the truth. Please," I begged as I shifted to stare at his side profile.

"Now I know why you didn't want anyone at work to know that we were together." He turned to face me. "Fine, tell me the truth. Are you dating Kent Plack?"

Am I? It's not real. It's just a contractual agreement. "No, I'm not dating him," I told him.

He squinted at me as the elevator door opened. "I don't believe you."

My heart dropped at his words. He walked in, and I stepped inside right behind him. "You have to believe me because it's the truth. I'm not really dating him. It's all for show. It's not real. I'm dating you and only you, no one else." I looked to him for understanding, but what I'd said didn't even make any sense.

His face showed no emotion, and I knew he still didn't believe me. The look in his eyes told me he didn't want to know anything further. If he walked away when the elevator opened on the first floor, I knew I'd never get a chance to tell him my side of the story. Then, I would always wonder about the what-ifs between us. I watched the numbers decrease with our descent, and I made an impulse decision. I lunged myself toward him, hugging him with my head on his chest.

"Please, please, please believe me. It's only you. I wouldn't play you or anyone else for that matter. Give me a chance to explain. Please," I begged. Squeezing my eyes tightly, I was hoping he wouldn't push me away.

He didn't.

After a second, I felt his body loosen in my embrace. The doors opened, and I released him. I met his eyes, and his face turned serious.

"Fine. Explain."

SITTING IN A small pizza joint, I stared at the sugar in front of me. Brian had ordered us drinks, not dinner, which didn't look very promising on my end.

Not making eye contact gave me more strength to get the story out right away. In the end, I couldn't tell him the truth. I just couldn't tell him about my pathetic childhood. I didn't want to delve into my deadbeat mother who had put me into this mess. Maybe I wanted to seem like I had it together, that my life had been just like his while growing up. I didn't want him to look at me any differently. I wanted him to see me—the girl I was today, not the circumstances that had gotten me here. I decided to tell him as much of the truth that I felt comfortable with.

"I'm a victim of identity theft," I said, reaching for the pepper shaker. "Someone used my social security number to rack up debt in my name." I stole a glance as he observed me, and my eyes dropped again to the pepper shaker on the table. "I've tried to contest it, but it's going to cost me money that I don't have. In the end, I'm in a lot of debt, but it's not my fault." I exhaled a heavy sigh. "It's not like I can tell you these things when we just started dating." I said, peeking up at him.

Brian's face turned sympathetic. "I wish you felt like you could tell me anything."

I didn't want his pity. Moving to this big city, starting over, and meeting this great guy were the most normal things that had ever happened to me. My life was just beginning to fall into place.

"I know. It's just that we're not there yet, Brian. We're in the new, exciting stage of dating. I'm supposed to wait to dump this stuff on you in stage two of the dating phase," I said, meeting his eyes. "Plus, I don't tell everyone my problems. The only people who know are Kendy, Kent, and now, you."

Brian's face blanched at the mention of Kent.

"Now, on to how Kent is involved..." I looked to my entwined hands gripping the pepper shaker. *Get this all out and then be done.* "He's going to help me with my debt problem, and in return, I'm helping him."

I dared to glance up to gauge his reaction, but he

163

gave none.

"His parents want him to get married or else they will take away his trust fund. I've agreed to marry him—on paper only—so he can access his money. Then, after a month, we'll get divorced, and he'll pay off all my debt," I revealed, releasing everything in one breath. *There, it's all out.*

I tilted my head to look at Brian.

"That's crazy," he said incredulously. "Don't do it."

I let out a long sigh, thinking of everything I'd overcome to get here. "I know you've lived a normal, stress-free life, but you have no idea what I've been through or what I'm going through right now. Every day, I have creditors calling me. The worst part of this all is that none of this is my fault. I didn't cause this, but I'm the one suffering.

"I've done all I can to get myself far from Bowlesville. I've worked so hard at random jobs through college to get here and into Financial State. I really do make good money for a new graduate, but it's not enough. I will move up and make more money. I know I will. I'm determined to, but that's going to take time."

"I don't want to lose you over this, but right now, Kent is giving me an out, and I'm taking it," I said in finality.

"Does he want more from you?" Brian asked.

"No, I told you, it's not like that." I shook my head. "This is only an arrangement, a one-month arrangement. It's purely platonic."

Of course Brian would be jealous. I would be, too, if our roles were reversed. This situation was far from ideal, but I was born into an abnormal world, so I should be used to it. Still, every part of me wondered if I'd had done something, committed some crime in another life that had doomed my future, and complications were just part of my life now.

He looked at me and smiled.

"What?" I asked, confused by his amusement. This situation, my life, was no laughing matter.

"This is the first time I've seen you so intense." The corner of his mouth lifted. "He doesn't want you?"

"I told you already, no. He said we could date whom we want and do what we want. The show is really for his parents. I mean, everyone else has to believe we're dating, too, but it is only temporary. A month after we're married, we'll file for divorce." I grimaced at how ridiculous that had sounded. Using marriage and divorce in the same sentence should be banned.

He placed his hand over mine on the table, startling me, as he leaned in. "I don't like your arrangement, and I can't tell you where this, where us, is going," he said, looking at his hand on top of mine, "but if this is what you have to do, then it's what you have to do. I believe you when you say nothing is going on between you. Still, this situation is just plain weird. You know what I mean?"

I nodded in agreement as I bit my lower lip. My whole life fell in the bucket of weirdness.

"I haven't met anyone that I was this into. I like you, Beth, and I want to see where this goes. Maybe we should take it slow until this arrangement is over," he said. "Even if it looks, sounds, and seems crazy."

I looked down at his hand on top of mine, thinking he was seriously a godsend. "I'm glad," I said softly as the tension in my shoulders finally relaxed.

He chuckled with amusement.

"What's so funny?" I looked up at him.

"You're cute when you're serious. That pouty lip of yours is irresistible. I've never seen you like this before."

"I guess that means we've moved up to stage two of dating." I placed both of my hands in his.

"One month?" he asked.

I nodded at his adorable face. He leaned in for a kiss, and I gave him a peck on the lips.

"So, what else does this movement to stage two entail?"

His look was devilish, and I laughed at the look he shot me.

"You'll find out after we leave." I gave him a longer kiss on the lips, reveling in their softness.

He pulled back to look at me. "How do I get to stage three?"

"Don't push your luck," I whispered.

"Okay, I was just asking," Brian said, playing innocent. He pulled his wallet from his back pocket. "Drinks are done," he said, raising his hand to our waiter. "Check please."

IT WAS A typical evening in Barrington as Kent and I sat on opposite ends of the couch. A week had passed and we were coming to his parents' house almost every other day. We were watching TV while we waited for his parents to come home. As soon as we heard the front door open, Kent startled me by grabbing my hand, jerking me forward, and pulling me onto his lap. I laughed, hit him, and moved away, but he gripped my wrist and pulled me back.

"Get over here," he said as both dimples appeared.

"Stop," I said playfully, shoving his hands away.

I tried to maneuver away from his grasp, but he linked his arms around my waist, pulling me to sit on his lap. I pinched his hands to release me, and he just laughed it off while using a strong hold to draw me closer against him. I couldn't help the laughter that escaped my lips as I tried to break from his tight grasp. Amusement crossed his face as he used all his might to keep me still. I wiggled in his hold while pinching his wrists.

"You think you're funny," he said, whispering in my ear.

"Very," I replied, leaning forward to bite him to let go of me.

His chest moved up and down in laughter as he gripped me tight, while he moved his arms lower, so I couldn't get a good direct bite. When his parents strolled into the family room, I stilled and pushed myself off of Kent's lap. My cheeks warmed from embarrassment as if we had been caught doing something inappropriate.

"Hi, Mrs. Plack. Mr. Plack," I greeted, briefly looking at each of them.

A beaming grin appeared on Mrs. Plack's face. "Call me Karen. And Beth, I'm glad to see you again. You guys are too cute." Her eyes lit up as she headed toward the kitchen, tugging Mr. Plack behind her. "We're having steak today," she called from the hallway.

Mr. Plack chuckled softly, also entertained by our show of affection.

"You!" I scolded, pointing my finger at Kent.

He nipped at my finger, pretending to bite it, and I pulled my hand back, laughing.

DINNER WAS EXCEPTIONAL. I learned that even though they had help, Mrs. Plack cooked dinner most nights unless she had a late-night charity function. We continued to sit at the table as Mrs. Plack talked about Kent's childhood. By the end of dinner, she had the whole table laughing.

"Jack, do you remember when Kent ate dog food?" Tears from hysteria formed in her eyes as she recalled the story.

"It was a dare, and for your information, I won a dollar," Kent said, feigning boredom. He tried not to smile but failed.

"You'll do anything for money," I said, joining in.

He swiftly kicked me under the table and his eyes widened when I kicked him back even harder.

"Tell me, Kent, what did it taste like? What was the brand, Kibbles 'n Bits?" I asked, playfully poking at his side.

Everyone erupted into laughter.

"Funny girl." He gave me a sly smile as he pinched my leg under the table.

The conversation continued with Mrs. Plack reminiscing about Kent's high school years. I chimed in with snide comments every once in a while. Most of the time, Mrs. Plack and I were hysterical with laughter from making fun of Kent. The men, not even close to our level of giddiness, looked at us in amusement.

Mrs. Plack rubbed her eyes. "Sorry, there are only a few times when I get to relive Kent's younger years. So, Jack, how was work?" She laughed at herself for trying to change the subject into a more serious conversation.

I reached for my glass of water and took a sip as I attempted to compose myself.

Mr. Plack filled us in on Plack Industries and their overseas operations. I watched as Mrs. Plack looked to her husband in approval. Her eyes never strayed from his and he drowned in her attention.

She cracked a joke about him being too serious at work, and his eyes lit up. When she spoke to him, she leaned in, and her hand rested lightly on his arm. It was as if they were the only two in the room, and I was in awe of their marriage. I studied their relationship in silence and wondered if I'd have that one day. Resting my hand on my chin, I gazed at them, soaking in their interaction. I didn't even realize that I was smiling.

In my peripheral vision, I noticed Kent observing me as I was studying his parents. I gave him a *what* look, and he lightly placed his hand on top of mine as it rested on the table. He began massaging my hand, making circles with his thumb. My hand tingled where he touched, but I didn't pull away. I glanced back to his parents to pay attention to their discussion.

We had been so engrossed in our conversations during dinner that I didn't feel the time passing by. When we got up to leave, I peered down at my watch and noticed it was already ten in the evening. At the door, Mrs. Plack engulfed me in a big hug, and this time, Mr. Plack surprised me by doing the same.

At the dinner table, I'd felt like myself. I'd been comfortable and at ease. At times throughout the evening, I'd forgotten that it was all for show, but Mrs. Plack's warm embrace had brought me back to reality. I had to remind myself that my time with this family was not permanent, and it would end. That was the part that saddened me most.

ON THE CAR ride home, I stared out my window, watching the cars on the interstate. The night with his family had reminded me how much I missed my Nana.

Our dinner table had always been filled with joy and laughter, so much so that I would frequently forget that I didn't have a biological mother or father around. Nana had always filled that void, that spot they had abandoned. I missed her so much that my heart physically ached for that family bond. It had always been me, Nana, and Kendy. Now, Nana was gone, and because of Kendy's work schedule, I hardly ever heard from her. As a woman, I needed, wanted, and craved that family connection.

Kent broke me from my thoughts. "You know, our conversations at dinner usually consist of my father talking about Plack Industries, so you can imagine how boring dinners are. You brought laughter to the table tonight," he said, glancing back at me and then to the road ahead. "You and Mother were bantering back and forth like you two were in your own little happy world. You're a lot like her," he said wistfully. "You're genuine and fun-loving, and you bring laughter wherever you go. Mother is just like that. That's why she spends a lot of time at St. Jude's and nursing homes. It's no wonder Brian has fallen for you. It's because you're so easy to love," he said.

I lifted an eyebrow, giving him a sly smile. "Kent, I think that's the nicest thing you've ever said to me." I was touched by his sentiment.

When we reached my apartment, Kent escorted me

to the door. He gave me the longest lingering embrace. "Beth, thanks for spending time with me and my family and for making dinner enjoyable."

His hugs were always safe and comforting, but this time, it felt different as his hand lingered on the small of my back.

I was the first to disentangle from the embrace. "Anytime. I love your family," I said, glancing up at his face.

When I walked into the apartment building, I still felt his eyes on me as the glass door shut behind me.

KENT PICKED ME up from work, and we drove to his parents' house.

We were plopped on the brown leather couch waiting for his parents to come home from a charity event, as we had done two nights before and two nights before that.

I wondered if his parents' found it odd that Kent was stopping by more often. When I confronted Kent about it, he'd said that his mother was just happy that he came around and that his father probably thought that he gave up his partying ways for me. Either way, according to Kent, they seemed happier to have us around regularly.

As Kent watched the news, I yawned, stretched, and got up to walk around the study.

Floor-to-ceiling bookshelves were stocked with books. I ran my hand against the cherry wood desk and picked up a framed picture of a little boy. He was un-recognizable, but it could only be one person. The chubby boy had glasses, a mouth lined with braces, and looked no more than twelve years old. I squinted as I held the

171

picture frame closer to my face. When I looked in Kent's direction, I started to giggle.

Hearing laughter, he turned in my direction. "What's so funny?" he asked, narrowing his eyes at what I was holding.

"Is this you? This nerdy-looking guy?" I laughed, tapping the frame.

He pushed himself off the couch and walked toward me. I showed him the picture, and he tried to reach for it. Raising the frame above my head, I ran to the other side of the room.

"Not funny. Give it to me," he commanded, stalking toward me.

"Make me." I stuck out my tongue and waved the picture frame in front of him to taunt him. "Wow, this doesn't even look like you. Who knew you were such a nerd?"

"Beth..." His tone sounded like a parent scolding a child.

I studied the picture again and started to laugh. "You rock glasses pretty well. You should totally bring them back."

He lunged toward me, and I squealed as I propelled myself toward the opposite end of the room. I shook the picture frame in front of me again.

At my immature gesture, a dimple hit his face. "Is this a challenge? Because if it is, just so you know, I always win."

"I want to see you try."

I widened my eyes to mock him, and he shook his head as a mischievous smile slowly crept up his face. He dashed in my direction, but I swerved toward the other side of the room. Kent's stance changed, and he propelled himself forward once again as I moved by the couch. He closed in with a slight smirk on his face, like he was going to win. Determined, I veered right, but I was too slow as he grabbed me by the waist. In a football-like tackle, he pushed me onto the couch.

"No!" I clutched the picture frame to my chest with all my might.

"Give it back."

He was on top of me and had me trapped between his knees. I tried to buck him off, but he was too heavy.

"Give it here," he commanded with a boyish smile.

"No!" My hair was splayed all over the couch, and I blew my bangs out of my face, catching his amused look.

A slow, conniving smile encompassed his face. "Fine." His fingers started to torture me as he began tickling my sides.

"Stop!" I squealed.

I tried to buck him off me again, but failed as his fingers accelerated in their torture. I was laughing so much that I was almost crying.

"Give me the frame," he said as both dimples emerged. "You don't want to give it to me?"

"Never!" Instead of using my hands to protect myself from his torment, I continued to clutch the picture frame against my chest.

"Okay then."

His knees tightened on my sides, so I could barely move, and he went in for the kill. He tickled me with full force, causing me to laugh so loud that no sound left my lips, only hoarse huffs.

"Please...st-st-stop." I could barely form words while I was dying of tickle pains from his evil hands.

"You never listen to directions, do you?" Kent leaned

in with a smile on his face.

His hands continued to torment me. My cheeks hurt from laughing, and my eyes were shut in torture.

I felt his hands slow down and still to a stop. When I opened my eyes, Kent was a few inches from my face. His eyes bore into mine, and I stopped breathing. Stopped. Breathing. Temporarily, he looked lost, but he was still breathtakingly beautiful.

The air shifted around us, and suddenly, my every nerve was aware of his whole body on top of me. His one hand on my arm, his chest was flush against mine, his knees were on either side of my legs, and his lingering touch was on the side of my face. His scent filled my nose, and for once, I felt an undeniable urge to close the gap between us to meet his lips.

We both turned when his parents entered the room.

I blushed at the position they'd caught us in—me lying on the couch while Kent hovered above me, trapping me between his knees.

Mrs. Plack had a small smile on her lips "Oh, please don't let us interrupt you." She tugged Mr. Plack's arm and pulled him toward the kitchen.

Kent immediately stood, and he reached for my hand to pull me up into a sitting position.

"Excuse me." He didn't meet my eyes as he turned and exited the room.

I had a strong awareness of my heart beating loudly in my chest. I placed my hand on my cheek to stop the tingling from Kent's touch that was still present even though he was no longer here.

What's happening?

After a few minutes, I searched for Kent. I found him sitting in the billiard room. His thumb and pointer finger pinched the bridge of his nose. From his side profile, I noticed every feature —from his straight nose to his chiseled jaw line to his full lips. I waited and listened to him taking deep breaths in through his nose and out his mouth. His brow was furrowed in concentration. He didn't even know I was standing there, so I knocked on the wall beside me. His head shot up to my direction, and his eyes locked with mine. He seemed so lost, and all I wanted to do in that instant was to console him.

I walked toward him until I was a few inches away. "What's the matter?" I asked, placing my hand on his shoulder. "Were you teased as a kid?" I whispered.

He glanced at my hand touching his shoulder. "No," he said as he placed his hand on top of mine. A feeling of warmth flooded where we were connected. "Never." He shook his head slightly. "Sometimes, I'm sure of myself, and other times, I'm not," he said, mostly speaking to himself.

We stared at each other as an uncomfortable silence built in the air between us.

I realized I still had the picture in my other hand. "If it's not that, then I'm the winner," I said, breaking the awkward silence.

I gave him a cheeky grin as his eyes focused on the frame in my hands. "Yes, I was a bit chubby in my younger years, but kids were afraid to make fun of me because they knew I'd beat the living shit out of them," he said.

"Or eat them." I giggled.

When I was momentarily distracted, he snatched the picture frame from me and shrugged.

"Not fair." I pouted.

He studied my face with seriousness in his eyes. It was a look that I'd never seen before.

He glanced to my hand before reaching for it. "Come on, let's join my parents for dinner."

We entwined our hands as he led me into the dining room, and I wondered if he could feel the electricity that I felt from where we were connected.

Chapter Eleven

"HAPPY BIRTHDAY!" I stepped into Brian's car and gave him a kiss on the lips.

"Hey, sexy," he replied, appraising me with his eyes.

He used one hand to entangle with mine while the other remained on the steering wheel. He pressed on the gas to lead us to our destination, a suburban bar outside the city, where we'd meet his high school friends.

"I'll give you your birthday present later," I said, giving his hand a squeeze. I looked to the traffic forming in front of us, thinking of the Chicago Cubs tickets I'd purchased, which were sitting on my kitchen counter.

"I can't wait. I hope it's you unwrapped." He winked.

"Eyes on the road," I warned, squeezing his hand back.

I wondered if today would be the day I let him seal the deal. We were way past date number ten, and I knew we had been leading up to this point. I'd made him wait long enough, almost to the point of his combustion, but the anxious, giddy feeling I'd had when we first started dating was no longer there. I knew this had to do with Kent and how the lines were blurring between us, and I mentally cursed him for it.

"How long is it going to take us to get to the bar?"

"About forty-five minutes," Brian said, glancing at

the clock on the dashboard.

My mind drifted to Kent as we left the city lights behind us. I'd invited Kent to Brian's birthday party when things were not so gray between us. Now, an uneasiness was building inside me. I worried about Brian's interaction with Kent tonight, how Kent would feel at seeing Brian and me together, and worst of all, how I would feel when I saw Kent, especially now that the friendship lines were no longer clear.

"Hey, Kent is coming tonight, remember?" I said.

Brian and I didn't speak of Kent often. It was the one bad word in our relationship. The four letter K word never failed to put Brian in a foul mood.

"Yeah," Brian said under his breathe. The look on his face showed his displeasure.

"Be good. He asked about your birthday, and I wanted him to join us."

"I'm always good," he stated, gripping the steering wheel tighter.

I raised an eyebrow as I gave his hand a squeeze, and he loosened with my touch.

"It's not like I don't like him. I just don't like the situation," he said.

"Okay, just remember that when you see him. He's saving me from a lot of debt, so be good."

Brian gave me a quick kiss on the lips and placed his eyes back on the road. Hopefully, that kiss had meant that he would play nice.

A line of people spanned from outside the door to down the block. Given that this was a bar in the suburbs, the crowd surprised me. When Brian spotted some of his friends in line, he ushered me through the herd. I introduced myself to the group, and we exchanged pleasantries.

Scanning the crowd, I noticed Kent beyond the mass. As I saw him gilding forward, I excused myself.

"Hey, I'll be back," I whispered as Brian continued to reconnect with his friends.

My eyes locked with Kent's through the pack of people, and a small smile formed on his face.

"I'm so glad you made it," I exhaled.

Pulling me into a hug, he wrapped both arms around me and placed his head in the crook of my neck. I felt his deep intake of breath through his nose, taking in my scent, and as he exhaled, his whole body relaxed. His breath tickled my neck, and every nerve in my body felt that electricity between us. I closed my eyes, and for a moment, I basked in his embrace. Then, I remembered that I was here with Brian, so I moved from Kent's touch.

"I had no idea this place would be so crowded. Did you find it okay?" I asked, touching my hair nervously.

"It wasn't that difficult. You asked me to come, so I came."

The way he gazed at me sent a shock from the pit of my belly all the way down to the tips of my toes.

"Well, I'm glad you came. Let's get in line," I said, ignoring the tremor in my voice.

He devoured my ensemble with his eyes, and I swore that I stopped breathing.

"You really look great tonight, Beth," he said softly.

I warmed from his compliment and the way his eyes took all of me in. "Thanks. Let's get in line," I repeated.

He reached for my hand, but mine stayed in place. It would have been easy to meet him and link our fingers together. During this charade, it had become natural for him to extend his hand and for me to grab his in return, but tonight, I was here with Brian, and I had to remember that.

From my peripheral view, I could see Brian heading toward us, just on cue, and as he approached, the uneasy, nervous feelings I'd felt in the car rushed back.

"Hey, Kent. Thanks for making it, man," he said, gripping Kent's hand firmly.

"Any reason to drink. First round is on me for your birthday," Kent replied, taking a step away from us.

"The line is moving, so we should go." Brian affectionately kissed me and grabbed my hand to lead me through the crowd.

I glanced behind me. Kent had his hands fisted at his sides while looking at my hand linked with Brian's. I couldn't read his face.

INSIDE, THE MUSIC roared, and the dimmed lights highlighted our surroundings. The place was packed with people standing shoulder to shoulder. We pushed ourselves to a spot against the bar and made room for all of Brian's friends.

As promised, Kent took the first round. When he ordered shots of tequila for everyone, I made a face. This was going to be a fast night. I had to pace myself because it was Brian's birthday, and I would be the designated driver.

I licked the salt off my hand, downed the shot, and sucked on the lime quickly, feeling the liquor go down and burn the back of my throat. "Kent Tequila? Really?" I scrunched my face, feeling the aftertaste.

"Beth, it's not like you can't drink," Kent said above

the music.

My thoughts flickered back to the first time we'd gone clubbing together. It felt so very long ago, and I smiled at the memory.

Brian reached for my hand. "Hey, some of my friends just arrived. Let's go say hi." He looked to Kent and gave him a nod. "Excuse us."

I felt Kent's eyes burning a hole through me as Brian and I drifted through the crowd. After a while, I peered behind me, and two girls were standing by Kent's side, flirting with him. I cringed inwardly, noticing as each girl tried to top the other while vying for his attention. I watched as Kent laughed at something the shorter one had said, and then the taller one leaned in to whisper something in his ear.

I figured that Kent would pick up two attractive girls within the first fifteen minutes of being in the bar. I glanced to either side of him, and I noticed other girls were also eyeing him. From his clothes, to the way he carried himself, Kent looked like he had money. I couldn't decipher if women were after him for that or if it was his handsome face and fitted shirt over his toned body.

He bought drinks for the girls still talking to him, and I wondered if he would take one or both of them home tonight. I knew it was his usual routine, but today, it left a bad aftertaste in my mouth.

Today, I didn't like it.

I wanted to take him by the collar and tell him, *You deserve better than those girls. Don't do it.*

But I had no right to. I couldn't be protective when this was the lifestyle he'd chosen to live. Most importantly, because he wasn't mine, I had no right to challenge what he decided to do.

When he caught my stare, his smile disappeared. His face turned serious while the barflies continued to laugh around him. As they tried to get a reaction from him, he ignored them completely while he stared at me so intently that his look alone sent shivers down my spine. I felt a gravitational pull toward him, his eyes beckoning me forward, and in that brief second, it was as if we were the only two people in the room.

I finally shook myself out of the trance and broke the awkwardness in my usual Bethany way. I shot him a cheesy smile, pointed to the girls, and gave him two thumbs-up. He didn't return my smile. Instead, he slowly and painfully tore his eyes from mine, which left me feeling empty.

Standing behind Brian, I placed my arms around his waist. He pivoted around to wrap his arms around me, and he placed a kiss on my lips. I tasted the beer he had just drunk as he tipped me back.

Bringing me forward, he leaned down and nuzzled my ear. "For my birthday, I want to take you home," Brian said, lightly tracing his fingertips at the small of my back, just under my tank top before the top of my jeans.

Instead of my hormones raging at his words, my first thought was Kent.

Brian pulled me in tighter against him as he kissed me more deeply. I felt his tongue enter me. I knew he was starting to feel the alcohol because this was not typical Brian behavior. He wasn't normally overly affectionate in front of other people. Part of me thought he was staking a claim on me because Kent was here.

When Brian released me, I wasn't sure why, but my eyes flipped toward Kent's direction. His mouth was set in a straight line. The women continued to talk to him, but he was oblivious to their one-sided conversation.

The feeling of butterflies fluttering in the pit of my stomach was back, and I looked away. I was physically by Brian, standing next to him with his arms around me, but my thoughts were at the opposite end of the bar.

THIRTY MINUTES PASSED, and I noticed that Kent had bought more rounds of drinks. More women were surrounding him. He pounded back shots, and by the speed he was going, I would have to ask Brian or one of his friends to carry Kent out.

"Excuse me, I'll be back," I said to Brian. One glance at his glossed over eyes indicated he was equally wasted.

I moved toward the opposite end of the bar to control the train wreck I knew was going to happen.

When Kent glanced up, he smiled slyly. "Beth, let's have a shot."

The girl beside him giggled like an idiot, and I moved past her to get into Kent's face. "I think you've had enough. At least pace yourself," I said, taking the drink out of his hand.

"Don't ruin my fun. I just started," he slurred with a drunken smile on his face.

A busty blonde maneuvered in front of me, leaning into him. "Yeah, don't ruin his fun, honey. The party just started." She placed her hand on his inner thigh and peered up at him through her fake eyelashes. "Unless you want to take this party to your place," she said, brushing her chest against him.

Women had no shame. I felt my temperature rise as I glared at the little skank in front of me. I turned to face

Kent and shoved the girl off of him. "Just so you know, you're not driving," I stated.

"Bitch," she snapped. Her sweet face turned vicious as she lifted her hand to smack me.

Kent blocked her path and gripped my hand as he pulled me through the crowd. Before I knew it, we were outside the bar. The brisk air hit my arms, causing goose bumps, and I jerked my hand away from his to wrap my arms around myself.

"What are you doing?" he asked, leaning closer to get in my face.

"Nothing. I'm just telling you, if you're going to take that whore home, you can't drive," I snapped, rubbing my shoulders. "Where are your keys?" I placed my hand out and narrowed my eyes at him.

His eyes moved to my lips before slowly dropping down to my low-cut top. Finally meeting my eyes again, he gave me a look that was so intense and so hot that it bore straight into my deepest core, warming me in the cool air.

He shook his head. "I'll be fine," he said, turning away from me.

I grabbed his arm and jerked him to face me. "I want your keys, Kent. Give me your keys. Don't be stupid!" I yelled.

People turned toward my direction and I didn't care that I was causing a scene.

He took a step forward, grabbed both of my elbows, and pulled me into him until his face was inches from mine. "Why are you doing this to me, Beth?" he yelled.

I could smell the liquor on his breath. He was so close that it was unnerving. He looked to my lips. "What do you want from me?" he whispered.

I felt that electricity, that zing between us again. The hold he had on me, just with his chestnut eyes catching my emerald ones, was intense. I fell silent. I couldn't form words. I couldn't move. I couldn't breathe.

"What do you want?" he whispered again.

One of his hands slipped from my arm to my waist, grazing my flesh between my tank top and jeans. Warmth spread throughout my whole body, initiating from where his hand met my skin. His fingertips dug into my back, my bare skin, pushing me closer to him.

"Your keys," I said breathlessly, looking into his chestnut eyes.

"Come with me. Drive my car home. Make sure I make it back okay. Leave with me," he said softly, looking at my lips.

A few more inches, and it would be so easy to feel his lips against mine.

And I wanted to.

I wanted so badly to close the gap between us, to finally allow our lips to meet.

I'd never felt such an attraction, a pull so strong that it took all my willpower to close my eyes to compose myself.

Everything is changing.

I felt it, the charged air around us, his look, his stance, his more than friendly touches.

I had to rein things in—now.

I had to get things back in order. If I wanted to save our friendship, to get any form of normalcy back between us, I had to right things.

Maybe in another lifetime when Kent isn't with a different woman every night...

When he held some sort of job or showed some sort

185

of responsibility, maybe, just maybe we could be together. But he could never be the man I wanted for myself, the one I pictured for myself because I would never force a man I'd grown to care for to change, not for anyone, particularly not for me.

"I'm here with Brian," I whispered, speaking mostly to myself. "I'm going home with him."

Those words broke the connection between us, and as soon as his touch left me, I felt empty.

He staggered, moving back, and his gaze seemed unfocused. I knew those words hurt him, but they needed to be said, not only for him but also for me. I had to remind myself that I'd come with Brian. I was here with him.

"I just want your keys, Kent. I don't want you driving home drunk."

My eyes flickered to the bar behind me and back to meet his face. There was a tightness around his eyes that made my heart hurt. I didn't like his demeanor, and I didn't want to yell anymore. I wanted to know he was safe, but most of all, I wanted to erase that desolate look on his face.

I reached out for his hand. "Please, can I have your keys?"

I gave his hand a squeeze, and he looked down to where we were joined.

"I don't want you driving drunk. I don't want you to get hurt," I whispered, my heart hurting for a reason I couldn't place.

He furrowed his eyebrows, still looking to where our hands met.

A moment passed between us, and he pulled out his keys from his pocket, dropped them on the ground, and turned toward the busy street.

"Beth," he said, still facing the other direction as his shoulders slumped, "you deserve happiness."

With that, he walked away.

THE NIGHT WENT from bad to worse. By the time it was over, Brian was piss-ass drunk. He was a sloppy drunk, so much so that we were kicked out of the bar by two burly bouncers. He had drunk himself into oblivion, and he was throwing up out the window all the way back to Chicago. It took his roommate and me over an hour to get dead-weight Brian out of the car, into his apartment, and undressed. It also didn't help that Brian's roommate was nowhere near sober.

I took a cab back to my apartment because my feet ached and my back hurt, and I was unbelievably tired and pissed off. All I wanted was to fall asleep in my own bed and not next to Brian, who had been snoring loudly when I tucked him in.

When my head hit the pillow, I tossed and turned. I wanted to shut off my mind to all that had happened and all the confusion going on in my brain, but sleep wouldn't come. It wouldn't come because I was worried about Kent, wondering if he'd made it home safely.

I ended up calling him over and over, but he never answered.

I didn't know when sleep had finally taken over, but I knew it had because I woke up the next morning with the phone right next to my ear while a woman's voice said, "If you'd like to make a call, please try again."

MY POUNDING ON the door accelerated louder and louder while the beat of my heart raced in my chest. I'd been calling Kent for two days, and he hadn't picked up. The last time I'd seen him was when he left the bar drunk.

When he opened the door, I released the breath that I had been holding. His hair was disheveled and he looked like a mess but I didn't care. I was just so relieved to see him in person, safe in front of me. As I walked in the room, I noticed all the shades were drawn, and his apartment reeked of a foul smell.

"Where have you been? I've been worried about you. I was about to call your mom, but I didn't want to worry her," I said, pushing past him and barging into the condo.

"Not feeling well." He slouched and made his way toward the couch.

I followed behind him and surveyed the room. Liquor bottles and beer cans were on the floor, and shot glasses and tumblers spanned every inch of the coffee table.

I dropped my bag on the hardwood floor and started to draw up the shades. I heard Kent huff as I drew up the first set. He pulled a pillow over his head to block the sunlight from hitting his face.

"Did you have a party and not invite me?" My head lifted toward his bedroom, and I was relieved that there wasn't a woman in his bed.

I walked to his kitchen, got out a garbage bag, and started tossing out the cans and bottles, one by one. With each drop into the bag, I could feel my temperature rising. "Do you want to die from alcohol poisoning or something?" I asked, hearing the bottle drop with a ping as it hit the bottom of the bag touching the floor.

"Seriously, what's the matter with you? I don't want to be your mom, but what the hell is this? I mean, you can party, but party responsibly," I scolded.

I stomped toward him and lifted the pillow from his head. "Are you hearing me right now? What's the matter with you?"

He lifted his head to look at me. The bags under his eyes were noticeably dark. "What do you care?"

I was taken aback by his tone, but I let it pass. "I care that you don't die," I said, glaring at him. "I've been calling you. The least you could have done was call me back to tell me you're alive."

He sat up so slowly as if every bone in his body ached, and he placed his head in both hands. "How's Brian?" he asked, his voice sharp.

I reeled back, startled by his question. "Okay," I replied, unsure where this was headed.

"Did you give him his birthday present?" Kent snapped, lifting his head to meet my eyes, his jaw clenched.

I flinched at his words, the tone of his voice, and the look he was giving me.

I didn't want to talk about this. I didn't want to relive the other night or talk about how it had taken me forever and a half to get Brian home in one piece. "I'm not talking about Brian with you," I said, pulling the garbage bag tighter to my side.

"And why not?" he asked as he stood up. "You tell me everything." He inched toward me, reeking of alcohol. "Tell me, why doesn't he know about mommy dearest?" His eyes grew dark.

His proximity quickened my pulse and warmed my

insides.

"I just haven't gotten the chance to tell him every-thing yet," I said, moving away, as his look raked me in.

Kent stalked until he was a foot away from me, and I couldn't breathe.

"Why do you tell me everything?" he asked.

"I don't know," I whispered.

When he took a step forward, I took a step back, afraid of what I'd do if he got too close.

"Why do you tell me and not the guy you're dating?" Kent asked, towering over me.

"I told you, I haven't gotten around to it," I said, to-tally aware of his nearness. My pulse quickened at his proximity and I did all I could to steady my breathing.

"Why not? You've been dating long enough. Does he know about Nana?" he said, taking another step in my direction. "Why do you tell me when you're in a relation-ship with him? I just want to know why."

I backed up farther until I felt the coffee table hit the back of my knees. There was nowhere else to go, and my whole being was hyperaware of his body by mine.

"What's the matter with you? I told you, I don't know. I haven't gotten to it yet."

He aligned himself in front of me, his face inches from mine. He looked briefly to my lips and then back to my eyes. "Why do you confide in me? Why me?" he asked so softly, his warm breath on my face.

My heart stuttered in my chest. He was so close that I could taste him, and every ounce of my body wanted him nearer.

"Why?" he asked.

I closed my eyes. Before I could do something I would regret, I pushed him away from me with both hands, dropping the garbage bag I'd been holding. "Leave me alone. I told you, I don't know why. I came to drop off your keys. I made Caroline drive me this morning to pick up your car."

I turned to walk out the door. "I'm glad you're alive. When you're normal again, you can call me." I shut the door behind me while my heart pounded loudly in my ears. I stormed into the elevator, and as soon as the door shut, I used the wall as support while I tried to calm my raging pulse.

What the hell is happening between us?

TWENTY-FOUR LONG-STEMMED ROSES were delivered to my desk the next morning.

Caroline peeked over her cubicle, beaming at me. "Oh, Beth, you live the life," she said.

Little did she know, the life she thought was so great was becoming really hard to maintain.

I opened the card, knowing it could be from only one person.

I'M SORRY. FORGIVE ME.

BE READY AFTER WORK. WE ARE HAVING DINNER WITH MY PARENTS.

WE'RE GETTING ENGAGED TODAY.

I blinked a couple of times, my eyes zoning in on one word. *Engaged.*

I placed the card away in its envelope and smiled

awkwardly at Caroline before I headed toward the conference room. I shut the door behind me and called Kent from the office phone.

He picked up on the first ring. "Did you get them?"

"Yeah. Thanks," I said, fiddling with the ends of my hair. "Today? Why today? Aren't we supposed to talk about these things? I mean, that's not fair to spring things like this on me at the last minute. I have to prepare." I was pacing back and forth while pulling at the ends of my ponytail.

"Are they beautiful?" he asked, ignoring my question. "Am I forgiven?"

"What?" I shook my head. "The roses? Yeah, they are beautiful. Kent, does it have to be today?"

"Am I forgiven?" he asked again, his tone laced with underlying worry.

"Yeah, okay, you're forgiven," I huffed. "Listen, I'm at work. Why today? Why didn't you give me advance notice?" I could feel my temperature rising with anxiety as I dug my black heels into the industrial gray carpet of the conference room.

"I just thought it was time. I've been doing a lot of thinking, and I think it's time."

My thoughts moved to Brian. I was glad that he had a client call this evening. Ever since I'd told him about this arrangement, I'd been walking on eggshells, trying not to mention Kent's name. I figured if we didn't talk about Kent or my past, then everything would turn out okay. A month would pass, the arrangement would be done, and maybe I could get past the confusion with Kent.

"Okay, let's just get this done," I replied.

"Beth," he said before letting me off the phone, "know that you can still tell me anything. You know that, don't you?"

"Yeah," I said, glad that my old Kent was back.

I hung up the phone, walked to my desk, and admired the beautiful red roses positioned by my computer monitor. I turned toward Caroline. "Hey, do you want to take these home?"

"Why? They're so beautiful."

"I know. I'm just allergic to flowers," I lied.

"Well then," she said with a big smile on her face, "hand them over." She strolled over to my desk and reached for the vase.

"Take them home today, please." *Before Brian sees them.*

"Sure thing. I wouldn't want you sneezing everywhere."

Chapter Twelve

AFTER KENT'S CALL, I couldn't work, I couldn't eat, I couldn't do anything, except think of dinner with his parents. Dusk approached as my heels clicked against the sidewalk while I was waiting for Kent to pick me up. We were going to meet his parents at The Peninsula Hotel.

All the pent-up anxiety that had bubbled up inside of me after I'd talked to Kent this morning had led into a full-on panic attack when I stepped into the car. "I can't do this," I said, mostly to myself. I looked down at my clenched hands, my palms sweaty. All the nervousness from the first day when we'd pretended with his parents rushed back to haunt me.

Kent reached for my hand and squeezed it as he pressed on the gas to take us closer to our destination.

Breathe in and out, in and out. I tried all the tricks in the book, trying to calm my nerves, but nothing seemed to work. The jumpy, anxious feeling was building inside every part of my very being. From the queasiness in the pit of my stomach, I thought I was going to hurl on the dashboard. I'd pulled it off this far, but now was the real deal. With every lie, I'd fallen deeper and deeper, getting further away from reality. *You agreed to this. Breathe, Beth. Breathe.*

"You'll be fine, I promise," he said, releasing me and

putting both hands on the steering wheel.

Once I did this, I couldn't go back. We would be engaged, and the planning would be full force and straight ahead. As he drove down Michigan Ave, I stared at the designer stores to my right. Marc Jacobs, Burberry, and Ferragamo passed by me. It was sensory overload. I saw the stores, the lights, and the cars as my mind raced a mile a minute, thinking of what would happen and what I would say at dinner. I concentrated on one thing to prevent myself from passing out—my breathing.

In and out.

In and out.

Before I knew it, we were parked in front of The Peninsula Hotel, waiting at the valet.

"I can't do this," I said a little too loudly. I looked to him with wide eyes as I clenched my jaw.

The valet attendant approached and waited by Kent's door, but Kent stopped him by locking the door and putting up one finger, signaling to give us a moment.

"Come on, Beth."

I stared at him, and then I shut my eyes tightly and shook my head vigorously from side to side.

He placed both hands on the sides of my face, to still me, forcing me to open and meet his eyes. "I promise you, you will be fine. You won't even have to say a word. We're almost there, Beth. Just a little bit further, and we'll be married. Then, it will be over, and I can pay off your debt."

I listened to the intensity of his words.

But I want marriage to be forever.

"Stop it," Kent said. "Don't think of backing out now. Everything will be fine. Don't you want to be out of debt?"

The valet attendant knocked at Kent's window.

Kent's demeanor changed as he twisted to face the attendant. He shot him a look. "What?" he mouthed. He held up one finger again in warning. Then, he turned to me slowly, framing my shoulders with his hands. "Beth, listen to me. Do you want to be out of debt?"

When I didn't answer quickly enough, he shook my shoulders gently and smiled. "Yes or no?"

I nodded, but before I even had a chance to speak, he had his hand on the door.

"Good. Let's go before you change your mind." He stepped out of the car, and walked right past the valet attendant holding his door. He approached another attendant and gave him the keys.

Walking to my side, he opened the passenger door and offered his hand. "Are you ready?"

Am I ready? I don't think so.

I didn't have time to overanalyze my thoughts further as Kent reached over, interlocked our fingers, and pulled me inside The Peninsula Hotel.

He took the lead through the lobby, and I held on to him, gripping his hand for support. I thought I would fall while walking on the marble floor, so I concentrated on stepping one foot in front of the other. I concentrated to my black heels clicking against the marble floor. I looked up when he stopped in front of the extravagant floral arrangement of pink and cream hydrangeas, roses, and peonies. The scent of the fragrant flowers filled my nose. He pulled me to face him and used both hands to frame my shoulders. It was only then that I realized he was in a suit that was similar to the navy suit I was wearing. As always, he looked handsome, and when I peered up at him, I felt the same butterfly feeling, that jolt of electricity between us. For a brief moment, the nervousness and the anxiety dissipated as I stared into his chestnut eyes.

"I just want to say sorry for a couple of nights ago. I was going through some stuff, my own stuff." He shook his head. "I'm just confused. All I know now is that I want you to be happy. Whatever gets you there, I want to see it happen."

He stepped back to pull something out of his inside jacket pocket, and my eyes widened at what he was holding in his hands.

It was a red velvet box with one word etched in gold. *Cartier.*

"I went shopping," he said, a dimple emerging on his cheek. "I saw this, and it reminded me of you. It's perfect and beautiful," he said, staring at me intently.

He flipped the top open, and inside sat a single round solitaire on a thin band that I assumed was platinum.

"Fit for a princess." He reached for my left hand and slipped it on my ring finger.

I looked at the rock that spanned half of my ring finger. The diamond was supposed to represent love and promises of the future, but most of all, it was supposed to represent forever. And I knew that didn't apply to us.

The crowd around us erupted in applause, breaking me from my thoughts. I hadn't even known that anyone had noticed us, and I blushed at the attention we were getting.

"Kiss!" someone yelled as the oohs and aahs quieted down.

Kent pulled me closer, wrapping his hands around my waist. He looked younger, smiling like a little boy. "Maybe I should have gotten down on one knee," he whispered.

My eyes noticed the expectant people surrounding

us.

"Kiss!" someone yelled again. "Do it."

His face was so handsome, but more than that, his chestnut eyes were shining. His closeness was unnerving, but it wasn't enough because I wanted to be closer. I was hyperaware of his whole self in front of me and when he leaned in, I slowly closed my eyes.

What am I doing?

He kissed me at the corner of my mouth, and when I looked up, everyone was cheering.

"Do you like it?" Kent asked, looking toward my left hand.

"It's big," I said, peering at the rock on my finger. I didn't know anything about rings, but the size of the diamond spanned knuckle to knuckle.

"Big?" He looked at me, expecting more.

"Big and beautiful," I smiled, "and really heavy." I entangled our hands together to prevent the onlookers, especially the women, from getting closer to look at the ring.

He kissed the top of my hand once before leading me into the restaurant. "Let's go. My parents are waiting for us."

My hand tingled from the spot where he'd kissed. The lines were getting gray again, and I didn't know how to stop it. Why he did this, I didn't know, and why I let him made me feel guilty.

"What?" he asked.

"I'm nervous," I said softly as we walked past the greeter. "And you can't do that anymore. It's not fair to Brian."

His smile disappeared as he pulled me forward, and we made our way to the table where Mr. and Mrs. Plack were seated.

Mrs. Plack, as usual, was prim and proper in a cardigan sweater. She was laughing at something Mr. Plack had said. They were cute as always, looking as they should, like an older couple in love. When she saw us approaching the table, her face lit up, and they both stood to welcome us.

She kissed Kent on the cheek and enveloped me in a big hug. She grabbed my hand to squeeze it, lifted my hand and gaped at the ring. Her eyes widened at Kent in shock.

"Surprise! We're engaged," Kent said, observing his mother's reaction.

Her mouth was slightly ajar as she blinked a couple of times. She was stunned into silence.

Mr. Plack mirrored her shock, but he didn't even try to hide it. "Are you crazy?" he asked, placing both hands on the table and leaning in.

Mrs. Plack sat down and tugged on Mr. Plack's jacket to force him to sit with her, but he didn't budge.

"Jack," she whispered, looking around us.

"What are you thinking?" Mr. Plack cried out, looking directly at Kent.

"Jack..." Mrs. Plack pulled him down more forcefully.

"Karen, this is crazy," he snapped, as he briefly glanced at his wife before sitting.

When Kent took his chair, I followed suit and sat down. I fidgeted in my seat as an audience of spectators slowly built around us.

Kent's face remained resolute. "I know we haven't known each other long, but you and Mom were engaged less than a year before you got married, and you two have been together ever since."

199

"We were engaged in less than a year, but we had known each other for five years before that. You can't compare the two." Mr. Plack's voice was hushed as he tried to keep his temper under wraps.

I glanced at Kent, and his face mirrored the same frustration as his father's.

"Kent, you think marriage is just a walk in the park. Do you even know how to unselfishly take care of another person, to put someone's needs above yours, to love someone unconditionally?" Mr. Plack looked to his son in expectation.

"Of course I do," Kent said, meeting his father's stare head-on.

They were both stubborn, and I wondered who would back down.

"You don't even know how to take care of yourself, let alone another person. You're selfish and spoiled, and living off a whim is not justified."

"Jack..." Mrs. Plack said softly, placing her hand on Mr. Plack's arm to calm him.

"Don't pretend you know anything about our relationship. I care for her," Kent scoffed, reaching for my hand. "I do," he said, meeting my eyes.

My ears warmed, and I tugged my hand from Kent before adjusting the salt and pepper shakers on the table.

"Oh, and love saves the world," Mr. Plack mocked. "Marriage is through sickness and health and good times and bad. Do you understand the magnitude of this type of commitment?" Mr. Plack stood up, looking to his son. "Do you even know anything about each other? Have you had your first fight yet?" His voice was slightly raised now as he leaned in. "You're spoiled, son. That's the truth, and the uglier truth is that it is our own fault.

But your actions have never drastically affected the life of someone else."

"Jack, stop," Mrs. Plack pleaded.

Mr. Plack suddenly realized that I was there. "Beth, know that this hostility is not meant for you. It's just too soon. You're a bright lady. Why would you want to jump into something like this so soon?" He paused slightly and furrowed his brow. "Did you guys have an accident? Are you pregnant? Is that what this is all about?"

"No!" Kent and I spoke simultaneously.

I felt my face heat up, the warmth spreading to my ears. I wished I were anywhere but here at this moment. I placed my hands together on top of the table, cutting off the circulation and concentrated on the paleness I was causing due to the lack of blood flow.

Mr. Plack ran one hand down his face in frustration. "Kent, are you ready? Marriage is forever, son. Are you ready for that till-death-do-you-part stuff? Are you ready for forever? Because that's what marriage is."

"I am." Kent's voice was steady, but his eyes wavered, giving him away.

"You're not," his father laughed once without humor. "You have a lot of growing up to do before then."

Mrs. Plack slammed her hands on the table, shaking our wine glasses on the table. "Stop, both of you," she said softly. There was an undercurrent in her voice that caught the attention of both Plack men, bringing them to silence.

She looked to both Kent and me. "Why the rush? Why not wait, even just a year?"

I lifted the glass of water to my lips, feeling nervous from the tension of this conversation.

Kent paused, looking at his father first and then his

mother. "She's a virgin, and she won't have sex until she's married. I love her, and I can't wait."

I coughed up my drink, sputtering water onto the table. Dribbles of liquid leaked from the sides of my mouth.

Still coughing like an idiot and most likely choking on my own spit, I stood. I thought I was going to die right then and there. There was an intense ringing in my ears, and at that very moment, I wished for death.

"Sorry. Excuse me." I said, not meeting anyone's eyes. Before I could catch a reaction from anyone, I walked away.

I rushed toward the restroom, almost knocking over someone on the way. I gripped the sink and looked at myself in the mirror. I twisted on the faucet to wet my hands and splash water on my face.

How the hell can I move forward from this?

When two women walked into the restroom, laughing, I moved to the handicap stall. If I was going to have a panic attack or throw up, I was going to do it in private. I leaned against the wall for support. My eyes focused on the gray ceramic tiles on the restroom floor as my mind flickered to thoughts of Nana.

It was the first time I'd thought of her during this whole mess. Subconsciously, maybe I'd put her in the back of my mind. I didn't want to think of her because it saddened me. She would be so disappointed in me, and knowing that broke my heart. She hadn't raised me to be this person—a person who manipulated people, a person who lied to get what she wanted. For once, I just wanted the easy way out, and in the back of my mind, I knew she wouldn't have agreed. I looked to the ceiling, blinking back tears that I knew would surely come.

"Beth?"

It was Mrs. Plack.

Things could not get any worse.

She knocked on the handicap stall, and I was sure we were the only two in the restroom now since her voice had echoed through the stalls. There was no way I could hide in there forever, so I let her in. She gazed at me, and my eyes dropped to the floor. I couldn't even look this lovely woman in the face.

"Honey, are you okay?"

I nodded once. When I met her eyes, they were full of sympathy but also full of warmth.

"It's okay. There's no need to be embarrassed. I think saving yourself for your husband is very rare nowadays."

Please.

Someone.

Kill.

Me.

Now.

"The fact that you love him and have not given into temptation makes you a very strong-willed woman. That's very commendable."

Oh my word…

I lowered my gaze to the floor and nodded again. This would have been comical in any other circumstances, but the guilt is what prevailed.

She moved in to lift my chin. "I know you love him, and he loves you. I can see it. I see it when you both look at each other and when he touches you. I've never seen him so happy."

Her smile was genuine, and the guilt overwhelmed my body ten times worse as I stared into her warm chestnut eyes that were so much like Kent's.

"But, honey, don't let him force you into doing

something so soon. You two will get there. Guys will be guys." She moved back to give me space. "At the end of the day, you two are adults, and I truly believe you're it for him." Her eyes were lined with unshed tears as she pulled me toward her, wrapping her arms around me. "Thanks for making him so happy. I can't wait to plan this wedding," she whispered.

"Me, too," I said, shutting my eyes tightly.

As she hugged me, I should have felt relieved that Kent and I had pulled it off, but that was far from what I felt.

THE RIDE HOME was quiet.

I had to break the uncomfortable silence in the air. "So, I can't believe we're engaged," I said. "You were very convincing, especially the part about me being a virgin."

He laughed once. "I thought of that on a whim. Pretty good, huh?"

"Priceless," I replied.

"No, my father's face was priceless. His face was not of anger. It was of realization. Yeah, he and my mother were friends for a long time, but as soon as they became romantically involved, he married her as fast as he could because she wouldn't let him seal the deal beforehand." Both dimples emerged. "I might not look like my father, but we are alike in more ways than I'd like to acknowledge."

He stared at the open road in front of us. "He was starting to really get on my last nerve. He asked if getting married was your idea. I didn't want him thinking that you wanted to get married quickly to trap me, so I told

the truth—that this was my idea, that I wanted to pro-
pose, and that I wanted to get married. When my mother
went to the restroom to get you, that's when the real party began."

Kent rubbed the back of his neck with one hand, while
the other remained on the wheel. "He started rambling
on about how I was irresponsible and how I couldn't take
care of a family if I didn't hold a job. He started to tell me
how money was not everything and that holding a job
was part of the responsibility of being an adult. He firmly
asked me to work for the company. He kind of demanded
it." He ran one hand through his hair, gripping at the tips.
"After I blatantly told him no, the waiter came to our table to tell him to quiet down, and he asked us if we'd like
a private room. That's the part that was truly priceless,"
he said, pressing his foot on the brake as the yellow light
turned red.

If I were a parent, I'd want the same thing for my
kids. I'd want them to hold a steady job and have a family
of their own to grow old with. *Isn't that what every parent
wants?* And when that happened, I'd feel like I had done
my job and that I'd raised my kid well. I'd feel like an ac-
complished parent. I couldn't help but sympathize with
Mr. Plack, who wanted what any normal parent would
want for their child.

"Why don't you just work for the company?" I
prodded.

My question surprised him, and his jolly mood
turned sour.

"Because I won't," he said as the corners of his mouth
turned downward. He pressed on the gas as the light
turned green.

"You'd rock it. I know you would. Your grandfather

and father have already set up the groundwork. Plack Industries is a top company in its industry. I just don't understand why you don't want to be a part of that legacy."

"Because I don't," he huffed.

I could see the whites of his knuckles as his grip tightened on the wheel.

"I mean, it would take time, but in the end, if you just learned the business from the ground up, you'd excel. You could lead the company to greatness."

"Please, Beth, not you, too." Kent turned to face me as he pulled the car to the right, outside of my apartment. "I have no idea how to run a company, let alone how to lead thousands of employees. Do you think it's easy? I see my father work his butt off, day in and day out. I see him frustrated at work before coming home, only to be frustrated again the next day."

"I'm sure he gets frustrated, but there is a level of frustration at every normal job. It's a cycle. I know running a company can't be easy. I mean, you are leading a whole corporation. It can't be easy, but you'll learn. You'll learn, just like your father learned. You'll have a whole team to help you, to back you up. I think if you would just try, then you'd be amazing. What are you afraid of?"

"I'm afraid of failure! There, I said it."

Real fear filtered through his eyes. It was the first time I'd seen him so exposed.

"I've excelled at sports and school. I was sure of those things when I started. I didn't have any doubt that I would do well. I can't see this one, Beth. I can't see where this road will lead me, if I take it. I'm afraid of running this great company that's doing fine into the ground. My father and grandfather have such high hopes for what they've built. I can't bear to let down that legacy."

The image of the confident, arrogant man was no

longer present. In front of me sat a typical guy afraid of normal life things, like not living up to expectations. It was the first time I realized that regarding this part of his life, he put up a front. He looked so vulnerable and lost. As many times as he'd done it for me, the only thing I wanted to do was comfort him.

I placed my hand over his. "I don't know what you're afraid of. You're so capable, Kent. I know you are. If you would just try to be as great as I know you can be, as your family believes you can be, I know you can do just that. You could take this company to new heights. I know you would never, ever stop until you did just that. I believe in you."

He was silent as I spoke, and when I finished, he placed his free hand over mine, sending sparks up my arm and down to the bottom of my toes. There was an electricity in the car, and it was so palpable that I could taste it. The connection between us was so strong that I had to close my eyes to break it. I pulled myself from his touch and reached for the door to leave. I had to get out of the car, away from him, and away from this feeling inside me.

He took hold of my hand again and pulled me toward him.

I closed my eyes and shook my head. I was a good girl, and I was already spoken for. I thought it was going to happen. I thought he was going to kiss me.

And the crazy thing was that I wouldn't stop him.

But he kissed my forehead instead. When he pulled away, he gazed at me with a look of intensity that warmed me all over.

"Good night, Beth."

I nodded once and stepped out of the car, feeling his eyes following me into my apartment.

Chapter Thirteen

WIDE EYES STARED back at me in the full-length mirror. Only two weeks later, and Mrs. Plack had organized an engagement party. I stared at my black Alexander McQueen cocktail dress and bright red pumps, and sighed outwardly.

Taking a step toward the balcony that overlooked the backyard, I watched everyone below mingling among themselves. Cocktail tables and tents spanned the back of the Plack estate.

When Mrs. Plack had said she was throwing us a quaint engagement party, I didn't imagine that everyone from the city and my work would be invited. She'd even surprised me by inviting Aunt Diane and Kendy. I scanned below me and looked upon Brian as he stood by Caroline. I knew this must be especially hard for him. The buzz around the office had been bad enough, and here he was, at my engagement party. Inwardly, I cringed.

I'd felt the tension rising between us as this day approached. I wondered if he'd imagined all this when I'd initially told him about the deal. Not only was I living a lie, but by choosing me, he was also living in it too.

"You look stunning."

I turned around, and Kent loomed behind me. I wondered how long he'd been standing there, watching me. I hadn't heard him enter.

"Thanks." I took in his sharp black suit and skinny tie. "You look dashing yourself," I said, giving him a melancholy smile.

He offered his hand. "Ready? Everyone has been waiting for us."

I took a deep breath, and when his hand met mine, I found comfort in his touch once again.

When we were downstairs, I socialized with the guests. At Kent's side, Mr. Plack introduced me to hundreds of people. All their faces were a blur, and I forgot their names the moment after I'd been introduced.

When I finally distinguished Aunt Diane and Kendy among the crowd of unknowns, I excused myself from the Plack men and made my way toward them, almost running to their familiar faces.

Kendy jumped up and down as I approached, and she wrapped her arms around me, squeezing me so tightly in one of her trademarked hugs. I could barely breathe in her hold.

"I'm so happy for you, Beth Boo!" she said, using her squeaky voice.

I stifled a laugh because with all this pretending, Kendy played the part very well. I wondered if she was secretly enjoying the acting. It was Aunt Diane's turn to engulf me into an embrace, and I squeezed her back tighter, realizing I'd missed them so much. They were the only family I had left.

Continuing to make my rounds, I tore myself away from both of them and searched for Brian. In the corner, right by the bar, I found him staring at the drink in his hand while Caroline and Jim conversed next to him. When Brian saw me, his face lit up.

"Hey, engaged one. Congrats!" Caroline said, stepping in to reach for my hand.

"You owe me one. I introduced you to your future husband," Jim said, raising his wine glass.

"Thanks. Yeah, I owe you big time," I said, my eyes drifting to Brian's.

Caroline continued to talk about how grand the party was and how Karen Plack had gone over the top with the planning. I couldn't agree more. I'd had no idea that this was what Mrs. Plack considered intimate. Caroline pointed behind me, directing my focus to Kent, who was trying to get my attention. "You're one popular girl tonight," she said before tipping her wine glass back.

I said my quick good-byes to Caroline and Jim.

I gave Brian a small hug and whispered discreetly, "Just a little longer."

He said nothing as he nodded.

I maneuvered through the crowd toward Kent, who was standing on the top of the steps, holding a wine glass. When I approached him, he took my hand. When I felt his fingers against mine, I instantly relaxed.

"My mother asked me to say a few words."

Kent cleared his throat, and one by one, everyone turned to his direction.

"I'd like to take this time to thank everyone for coming. It means so very much to us that everyone we care for, who has impacted our lives in one way or another, is here to celebrate with us. I never thought I'd be up here, saying this speech, and about to get married. But then, I met Beth."

I glanced at Mrs. Plack, and tears were in her eyes while Mr. Plack's arms surrounded her.

"And to my beautiful fiancée and future wife…"

I looked to him as he continued to speak. His gaze raked my face with such intensity that it sent butterflies straight to the pit of my stomach.

"Thanks for being there for me and for being who you are—innocent, fun-loving, and honest."

His voice dropped slightly, and when his eyes fixed upon me, I felt that undeniable connection, that electricity between us.

"You make me look at everything in a new light. You're the reason I get up every morning and the reason I laugh every day." He leaned into me and framed my face with both of his hands. "I will never care for anyone the way I do for you. My life began when I met you."

His speech left me breathless. The intensity of his brown eyes consumed me. Absolutely consumed me. I was drowning deep into a sea of chestnut and for a moment, I forgot that we were surrounded by a mass of people. When he bent down, I held my breath, closed my eyes, and let his lips meet mine for the first time.

My body responded automatically, and I was free-falling into an empty space of bliss. I didn't want it to stop—ever. My heart raced in my chest, and I couldn't think of anything but this kiss and his lips, but I needed more. I wanted more. I gripped his shirt, fisting it with one hand and pulled him toward me until my body was flush against him. I heard myself moan against his mouth as I tasted mint on his lips. His masculine cologne filled my nose. I was engrossed by everything that was Kent Plack, and it was not enough. We were not close enough even though we were basically molded into one body.

His kiss was all-consuming, touching my whole mind, body, and soul and I swore, if he released me, I'd die.

I tilted my head, wanting more of him, because our nearness was not enough. I felt just the tip of his tongue against mine, and before I opened wider to let him in, his hands moved from my face to frame my shoulders. He began pushing me, moving away. My eyes were still closed as my brain screamed, *No!*

His body was no longer flush against mine. He took a step back, and the only thing left touching was our lips. He slowed his movement to a few pecks, and he distanced himself slowly as if he didn't want to break from our connection either.

Opening my eyes just confirmed my thoughts. His eyes told me that he wanted more, that he needed more of me and what I could give him. His look alone, a look of desire, transformed the butterflies in the pit of my stomach into something else—something deep, dark, and not so innocent. We stared intently at each other, his chestnut brown locked onto my emerald green. His breathing was hard and labored as if he had just run a race, and all I could feel was the pounding of my heart in my chest.

And then, I heard it all around me.

Applause.

The applause broke me from my trance. I blinked, noticing the consistent hollers around us, and I blushed pink, feeling as if everyone had interrupted something that passed between us. Immediately, my senses heightened. I realized where I was, and what I just did. My head flipped up to scan the crowd for Brian. I saw him standing next to Kendy. His mouth was set in a straight line, and his hands were fisted in front of him. Emotions rushed through me in that one instant. Confused, dazed, and angry with myself, I wanted to hit something.

Kent pulled me to his side. "Once again, thank you

for coming," he announced.

My arm wrapped around his waist, and I pressed my fingertips into his side. "Yes, thank you all for coming," I said, facing the crowd.

I dug my fingers a little harder, and from the corner of my eye, I saw Kent's teeth clench through his smile.

How dare he! How dare he kiss me in front of this crowd and how dare I kiss him back.

It was the WTF moment, and I had absolutely no idea what had just happened or what had just passed between us. When the applause and commotion died down, I disengaged myself from Kent. I ignored him as he yelled out my name while I walked away before half-running through the crowd to look for Brian.

People stopped to congratulate me once again. My body went through the motions of nodding my head and accepting half-hugs, but my eyes were scanning the crowd for Brian.

I walked the grounds, but I couldn't find him.

"He left."

I wheeled around, and Kendy was standing behind me.

My stomach dropped as I took in the discouraged look on her face. "Where did he go?" My voice was barely a whisper.

"Probably home."

"Okay."

I made my way to leave, but Kendy reached for my arm, drawing me back.

"Beth, you can't leave your party. He's upset. Just let him be for now."

"I'm not sure why Kent did that, but I have to apologize to Brian. I have to talk to him," I said, clenching my dress with both fists.

Kendy shook her head and exhaled a heavy sigh. "You're so blind. For someone who had straight As all through high school and college, you have no idea, do you?" she huffed, scanning my face. "Kent is in love with you, Beth."

I reeled back as if her words had slapped me in the face. "He's just that believable. He has more to lose than I do, so he has to be," I contested.

"He's believable because he's living the truth," she said, exasperated. "You should start living yours," she said, taking a step closer. "I've known you all my life, Beth. No one knows you better than I do. I know how you are, how you think, how you've tried all your life to be perfect, to make the right decisions, so you don't turn out like Jamie." Her face was sympathetic. "You're not her. You can't control everything, and you especially can't control who you fall in love with."

At her words, I blanched. Stepping back, I shook my head. "I'm not in love with Kent," I whispered, staring at her in disbelief.

"Then, why did you kiss him back, Beth? Why, when you look at him, it's as if he's the only guy in the room? Why, whenever we are on the phone playing catch-up, you briefly mention Brian, but your voice hitches a tone higher when you talk about Kent?"

"Stop! Kendy, whose side are you on?" I yelled, pulling away from her.

She reached for my arm again. "Beth, I'm on your side. I've been on your side since you were six. I will forever be on your side. I just wish, instead of doing what you think is right, for once, you would do what's going to make you happy. Follow your heart."

"I'll fix this," I said mostly to myself.

I left Kendy and stomped back to the foyer. Kent was surrounded by a group of people when I walked up to him. Engrossed in the conversation, he barely noticed my arrival.

I tapped him on the shoulder. "Can I talk to you?"

He cast me a glance and smiled. "Sure, baby, one second."

I waited the longest two seconds of my life, and I tapped him again. "Hey, can we talk now?"

"One sec."

I widened my eyes. "Now," I demanded.

The group of four stared in my direction. I didn't care if I looked like the controlling psycho fiancée. We needed to talk and it needed to happen on my terms.

Kent smiled, entertained by my reaction. "Sure."

I took hold of his hand, ignoring the warmth I felt, as I pulled him through the crowd, into the house and in the study. I shut the door and locked us in. "I'm sorry, but what was that?" I asked, exasperated, pointing to the door behind me. I was determined to get things back in control.

"What was what?"

When the dimple emerged on his face, I lost it. How Kendy could believe I would fall in love with a man who could possibly drive me to jump off a cliff was insane.

"That kiss!" I said. "What was that? You can't do that. Why did you do that? You just can't," I said in one breath.

He scanned my face. "I had to make it believable, Beth," he whispered.

"It was believable all right. Brian believed it, and he left."

At Brian's name, his eyes dropped to the ground. "I

215

forgot about him," he said, talking mostly to himself.

"Well, you can't forget about him. In all of this, he's been the most patient. He's upset. I saw it on his face. He's upset, and Brian never gets upset." I shook my head. "I hope I haven't lost him."

He lowered his head, pinching the bridge of his nose, as he shut his eyes. "You haven't. He's not stupid enough to leave you."

"You don't know that! He's the last person I want to hurt, okay?"

"I'm sorry." Kent said, lifting his head to meet my eyes. "I don't know what came over me. If you want, I'll talk to him."

"No, I'll talk to him myself." I turned to walk away as I heard Kent call my name from behind me.

I ran out of the room, down the hall, and straight outside. I rounded the corner where there wasn't a person in sight and gripped my shoulders tightly as goose bumps formed on my arms from the brisk air. I looked up at the clear night sky and to the twinkle of stars that weren't present in the city. I used the white brick of the house to support me as I slid down to the ground. I allowed my head to drop into my hands as I took three deep breaths, breathing deeply through my nose and exhaling through my lips.

I squeezed my eyes tightly, seeing only darkness. I was frustrated that Brian had left, confused as to why Kent had kissed me, and even more taken aback that I'd let him. I convinced myself that it had been because of this charade, the lie we were living, and that was the reason I had been so confused.

But Kendy's words from earlier rang in my head, and I wasn't sure of anything anymore. I couldn't control how

I felt or how Kent's touch and the way he gazed at me made my heart stutter. Maybe I was in love with him. Maybe I wasn't. I didn't know anymore.

All I knew was that I couldn't be with him. He lived his life on a whim. He loved the lavish lifestyle of being with different women all the time and he held no responsibilities. The one thing I valued most about myself was the fact that I was responsible.

I had met my other half. He was just like me. He was hardworking, we shared the same values, and he was someone who I had always pictured myself ending up with. That was Brian.

But why did I kiss Kent back?

I shook my head, continuing to take the deep breaths through my nose to try to calm my raging pulse.

The more I couldn't control my feelings, the more frustrated I felt because in my whole twenty-three years of existence, I'd never felt so out of control.

THE NEXT MORNING and into the afternoon, I kept calling Brian. I left multiple messages. Although I was confused as hell about everything going on in my life, I knew I needed to do the right thing, which was to fix things. I always did the right thing.

After leaving my apartment at noon, I grabbed a sandwich from the deli. As I was eating lunch, I glanced at my phone for the hundredth time. *Still no missed calls.*

As I headed back to my apartment, I spotted Brian leaning against the exterior door, looking lost in thought. His baseball cap was angled low, so I couldn't see his eyes. As I approached closer, he glanced up. He looked so forlorn that I just wanted to give him a hug to console him, so I did.

Tiptoeing, I wrapped my arms around his neck and buried my head in the nook of his neck. "You left," I whispered.

His broad arms encompassed my lower back. "I'm sorry." He squeezed me tighter. "I just didn't want to ruin your night."

I inhaled his masculine musky scent. "You ruined my night by leaving," I said.

His chest expanded. "Would you be mad if I told you that hearing you say that makes me happy?" He released me and moved to grab my hand. "Let's walk."

I glanced at our hands laced together as he led me across the street toward Millennium Park. I stared at the silvery bean statue gleaming in front of us. Gazing straight ahead, Brian seemed wistful, deep in thought. I looked to him, but he continued to blankly stare at the park ahead of us.

With each step forward, dread washed over me. It was as if I was walking along this long cliff, knowing there was a deep, deadly drop at the end. My heart constricted because I knew where this was heading. We reached the park and stopped at a bench in front of the statue. Brian released my hand, and I immediately hugged him. I wanted to be close to him to apologize for what I had done, for putting him through all of this mess.

I tapped my forehead lightly on his chest. "Don't say it," I whispered.

"You don't even know what I'm going to say," he said softly, as he wrapped his arms around my waist.

"Whatever you are going to say, I don't want you to say it." I bit the inside of my cheek to stop all the emotions running through me.

Releasing me, he tugged my hand and pulled me down to sit on the bench. He inched away from me and placed his forearms on his knees. His head hung low as we both fell silent. My eyes focused on an older couple holding hands, walking at the other end of the park. I wondered how we'd ended up here because this was not how it was supposed to be. This was not how I'd planned it to be.

Brian moved to face me and held both of my hands in his. "I can't do this anymore, Beth."

The back of my eyes instantly burned. I'd known this was where we were headed when we took this walk, but I hadn't really been sure until now. I had hoped it wasn't going to happen, but he'd just confirmed my fear.

"Brian—" I said, staring down at our hands linked together.

Stopping me before I could even continue, he huffed, "It's not friendship anymore for him. I see it. I see the way he looks at you. It's so familiar." His eyebrows drew in. "It's the same way I look at you."

"It's not like that," I said.

"I know the symptoms, Beth. He's in love with you."

He heard my sharp intake of breath.

"He's not in love with me." I shook my head, trying to deny it. But Kendy's voice and what she said the night before rang loudly in my ears.

Brian's smile turned wistful. "After spending so much time with you, how can he not be? It was only a matter of time."

This is not happening. This is not how it's supposed to be.

Brian was supposed to be my happily ever after. I didn't know if I was ready to let him go. "He's not. I can promise you that he's not. He's not, Brian. He's not in love with me," I said.

Brian closed his eyes. "I took the job in New York."

The air was knocked out of me, and my shoulders sagged. My argument had been for nothing. He was leaving me.

I stared at my pink flip-flops on the ground as a lump formed in the back of my throat. "When did you take it?" I asked, my voice barely audible.

"I took the offer this morning, Beth."

He moved to touch me, but I recoiled. I knew tears would flow if he touched me.

"I want you to come with me."

At that, my eyes flipped up to his face. I looked into eyes that were bluer against the backdrop of the clear sky.

"Beth, this is a good opportunity for me, and I'm sure with recommendations, you can get an underwriting job there. In New York, you will be able to move up faster." He looked at me with expectation and hope.

"It's too late. I've set things in motion. The wedding is in less than a month. It's too late," I pleaded.

"I know this is your way out of debt, Beth. He's offering you so much, and it's selfish of me to ask this of you." He paused, briefly closing his eyes. When he opened them, I saw such sadness. "I'm asking you to choose. I am asking you to choose because I can't watch you walk down the aisle with another man when I've fallen for you. I can't do it. It'll break me."

I looked into this man's eyes. He was the ideal male and the kind of person every little girl dreamed of marrying. He was a man so like myself in so many ways when it came to work and values and life.

But then, my thoughts drifted to Kent. Although he

had many faults, too many to count, in the end, I couldn't do it. I couldn't go back on my agreement when it had been set in place before I became serious with Brian. Kent would be broken from my betrayal, and most of all, I couldn't do that to him.

"I can't," I said.

Brian's eyes filled with such anguish, losing the tinge of hope he'd just had a moment ago. When I reached to touch him, he reeled back, nodded twice, and stood. He left me on the bench, never once glancing back.

I stared at my pink flip-flops as I gripped the bench, feeling the cold steel underneath me, while I wondered why I was always picking Kent when the perfect guy was right in front of me.

I HADN'T CRIED last night. When I'd called Kendy and she didn't answer, I hadn't bothered leaving a message. I'd had the urge to call Kent, but I hadn't. That would have been the ultimate wrong thing to do given that he had been the main reason Brian and I had broken up.

I did what I did best and treaded through the day. I got up for work and walked into the office with a fake smile on my face. I'd debated on calling in sick, but I hadn't. I would have to face Brian sooner or later. Even though I dreaded seeing him after what had happened, it still saddened me that he would be leaving for New York.

"Good morning, sunshine," Caroline said, glancing up at me from her computer as I walked into my cubicle.

I dropped my bag on my desk. "Hi," I said, placing my laptop into the docking station and adjusting my chair.

"The engagement party was so much fun. Seriously, Karen Plack knows how to throw a party. Are you ready? Less than a month, and you will be married."

"Yeah, I'm excited," I said in a fake cheery voice, when all I wanted to do on this Monday morning was crawl back under the covers and into bed.

My eyes stayed glued on my computer screen the whole day. I walked the entire length of the floor to avoid passing Brian's desk. It was just too soon to see him.

Just when I thought I was in the clear while I was packing up to go home, I saw him approaching our desks, carrying his bag and a file folder. He walked directly past my cubicle and to Caroline, not once looking my way.

It hurt.

"Caroline, can you give this to Jim?" He handed her a file. "Oh, and hey, make sure you come to happy hour in a couple of weeks for my going-away party."

He smiled his easy smile that I used to see directed my way.

"I'll be there," Caroline said. "Aw, you're going to miss the wedding. You're leaving before then."

That was when he acknowledged me. "Oh yeah." He angled himself in my direction. "It's okay. You won't miss me. I'll be the last thing on your mind that day."

Stab.

"But I do wish you happiness and luck with Kent. He seems like he makes you really happy."

Stab.

"You must see some really good qualities in him that I can't see. But hey, he has money, and money rules the world."

Big stab.

A knife could have cut the thickness in the air. I forced

a smile on my face, but I felt my cheeks flush because I was embarrassed that Caroline was listening. That feeling transformed into annoyance, and that feeling was directed to the blue-eyed male standing in front of me.

He had every right to be upset. I could admit he had been the most unselfish person in this situation. So, if he was upset, that was justified. What was not justified was showing anger that he had never shown me in front of Caroline, someone who knew nothing of my situation.

Caroline's eyes widened as she fixed Brian with a stare and glanced back in my direction.

I twisted to face him, still smiling. "He does have great qualities—ones that I'd rather not repeat in front of Caroline," I insinuated, deepening my voice.

Caroline's face developed into amusement while Brian looked like he'd swallowed something spoiled. He fisted his hands as if he was going to punch something. He straightened his back, and I could see him working the muscles of his jaw. When he stomped down the hall, I followed. He walked into the elevator, and I stepped in right behind him.

"What was that?" I snapped.

He flipped around to face me, and I rocked back a step. I'd never once been afraid of Brian, but this time, I had to admit that I was a little scared. His anger was brewing, and I knew he was holding back.

"What was what?" he asked slowly, hands fisted to his sides. "Me telling the truth, and you basically admitting you're a slut?"

I flinched. It was as if he'd slapped me on the face, hard. I pulled the emergency button, and the elevator halted with a jerk as the alarm rang loudly around us.

"Slut? I have been intimate with a total of one person,

and that was in high school. I have never slept with Kent—ever. The first time I ever kissed him was at the engagement party, and that was his doing."

I pointed toward the elevator door. "That insinuation back there was not meant for you. That was meant for Caroline, and I said it to save my butt. She doesn't know my situation, and for you to basically tell her was not cool. That's not right. You're mad? Fine, be mad at me. Don't bring other people into it," I snapped.

"What the hell did I do wrong?" he yelled inches from my face.

I reeled back at the increased fury in his tone, distancing myself from his anger.

"I gave it my freakin' all in this relationship. I waited for you, for all this crap to go down. I've been patient. I want to know—what did I do wrong?" He ran one of his hands through his hair until he reached the base of his neck.

"I have told you from the beginning what Kent and I were. I told you about our situation, and you still wanted to be with me. I told you everything. I've never lied to you. You were asking me to back out of a deal that I'd made before you and I were serious. You knew all of this," I responded. "Why are you so upset? You're the one who broke up with me. You left me," I said, placing both hands on my chest.

"I left you because you broke my heart. I did it for me, not you. I couldn't take it anymore. Can't you see that?" A look of incredulity crossed his face and he backed away slowly as his eyes turned cold. "You're so selfish. I can't believe I never saw that in you. Love truly is blind," he said.

It was another slap in the face. This time, it had been

harder because I realized it was the truth.

I was the girl who always did the right thing, who always walked the straight line, and who always put other's needs above her own. I was the girl who thought before I acted, who contemplated the consequences before I did anything. And I'd worked hard my whole life to get to where I was today.

For once in my life, I hadn't been thinking. I'd acted on impulse, and I'd wanted the easy way out.

I pushed the elevator button to continue our descent to the first floor.

"You're right," I whispered. "I wanted to be debt free, and I wanted to keep the perfect boyfriend after it was all done. If I was selfish along the way, I'm sorry. For once, just once, I just wanted it all."

The elevator doors opened on the first floor, and I stepped out. This time, I was leaving him behind.

Chapter Fourteen

THE NEXT FEW days were torture. I called in sick, missing my first days ever at work, and turned off my phone. I didn't even want to talk to Kendy, and there was no way in hell I was going to call Kent.

I contemplated Brian's words. I'd never thought I was being selfish because I had always been honest with him, but realistically, I now knew I was. I'd made him choose me, and in the end, when he'd wanted me to choose, I'd chosen Kent.

The banging on the door did not let up, and I knew it could only be one person. It was just a matter of time when he showed up at my door. I had done the exact same thing weeks ago when he didn't answer my call after Brian's party. Plus, this was our longest stint in not talking to each other.

I placed the pillow over my head to avoid the banging, but the loud knocking continued. I was worried that my neighbors would get annoyed, so I finally pushed myself off the couch when he wouldn't relent. It was only when I rose to my feet that I realized it was evening.

Unlocking the door, I turned the doorknob and pivoted back around to plop on the couch. I positioned the throw pillow over my head as I decided that if I wanted to wallow in self-pity and guilt, I should be allowed.

"Where have you been? Do you know that I've been calling you? Did your phone die?" He tugged the pillow from my head. "What's going on?" he asked, a look of concern etched on his face.

"I want to be alone. Can you please just do that? Let me be." I pulled the pillow from his hands and placed it back on my face.

"Are you sick or something? You don't look well."

I huffed, ignored his comment, and flipped onto my side, facing the back of the couch.

"Do you want me to make you an appointment or buy you some medicine?"

"I just want to be left alone."

"I can't," he said quietly.

I felt the couch indent right behind me, and he fell silent. The silence seemed to last forever, and I could feel his eyes burning a hole in my back. After a while, he tugged on a strand of hair as I continued to face the back of the couch.

"Beth…" he sighed. "About the other night, I…" He paused, unable to continue.

After a minute, I flipped to my back and lifted the pillow from my head. I stared up at him from under my lashes and our eyes locked, my emerald to his chestnut brown.

"There you are." He used his finger to brush a strand of hair from my cheek, and the familiar warmth spread from his touch.

"We broke up."

"I'm sorry," he whispered, his eyes raking over my face.

I moved, shifting my weight on my elbows. "Are you?" It slipped out before I could stop it.

"Of course I am," he huffed. "I want you to be happy." He ran a hand through his hair, grabbing a fistful at the top. "What happened the other night was impulsive. I was so engrossed in the whole charade and playing a part that I wanted to make it believable. I was confused, and I certainly didn't mean to get between you and Brian."

Chestnut eyes bore down at me, and it sent that butterfly feeling from my chest to the pit of my stomach.

I wanted to ask him what he was confused about, so we could sort it out together.

I wanted to ask him what he was doing.

What are we doing?

Why do you look at me that way?

When you do, why do I feel the way I do?

In our old relationship, I could have asked him just that. I could have said, *What the heck is going on?*

But we had crossed some invisible line, and I didn't feel comfortable asking him what I honestly wanted to ask him anymore.

"I just want this whole thing planned, done, and over, okay?"

I wanted to move forward, and once it was over, maybe we could get back to where we had been before—before all the lines had blurred and turned gray.

He nodded his head in reply. "Okay."

AND SO, IT began. We were meeting with the wedding planner and his mother in Barrington. I put it in my head that I'd get through this, and now that I knew there was an end date in sight, it was easier to trudge through the day.

When we walked through the door, shopping bags were lined by the stairs.

Karen greeted us as we approached. "I'm getting excited," she said, her eyes lighting up.

Kent glanced at his mother and a small smirk displayed on his face. "Mother, what did you buy? Did you buy all of Neiman?"

"Well," she said softly as a shy smile crept up her face, "Neiman, Saks, and Barneys." She took hold of each of our hands and tugged us toward the staircase where bags were scattered on the marbled floor. "I know we haven't talked about it yet, but I was thinking peach. Do you think peach is a fun color? Of course, it's your choice, but I just wanted to show you everything. It's better if you get a visual. Look," she said, rambling on.

I scoped what was visible inside, and everything peach-colored—from candles to napkins to tablecloths to glass hurricanes, and imitation flowers—filled the bags. The color was not a pretty light peach. It was more of an ugly bright, almost neon, peach and I had to keep my facial features steady to hide my distaste.

"Mother, isn't this the wedding planner's job? And don't we rent most of these items?" Kent chuckled.

"Oh, I know, but I figured we could use some for the wedding shower and donate what we don't use to charity." She reached into a Barneys bag and lifted up a peach silk nightgown, holding it by its thin straps. "Look. I thought it would be perfect for your first night together."

She gave us a look, and I flushed at her comment.

Kent leaned in behind me, and his warm breath tickled the back of my neck. "Don't worry. She's not on something. This is her natural high. This is how Mother gets when she's excited," he whispered.

"So, what do you think?" Karen's eyes were shining. "Everything is returnable," she stated when I didn't answer right away. She glanced at the bags in front of us. "Maybe I did go a little overboard."

I smiled at this sweet woman, bursting in joy over her son's wedding. I didn't have the heart to tell her the truth. "I love it. Peach is my favorite color."

She clasped her hands together and practically jumped on me. "Oh, I think it will look perfect. It is such a young, fun color. It doesn't fit me, but it fits you perfectly. I can't wait to show Mary." She released me and rummaged through her purchases.

"Mary is the wedding planner," Kent said, taking my hand. He brushed a lock of hair away from my face. "Thank you," he whispered as his mother scattered about.

"Wait till I tell Kendy that she's wearing peach. It will be worth it."

I let him lead me into the family room. He pulled me to sit next to him in front of the TV, grabbed the remote with his free hand and flipped the channel to the news. I felt warmth where our thighs touched, and I cursed the butterflies in my stomach that were back.

"Kent..." I said.

When he turned toward my direction, everything came flying out all at once. "I don't want a shower or a bachelorette party. I don't care what we do, but I don't want this long, drawn-out process. I want to get married and divorced, okay? That's all. The end."

"Okay," he said, as his eyebrows pulled together.

"I know your mom is excited, and I don't want to be the one to let her down. So, you tell her, okay? You set the expectations," I continued.

"So, she's being the monster-in-law already?"

"No, I just want this to be as painless as possible." I wanted everything back to how it had been between us.

The doorbell rang, and I jumped. He placed his hand on my leg to calm me.

I widened my eyes at him when I heard a woman's nasally voice greeting Karen down the hall. Her voice was getting annoyingly louder and closer to the family room.

When they entered the room, the wedding planner's eyes locked on mine. She was studying me from the top of my head to what I was wearing to the color of my socks. She must have been in her early forties. A silver clip held her low ponytail, and her black skirt suit reminded me of a scary teacher in designer clothing. Thin black-rimmed glasses sat at the tip of her nose, and I swore, all she needed was a ruler.

I slid closer to Kent, and as he sensed my uneasiness, he squeezed my knee to placate me, silently telling me things would be all right.

"Beth and Kent, this is Mary. She's our wedding planner. How exciting is this?" Karen was almost jumping from her delight. "She has over twenty years of experience, and she is the top wedding planner and owner of One Fine Day," Karen said, clasping her hands together.

I stood up at attention, and Kent stood beside me. While Mary analyzed me, observing me through her glasses, my palms began to sweat.

"Hi," I said, breaking the silence, sporting a forced smile on my face. I stuck out my hand awkwardly to greet her.

She stared at me and then to my outstretched hand for a second before an eerie smile popped up on her face. She was scary. Her teeth were the straightest and whitest teeth I'd ever seen. Kent stepped in front of me to act as

231

a barrier between the wedding planner and me. I silently thanked the heavens above that I had him.

"I'm Kent, the son and fiancé," he said, giving her his fake smile that didn't reach his eyes. "We're very excited that you have availability to take us on. How lovely."

He studied her just as she had studied me earlier. She shifted her weight, and the confidence she'd had seconds ago was no longer present. It was times like these that I really loved the overly confident, cocky Kent.

"Regarding this wedding, Beth and I work a little differently. Just so you know, she's the boss in our relationship, but I'm the leader when it comes to the planning. I've been dreaming of this day ever since I was a little boy playing with my Barbies."

I looked to Karen, and her mouth slipped slightly ajar at his words.

"That being said, I will have the executive decision on all—from venue to cake to centerpieces. My sweet buttercup over here has allowed me to take the lead as she knows I'm into the details." He pulled me closer to his side. "I'm a metrosexual male, so she says, and details do matter to me. But she would like to choose her flowers, shoes, and dress. All else, you direct your questions to me or my mother."

At Kent's tone, Mary's demeanor changed. She was not standing as straight as she had been earlier. I wanted to reach over and give Kent a high five, right in front of her.

"This wedding is to be planned in one month and not one day past that," he added.

"One month?" Karen and Mary asked in unison.

Kent softened his voice as he addressed his mom, "Mother, I don't want to wait any longer. I love her. One month is plenty of time to plan."

"A month is not a very long time to plan such an extravagant event as this," Mary said, lifting her nose to him. Her expectant eyes looked to Karen for concurrence.

"Mother, I can't wait longer than a month. If you want me to tell Mary about the details and the real reason I want to marry Beth quickly, I can."

I grabbed his arm. "No!" I warned, an undercurrent in my tone.

Karen put her hand on her head and conceded. "Sorry, Mary. This has to be planned within the month."

Mary cast Kent a look, and I was glad he hadn't seen it because I didn't want any more drama to occur.

"Noted," she said, moving toward the door. "I will need to get a few things from the car. Excuse me."

When she walked stiffly out of the room, Kent wrapped an arm around his mom. "Thanks, Mother," he said, as he kissed her on her forehead.

"Barbies, Kent?" She gave him a look of incredulity.

"Mother, that woman is too much to stomach." He grabbed my hand and started to lead me out of the room. "In all seriousness, Beth has allowed me full rein on the plans, and being the good son that I am, I'm allowing you full planning rights."

As we rounded the corner, I briefly caught Karen's face—wide-eyed and a cheeky grin of delight. I'd never seen her so happy.

WALKING HOME AFTER work, I once again found Brian leaning against the exterior glass door as I approached my apartment. His baseball cap was tipped low as he kicked a stone on the ground. I wanted to walk past him, enter the building, and pretend he wasn't there, but I couldn't. All those things he'd said in the elevator were true. He was the one who had gotten hurt.

"Hey," he said, peering at me from underneath his cap. "I'm leaving today."

"I know." I stopped a few feet away from him.

When Caroline had asked me to go to his going-away party, I'd made up the lamest excuse of having already committed to a charity event with the Placks. In reality, I had gone home and watched TV all night. I'd known he wouldn't want me to be there, and if anything, I had been too ashamed to go.

He tipped back his hat. "Listen, I just wanted to say I'm sorry."

"Brian, don't—"

"No, I shouldn't have said those things back in the elevator. I didn't mean it." He took his cap off and scratched his head. "I was just angry, but being angry isn't going to get me anywhere." He shook his head. "I guess I just wanted to say I'm sorry, and I wanted to say good-bye before I left. I didn't want to leave on bad terms."

I looked at my shoes and focused on the ground as everything he'd said in the elevator rushed back to hit me. "I'm the one who's sorry. You were right. I was the selfish one." I met his eyes. "I never cheated on you. You have to believe that. When I was with you, I was only with you. I'm sorry I had to drag you into all of this. You have to know, I never meant to hurt you on purpose." I looked to my hands. "I just wanted to keep the perfect boyfriend and the best friend and be debt free. I was the selfish one. For once, I just wanted it all. It's okay to be angry with me. I get it."

"Beth, I didn't come here to make you feel guilty."

"I know."

"In the end, I know that even if I waited, it still wouldn't be enough."

I shook my head, but he held up his hand to stop me from speaking. "I could have tried all I wanted, and I could have moved heaven and earth, but you can never force someone to fall in love with you. It doesn't happen that way. Love just happens. In the end, I wasn't enough."

"That's so not it. You're more than enough," I said. "You're everything any girl could ever wish for. You're perfect."

"Not perfect enough," he said, giving me a small smile.

"No, Bri—"

He gripped my hand and pulled me into an embrace. "Take care of yourself, Beth."

I closed my eyes and relaxed in his arms, taking in his musky scent for the very last time. "You're going to do great in New York."

"I know," he said.

I laughed.

"If I could only have the luck I have at work with relationships, I'd be golden."

"Brian…" I said, sighing into his shoulder.

"I'm just kidding." He released me and gave me one small peck on the top of my head. "Good-bye, Miss Bethany Casse."

I watched him walk across the street until he was a stick figure among the crowd.

And he never looked back.

BITING MY PINKIE nail, I sat and took in the display of couture wedding dresses in front of me. Headless full-body mannequins were draped in elegant gowns surrounding the reception area of Neiman Marcus's bridal salon.

I glanced down to my typical loungewear of jeans and gym shoes. I wished I'd dressed up more for the consultant to notice me. The tall blonde with the sleek long hair didn't glance my way. I'd been sitting here for twenty minutes, waiting for Mrs. Plack. I was surprised that the bridal consultant hadn't asked me if I wanted to look around.

My phone vibrated beside me, and I reached in my purse. Kent's name flashed against the screen right before I picked it up.

"Hey, Mother is running late. She just called my cell. She's just about there. Are you excited?"

"I'm excited to spend the day with her, but I'm not excited to go wedding shopping," I said, pouting at the phone.

"You're supposed to be happy. Play the part. Mother is thrilled to spend the whole day doing what girls do best—shop till they drop." I could sense his smile on the phone. "Well, try at least. She's ecstatic that she gets to spend time with you."

I glanced at the blonde-haired consultant in front of me and the row of couture dresses and sighed. "Fine, I'll fake it till I make it," I said, still pouting.

"Beth, thank you. I'm forever indebted to you."

"Uh-huh. Yeah. Sure." I ended the call just after I

heard him chuckle.

Karen Plack sauntered toward me, giving me one of her warmest smiles. She enveloped me in a bear hug, and I took in her sweet scent of apples and cinnamon, everything a mother should smell of—not alcohol and cigarettes, like my mother.

She released me and held me at arm's length. "Beth, are you ready to shop for that perfect dress?" she asked, her eyes alight.

"Am I ever," I replied a little louder than expected.

The blonde-bobbed bridal consultant greeted Mrs. Plack immediately. Shaking her hand firmly, she said, "Welcome to Nieman Marcus. We are so glad you came in to visit us today. I'm Crystal Kensington, and I will be assisting you in finding that perfect wedding gown."

The inflection of her voice annoyed me, and the fact that she hadn't acknowledged me earlier annoyed me more. It was most likely because, although Karen never tried, she looked like money with her cashmere sweater, Chanel purse, and the big rock on her finger. I looked like the help in my comfortable clothing of jeans and a light sweater. I'd already been warned that today was shop-till-I-drop day with the future mother-in-law, so I'd automatically dressed for comfort.

"Oh, lovely," Karen said, clasping her hands together. She wrapped one arm around me and held me close. "This is the beautiful bride-to-be, Beth Casse. Today is her day. I want to make sure she gets everything she wants."

Only then did Crystal Kensington glance my way to give me her fake smile. "Beth, nice to meet you," she said, taking my hand.

I caught her glancing at Kent's largely obnoxious engagement ring on my finger before she took in my appearance. "Let's move this way, shall we?"

She led us through the hall and to an open-spaced area lined with rows and rows of bridal gowns. "I'm sure we'll find you what you need. We hold accounts with every top-end designer, and we have the latest gowns from this year's wedding season."

We followed her as she continued to walk down the row of gowns. "We have the latest styles with fabrics imported from Europe—duchess satin, iridescent taffeta, organza, chiffon, beaded silks. We have it all," she boasted, running her hand against the gowns as she strolled down the aisle.

As her high-pitched voice continued to echo through the room, I felt my anxiety rising and the queasiness in my stomach climbing to my throat. It was too much to take in, and I slowly trailed behind them.

"Beth?" Karen asked, turning around, realizing I'd fallen behind. She walked toward me, her face etched with concern.

"I'm sorry. What was that?" I asked, not hearing her. I gave her a small smile and tried to recall what she'd just said.

"Will Kendy be getting her dress here?" Karen asked, giving my hand a squeeze. "Are you okay, honey? You don't look well."

Maybe my smile looked a little pained.

"I haven't discussed details with Kendy, but when I saw her at the party, I just told her to get a dress at home," I said.

Crystal made a face at my comment, and my annoyance jumped up a notch at this snooty bridal consultant that had barely even spoken a word to me. I was already not feeling well.

"Karen, there's also this other place down the street I want to try after this."

"Whatever you want, honey. This is your day."

Crystal stood at attention as my words sank in. She gave me her winning smile as she sensed her commission slipping through her fingers. "Ms. Casse, we do carry the most designers. Let's try on some dresses, shall we?"

Mirrors surrounded me as I was elevated on a circular step in the dressing room that was as big as my apartment. The Monique Lhuillier wedding gown clung to my body tightly from my bust to my waist and flared to a Cinderella-style organza skirt accented with pickups. I couldn't breathe as every time I exhaled my rib cage pushed against the bodice of the dress.

Through the mirror, I noticed Mrs. Plack's smile, displayed full of awe. It seemed as if she might cry, and I thought I might too, but not for the same reason. I tugged the piece of white paper attached to the dress I was wearing, and my eyes widened at the fifteen-thousand-dollar price tag. I dropped the paper as if I'd been burned, and I couldn't prevent my jaw from dropping as I thought of what other useful purchases could have been made with that kind of money.

"Honey, don't look at the price tag. Jack and I have been looking forward to this day. Please don't be shy. I want everything to be wonderful," she said, searching my face. "Don't let the money stop you from getting what you want."

When she moved closer, I realized that she was holding back tears. Her eyes filled with such strong emotion that the warmth in them moved me.

"You're going to make a lovely bride, Beth."

I bit my lip to prevent myself from tearing up as well.

She had never referred to herself as mom, and Mr. Plack had never done the same with dad before. But for a small moment, I secretly wished that I were marrying into this loving family to have a mother to do these things with, to have that motherly touch. With Nana gone, I craved and missed that bond so badly.

"What do you think?" My voice was slightly hoarse.

"I love it on you," Karen said, touching the beading by my waist.

"Me, too," I lied. Actually, I hated it, but looking at Karen's face, I just wanted to see her happy.

"Honey, it's the first dress you've tried on. Are you sure you don't want to try on others?"

I nodded. I didn't want to try on any more when I knew I'd hate them all. *Why prolong the daylong torture of trying on dress after dress when I know my real dress is not here or at any other upscale department store?*

"You sure you don't want to try on any more?" Karen asked again, surveying the dress one last time.

"I'm sure. I love it," I lied again.

Karen grabbed both of my shoulders to face her. "Beth, you are going to be such a beautiful bride." She enveloped me in a hug as I saw Crystal Kensingston smile at the buy we were about to make.

AS WE WALKED into the Club International restaurant of the Drake Hotel, I took in the private dining room cloaked in oak wood as we faced a large Gothic fireplace.

Karen's eyes crinkled at me as we were seated. "I'm so excited. We have the dress."

I returned her smile, pleased at her contentment and

delighted that I was in her presence. Her carefree aura was contagious, and just being around her made this experience less painful. I would never cease to wonder where this wonderful woman had come from.

After the waiter took our orders, Karen turned to me. "I can't wait for the big day. We're only a couple of weeks away." She sipped her tea and placed the fine china cup, rimmed with a gold trim, back on top of the saucer .

"I know. It's all happening so fast," I said.

"Thanks for being patient with him. Kent is not a very patient man. He takes that after his father, but what Kent lacks in patience, he makes up with his big heart."

She took another sip of tea as she leaned back against her chair. "Right after we were married, we tried for years and years to conceive. We consulted the best doctors, and they couldn't find anything wrong. Jack suggested that we adopt. I wasn't against adoption, but I loved Jack so much that I wanted the flesh of his flesh. I wanted his child." A melancholy smile passed her face as she recalled the struggles of her past. "Then, I decided to throw in the towel and call the adoption agency. I knew Jack would be the perfect father, just like his father, and I wanted to see that happen…and that's the week I found out I was pregnant."

She took a deep breath. "The first time I held our little boy in my arms in the delivery room, I studied every feature from the dark fuzz on the top of his head to his cute nose to his big, round brown eyes, and I knew there was nothing more beautiful," she said. "That's the first and only time I've ever seen my husband cry." She shook her head to bring herself into focus.

"And so, as you can tell, he is spoiled. We showered him with love and everything he's ever wanted. He was our one and only even though we kept trying through my child-bearing years." She fiddled with the rock on her ring finger. "He is how he is because of his upbringing. I take full responsibility for his spoiled side and his obnoxious side and the side of him that doesn't like the word *no*. But I also take responsibility for his softer side, his loyal side, the way he loves, and how when he cares, he cares deeply. He's always pampered this old woman, and he's spoiled me rotten, just like his father." She chuckled. "I can only imagine how he'll pamper you for the rest of his life."

I was privileged to know Kent's softer side, a side only a few people had been allowed to see, a side of him that he'd allowed me to see. If someone had told me that first day when we met that he'd turn out to be one of my best friends in Chicago, I never would have believed it. But I'd grown to care for him and his well-being, and overall, I liked being around him. I enjoyed his company.

"So, are you up for more shopping? We still need to pick out the cake and the flowers. Oh, and also we need to choose your shoes!"

I thought I made a not-so-cute face because Karen laughed.

"I'm sorry. I've never had a daughter to do this with. I guess I'm a little excited, if you can't tell already."

I made up my mind that every decision I had to make in planning this wedding would be to make her happy. I'd have my time later to choose what I wanted when I planned my own wedding.

LICKING MY FINGERS, I pulled out a napkin from my

pocket and wiped the remnants of chocolate from my hands. *Who knew cupcakes from a truck are more delicious than the ones bought from a cupcake store?* Seriously, it was the best thing ever.

I glanced at the clear plastic container in my hand that held a little piece of chocolate heaven, and I had to restrain myself from taking a bite of Kent's cupcake. Instead, I dipped my finger into his frosting and brought it to my lips. *He'll never know.* I closed the container and slipped it into the clear bag.

I waved at the security guard as I entered Trump Tower, swinging the bag with every step. When I keyed into Kent's place, I was unpleasantly surprised.

"Hey."

"Hi, Luke." The smile I had left my face instantly.

"What do you have there?" he asked, nodding toward the clear plastic bag I was holding. "Did you bring me something sweet?"

Sitting on the couch, he had one hand behind his head while the other held the remote control. He flipped through the channels while his eyes followed me through the room.

"It's for Kent." I dropped my gaze to the floor and backed up until I felt the door flush against my back.

"Oh, that's too bad. I like sweet." His voice was low, hoarse.

The undercurrent in his tone gave me the chills but not the good kind.

My eyes scanned the apartment. "Sorry, is Kent here?"

"No, he's not. Come and take a seat. He should be back soon," he said, patting the empty spot next to him.

I shook my head and felt my shoulders tense. "It's okay. I'll just come back later." I shifted my weight from one foot to the other and averted my eyes from him to the TV.

"Come on, keep me company."

"Uh...do you know where he went?" I asked, fiddling with the straps of the cupcake bag.

Luke shook his head. "No, but I'm sure he'll be back." He patted the seat next to him again. "Promise, I won't bite."

I sat at the edge of the recliner next to the couch. An awkward tension occupied the air, and I shifted in my seat, tapping my foot against the floor. I decided I would wait ten minutes tops and then leave.

"I thought I'd pay Kent a visit since I haven't seen him in weeks." Luke dropped the remote on the table in front of him and shifted to face me, resting both elbows on his knees. "So, I see you have a key, too?"

"Yeah, he gave it to me. You know, in case he gets locked out and stuff," I said, glancing at him once before moving my eyes back to the TV.

"You surprise me, Beth."

When he moved closer to the recliner, I moved my knees in the other direction, feeling my jaw lock and my body stiffen at his closeness.

"When he brought you to the club, I thought you were just another one of his girls, but you're not his usual type. He likes blondes and the not-so-sweet ones."

Warily watching him, I shifted in my seat as he moved closer.

"I'm curious about you," he said, inching forward slowly. "You know the night after we went out clubbing, he called me to tell me you were off-limits. I wasn't even allowed to breathe in your direction. He wasn't asking. He was warning me, and I wondered why." His eyes inspected me from my face to my chest, resting there, before looking back up to my eyes.

"When I would invite him out, he'd say no because he was with you. When I'd invite myself to your dinners, he'd say that you guys were basically done for the evening. I got the hint after a while. After that, I realized one thing…" He inched forward, leaning into me. Our knees were almost touching, and the first instinct I had was to recoil. "He's protective over you."

I froze at his closeness, the hairs on my arms standing at full attention.

His eyes narrowed and watched me like a cat. "So, I wondered why. Why would a playboy millionaire give up going out and getting different pussy every single night?"

My eyes widened at his vulgar statement, and I reeled back. When I glared at him, he laughed.

"You wanna know why?" He shifted closer, so he could whisper in my ear. "Because he's getting some good pussy at home, that's why."

He gripped my knee to the point of pain, and I shoved his hand.

"Get your hands off me!"

I jolted up from the couch, but he grabbed my wrist and yanked me back down.

"I want to try this flavor. I want to try sweet for once. Maybe after, I'll be a good boy, too."

"In your dreams, bastard."

I rammed both hands into his chest, but he gripped my wrists tightly, cutting off the blood circulation. He pushed my shoulders to the seat with such force that my neck whipped against the couch, my head bouncing off the cushions. All at once, he was on top of me and had me trapped between his knees.

"Get off of me! Get off!" I screamed. I thrashed back and forth, but my efforts were useless.

I couldn't move as he moved my wrists with one hand above my head.

"Stop!"

I tried to buck him off of me, but he was too strong.

"Help!" I screamed at the top of my lungs.

The first of the tears started to roll off of my face as I realized where this was heading. When I felt him aroused against my leg, I whipped around more. He tightened his knees, and with his free hand, he caressed my breast.

"I like them nice and full." He licked my tears off my cheek.

"Help!" I let out the loudest scream until my voice was hoarse. All I could hear was my muffled sobs, and all I could taste were my own tears as fear shook my body.

He covered my mouth with his hand, and I bit down hard enough to taste blood.

He closed his eyes, and when he opened them, he had a small devilish smile on his face. "The difference between Kent and me is that I like it rough."

With his free hand, he pulled up my skirt.

"No! Please! No!" I begged.

When he tightened his grip with one hand and started to unbuckle his belt with the other, my mind screamed for me to fight. Drawing enough saliva from the back of my throat, I spit in his face. The sound of the slap across my face resonated throughout the whole condo.

"You want it rough, too?" he scowled.

I spit in his face again, and he slapped me harder, my teeth shifting from the impact.

"Get the hell off her!"

Luke and I turned to the door to see Kent.

Before I knew what was happening, Kent exploded from the door, yanked Luke by his collar, and had him suspended against the wall.

"What the hell do you think you're doing?" Kent yelled, shoving Luke against the wall so hard that his head banged against it. "What are you into now? Rape? What are you thinking?"

"Get off me! I-I can't breathe," Luke said, clawing at his own throat.

"What? You can only handle fighting with women? Is that it?" Kent had both hands tightened against his windpipe. "I should kill you. I'll call the cops and tell them it was self-defense." Kent's jaw was taut, and there was a tightness around his eyes that I didn't recognize. "I'm going to kill you for touching her. I told you to stay away."

Luke's face blanched as Kent continued to use both hands to hold him up against the wall, his face inches from Luke's.

"Stop." I slowly stood from the couch and pulled down my skirt. I was frightened at the intensity of his words, frightened at Kent's stance, and scared that there was some truth in what he'd just said. "Kent, stop." I held my cheek that was still pulsing from the earlier impact. "Please," I begged, edging closer toward him.

At the sound of my voice, Kent turned and loosened his grip, which gave Luke an opportunity. Luke pushed Kent and fell to the ground on all fours, coughing and gasping for air.

"You're going to pick that whore over me?" Luke said, using the wall to steady himself.

I heard the impact from across the room as Kent's fist rammed a direct hit into Luke's face. Dribbles of blood flowed from Luke's nose.

"Did you fucking hit her?" Kent asked, glancing back at me as I held my cheek.

Luke staggered and got up again, and the second punch was even louder.

Kent pulled back to take a third swing. "I'm going to mess you up for hurting her, you bastard."

But I grabbed his arm before he could follow through. "Please. Stop. Enough." I used both hands to pull his arm down. "Please. Stop." I couldn't stand any more violence and I didn't want to see any more blood.

Kent turned to Luke, who had fallen on the ground. "Get out!" he yelled, pointing at the door.

Luke used the wall to assist himself into an almost standing position. Blood was everywhere—on the floor, on his shirt, on his face. "You're going to let our friendship end because of that girl?"

Kent narrowed his eyes at him. "We're not friends, Luke. We have never, ever been friends. You think just because we used to get drunk every night and we'd pick up girls to screw that we had a friendship?" he asked. "We're not friends. We were people who partied together. It's not the same thing," he snapped. "Get the hell out of my condo."

Luke spit blood onto the floor and glared at me. "You think he can settle down with one girl? I've known him since we were eighteen, and he's never settled down. He never will. He will leave you so fast, you'll be crying from a broken heart." He glanced back at Kent one last time before he spun around, stormed out, and slammed the door behind him.

All of a sudden, the fight left me. I felt instantly tired and dropped onto Kent's couch.

Kent was still facing the door as his hands stayed fisted at his sides. "I should go after that guy and beat him senseless."

"He's not even worth it," I said, holding my cheek, feeling a pulsing pain that spread throughout the whole right side of my face.

Kent turned toward me, his eyes softening. "I'm sorry."

He walked to the kitchen, opened the fridge, and took out an ice pack. "I forgot that I'd given him a key." He sat by me and lightly brushed my hair away from my forehead. "If anything happened to you…" He shook his head, shutting his eyes tightly, as a shudder ran through his body.

He removed my hand from my cheek and placed the ice pack on it. I flinched at the coldness.

"Shh…stay still," he said softly, running his finger up and down my jaw line.

His face was so desolate, so sad. I felt a sudden need to console him. "I bought you a cupcake," I said, looking up at him.

He peered down at me, holding my eyes, his chestnut brown to my emerald green. "I've never wanted to hurt someone so badly." He squinted and shook his head to compose himself. "I still want to kill him."

"But if you kill him, then you'll go to jail, and you won't be able to eat your cupcake," I said.

"Beth, it's not funny," he said, gazing down at me.

He was right. I always used humor as a defense mechanism of some sort. I shivered at the thought of what had almost happened.

"I know. I'm just glad you showed up when you did," I said. "Jesse didn't care if I was there. He'd still hit my mom." I cringed at the memory. "You know, she's feisty and has a mouth on her. Sometimes, I thought he did it to just shut her up." I glanced up at Kent through my lashes. "But you know what? No one ever deserves this," I said, placing my hand on top of his that was still on my cheek.

"No. No woman ever deserves to be hit by a man—ever. He's a coward if he does." Kent adjusted the ice pack. "My father would never even think of raising a hand to my mother. Even at his angriest moments, he would never do that." He lifted the ice pack and shook his head. "I think you might have a bruise by the morning."

"I just hope it's gone before the wedding, or people will think you beat me," I said, trying to make him smile. It didn't work. "I'm just trying to make you feel better. Listen, I'm the one who got slapped in the face multiple times. You should be the one trying to make me feel better." I just wanted to forget what almost happened and move on.

"You're right. I'm sorry." He placed the ice pack on the low coffee table. "What would make you feel better?"

I looked at him, crinkling my nose. "Can I have a bite of your cupcake?"

He shook his head as he reached for the bag that held the chocolate treat. "Sure."

Chapter Fifteen

"BREATHE IN, BETH," Kendy commanded, standing behind me while working on the buttons on my dress.

I sucked in the deepest breath of my life. "Seriously, I am," I whined.

I wished I hadn't visited the cupcake truck the day before and the day before that and the day before that.

Kent and I had been determined to try every flavor the week before, and we'd succeeded after tracking down the cupcake truck around the city using social media. And today, my wedding day, I was suffering from one too many cupcakes as Kendy had been trying to squeeze me into my dress for the last fifteen minutes.

"Okay, there." Kendy finally finished with the top button and patted my shoulders.

Finally, I let out the breath that I'd been holding in, filling out the gown. By the end of this night, I swore, I'd have button marks etched into my skin. The bodice was squeezing the life out of my stomach, and the top was pressing tightly against my chest. One wrong turn, and I was convinced that one of my boobs would fall out.

"Wow, cleavage." Kendy giggled as she stepped around me to take me in.

I would have hit her, but I could barely move, let alone raise my hand. "Shut up."

Kendy looked cute in her bridesmaid dress, the style complementing her petite figure. When I'd told her the bridesmaid dress would be peach, she'd almost vomited in her mouth. When I'd shown her the ugly peach dress, she cried, and when she'd tried it on, she'd nearly died.

I'd nearly died, too—of laughter.

We'd both decided that we would make them into curtains for Aunt Diane. She loved the color peach, but of course she did because that color had been in during her time.

Kendy twirled her finger, signaling me to turn, and I sighed as I cooperated.

When I pivoted to face her, her eyes were shining. "Beth Boo, you look amazing," she squealed.

"Please, Kendy, this is not my real day. Don't make it feel like it is," I begged. "Okay, Miss Peach?"

We both laughed.

Tugging me toward her, she gave me the biggest Kendy hug. It was the type of hug where I couldn't breathe because she'd wrap her arms around me to the point of suffocation.

"Okay, nothing is going to fall out there," she said, patting my backside. "I'm just telling you the truth. You make one gorgeous bride." She gave me one last squeeze and pinched my butt cheek. "Are you ready?" she asked. "It will be over before you know it."

The knock on the door broke us from our embrace.

Aunt Diane peered in. "Bethany, you look darling." The crinkle in her eyes showed her delight. "Honey, everyone is waiting on you. Come here, and let me give you some lovin'."

I nodded, smiled and hugged Aunt Diane as asked. It was a fake smile that I knew would be plastered on my face the whole day, so I'd better get used to it.

When Aunt Diane released me, Kendy linked her arm through mine and led me through the door. "Come on, let's go."

I walked out to a sea of paparazzi. The flashes of light, the oohs and aahs, the tightness of my dress, and the hunger in my stomach had me seeing double. The forced smile remained on my face as the photographers started positioning me back and forth and forth and back while shooting away with their cameras. They had me posing in every direction with my flowers, without my flowers, with Kendy, without Kendy, with Aunt Diane, and with them both.

My breathing accelerated as the seconds progressed, and I wobbled when the photographer continued to position me. I heard the thumping of my racing heart in my ears, and all of a sudden, I felt a dizziness that left me unsteady. Before I knew it, I jolted to the bathroom, locked the door and dropped to the floor before I started dry-heaving over the toilet.

"Beth? Open the door, honey. Are you okay?" Kendy asked, her voice laced with anxiety as she jiggled the knob.

"Give me a minute." I stood and gripped the sink with both hands, using it as support, as I stared at the wide-eyed girl in the mirror. Flipping on the faucet, I cupped my hands and rinsed water in my mouth.

"I just need a minute." I patted my mouth with the white hand towel that had been hanging on the wall and slid against the wall, sitting next to the toilet. My dress pooled at the bottom of my feet, and the train trailed along the white marble tile. My eyes focused on the tile on the floor noticing the specs of cream against the white marble.

As the minutes dragged on, I ignored the knocking and the yelling outside.

I didn't even know how long I'd been sitting there, staring at my hand and the gigantic rock on my ring finger. I didn't think I could go through with this. The day had just begun, and given how it was going thus far, I knew I wouldn't make it down the aisle without another round of dry-heaving or full-on panic attacks.

I ignored the violent attempts Kendy was making to get me to open the door.

"Did you hear me, Bethany Marie Casse? I'm going to break down this door. Do you understand? Open this door now!"

I even ignored her desperate pleas of concern.

"Beth Boo, are you okay? Open the door, hon. How do I know if you are okay if you don't open the door or even talk to me?"

Even her empty threats did not break me from my trance.

"Bethany Marie Casse, damn you. I swear, I'm going to tell the world about you-know-what. You know, that tiny little secret you're hiding. I'm going to tell them all."

His voice was what broke me.

"Beth?" Kent's voice was filled with concern. "Beth, open the door." He knocked lightly. "Let me in."

I picked up my train, opened the door, and peered at him through my lashes. He was so beautiful that I wanted to cry. It was his face that I'd wanted to see—because only he knew what I was going through, because we were the only two that were living this lie together.

When I moved to let him in, he pushed the door open and shut it behind him.

Instantly, I threw my arms around him, and almost started to cry. "I hate this," I whispered against his neck.

His arms wrapped around my lower back. "The fact that you hate it makes me think I hate it more."

We held each other in silence. He buried his head into the crook of my neck, taking in my scent, as his breath tickled my skin.

He spoke first, "Don't do that again. You scared me." He squeezed me tighter, pulling me closer against him and took a deep breath. "Kendy didn't know why you wouldn't answer the door. I ran here as fast as I could."

"I'm sorry," I said, closing my eyes. "Seriously, why are we doing this again? Because I don't think I can pull this off."

For once, the reassurance he had always given me about why we were doing this was not there. "It seemed like a good idea at the time," he said. He sounded nervous, which made me feel slightly better.

Releasing me, he took a step back. His eyes slowly raked over my face and then my dress, taking me all in, which warmed me all over.

He met my eyes, unwavering. "God, you're beautiful," he whispered as he took hold of my hand.

I felt my cheeks flush as his look of intensity consumed me and drew me in. That pull, that electricity buzzed between us as our eyes locked, his chestnut brown to my emerald green and all I could hear was the sound of our breathing.

I pushed my boobs together, breaking the awkwardness. "Look."

It worked as his eyes widened in amusement. "Interesting," he said, a dimple peeking out from his cheek.

"I mean, I always knew I had them, but in this dress… yeah…interesting."

He shook his head once, and then he pulled me into a soft embrace again. "I couldn't do this…I wouldn't want to do this with anyone else," he said. "Let's eat, have fun, and get drunk, okay?"

Releasing me, he pulled something that was wrapped in a paper towel out of his pocket. "Fries? I know you haven't eaten."

"Oh God. Mr. Plack, I love you," I said, snatching the paper towel out of his hand. Greasy, old fries never tasted better.

He observed me in silence, and I smiled at him as I chewed every single fry. My stomach grumbled as if it were showing gratitude for feeding it.

"I'm ready," I said, breaking the silence after devouring the last of the fries. I wiped my greasy hands on the expensive designer dress and reached for his hand.

He took it and kissed the top of my hand "You're truly the most beautiful bride I've ever seen," he said, his eyes never leaving mine.

I bet the flush on my cheeks was brighter than the pink blush I was wearing. "Let's go." I pulled him toward the door.

As we exited the bathroom, the paparazzis started again, blinding me with their flashes. I turned and buried my face in Kent's shoulder, shielding my eyes from the lights of the cameras. His arms wrapped around me in protection.

"Okay, enough pictures for the moment," Kent commanded.

Cheering and clapping erupted, and I glanced up, noticing everyone in the room.

Mr. Plack had Mrs. Plack in an embrace. Kendy stood next to Aunt Diane. Kendy motioned at Kent's arm wrapped around me with her eyes and an all-knowing I-know-what-happened-in-that-bathroom look even though the only thing that had happened was I'd eaten fries.

"Nervous jitters, but she's fine now," Kent said, breaking the applause.

One by one, they came to greet us.

"I thought you had smartened up and changed your mind," Mr. Plack said while winking at his son.

Mrs. Plack held my hands, taking in the sight of me. Her lips slowly quivered, and she covered one hand over her mouth. As her tears threatened to overflow, she stepped in to give me the biggest bear hug. "You're so beautiful, Beth."

"Mother, you said you'd try to control yourself," Kent said.

She reached up and touched his face. "I'm just happy and so very proud of you." Her tears pooled in the corner of her eyes.

"Okay, everybody, let's go, let's go, let's go!" Mary clapped her hands, catching everyone's attention and breaking the moment. "We are already fifteen minutes behind schedule. I'm glad I allotted time for mishaps such as this." She moved Mrs. Plack out of my arms and pushed Mr. Plack in the direction of the door. "Kent, let's go. You've already broken one of the most important rules. You've seen the bride," she said, a look of disgust on her face.

"No!" I gripped Kent's hand in both of mine. Immediately, the sound of my heart beating in my ears started to accelerate again. I didn't want to let go of my lifeline.

Mary glowered in my direction, giving me a subtle evil eye. "Honey, you'll see him in a minute," she blurted out.

I wanted to *honey* her right in the face. I shot her the evil eye right back, but mine wasn't as subtle.

Kent coughed to cover his laugh. "Give us a few seconds, please. Everyone out."

Mary shot me a look before turning to stomp out the door, and the rest followed.

"The best thing about this day being over is that I'll never have to see that lady again," I muttered. "I swear, for the amount of money your mom is paying her, she should at least be nice, right?"

Kent placed both hands on my shoulders and moved me to face him. "Forget her. I'll meet you down the aisle, okay? Don't worry about anyone else. I'll be down at the end of that aisle, waiting for you." He grabbed my chin to meet my eyes in the most intimate stare. "Okay?"

My breath caught.

I could see speckles of gold in his chestnut irises. "Fine," I said, pivoting toward the door. "I can't believe you stuck greasy fries in your tuxedo."

He shook his head and laughed as he followed me out. "I can't believe you wiped your greasy hands on your fifteen-thousand-dollar dress."

Chapter Sixteen

"CANON IN D" played in the background. The nervous, jittery feeling that had caused my dry-heaving over the toilet rushed back, but I tried to concentrate on my pointed Christian Louboutin shoes. Mary allowed Kendy to walk down the aisle first.

Now, I stood alone, left behind the closed doors, waiting for my cue.

Of course, I had no father to walk me down the aisle. When Mr. Plack had offered to walk me, I had been touched by his sentiment, but I'd declined. In the end, I'd wanted to walk down the aisle alone because I was the only one responsible for myself, and that was how it had been for some time.

The only person who would have had the privilege to walk me down the aisle was Nana, but even if she were alive, she wouldn't have shown up here today. She had always been proud of me, but I was sure that today would have been the first time she'd be disappointed. The thought of disappointing my Nana had the first tear falling down my face.

"You're up," Mary said, pushing the door open. "Ready?" she asked.

I nodded once even though my insides were saying no.

Flickering candles lit the room, and peach flowers sat atop pedestals lining the aisle. Over two hundred people occupied both sides of the room, standing in front of chairs draped in white and accented with peach sashes. I felt claustrophobic as I looked at the crowd to the left and right of me. I didn't want to faint, so I focused on my pointy shoes and concentrated on placing one foot in front of the other.

My mind drifted to Nana and how I wished she were still here. In my mind, I told her that I was sorry. I was sorry for doing this, for choosing the easy way out, for not living up to the woman she'd brought me up to be. That even if I wanted to, it was too late to back out now. I told her that I wished she were here even though she would be disappointed. I just wanted her near me. I was sad that she would never see me really walking down the aisle toward the man I would truly marry. I told her I missed her so very much. I missed her every day, every single minute.

One by one, the tears flowed down my face, and I could taste the salt on my lips. A few women in attendance, whom I didn't know, were crying also, but the reason they thought I was crying was not the reason at all.

Finally at the altar, I saw Kent and felt comfort.

He had a look of reverence and of awe on his face, and when he pulled my veil over my head, his brow furrowed with concern. He cradled my face in his hands and wiped the tears under my eyes with his thumbs, forgetting about the people around us. My eyes drifted to the crowd and I placed my hands on top of his and pulled them down, tugging him to face forward toward the officiant.

As the officiant started to speak, Kent turned in my direction.

Why are you crying? he mouthed silently.

"Later," I whispered, facing forward.

I didn't hear a thing the officiant was saying. It was as if someone had pressed the mute button and the whole time, all I heard was mumbling. I wasn't paying attention, and when it was time to repeat my vows, I missed my cue—twice. Kent had to squeeze my hands to break me from my trance.

When the officiant said, "You may kiss the bride," I knew the worst was over. It was done.

As Kent leaned in for a kiss, I wrapped my arms around him, and his eyes widened in surprise right before I kissed him full on the lips. He smiled as I did it. It wasn't a kiss of passion. It was a kiss of celebration. It was a kiss that was thankful because this whole ceremony and hoopla was almost over. Now, I could dance and get crazy drunk.

The applause roared to a deafening volume, and Kent had to be the one to disentangle me from his arms. His dimple emerged as he looked at me and linked my arm through his before we walked down the aisle. At the end of the aisle, chaos erupted. Everyone was hugging him and hugging me, congratulating us, but I didn't know a single soul.

Kent pulled me close. "Let's get drunk," he whispered in my ear, sending tingles down my spine.

"Let's," I agreed, smiling along with him.

WE WENT STRAIGHT to the bar and bypassed the line as we rocked the we-just-got-married card. The first shot we took was Crown. Having nothing in my stomach, except for old fries, I already knew this was going to be a short night. Kent shook his head after taking the shot, and when I raised my hand for another, he grabbed it and entwined it with his. With my free hand, I reached for the cranberry and vodka beside me.

"You have to pace yourself. I want our first dance before you pass out on me." He led us to the sweetheart table where we sat while staff in white jackets served us dinner.

"Do you even know half these people?" I asked, taking everything in.

"No, they're all business associates of Dad," he said, scanning the room of two hundred.

Tall, extravagant candelabras overflowing with white cymbidium orchids sat atop circular tables draped with peach linen and lined with bone china plates rimmed with gold. I watched as people mingled among the tables with their drinks in hand.

I lifted my glass of cranberry and vodka to my lips as Kent observed me. "I'm glad you don't know any of these people. Just a fair warning, I might embarrass you," I said.

He looked upon the crowd and shrugged. "Don't worry, these are Mom and Dad's friends."

I inwardly cringed, glanced at my glass, and contemplated if I should sip instead of gulp my drink down. "I don't want to embarrass them either."

Kent nudged me and pointed to the outer rim of the dance floor. "Look at her. She's having a good time. I doubt she'll even remember what happened in the morning." He chuckled.

Mrs. Plack was animated as she used one hand to tell a story to a crowd of older women while the other held a glass of liquor. Kent and I cast each other a look, and we both laughed.

"Funny how the last time I saw her like this was five years ago at our Christmas party," he said before lifting the wine glass to his lips.

One by one, colleagues of Kent's father approached our table to congratulate Kent and meet me. I smiled at each introduction, feeling my ears warm from the liquor.

The food had come and gone, and I made sure the drinks kept on coming. Kent smiled and nodded as he pretended to be interested in people he hardly knew. It was a large contrast to the Kent I'd first met, who would have had no problem blatantly telling them he wasn't interested in conversation.

I giggled at him trying so hard.

When he moved to face me, his smile turned genuine. "What?"

"Nothing." I giggled again.

"Mrs. Plack, you are drunk, or at the very least, you're getting there."

"I am not drunk," I said, blinking and smiling like a crazy person. I could feel my whole body warm, and I had to admit the liquor was making me feel pretty good.

I swayed to the sweet melodies played by the twelve-piece band as the woman singing at the microphone enthralled me, pulling me in with her sultry tones. When she announced it was time for speeches, I guzzled the cranberry and vodka in one gulp.

Mr. Plack stood and walked to the center of the dance floor. "We want to thank everyone for coming today to celebrate our Kent and Beth," he said, lifting up his glass. "Kent, I know we don't always see eye to eye on things, but know this—I love you, son. I will always want the

best for you. You might not always make the right decisions, but the decision you made today is the smartest
one you've made yet. When I see you two, I see myself
and your mother thirty years ago." He looked lovingly to
his wife and smiled.

He tilted his glass toward my direction. "Beth is an
amazingly driven young woman, full of life and spunk.
Karen and I tried years and years to conceive, and when
we finally did, we were blessed with Kent. We tried years
after that to conceive again. We wanted a little girl to
match that little boy, and today, I can say we've found
her. Our family is now complete. Thank you," he said,
bowing slowly to me.

Mr. Plack faced the crowd and raised his glass.
"Everyone, let's lift our glasses and toast to Kent and
Beth. For a life filled with lots of love, happiness, and
grandbabies." He chuckled.

The crowd cheered, and the liquor could not dissi-
pate the guilt rising again inside of me. The sounds of
everyone clinking their glasses had Kent twisting toward
my direction. He puckered up, and I placed a small peck
on his lips. The crowd roared in response.

Kendy was speaking on my behalf, and right before, I
had warned her that I wanted her speech to be short and
sweet, not personal. I shot her a look before she stumbled
onto the middle of the dance floor. I already knew she
had a few drinks in her, which made me nervous. People
were always a little too honest when they had a couple of
drinks in them.

"Hi, everyone." She hiccuped. "For those who don't
know me—which is, like, ninety-nine percent of the people in this room—my name is Kendall to most and Kendy
to Beth. I've known Beth most of my life. We grew up

together."

She turned to me, and although I had a smile on my face, I warned her with my eyes, secretly saying, *Hurry up.*

"In first grade, I was there when she had a little bathroom accident in class, and I helped her change out of her piss-filled clothes," she said, exaggerating with her one hand. "In fifth grade, I was there when Catherine picked on her at recess, and I was also there to ram little Cathy's face into the ground, shoving dirt in her mouth." She shrugged her shoulder as everyone responded with laughter.

"The only time I wasn't really there was when she moved to Chicago, and that was only because I couldn't be there—like, physically be there." She jutted out her lip into a fake pout.

"But that was when Kent took my place," she said, her voice softening. "I'm not going to go into details, but I clearly remember her telling me of a time when a guy touched her inappropriately, and Kent stepped in to show him who was boss."

She turned to Kent. "Thank you for taking care of my best friend. She means the world to me, the absolute world. I'm jealous because you've taken my place, but I know she's well taken care of when she's with you," she said, looking to both of us. "Everyone, let's toast, so Beth can stop giving me the evil eye to get this over with." Kendy lifted her glass. "Cheers!" Tilting her head to the ceiling, she downed all of her champagne.

I didn't want to face Kent after Kendy's speech because that shyness had rushed back again, so I reached for my third cranberry and vodka and took a sip from the glass, giving myself something to do.

265

"And now, it's time for the first dance," a member from the band announced.

Kent stood in front of me with one hand behind his back and the other offering to take mine. When I placed my hand in his, a tingling sensation started from my fingers and traveled all along my arm. He led me to the dance floor, twirled me around once, and swiftly jerked me toward him, which made me smile. He held me close, placing his cheek right above my temple.

The band was playing the song, and I recognized the lyrics. The words spoke of a man being lucky to fall in love with his best friend, and the chorus said that to be with her was to be at home. I snuggled closer to Kent, finding comfort in his arms.

I didn't know what it was, but in this moment, it felt like home.

Maybe it was the music or the lyrics. Maybe it was the whole charade of a wedding. Maybe it was everyone here, celebrating us, cheering us on.

Or maybe it was just him.

In any case, I didn't think anymore. I just basked in his closeness and reveled in the warmth of his arms around me.

As we moved slowly to the music, he placed his forehead against mine and closed his eyes. His cologne filled my nose, and I could almost taste the sweet red wine on his lips. When his hands tightened around me, I became hyperaware of him, his whole self. I felt his fingers gripping at my waist and his knees by my knees. He held me in the most intimate of holds, yet still, it wasn't close enough.

When I opened my eyes to meet his, there was a need, a want in them that mirrored mine. Desire pooled in the deepest part of my belly, and I read the same longing in his eyes. He lowered his head, met my lips, and slowly nipped my tender bottom lip. His lips were soft and warm, and I craved him, all of him.

This was not a peck like earlier at the ceremony. This was a promise of more. I felt it in the pit of my stomach, and for once, I accepted it. I pulled him closer, and when I sucked on his bottom lip, I heard his small intake of breath as a shudder ran through his body.

I moaned into his mouth, closing my eyes and letting him take the lead, as my heart raced, and my whole body meshed into his. His kiss was addictive. I wanted more of him, all of him, in that second.

"The dance floor is now open," someone announced, breaking that bond between us.

When Kent pulled away, we were both breathing hard. It took a few seconds for me to compose myself.

Realization set in, and I remembered that the crowd among us, including his parents, was watching us. I couldn't believe I'd forgotten about them, about everyone, to the point of almost dropping my panties on the floor.

I stepped away slowly to clear my head. I could see the yearning in Kent's eyes, and the look of need was still on his face. I smiled to the audience and cutely bowed to my husband before I walked back to the sweetheart table. I felt him following behind me, but I didn't meet his eyes.

"I'm going to dance with Kendy," I said in my most cheery voice to hide my nervousness. I didn't even wait for a response as I was almost running toward Kendy as she was getting her groove on the dance floor.

Kendy was a happy drunk as she swung our hands together while bouncing to the beats of the band. When

"The Twist" came on, Karen joined us on the dance floor. She was so uninhibited with the liquor in her. I danced along with the both of them, enjoying their company, and for a moment, I truly let loose for the first time during this whole wedding fiasco.

I caught Kent staring at me from across the room. I stopped in the middle of the floor, a large contrast to the moving bodies around me, as the residual smile slowly left my face. It was as if we were the only two in the room. He pulled me in with that same look he had given me earlier that made me feel things in the pit of my stomach.

I had to break that connection between us because it made me nervous. I gave him my cheesiest smile and shook my arms in a silly dancing motion. That seemed to work because the look was gone, and both of his dimples emerged. He placed his drink down on the table, stood, and approached the dance floor.

Damn.

It hadn't been an invitation, and Kent never danced.

When he entered our dance circle, Kendy and Karen moved to make room. He attempted to do the twist, which broke the awkward feeling I'd had a second before. I burst into laughter. For once, he was so uncoordinated, and him dancing the twist was so unlike Kent.

When "The Electric Slide" came on, his father came to join us. The bandleader stood at the head of the dance floor, leading the crowd in a short tutorial of the electric slide. I held Kent's hand as we went left and right and pointed to which direction we had to go next. When the band played the full rendition of "The Electric Slide," I was pleasantly surprised that Kent was a quick learner.

A slow song came on after, and he pulled me toward him. "So strange, but I'm having so much fun." He exhaled.

"With some help, you could move up to a moderate dancer," I teased. "We'll get you Dance Dance Revolution on the Xbox."

"What's that?"

I shook my head. "Never mind."

The song playing was "Unforgettable" by Nat King Cole. Kent's touch became intimate, and after he pulled me closer, his fingertips made tiny circles on my back. I was so close to him that I could feel the rise and fall of his chest as he breathed. That feeling came back again, and I knew I was playing with fire. I couldn't give in to temptation, not when I hadn't sorted out my feelings or thought things through. I couldn't risk one move changing everything between us, turning our friendship upside down, forever. I could feel his breathing accelerate, and mine mirrored his.

The band broke our connection again. "We are going to take ten and then play our last round. Stay tuned."

Relieved, I moved away from Kent. That look of want was back. He looked to my lips, and I wanted to pull him closer and ram my mouth against his, but instead, I looked to the bar.

"Want a drink?" I asked breathlessly and not meeting his eyes.

"Sure," he replied.

I turned to walk toward the bar, and he followed. Kendy and Aunt Diane were right behind us. He slowed until he was in line with them, and I felt that the almost event had been averted.

WHEN THE ELEVATORS opened, I hopped onto Kent's back and linked my arms around his neck. He raced toward our hotel room in a full-on sprint, causing my arms to tighten around his neck. The wedding reception had not been as bad as I'd expected. I'd drunk a lot and danced a lot, and by the time it had ended, I'd been in a happy, jolly mood.

"That was truly priceless. I will forever have the image of my mother practically giving my father a lap dance and then crying on his shoulder because her son is all grown up burned into my brain. And let's not forget when she passed out on that chair. My father will have a fun time carrying her to their room." With one hand, he swiped the key that opened the door to our honeymoon suite.

I was dying from uncontrollable laughter as he stepped into the room. I dropped off his back, and my eyes widened as I took in our surroundings.

The suite was complete with a full ten-person dining room table, a bar, and even a small baby grand piano in the center of the room. The twinkle of the city lights surrounded us as floor-to-ceiling windows spanned the whole living room.

"This is amazing," I whispered, dropping my Louboutin shoes on the floor.

"Yeah…amazing," he said, staring at me. "I've never had so much fun. Thank you," he whispered.

"Anything for my husband," I said, fluttering my eyes at him.

He laughed at the look I'd given him.

I surveyed the room and walked in farther. I stopped in the bedroom in front of the palatial king-sized bed. "You know what? Besides the getting ready and that awful ceremony when everyone was looking at us, that wasn't so bad," I said, trying to unclasp my necklace.

His hands came on top of mine. "Let me," he said, pushing my hair to one side of my neck.

It tickled where his fingertips lightly touched.

"Here," he said, facing me and dropping the necklace in my hands.

"Thanks," I said quietly.

His smile was disarming. He was truly handsome with his sly grin on his face, still wearing his tux. I didn't think I'd really taken in the whole ensemble until this moment.

"You look handsome today." It just came out.

One eyebrow lifted. "Don't I always?"

It was such a Kent thing to say, and I laughed.

"Thank you, Mrs. Plack." He bowed. "I'm glad you find me extremely handsome. For me, I find you extremely beautiful today in that dress, but you already know that," he said slowly.

I sat on the bed, looking at my gown. "Yeah, I'll admit that this is a pretty dress, but I still have no idea why someone would pay that much money for just a dress."

He sat down next to me and touched the beads of pearls and crystal on my waist. "It's the artistry of this dress, the intricacies of every bead being hand sewn," he said quietly.

His hands moved farther up, stopping right under my breast. "This is not synthetic fabric. It's silk, and the way it bunches right here tells me the designer is a perfectionist," he whispered, his voice dropping.

I stopped breathing as his eyes darkened.

He ran his finger in a straight line across the top, right above where the fabric met my flesh. "It's not just a dress.

It's every detail, every stitch. It's how the seams lay perfectly flat," he said, looking at where his finger paused.

When he met my eyes, I bit my lower lip, and his eyes flashed. I felt the air shift. His look was making my temperature rise even though the room was fairly cool. Desire pooled in the deepest part of my belly but I knew that one wrong move would change everything.

"You're such a metrosexual male." I laughed awkwardly, moving from his touch.

"I'm not an expert on dresses, but I do know the difference between a store-bought suit versus the finest handmade tailored suit. There is a difference," he said.

I stood up, turned, and grabbed the suitcase off the floor. "I'm going to change. I'm getting tired." I walked into the bathroom and shut the door behind me.

I dropped the suitcase on the black marble tile and glanced at the mirror, taking in my flushed reflection. I looked to the buttons lining the back of my dress and sighed before pivoting to walk out of the bathroom.

"Kent, can you do me a favor? Can you unbutton me?" I asked, turning to face the bathroom.

I felt him before I heard him, and when his hands moved to the top button, I held my breath. There wasn't a nerve in my body that didn't feel him slowly undoing each and every one. I heard his breathing deepen while he tugged and released each button. The loosening of the bodice should have allowed me to breathe easier, but his proximity prevented that. He stopped right above my blue lace panties and placed both of his hands on my hips.

"There," he said breathlessly against my neck.

I didn't move. Part of me wanted him to lower his lips onto the crook of my neck. I heard him exhale as I felt his eyes on my naked back. That electricity was in the air again, and if I turned around, there was no doubt what would happen next.

"Thanks." Holding the dress up at the sides, I walked back into the bathroom.

I splashed my face with the coldest water, but it was not bringing down the heat rising inside me. That was when I decided to take the coldest and longest shower of my life. I rinsed all the shampoo out of my hair and scrubbed my face raw, removing the caked-on makeup from earlier.

It was almost an hour later when I walked out of the bathroom. Kent had positioned himself in the middle of the king-sized bed, wearing gray pajama pants and a white T-shirt. He had the remote in his hand as he flipped through the channels. I frowned when I noticed him lying comfortably on the bed.

"Don't worry, I'll sleep on the floor." His mood was different from earlier, which made me relax.

I plopped on the bed next to him, combing my wet hair with my fingers. The events of the day were finally catching up to me, and I let out a big yawn.

"Why were you crying earlier?" he asked. I was confused at his question, but he continued, "At the ceremony, you were crying."

I thought back to when I walked down the aisle. "I missed Nana," I said, glancing at him. I took a deep breath. "And I know she would have been disappointed in me. Nana wasn't all about survival of the fittest, doing what you can to survive. Nana was all about doing the right thing, and for the first time since she raised me, I just know she wouldn't have been proud of me."

I looked at the engagement ring on my finger. "It's not me—this gigantic rock, the expensive fancy dress, the

big wedding. Taking the easy way out is not me. I'm pretending to be someone I'm not." I looked back up to him.
"On my wedding day, I always pictured myself walking
down the aisle in a short linen summer dress. I imagined
getting married in my backyard, surrounded by a garden
of wildflowers, and by the closest of family. Also, a big
part of me wishes Nana could be there on the real day."
I frowned at the thought of never having the chance to
see her again. I missed her the most when I needed her or
wanted her to experience my happiest moments.

I was surprised when Kent took my hand in his.

"Come here." He pulled me toward him. "Can I just
hold you tonight? I promise, I won't try anything crazy.
Plus, tomorrow at brunch, I can honestly tell my parents
we slept together."

I knew this was dangerous, especially with the near
misses throughout the day. I studied his face, which
didn't show any indication of his earlier mood. I really
shouldn't have, but I wanted him near me.

I laid my head on his chest. I was so close that I could
hear the thumps of his heart beating. I exhaled a long
tired sigh, feeling my whole body loosen in his embrace.

"Don't ever doubt that Nana would be so proud of
the woman you've become today," he said, running his
fingers through my wet hair.

His T-shirt smelled of detergent. It was like sleeping
on newly laundered sheets. I nestled close and fell asleep
to the rhythmic motions of his fingers running from my
scalp to the ends of my hair.

Chapter Seventeen

I WOKE UP to a big puddle of drool on my pillow. I wiped my crusty mouth with the back of my hand. When I moved, I felt Kent behind me, spooning me—and he was erect.

"Kent!" I whined, hitting him with my arm.

He flipped onto his stomach. "Sorry. That tends to happen in the morning." He chuckled, his words muffled against the pillow.

I took my pillow and whacked him on his back, again and again, until he flipped over and grabbed it from my hands. The phone rang, and I jumped off the bed before he could hit me back. Instead, he flung the pillow across the room, hitting me on the head.

"Hello?" I laughed, narrowing my eyes at him.

"Good morning. I hope I'm not interrupting anything."

"Hi, Karen. Good morning. No, Kent is just being silly."

"Come to bed, baby. I want more!" he yelled, so his mother could hear.

I widened my eyes at him as he placed both hands behind his head and gave me a wink.

"I'll call back later," Karen replied, letting out a delightful laugh.

"No, he's just hungry," I said.

"I'm hungry but not for food, baby!" he yelled even louder.

I squinted at him and pointed my finger in warning.

"You guys are too cute." She chuckled. "I called to tell you that I'm not feeling too well this morning. I think I had a tad too much fun last night. We're headed back to Barrington, so I'll have to cancel brunch. I'm sure you two had a long night, too."

I felt her smile on the phone.

"Okay, I hope you feel better, Karen."

"Yes, nothing an Advil, some sleep, and a dark room can't fix. And, Beth?"

"Yes?"

"Please call me Mom."

I fell silent at her words. *Mom.* I bit my cheek, touched by her sentiment. "Okay," I responded.

I blushed when Kent started moaning loudly.

"I have to go, Mom."

"Okay, we'll stop by this week. Have fun, and just so you know, your dad and I extended your stay for another night. You know, just in case you wanted to stay longer."

I blushed at her inward thoughts. "Thanks."

I hung up the phone, picked up the pillow off the floor, and threw it with a direct hit on Kent's face. He let out a low laugh.

"When did you start acting so goofy?" I asked.

A dimple popped on his cheek. "When I met you," he said, throwing the pillow back at me.

He missed as I sauntered toward the bathroom.

I COULDN'T AVOID the move.

Mr. and Mrs. Plack helped Kent move me into his condo and into his room. It was funny—watching them make room for my things, moving Kent's belongings in the process—when I knew I'd move it all back into my apartment once the arrangement was over. Throughout the whole ordeal, I made faces at Kent behind his parents' backs. When they left, I moved some of my stuff back into the spare bedroom.

"You know, when they visit in a couple of days, you're going to have to remember to move your things back before they get here," he said as he flipped through the channels on the TV while plopped on the couch.

"I know," I whined, sitting next to him.

I thought about what would happen in three weeks— at the end of our arrangement. At that point, I'd be moving everything out. I wondered if I'd see his family again.

"It's going to be hard. They love you, and they'll never forgive me," he said, reading my mind.

I gave him a nudge on the shoulder. "It's okay. They'll love the next one just as much."

As crazy as these months had been, I had become part of a family, and I hadn't felt that in such a long time. The openness and warmth that the Placks had shown me, by taking me in and showering me with affection, had been so overwhelming, but it was the kind that had left me with this fuzzy, bubbly overjoyed feeling, especially when Mrs. Plack would warm me with her hugs. I would miss that once this was over.

I peered up at Kent and thought of everything we'd been through. I knew I'd miss him the most. I wondered what our relationship would be like after this deal was over. He was my best friend in this new town that I'd moved to. As much as I'd felt confused as hell over these past few weeks, I knew I'd miss seeing him every day. I'd miss his newfound goofiness. I'd miss his dimples peeking up at me when I made him smile. I'd even miss his air of confidence. I'd just miss him. I'd miss it all.

I frowned, purposely making a sad face. "I'm going to miss your family, but most of all, I'll miss you." I didn't care that saying it would only intensify the confusion building between us. It was the truth, and I felt that the sappiness had to come out.

He turned to my direction, his stare warming me. "There won't be a next one." His eyes showed such sadness, mirroring my own.

He placed his palm against my face. I leaned into it, closed my eyes, and listened to the sound of us breathing. When I opened my eyes, he was gazing at me with such intensity. His look alone set me ablaze. He stared at me for mere seconds as if he was going to make a move or he was contemplating it, but immediately, he dropped his hand from my face.

"Who else would want to marry this fool?" he said, pointing to himself. "Plus, I can't do relationships." He moved from the couch toward the kitchen and opened the fridge.

I secretly huffed at his revelation. After the near misses right up to the wedding and even during, I had to be careful. Just with Kent in the vicinity had me yearning to be near him, and I didn't want to be the one to make that first move. I was starting to realize what I wanted, but what I wanted was something he couldn't give me.

THE NEXT DAY at the end of the workday, I rushed out the front door, leaving Financial State. I felt the brisk air of fall hit my skin. As I turned the corner, I wondered what cuisine Kent had concocted for dinner. It was funny how as soon as I'd stepped out of work, I had already started thinking about dinner and wine with Kent.

Stopped at a crosswalk, a strong hand gripped my right arm with force, and a sharp object pushed against my side, jolting me from my state of calmness. The pounding of my heart resonated in my ears, and I dropped my laptop bag automatically, freely giving it up to my attacker. *They can have it.*

And then, he spoke, "Hi, Beth." The stench of alcohol from Jesse's breath was strong enough to wake the dead. "Listen carefully. You move, you shout, you draw any type of attention our way, and I'll kill you. I'll shoot you dead." I tilted my head in his direction and flinched at the sight of him.

I stiffened at his words, feeling the jab of what I assumed was a gun underneath his jacket pointed directly into my side. I looked around us. With the buzz of rush hour, everyone was scurrying home, paying no attention to this homeless-looking male next to me in a worn black jacket and jeans. I looked to the crowd passing me by and begged for help with my eyes, but no one made eye contact.

"Move," he said, probing me forward as he draped one arm around me, pulling me to his side.

Dread washed over me as I stared into the depths of his pupils. His black eyes were deep and soulless. He pushed me down the street with one arm draped across my shoulders and the other hand digging a gun into my side. We turned into an alley, and he shoved me face-first into the backseat of a car. He tied my hands and slammed the door behind him.

I'm dead. The number-one rule when one was kidnapped was to never, ever go to a second location. I should have let him shoot me on the street. At least there, I would have had a fighting chance. *Why didn't I scream at the top of my lungs?*

"Sit up, and don't move," he commanded.

Two large black duffel bags on the floor caught my eye. I rooted myself against the seat and pushed one open with my foot. Wads of cash bounded by currency straps filled the duffel bag. I could only assume the other was filled with the same. I held my breath and swore I was going to pass out from the anxiety building in my chest.

"Where did you get all this cash?" My voice quivered, failing me.

He glanced at the rearview mirror, and his eyes flitted from left to right as he started to drive off. He ignored my question. "Where's your phone? Call your mom. I need to talk to her." When I didn't move, his voice hardened as he said, "I'm not going to ask you again. Call your mother."

"It's in my bag, and I can't exactly reach for it when my hands are tied. Where did you get all this money, Jesse?" I pressed, trying to keep my voice level.

"Shut up." He looked around, turned into another alley, and slammed on the brakes, throwing me forward and making me hit the seat in front of me.

He stepped out of the car, pulled me to a sitting position, and yanked the ropes off of my hands. "Call your mother from your phone. She'll answer."

I grabbed my phone and steadied my shaking hands to look for her number. When I pressed the button to dial, Jesse yanked the phone from my hands.

"Jamie. Jamie, baby, I'm sorry." He ran one hand through his hair, his eyes frantic. "I didn't mean to hit you. You led me to do it. We have money now. I did this for you, for us. We don't need anything else but the money and each other." He exhaled. "If you had just waited till I got the money and you drove the car, none of this would have happened. We could have been out of town by now." Paranoid, his eyes flittered to our surroundings. "Call me back."

Shit. He robbed a bank.

Dropping the phone on my seat, he surveyed the area before getting back in the car and driving off.

We stopped, stuck in bumper-to-bumper traffic. My eyes searched for anyone I could make eye contact with. I looked in cars and at the people walking down the street. Nobody was paying attention.

"Keep calling her. Tell her it's an emergency." His eyes observed our surrounding area as the traffic began to let up. "Do it!" he yelled, making me jump.

Sitting straighter on my seat, I quickly dialed her number. "Jamie, it's me. Call me back. I'm with Jesse. Please call me back."

"We need to leave and get out of town. I need to find her first," he said, mostly to himself. "Call her back. Keep calling," he commanded.

We stopped at a red light, and my eyes flipped up to focus on the police car right next to us. Jesse gripped the steering wheel with both hands, the whites of his knuckles evident. His head remained utterly still as he seemed focused on the red Toyota Camry in front of us, careful not to move his eyes to where the police officers sat to our right.

I took that nanosecond to make a stupid move. I

stared directly in front of me at the back of Jesse's head while doing it, and I only hoped I was texting the right information.

In Black Corolla with Jesse. On Madison and Wells. Help.

Trying to calm the tremor in my hands, I sent the text to Kent and deleted it.

When we passed a couple of lights, my phone rang, and I jumped. Glancing at the flash on my phone screen, relief washed over me as Jamie's name came up. I was glad Kent was not stupid enough to call.

"It's Jamie."

Exiting toward the highway, he reached back, and I gave him my phone.

"Baby, I'm sorry. I didn't mean to do it. What? Yeah, I'm calling from Beth's phone because I have her. No. She's fine. She's safe. We have enough money to finally get out of this place. I'm coming to get you, baby. Just tell me where you are." His eyes surveyed the highway, darting from left to right. "No, I can't do that. I'll let her go when I pick you up."

Cars swished past us as he stayed in the right lane, adhering to the speed limit.

"We don't got a lot of time here. Tell me where the hell you are, or there will be consequences to pay. Don't make me mad, Jamie. You know what happens when I get angry." He scowled at the rearview mirror, staring into my face.

A shudder ran through my body as I sent up a silent prayer to Nana, wishing this was all a terrible nightmare that I'd wake up from at any minute.

"Good. Be there. I'm coming to get you. Yeah, I'll let

her go once you are in the car."

Five minutes later, I noticed Jesse tense up as a cop car trailed behind us.

"Face forward. I don't want you looking around," he commanded.

I didn't think anything of it until another cop car pulled up to the left of us. I felt anxiety rolling off of him as he blanched and gripped the wheel, trying to pay no attention to the cops beside us. When the cop lights flickered, my head slammed against the backseat as Jesse pressed on the gas. Flashing lights and sirens indicated that the cops were on our tail.

We were in a full-on car chase on Interstate 90, and when I glanced behind us, the two cops had now grown into four. Cars moved to the right lane to get out of our way as we sped through the highway doing over ninety miles per hour.

He exited the highway and blew through a red light. I held on to my seat with both hands as he veered the corner. My eyes flickered to Jesse. His eyes were wide as he glanced toward the rearview mirror, watching the chaos around us. He turned a corner and hit the brakes as he realized we'd hit a dead end.

I jumped when he punched the dashboard. He reached for his revolver as he twisted to look behind us. We were surrounded by flashing lights on all sides, confined by law enforcement. Eight or nine cop cars had caged us in. Everyone, including Jesse, was ready with their guns out.

Anxiety rose inside me as he whispered, "I'm not going to jail."

"Sir, step out of the car. We need you to get out of the car," an officer said over a speaker.

"Get in the front—now!" Jesse ordered.

I did as I'd been told and jumped to the front seat.

Jesse gripped my upper arm and pushed me toward the door. "We're going to get out of here."

He yanked me out of the car and positioned me as a barrier between the law enforcers and himself. I flinched when I felt the cold revolver against my neck.

"Back away. I'll kill her. I swear it!" he shouted toward the crowd of policemen.

The ringing in my ears began to intensify as bile crept up my stomach and into my throat. My vision blurred as I scanned the chaos around us, and then I saw him.

Kent.

He was standing behind his opened car door. His eyes mirrored mine with pure terror and something more—helplessness.

As I looked into his eyes across the mass of chaos with the cars and the cops, all I wanted, all I wished for in that second was to feel his arms around me with his breath against my neck as he held me close. I wished I could have that just one last time.

Tears ran down my face as our eyes locked.

If I were to die this instant, there would be so many things left unsaid. Things I wish I would have said as I stared into his eyes, the warmest brown eyes—the eyes that had offered me comfort, the ones that had crinkled at me every time we laughed together, the ones belonging to the man who had taken me in and welcomed me into his family.

If I ever had a chance to talk to him again after this—after this crazy, unforeseen moment—I'd tell him, I'd scream out to the world those three little words that I would have never had the guts to say until this moment.

I love you.

I love you, Kent. Not just love you, care for you, but I'm in love with you, in a way where my heart is so full, full to the point of combustion.

And I just want you to know this, even though you might never give me what I need—for you to be with me and only with me, I need you to know that I've fallen for you. Because if I don't get to see the light of day tomorrow, you deserve to know your place in my life is profound, and I want to thank you for caring for me in a way I haven't felt in such a long time.

"Let's talk about this reasonably. Let her go, and no one will get hurt," the policeman said.

"No. I make the rules here!" Jesse yelled, prodding me forward. "I need everyone to back away. I will kill her. You hear me?"

He jammed the revolver further into the side of my throat, and my vision blurred as tears flooded my eyes and rolled down my face.

Directly in front of me, Kent gripped the car door for support. His eyes, which usually provided comfort, glistened with fear. I couldn't bear to look at him as panic inside me intensified.

"Okay, don't do anything drastic. Everyone, in your cars!" the cop yelled into his receiver.

One by one, the officers began to draw back. Jesse retreated backward, flopped me into the backseat, and jumped into the car. As he wheeled the car around to drive out of the dead-end street, I heard the first gunshot, held my ears, and screamed.

Jesse's eyes were wide as he looked around him. He hit the brakes hard, plummeting me forward toward the seat in front of me. The gun was still gripped in his hand against the steering wheel.

I didn't waste any time to think. I just reacted.

I propelled myself out the door and ran. I ran as fast as I could. All I kept thinking was, *Run.*

Run.

Run.

Run.

He could shoot me, but I kept running until I tripped on my own feet and fell to the ground on all fours. The impact of the fall scraped my knees while pain shot up my thigh. I glanced behind me. Jesse was on his feet and out of the car, and his gun was pulled straight out in front of him. This time, everyone had their weapons pointed at him as well.

I felt strong hands pull me up, and I yelped as an officer dragged me away from the scene. Words were exchanged back and forth between Jesse and the officers, but I didn't comprehend what was being said. The only sound that I kept on hearing was the ear-splitting boom of the gunshot earlier.

"She's my wife," I heard him say.

Hands reached under my knees and lifted me. When I glanced up, it was Kent, and automatically, I collapsed into his arms, held him tightly, and sobbed uncontrollably into his neck. I was shaking as he held me, the tremors from my cries taking control of my body. I didn't pay attention to where we were going. I just held onto him for dear life as if he was the air I needed to breathe.

"Shh...it's okay. I'm here. I'm going to take care of you," he said, pulling me closer toward him. He kissed my forehead and held me like a small child. He comforted me with his words telling me that everything was going to be okay, over and over again. Not once did he let me go. If anything he held me tighter.

I cried and cried until my tears ducts were dry, and when the sobbing slowed, I realized that we were in the back of a cop car. He placed both hands under my chin, searched my face, and wiped the tears under my eyes with his thumbs.

"Did he hurt you? Should we go to a hospital?"

I stared at him from under my lashes and shook my head. He gripped me closely, pulling me flush against him, and kissed my forehead forcefully.

"Thank God," he whispered.

THE COP OPENED the backseat of the car to peer in.

"Ma'am, we'll need a statement. Before that though, I think you should get checked out for any trauma. The crime scene is cleared and they've taken the culprit down to the station. There is an ambulance outside. In any way, did that guy use force on you?"

I shook my head to indicate 'No'.

"At the minimum, you should at least get that scrape on your knee looked at."

I nodded, and Kent scooted out of the car. As I stepped away from the car, Kent lifted me again and carried me to the ambulance. I nestled closely, resting my head against his chest, as I relaxed in his arms, taking in his masculine scent that calmed me.

He positioned me at the back of the ambulance truck, and a nurse tended to the scrape on my leg. I flinched at the sting of the alcohol wipe against my bloody knee and observed the nurse as she tended to my wound. Dazed and tired from what had happened, I zoned out as my adrenaline died down.

287

My head popped up when I heard Kent yelling. I saw him pacing back and forth with my phone in one hand and his other on his hip. "No. You cannot talk to her. You're the reason she got into this mess. I warned you and that bastard to never contact her. No. You can't. She doesn't want to speak to you. There is nothing you can say that she wants to hear."

When he glanced my way, I motioned him toward me.

"I said, no. What don't you understand? If you want to speak to someone, you can speak to Officer Daniels. He said he'd be contacting you, and you can bet I made sure he had your number."

I reached for his arm. "Just tell her that I'm okay. I don't want to talk to her, but just tell her I'm okay," I said, my voice hoarse.

"She said she doesn't want to talk to you, and she's okay. That's the end of this conversation." He hung up the phone, reached for my hand and squeezed it. Immediately, he softened at our touch. "Ready?" he asked, his warm eyes meeting mine, a contrast from his mood a moment earlier.

I nodded.

"Let's make your statement, and then I'm taking you home," he said, assisting me from the ambulance.

AS SOON AS we stepped into Kent's condo, Mom and Dad charged toward us and wrapped their arms around both of us.

Mom took hold of my hand, walking me further into the condo. When we were in the living room, her hands cradled my face, examining my features as if I could disappear in an instant. Her warmth that always surrounded her was amplified as she took hold of me, bringing me close and thanking the heavens above that I was okay.

Men weren't affectionate. They didn't usually show much emotion. But after Kent relived the day by telling his father all that had happened, his dad gripped him close and patted his back. Dad's eyes showed relief and thankfulness. It was the most I'd ever seen them interact on a physical level, and it showed me the amount of love Dad had for his son.

The high-speed chase was broadcasted all over the news, and by now, everyone had heard. Caroline, Kendy, and Aunt Diane had called to check that I was okay. After almost thirty minutes of reassurance, I tried to convince Kendy that she didn't have to drive down to Chicago. When Kent reached for the phone and ensured her that he would take care of me, only then did she calm down.

With the adrenaline long gone, exhaustion hit me, and all I wanted to do was sleep. I was glad when Kent sensed my mood and hurried his parents out. After we said our good-byes, I stood and watched him close the door. I wrapped my arms around myself to hold myself up as tiredness hit.

He walked toward me, searched my face, and slid one arm around me. "Let's get you to bed."

I changed into my pajamas and lay in my bed in the spare bedroom.

"You just stay there. I'll cook you something and bring it to you," he said, sitting on the edge of my bed.

He brushed a strand of hair from my face, and I leaned into his touch.

Staring up at him, I was so grateful that he was here

with me. My heart swelled as I thought of how he'd saved me today by calling the police, how he'd cared for me at the crime scene, and how he'd continued to take care of me now.

"I never said thank you. I just want to thank you, Kent, for calling the police today and for—"

"Beth, you don't have to thank me. All that matters is that you're safe…here…with me." He pulled me in by the nape of my neck and kissed my forehead tenderly.

I closed my eyes and exhaled, relishing in the warmth of his touch. In that moment, I felt so cared for, so loved.

He was the first to break contact as he backed away and moved from the bed. "I'll go get you something to eat."

KENT TUCKED ME in that night and brought me dinner in bed as if I were sick. I basked in his comfort and as he sat next to me as we watched TV together, I realized one thing. I'd realized that I was madly and deeply in love with my best friend. I didn't know when it happened or how it happened. I hadn't even had time to think things through or sort out my feelings along the way. It just happened. With everything that occurred earlier, all my true feelings rushed to the surface.

I snuggled closer to Kent as he continued to flip through the channels, holding me, as I nestled against his chest, taking in the scent of laundered sheets and pure masculinity. Finally, sleep claimed me as I lay in the comfort of his arms, once again.

Chapter Eighteen

AFTER A COUPLE of days, everything went back to normal. The gossip of what had happened and the concerned people asking if I was okay had lessened. I'd found out from Kendy that Jamie was going to testify against Jesse and that she'd only found out of his plan to rob the bank when she was actually in front of the building. Jamie was supposed to be the getaway driver, but she'd left the car as soon as he stepped into the bank. The prosecution was going to try to charge her with aiding and abetting until Jamie agreed to testify against Jesse.

Jamie had called Aunt Diane to check on me, but I didn't want to talk to her. I was glad she wasn't with the loser, but she had never been a part of my life. Just when I was getting my life together, I didn't want her to ruin it.

My days with Kent had turned into a routine. I would wake up for work, and when I walked out of my bedroom, Kent would already be up with a cooked breakfast on the counter. He would walk me to the elevator, seeing me off to work. Everything would have been fine if his hand didn't linger on mine when he would pass me the orange juice, if his knee didn't brush against mine when we would sit at the counter, if his embrace before I would step into the elevator was less intimate and shorter, and if his eyes didn't darken when they would meet mine.

It was driving me insane—absolutely insane.

It was fun living together because our laughter never ended, but it was torture at the same time. The near misses were escalating to a point of almost combustion, and each and every time, I'd wanted him to give in. I just wanted him to give in to temptation and cross that line because I would respond without restraint. I wanted him to say he'd change his ways for me and that he wanted me, and only me, to be his.

It was only two more weeks until our deadline. The closer that date approached, the heavier my heart felt. I didn't want it to end, but it was torture to feel this way toward him, knowing he couldn't give me the kind of commitment I needed.

Every night, Kent would cook me dinner. Where I was a good cook, Kent was exceptional as he was a perfectionist in the kitchen. His sauces were always flavorful, and he had to have the right amount of spices.

During the routine preparation of dinner, I would watch his muscles move under his T-shirt as he reached for bowls in his cabinets. I was his assistant, and although I enjoyed learning about the art of cooking, I enjoyed watching the art of Kent cooking more and found it harder and harder to concentrate.

"Can you stir the sauce?" he asked, putting the bowls on the counter.

I moved toward the stove, picked up the wooden spoon, and began to stir the sauce in the pan. The scent of tomatoes and garlic filled the air, and my stomach grumbled in response.

I felt him move closer behind me.

"Continue stirring," he said, placing his hand on mine stirring with the wooden spoon. "You don't want the bottom to burn."

He was so close that I could feel his breath against my neck. I could barely handle the heat, and it wasn't from the nearness of the stove. I leaned back into him because—well, I wanted to be near him. I bit my lip and rested against him as I felt a hypersensitivity wherever our bodies touched, his chest to my back. Right before I was about to turn around, he released my hand and backed away. "Keep stirring," he said, his voice deeper.

I closed my eyes to compose myself, to calm my raging pulse and yelped when my pinkie finger touched the edge of the pan. "Ow." I dropped the wooden spoon, and tomato sauce spilled on the floor.

He grabbed my hand and inspected it. "Let me see."

I forgot about the pain when he quickly placed my pinkie in his mouth, sucking it lightly. Our eyes locked as I watched him pull at my pinkie with his tongue. The warmth of his tongue on my flesh heated my insides to immeasurable temperatures, and I felt that yearning hunger in the pit of my stomach. That electricity between us was there, thick and palpable. The need and want in his eyes mirrored mine. I leaned into him ever so slightly. I wanted to kiss him. I wanted him to kiss me. I waited for it.

But he closed his eyes, and at once, he released me. "There. Better." He dropped my hand and picked up the wooden spoon off the floor. "You have to be more careful. Do you need a Band-Aid?" he asked, not meeting my eyes.

"I'll get one." I staggered back before almost running to the bathroom.

I closed the door and leaned against it, using it as support. I took deep breaths to calm my stammering heart in

293

my chest. I didn't know how to make it more obvious without stripping naked and yelling for him to take me. I wanted him but not only on a physical level. I wanted him to be solely mine, and only he could decide that, so he had to be the one to make the first move.

When I walked back to the kitchen, I caught Kent pinching the bridge of his nose. His eyes were closed as he furrowed his brow in concentration.

I didn't know how much I could take. Given all the tension rising between us and the feelings rising within me, I wondered if we could go back to our friendship as it had been before. More than that, I wondered if he felt the same and had feelings for me too.

KENT WAS SITTING on the couch in front of the TV when I walked into the condo after work.

"How was your customer call?" he asked, flipping through the channels with the remote in his hand.

"Long and boring." I dropped my laptop bag on the floor. "I could never be a banker. They wine and dine every day and have so many night functions. When I'm done with work, I'm glad I'm done for the day."

I walked over and plopped myself next to him on the couch. Closing my eyes, I rolled my neck from side to side to ease the tension from the long day. Working from eight to five in front of a computer and then logging off to attend a customer dinner had just been too much to handle. I was glad I didn't have to do it on a daily basis.

"Come here," he said, "I give the best massages. You look stressed."

He parted his knees and dropped the remote, as I

moved to sit in front of him. He began to knead my shoulders with his thumbs, and I eased into his touch.

"Mmm…you're pretty good at this," I said with my eyes closed.

"When will you figure out that there's nothing I'm not good at?" He chuckled.

I opened my eyes to watch the news as Kent continued to work my shoulders.

"Did you do anything today? Did you go to the gym?" I relaxed my shoulders, feeling the tension slowly ooze out of me.

His hands moved to my shoulder blades as he began retelling his day's events. His fingers were magic, and I began to feel each muscle relax with his touch. Moving his hands to the middle of my back, he used his palms to work the tension out and undo each and every knot. After a while, a slow sigh of relaxation escaped me. The tension of the day's hard work slowly disappeared as his fingers kneaded my flesh, and I found myself sinking into the couch. Moving further down, his hands massaged my lower back, and eventually, they shifted to my hipbones. I felt the pressure of his fingertips deepen against my skin and the sudden sensation of warmth flooded my body.

His touches moved slowly and intensified as feelings of relaxation transformed into something else. It was something deep and dark—and something a paid masseuse shouldn't be doing. I didn't even notice when he'd stopped talking. His hands continued from my hip bones to my thighs, massaging and kneading and touching. I didn't know what came over me, but I leaned back against him, wanting to be closer. His breathing changed, and I could feel his labored deep breaths coming through his nose and onto my neck. His hands shifted to my inner thighs where he continued to rub slower, deeper, and with heightened pressure.

Leaning my head back, I felt his tongue on my neck. Heat spread throughout my body. I felt tingly from where his tongue met my flesh. The sensation spread from the deepest part of my belly to the tip of my toes. He pulled me against him, gripping me closer, as his hands continued to massage my inner thighs. I felt him erect against my back, and I moved against him, fully turned-on, as my breathing accelerated, giving away my arousal.

It was all too much to take. All at once, he grabbed the side of my neck, turned my face toward him, and slammed his lips down on mine, his tongue invading my mouth. I gave it right back and opened my mouth to let him find passage, welcoming him, meeting him. He tasted of mint as I bit hard on his lower lip, and I was rewarded when a moan slipped from his mouth. His soft touches were gone, and he kissed me hard and rough, his tongue tasting mine.

Framing my face with both of his hands, he attacked my lips and moved my legs to straddle him in one swift movement. He grabbed my bottom and pushed me closer to him. I moved against his hardness and felt my wetness soak my panties. He lifted me, and I wrapped my legs around him as he carried me to his bedroom. His lips never left mine as he dropped me onto the bed and rested between my knees. I kissed him back, meeting his tongue, tasting and feeling him. He groped me through my clothes, every part he could get a hold of.

Spreading my knees apart, I felt his hand travel under my skirt, up my thigh, and to my center where he rubbed his hand against my sweet spot. When he moved my panties out of the way and his finger pierced me, I let out a small moan of pleasure.

"Oh, Kent," I exhaled, moving against him.

He pulled back slightly and as he peered down at me, lust filled his eyes. As if saying his name, released his sexual beast inside, he continued to create this sensual friction inside me with his fingers. His breathing accelerated, and when his mouth moved to my neck I turned to give him better access. He licked and sucked my neck, and there was no doubt I would have a hickey in the morning, but I didn't care. I ran my hands through his hair and tugged at the ends, hard.

He was flush against me, but it wasn't close enough. I arched my back toward him, rubbing myself against his chest, as I wanted to be even closer. My silk shirt was now an itchy barrier between us. Reading my mind, he withdrew his hand and loomed over me. I sat up a little as he lifted my shirt over my head and tossed it to the side. I tugged on the bottom hem of his T-shirt, and he complied, lifting the shirt above his head before throwing it on the floor. Slipping my skirt down and off, I was now only in a bra and panties.

Kent pressed himself on top of me, and his lips were on mine again. His hand moved to my back to undo my bra, and in a flash, it was off. As he moved on top of me, I was on fire and soaking wet. I ran my nails roughly over the muscles of his back and down into the back of his pajama pants. I squeezed his backside to press him down onto me as I lifted my hips to grind against him.

"Shit," he said, breathing harder, giving me a thrill.

His lips moved to my breast, sucking and teasing with his tongue. I was sensitive all over, and at that moment, I wanted to feel him in me. I moved my hands to his hip bones to slip off his pants, but he inched even lower, placing his lips on my belly, his tongue dipping into my navel.

"God, you're sexy," he breathed.

I started to get nervous as he trailed his tongue from my belly button down over my hip bone until he came to the elastic of my panties. He distracted me with soft nibbles as he slipped the wet fabric down my legs. When I felt his tongue touch my center, my body convulsed. Automatically, I tried to close my thighs, but his grip tightened. He lifted his head up, and his eyes bore into mine.

His lips returned to my core, and I tried to relax and enjoy the feelings he was sending throughout my body. My breathing intensified, and I realized sounds I'd never made before were escaping my lips. I fisted the bed sheets, not knowing what else to do with my hands, as his tongue flicked against my sensitive nub.

I felt a tightening in my belly and tingling in my legs as my body rocked into him. As he moved his tongue deeper into me, my thighs closed instinctively due to the unfamiliar sensations of my body building toward release.

He lifted his head and pulled me closer, tightening his grip on my thighs. "Baby, let me do this. I want to be the first to give this to you." His grip would not relent, and his mouth attacked my core, flicking his tongue directly over that perfect spot.

My brain was mush, and I was lost in feeling. The deep sensations in my belly began to rise again, and my legs began to tremble as the buildup started to intensify. Kent gripped my thigh with one hand and placed the other on my lower belly to hold me still. Loud moans escaped my mouth. I wanted more, yet at the same time, I was scared of the unfamiliar feeling building in my body.

"Let go, baby," he grunted before torturing me with his tongue. "Come on," he mumbled against me.

At that, I exploded. I let out a loud scream. Everything went into sensory overload, and my body rocked in ecstasy. Tingling intensified all over my body over and over and over again. Kent withdrew himself and pressed his lips to mine while I rode my first orgasm down, moaning in his mouth.

I laid on the bed, utterly spent and exhausted.

After a minute, I opened my eyes. He had flipped me over to lie on his chest, his hands running lightly through my hair. I listened to his heart beating as I felt the rise and fall of his chest against my cheek. I was satiated from the experience, but more than that, I felt so whole in his arms. I felt safe. It felt right to be there.

I thought of all that we'd been through. He had been my rock through all my struggles in a new town. He was my best friend. After everything we'd been through, I was glad that we'd ended up like this—me in his arms.

It was then I realized that it never would have worked with Brian. Although I'd tried to deny it for such a long time, I had always been in love with Kent. I'd been in love once, but this time it felt different. I'd never felt such a physical and emotional attachment with such heightened intensity, such magnitude to another person before.

It slipped out before I could stop it. "I love you," I whispered into his chest, nestling in even closer.

For a brief moment, my cheek lay flat on his chest as he held his breath.

I realized he was still aroused. As I reached in his pants to give him some release, to finally feel him in me, he grabbed my hand and rested it on his chest.

"I just want to lie like this," he said.

After a heartbeat, the rhythm of his hand moving slowly up and down my back contributed to my drowsiness, and before I knew it, I was asleep.

THE WARMTH OVERWHELMED me. I lifted my head to find that Kent had me in a death grip. His arms and legs were wrapped around me as if I was his body pillow—not that I minded at all. Not only did I not mind being in our own little cocoon of heat, but I also basked and reveled in it. If I could stay here forever, just the two of us, I would.

I kissed his forearm and turned to align my face with his. We were a breath apart, and I slowly took in his every feature. With the tip of my finger, I touched his perfectly shaped brow and his unbelievably and unfair long dark lashes that hit just above his cheekbones. I dragged my finger from the bridge of his nose to his lips, which were parted slightly in his deep state of sleep. I traced his plump bottom lip and inched closer to kiss him, to press my lips against his—because this time, I could.

He was truly the most beautiful man I'd ever laid my eyes on. And not even his hotness, his crazy good looks could measure up to how truly beautiful he was inside, how big his heart was, how he cared for his family, and more, how he cared for me. I loved him. And finally, he was mine for keeps.

The red digits from Kent's alarm clock on his side table flashed in my eyes. Painfully, I moved his arm to extract myself from his embrace, so I could get ready for work. I rewarded myself one last glance as I gazed at the handsome man lying on his stomach next to me and sighed. With my finger, I traced the defined lines from the muscles on his back. He didn't flinch and was still sleeping soundly.

I stopped to think about what had gotten us here today. I wondered if I'd avoided the inevitable by trying to deny my feelings for so long and if we would have made it here anyway. I never believed in fate. I'd always been the one who believed that everyone could shape their own future by the actions they took. But now, lying next to Kent, I believed.

I kissed his shoulder before jumping into the shower to get ready for work.

WORK WAS CRAZY busy. It was nonstop meeting after meeting in the boardroom about current clients. My butt was either stuck in a boardroom chair or stuck in my desk chair with my head in front of a computer, analyzing company financials. Preoccupied with work, I only had time to eat lunch at my desk. Because of the hectic day I was having, I would have thought the workday would fly by, but five o'clock could not get here fast enough, especially when I was anxious to see Kent.

After work, I shut down my computer, said good-bye to my bankers, and headed out the door. I was smiling, almost skipping back to Kent's condo when I stopped dead in my tracks.

And then I saw them.

Kent was with some girl.

Her arms were wrapped around him.

They stood right in front of the doors to Trump Tower,

right there for everyone to see.

Right there for me to see.

I felt sick as I took in the scene.

She had her arms wrapped around his neck, and he was laughing at something she'd said.

Heat flashed to my face, and I could feel my eyes getting warmer and warmer by the second. I wanted to scream and cry, hit him or her, hit something. I gritted my teeth. I didn't understand what was happening. *Did last night happen?*

Something inside of me believed that he'd wanted me to see this. I couldn't control the slight tremor in my hands. I didn't know what was going on, but all I knew was I needed to leave. And I needed to leave now.

I was a few feet away from him when he saw me. I made my way over to pass him. I didn't even want to acknowledge or talk to him because I knew I would cry.

"Hey, Beth." The remnants of his smile were still on his face as he stood there, entangled in the girl's arms.

At the look I gave him, his demeanor changed, and he stepped away from the woman. I stormed past him through the revolving door and felt him following behind me. A couple came out of the elevators, and I immediately stepped in and pressed the button to shut the door in his face. I pressed 55 and tapped my foot against the tiled floor, not reaching my destination fast enough. As I stepped out of the elevator, I rushed toward the condo and keyed in the door. The elevator pinged behind me, and I heard him call out my name, but I didn't turn around. I let the door shut behind me, but he caught it.

"Beth, wait. Are you upset?"

I wheeled around to face him, my hands fisted by my sides.

The fact that he'd asked me that question made me livid. "Upset? Why would I be upset?" I said in the softest voice possible.

He studied my face for a second before running both of his hands through his hair. "About last night. I know we haven't talked about what happened, but...I just don't want anything to change between us."

At this, I lunged toward him. All restraint was gone at this point. "You bastard. You don't want anything to change? Well, you should have thought of that before you touched me last night!" I yelled, pushing both fists at his chest.

He tried to block my hits as I kept pushing him. I was yelling and spitting, and my face was red from frustration. I knew I was not a pretty sight.

"I'm not one of your whores. Why are you treating me this way? How could you do this? How could you do this to me? To me!" I said, putting both hands on my chest.

I reeled away as the fight left me. Tears flowed down my face, and I looked directly in his eyes. "I'm not one of your girls." I shook my head. "Just because they can disconnect their emotions from any physical contact doesn't mean that I'm built that way because I'm not."

I wiped away the tears falling on my cheek with my sleeve. "After knowing me like you do, how could you not know that once you crossed that line, I'd think you'd want something more?" I asked, my voice breaking.

I tried to rein in my emotions, but the more I tried, the more tears fell. "I can't believe you. I...I trusted you," I said, stifling a cry. "I can't do this anymore. It's taking too much out of me. I'm done," I said, backing away from him.

"Beth…I"

"No, I don't want to hear it. Your actions speak louder than anything you have to say." I turned and stomped toward the guest bedroom. I scanned the room that I'd spent the last week in. I couldn't believe it was ending like this. My belongings were scattered everywhere. I would just send Caroline to pick up the rest of my stuff.

My hands shook as I scooped up my necessities, toiletries and a couple of suits. I pulled out my suitcase from the closet and felt Kent's presence behind me, standing by the door, but I didn't look at him.

"You're leaving?" he whispered.

I didn't turn around. I kept myself busy as I continued to pack my stuff, trying to keep my emotions under control, trying not to fall apart in front of the only person in Chicago I thought I could count on. I was tired, but most of all, I didn't want to cry anymore. I just wanted to leave.

"What about the deal? You can't leave," he said softly.

"You have access to your trust fund money. I've held up my part of the deal." I pulled the zipper to close my suitcase, and I plowed my way toward the bedroom door.

He blocked my path, ran both hands through his hair, and tugged it in frustration. "I'm confused. These past few months have confused me, and I don't know which way is up anymore. I just don't know what I want. All I know is that I don't want you to leave. Don't go."

I clenched my jaw, fighting the tears. "I'm sorry you don't know what you want. Sometimes, we don't get what we want. Welcome to the real world, Kent."

I made my way around him, stalked toward the kitchen, and grabbed my laptop bag.

He followed and paced back and forth, with both

hands running through his hair. I glanced at him as his eyes went wild. "You can't go," he said.

I ignored him and stepped my way to the foyer where he followed. I grabbed my jacket from the closet, and he stopped directly in my path, blocking the door to the outside.

"Listen, okay? Just listen," he said with a desperation in his tone. Kent looked down to the floor as if he was thinking of what to say. He paused and stared directly at me. His eyes changed from scared to now determined. It was as if he had stopped breathing. "Beth, please just listen. I don't know what to say. Just don't. Please listen. Just don't do it. Don't go."

"Move," I said, firmly meeting his eyes.

His face was resolute, but his eyes gave him away. He was shattered. "I don't beg, okay? I've always gotten whatever I wanted, whenever I wanted. I manipulate everyone I know—my parents and my friends. I don't want to do it, but if you walk out that door, I won't give you a dime. You won't get your money."

I took a sharp intake of breath. At that moment, I was at a loss for words. I wanted to cry again, but I was so mad that I couldn't. I knew the money could lead to my freedom from my past, the debt, and my mom. But it wasn't about the money. I wasn't mad that he wasn't giving it to me. I was mad at the fact that he was using it as leverage. Kent used money to manipulate people. He had even said so. The difference was that he was using it on me to get what he wanted. He was using it as leverage for me to stay.

I didn't even waste the effort to speak. I wheeled around and stepped out the door.

I WENT STRAIGHT back to my apartment after I'd left Kent's place. I'd known I would end up here after the divorce, but I couldn't have predicted that it would hurt this much when I did.

I was tired of crying, especially when I'd spent all my life living by the book and doing everything right. I refused to cry over things I couldn't control.

So, I didn't.

I turned off my phone and tried to sleep.

When sleep still hadn't come as dawn approached, I did what I did best. I got up for work and pretended that nothing had ever happened.

Twenty-nine missed calls greeted me in the morning. They were all from Kent. I pressed delete through all the messages, not listening to one word. I was tired of being used. There was nothing he could say to make things right. To me, actions always spoke louder than words. I'd learned that from past experiences. I'd learned that from my mom.

I busied myself at work, facing my computer. I didn't want to talk to anyone nor did I want anyone asking me about married life again.

On my way home, I saw Kent standing outside my building. I stopped and took the deepest breath of my life and stepped forward. His hair was in disarray, and his clothes were disheveled. It was one of the few times I'd seen Kent not put together. When he saw me, his eyes lit up. I glared at him and clenched my jaw.

"What do you want, Kent?" I said, as I tried to steady my voice.

I tried to walk past him, but he blocked my path on the sidewalk.

"I've been trying to call you." Bloodshot eyes bore into mine. It didn't look like he had slept. "I want you to come home."

I crossed my arms in front of me. "That's not my home. That was the set of some theatrical play—a play that turned awfully bad. Please move."

"I've paid off all your debt," he said softly, blocking my way. He stood taller, gauging my reaction.

I didn't know what to say, but I was definitely not going to thank him. His eyes fell, and his shoulders slumped at the look I gave him.

"Good. Thanks for consolidating my debt. Now, I can mail one check instead of twenty."

When I moved around him, he grabbed my wrist.

"Please," he whispered, his eyes pleading. "I-I can't take this."

I hated how I softened at his touch. I hated how I missed his scent, his presence, his very being.

I looked into his chestnut eyes, and all my feelings for him rushed to the surface. I thought I was about to lose it. I turned around and bolted in the other direction, hearing him call my name. I didn't know where I was going. I just knew I had to distance myself away from him, from the sight of him, from his very presence. I curved around a corner and realized I'd walked into a dead-end alley. I pivoted around, and Kent was right there, facing me.

"What do you want?" I yelled, tears falling from my face. "You think you own me? You think that just because you paid off my debt, I owe you something? I'm tired of people thinking that they own me." I staggered back. "Just because Jamie gave me life, she thinks she can use me and destroy me. Just because you paid off my debt, I now owe you something? I've never done anything to you. I've never hurt people deliberately, so why does this keep happening to me? Why do people keep hurting me when I've never done anything wrong?" I couldn't see. I was crying so much that his figure was a blur.

Kent reached for me, but I stepped back. I couldn't risk him touching me. My resolve would weaken, I know.

"Don't hate me," he said, his voice quivering. "Please."

He moved forward, but I retreated, taking another step back. I held up both hands to stop him from inching toward me.

"I know I don't own you," he whispered. "If you were mine, I could hold you while you cry." His voice broke. "If you were mine, I could take you home."

"I did it because I want you to be happy." He clenched his jaw. "I never meant to hurt you. Nothing happened between that girl and me. You have to believe me. I don't even know why I let her come that close to me." His eyes bore into mine. "It's just...these feelings...I've never felt these feelings before, and...I was scared."

His eyes filled with such emotion that I had to stifle a sob from escaping my mouth.

"I wasn't sure what I wanted. Being with someone was not what I had planned for myself, but as soon as you left, I haven't been able to function. I miss you, Beth. I miss you so much."

He ran his hand through his hair, and I clenched my jaw to prevent my face from showing any reaction.

"You know, I've always been content in my life. I've never been miserable, and I'm so miserable, Beth. And I know it's because you're not there. You don't understand.

I miss talking to you, Beth. I miss your face and your smile. I just miss you."

His face showed such anguish that I couldn't bear to look at him.

"I didn't know what I wanted before, but I do now. I know I want you. Without you, I'm not complete. I'm not whole. There's this void. It wasn't there before I met you, but now, it is." He took a step forward. "I know I can make you happy. I'd live my life making you happy, I swear it," he said, his voice breaking.

"If you want me to be happy, you'll let me be. You'll leave me alone," I snapped, trying to show no emotion.

I was done being hurt over and over again, especially by the people I loved the most. I'd been down this road before, and I didn't know how much more my heart could take. It was as if my heart was physically breaking, and my insides were being torn apart. I just had no more to give without losing myself completely. I was done with giving second chances.

His face fell at my words.

"I just want to be left alone, Kent," I whispered, my heart breaking into a million pieces. I had to save myself, protect myself, because I couldn't rely on anyone else to do it for me.

He staggered back and closed his eyes.

I stared at the man in front of me. He was the man who had hurt me, but he was also the same man who had been my best friend in a new city. And he was the man I'd fallen in love with, the man I was still very much in love with. With the fight all gone, I knew I didn't want to leave the tension between us like this.

When I touched his shoulder, his eyes opened to meet mine.

"You're a good man, Kent. You're selfish and spoiled, but you also have a good heart. You need to let the world see that side of you that your family and I have always known."

His eyes glossed over as I spoke. When he moved to reach for me, I stepped back. I knew I'd weaken if he touched me.

On the verge of losing it again, I walked past him. "Please...please, don't follow me. Good-bye, Kent."

Walking away, I stole one quick glance behind me. Kent was leaning against the brick wall, his head hanging in between his hands. He looked so defeated. My tears began to fall again as I continued to walk home.

Chapter Nineteen

I CRIED MYSELF to sleep that night and the few nights after that. Kendy would stay on the phone with me as I sobbed against the receiver.

"I'm sorry, honey. I hate hearing you cry," she said.

I didn't want to talk. I wanted to have someone with me, and if the best I could get was via phone, then so be it.

Many times, there would be silence over our long-distance call. And when my eyes were too heavy to keep open, we would drop the call together.

Funny thing was, if this were any other problem, I would have called Kent, and he would have been by my side the moment I hung up.

As tears continued to soak my pillow, I wondered if *leave me alone* meant *fight harder even though I continue to push you away because I'm tired of getting hurt, especially by the people I cared for the most.*

But the calls never came.

What was worse than breaking up with a boyfriend was breaking up with a best friend because boys could come and go but best friends were supposed to last forever.

NEWS SPREAD THROUGH the office. It was like reliving the past, and it brought me back to Bowlesville once again. The stares, the snickers, the hushed conversations that I was so familiar with occupied my workplace. There were even some dirty looks from women I hardly knew. I gritted my teeth, kept my face on my computer, and ate my lunches at my desk.

I will not cry in front of these people.

I will not.

I will not let them see me break down even though I am a mess on the inside.

Caroline didn't help the situation. She would bring me coffee every single day and put her arm around me. "I'm here for you whenever you are ready to talk."

Everyone would stare every single day, every single time she did it. I knew she wanted me to feel better, but I would have felt better if she just acted normal as if nothing had happened.

I didn't want to know, but I found myself asking anyway during one of our breaks. "Caroline, what are people saying?"

She shrugged. "I don't believe ninety percent of what I hear, and you shouldn't either." She placed her hand on top of mine.

"I'm okay, Caroline," I said, trying to reassure her.

"I know you didn't marry him for money," she snapped.

My eyes widened. I already knew that was one of the things they were gossiping about. The funny thing was that it was the absolute truth. I had married him for money.

I didn't deny it, but I told her my truth. "I loved him, Caroline."

She pulled me into a hug, squeezing tightly. "Then, what happened? Can't you work it out?"

I bit the inside of my cheek and willed myself not to cry. "I wasn't enough." I mirrored the same words Brian had said to me outside my apartment before he left for New York.

Now, I finally fully understood what he'd meant.

RENEE, MY BOSS, acted as she always had, which was exactly what I needed.

"What are you working on?" she asked, towering over my desk one day.

"Panchal Corporation. They are one of Jim's prospects. I'm looking through the financials right now," I said, glancing up at her.

"Good. I need another favor."

"Sure. Anything, Renee."

She looked at the papers in her hands. "Uh…I know you are going through some things, and I wanted you to know that if you need some time off, I understand." She held up her hand as I tried to interrupt her. "You're one of our best underwriters, and the quality of your work is exceptional. If you want to slow down for a little bit, you can. You do have vacation days."

I didn't want to see the sympathy in her eyes, but it was there.

"I'm dealing. Right now, work is the only thing keeping me going."

She nodded once. "Yes, I understand. I'm the same way." She straightened out her stance. "Well then, I'm going to get to another point. I'm building my team in California. You know we're expanding out west." She paused, gauging my reaction. "As I've mentioned before, I want you to come with me. Management wants me to have my team up and running before the end of the month. I'm moving in a couple of weeks. You're a top notch employee, and I'd like you on my team."

When I remained silent, she continued, "Financial State will pay all the relocation fees. If you have a lease, they will take care of that as well. Plus, there is a hefty sign-on bonus to entice internal employees to move. You don't have to answer me now, but I'd like a response by the end of the week."

Kent's presence touched every bit of my life in Chicago. Being in my apartment flooded memories of us hanging out and watching reality TV together. Every time I stepped into a restaurant, I would think of him and our love of food. If I stayed in Chicago, I knew my heart would never heal. I'd always be broken.

It was a no-brainer. I needed a second chance at a new start.

"I'll take it," I said, sitting a little taller.

THE NEXT FEW weeks trudged slowly, and the only thing that kept me going was knowing that I had an end date to my old life and a start date to my new beginning.

One afternoon, I glanced up to see Jim lurking near my desk. As soon as we made eye contact, he walked over. "Uh…I was going to go without you today, but Mr. Plack has requested your presence at their corporate headquarters downtown."

I glared at him, but he continued, "I know you've been through some things." His usual confidence was not there as he glanced at his shoes. "I tried to insist that you were no longer on the account, but he pressed. They're having their quarterly update today, and he'd like you to see where Plack Industries is heading, especially since you originally underwrote the loan for their restructure."

This can't be happening. "When are you going to grow some balls and for once tell your clients 'No'?" I couldn't bite back the disgust in my voice. I gave him my dirtiest look before charging toward the restroom.

He could have told them I was busy on another call. He could have told them I was sick. He and everyone in the whole dang office knew what had been going on. He could have lied, but if I'd learned one thing about Jim, it was that he would never tell his clients no, even if it was at my expense.

I shut myself in the restroom stall and wrapped my arms around my shoulders to hold myself together. I tried to steady my breathing as I fought my hardest to forbid the waterfall of tears to start.

I heard the restroom door swing open.

"Beth? Where are you? That stupid jerk. I told him off," Caroline said.

I heard her open every stall. She finally found me in the handicap one as I leaned against the wall for support.

"What the hell was he thinking? He's such a people-pleaser when it comes to his clients. He could have told them no. Damn bastard," she said, stomping her feet.

"It's fine. I'm fine," I said quietly, mostly talking to myself. I bit my cheek hard enough to taste blood, keeping

315

my emotions at bay.

Don't cry.

Don't do it, not at work.

"You don't have to go. I basically told him that you're not going." She stood in front of me and held my shoulders. "I told him no."

"It doesn't matter. I'm leaving anyway. I leave for California in a couple of days. Mom and Da—I mean, Mr. and Mrs. Plack have been nothing but nice to me. If Mr. Plack specifically asked for me to be there, then I'll go."

"Are you sure? Are you going to be okay?"

My eyes dropped to the ground, knowing full well I wouldn't be okay. "The problem is, I didn't only fall in love with Kent. I fell in love with his family, too. I'll be okay. I'll be gone soon anyway." The tears threatened to spill over. "It's just...I've tried everything to forget him. I've avoided every place we ever went to, everywhere that reminds me of him and now, I have to go see his family."

"Oh, honey," she said, pulling me to her side, "I'm so sorry."

Her gentle, consoling touch broke me as the first of my tears betrayed me and began to spill over. "Caroline, my heart...hurts." I dropped my face into my hands as my sobs shook my body. "It physically hurts, and all I wish for, all I want is for the hurt to stop. I just want it to stop." I cried, feeling warm tears wet my palms. "I wasn't supposed to fall for him. I'd forced myself not to fall, but then I did." I sobbed harder, collapsing into her arms. "Because I'm stupid. I'm so dumb."

I ugly-cried on her shoulder. She held me until my breathing steadied, my tear ducts dried out and finally, I had no more tears left to fall.

I DIDN'T LOOK at Jim or speak to him as we drove to Plack Industries' corporate headquarters in the city. I nodded at his comments as I stared blankly out the window and at the buildings in front of us.

Before we walked through the double glass doors into Plack Industries, I rubbed the back of my neck, bit the rest of my pinkie nail off, and took a deep breath.

I didn't want to see Dad. Memories of everything I'd had with Kent and the family I'd felt so much a part of would come flooding back even though it had just been a temporary arrangement.

The receptionist led us through the hallway and into the boardroom.

"This should only take an hour, maybe two hours tops," Jim said, taking a seat at the long chestnut table surrounded by black leather cushioned seats.

I rolled my eyes and didn't care that he'd seen it. I would never have to work with him again. In two days, I would be on my way to California—away from him, away from Plack Industries, away from it all.

When the doors opened, we both stood. Two women in suits followed two men into the boardroom. Right behind them, Mr. Plack strolled in. He nodded toward Jim. When his eyes reached mine, his face lit up, followed by a warm smile.

"It's good to see you, Beth." Mr. Plack came over and pulled me into a bear hug, patting my back.

"Hi, Mr. Plack." My ears warmed as I surveyed everyone in the room watching us, but Mr. Plack didn't seem to care as he held me a little longer than comfortable in a professional setting.

"Mom and I—we've missed you," he said, quietly backing away. He held me out at arm's length and studied me. "You've lost weight. Have you been eating?" he asked, his eyebrows pulling together in concern.

I nodded, feeling the warmth of my ears spread to my face as everyone stared at us. I'm sure they gossiped in this office, as they had done in mine. Most of the people in this room had most likely been to the wedding.

After a few seconds, he shook his head and turned around. "All right, we'll get started in a few minutes." Mr. Plack sat at the head of the table and flipped through his papers. "Jason, pass out the copies of those projections."

I reached into my purse, pulled out my pen, and opened my portfolio to a blank page. One by one, people filed into the conference room, filling the seats around the table. I glanced up when I heard a high-pitched female laugh, and I almost fell out of my seat when I saw Kent walking in, followed by a tall brunette. He looked annoyed at first, but when he saw me, his eyes widened. He was surprised to see me, too.

"Beth..." he said, his eyes lighting up.

The chatter in the room slowed to a dull hush as he took me in.

I gave him a small wave and lowered my head, focusing on the papers in front of me.

"Okay, everyone, grab your seats. Let's get started. I have an eleven o'clock meeting after this," Mr. Plack said.

The seats around me were occupied, and I released a soft sigh of relief. I wouldn't have been able to survive the whole meeting if Kent were right next to me. I didn't hear a word anybody was saying. I didn't even glance up from my papers. I could only feel his stare from across the room.

When the lights turned off and the third presenter walked up to the projector, I stole a glance. A small dimple emerged on his handsome face when my eyes caught his. I glanced away toward the numbers on the screen.

I didn't know why he was here. He'd wanted nothing to do with the company. I was so confused. I wanted to hide. I wanted to run. Most of all, I wanted to cry. I wanted to cry because over a month later, it still hurt being in the same room with him. It hurt because I realized one thing. I missed him so much even though I didn't want to.

The only thing that kept me in my seat was my hands gripping the sides of the leather chair. I bit the inside of my cheek and told myself to focus. *Focus on the numbers. Focus on the screen.* I had to focus on anything but the emotions running through me from just being in the same room with him.

When the lights flipped back on, I didn't glance in his direction. I could feel his eyes on me, burning a hole through me. His stare warmed the whole side of my face. I lifted my head, forced to look at him when he walked to the front of the room.

"Hi, everyone. I'm Kent Plack, assistant to the head of logistics for the roll out of this expansion. In other words, I got the job that no one else wanted."

The whole room chuckled, and even though I'd tried not to, the side of my mouth lifted slightly. His eyes warmed when he saw my smile, and he continued to talk about the renovations to the plants across the nation.

As he stood at the front of the room and pointed at the white board, I found myself drawn to him. He exuded confidence and wit. He knew what he was talking about, and my heart swelled with pride as he continued to speak. I'd always known he would be successful at anything he did. Watching him at the front of the room, taking charge and commanding the audience in this professional environment, I felt genuinely happy for him, happy for his family.

Although I couldn't have him for myself, even though I couldn't keep him, I knew I loved him wholly and fully because I wanted the best for him. I wanted him to succeed. And seeing the glint in Mr. Plack's eyes as his son spoke of the future expansion, I knew this was where Kent belonged.

When he concluded his speech, the whole room clapped, and the first thing Kent did was look in my direction. He raised his eyebrow slightly with his silent question, asking me if he had done okay. I met his eyes and nodded while I clapped slowly along with the group. It was only then that both his dimples appeared.

When the meeting ended, Jim walked toward the CFO and started a conversation. I picked up my purse and put my pen and portfolio away. I felt his presence before I even heard him.

"Hi, Beth."

I glanced up while gathering my papers from the table. "Hey," I said shyly. I looked around as people started to disperse from the room.

"You look great."

I continued to organize my papers. "You did amazing up there," I said, trying to change the mood.

I tried to block out the proximity of his presence, but I couldn't. He smelled of newly laundered sheets with a mix of his expensive cologne that exuded masculinity. It saddened me because at one time, just the scent of him had meant he was close, and it had been what calmed me when I needed it the most.

The brunette from earlier popped up in front of him. "Kent, want to do lunch today?"

"Sorry, not today," he replied, his eyes never straying away from me.

"Okay. Maybe tomorrow then?"

I felt a pang of instant jealousy as I took in her petite figure. *He's not yours to be jealous over*, I reminded myself.

"No, I don't know. Not now, okay?" He didn't try to hide the annoyance in his voice as he shooed her away.

She gave me a once-over before strutting out the door.

"How have you been?" he asked, a dimple showing on his handsome face.

"Good." Creating some sort of barrier between us, I held my portfolio tighter to my chest. I looked toward the gray carpet because staring at him made my heart hurt again.

He moved into my line of sight. "Do you...do you want to do lunch or something? I can drive you back to the office."

"No. I don't think that's a good idea."

"I found this new steak place, and I thought of you."

I shook my head, and his face fell.

"Every time I try a new restaurant, I think, 'Beth would like this place,' and then I wish you were right there with me," he said quietly.

I glanced around us. Everyone had already left the conference room. We were the only two people left in the empty boardroom. I stepped back and composed myself before the sadness in his eyes filtered into mine.

"Kent, I'm so happy you're working with your father. It seems like things are looking up for you. I always knew you could do it."

He reached for my wrist, and I weakened at his touch.

"It's because of this one beautiful girl who believed in me when I didn't believe in myself. She's the reason that my father looks at me from across the boardroom with pride in his eyes. Maybe that's why my mother hugs me a little tighter now, and I didn't even think that was remotely possible." He leaned in. "Your push is the reason I'm here."

I looked at where his hand met my flesh. "I'm happy for you. Good luck, Kent." I pulled my wrist back but the warmth from his touch was still present.

He leaned into me and my breath caught. "Beth, I...I miss you," he exhaled, his voice breaking.

I missed him, too, but I couldn't afford to say it, especially since I was leaving. I bit my cheek and gave him a sad smile. "I took a job in California. I leave in a few days." I'd had no intentions of telling him, but then again, I never thought I'd see him again.

He paused, taking my words in. "California?" he asked.

"It's a good opportunity. I'll be working for my same boss. It's going to be great," I said, speaking quickly.

"Is this because of me?" he asked, his eyes tormented.

"No, it's not," I lied, shaking my head. "It's because of me. I need a change of pace. I need something new."

He met my eyes and then looked to the floor. Jim peeked inside the conference room and signaled that it was time to go before he walked away.

"Listen, I have to go, but I wanted to say thank you... for being there for me with my mom problems and...for everything. I wish you would just cash those checks I send you for paying my bills."

"You earned it. That money is yours," he said. "Stop sending me checks because I won't cash them." He reached for my hand again and linked our fingers together. It was the most intimate of holds, the warmth of his hand spreading throughout my body. "I don't want you to go," he said softly.

I thought I was going to lose it at seeing the unshed tears in his eyes. I searched his face, and before he could say any more, I pulled back my hand. "I'm so proud of you, Kent. I wish you the best."

I turned and walked quickly out of the room, so he wouldn't see me cry.

ON MY HANDS and knees, I taped the last of my moving boxes. I glanced around me. My apartment was bare. No pictures remained on the wall, and throw pillows and blankets were packed away. Tomorrow, I'd be off to California to start a new life yet again. Hopefully, this time, it wouldn't be as complicated.

I stood, pulled my high ponytail a little tighter, and looked at the clock. I'd been packing all day, and I'd forgotten to eat lunch, so I grabbed my keys and headed out the door.

I found myself at a local cafe down the street, and as I took the last few bites of my panini, I mentally made a list of what else I needed to accomplish before the move. After eating, I strolled back toward my apartment, walking slowly to take in the city view for one of the very last times. The sounds of cars bustling around me and the train overhead filled my ears.

Then, I saw him and stopped. Just the sight of him

made my heart hurt. He took my breath away, and the flood of butterflies stirred in the pit of my stomach. I walked toward him at a painfully slow pace.

"Hey," Kent said. A dimple emerged as he lifted up a McDonald's bag. "McRib sandwich?"

I smiled, and his eyes lit up in response.

"I didn't know you ate McDonald's," I said shyly.

"I don't, but I thought if I ever did, I wanted my first experience to be with you."

I suddenly became wistful but I had to stop because I couldn't let myself feel this way. I didn't want to hurt anymore. I just needed a clean break. I was tired of feeling this way, gutted and heartbroken.

"I already had lunch." I fiddled with my keys and squinted up at him. "Kent, what are you doing here?"

"Can I come up?" he asked with a slight hesitation in his voice.

"I'm packing."

I didn't want to see the hurt in his eyes, but it was there.

His eyes dropped to the McDonald's bag that he was holding before meeting mine. "Come on, Beth. We eat together. That's what we do."

I sighed because it was the truth. It was what had brought us together as friends. I knew I shouldn't allow it, but in the end, it didn't matter. I was leaving tomorrow.

I walked past him and held the door open as he followed behind me. We were silent on the way up in the elevator. I stared at the red numbers indicating our ascent to each floor as I felt his eyes burning a hole on the side of my face.

When I walked into the apartment, I dropped my keys on the counter. He stared at the stack of packed boxes near the TV.

"You're leaving," he whispered.

"You knew this."

"I guess it just feels real now." He shifted and walked toward me.

I took a step back until I felt the kitchen counter behind me. "Kent..." I warned, putting both hands up to stop him from inching forward.

"I just want to talk."

"We've talked enough. I can't do this. It's like we're breaking up all over again even though we were never really together," I said, my voice trembling.

"Beth, hear me out. I'll regret it if you walk away and I never laid it all out on the table."

I bit my cheek and stared at my hands that were now clutched together.

"It's hard for me to do this, to talk about my feelings. I've been thinking of what I should have done, how I could have made things turn out differently. I realize I messed things up, myself."

I glanced up at the intensity of his voice as he inched closer.

"You know, I was so used to things being how they were, what I did day by day. It was routine. I was content. Life was just fine as I knew it—going out with Luke every night and living life as I did." He took another step forward. "Like I said, I was content and fine living that way. Then, I met you. Who knew eating, watching reality TV, and just talking was more than fine? It was fun. Spending time with you was what I looked forward to every day. Then, you left me...and I've never been so miserable. I've always gotten everything I've ever wanted. When you left, I felt like I'd lost it all. I've never felt emptier.

325

When you said you loved me, I got scared. I was scared of the unknown, scared of ever hurting you. Mostly, I was scared of my feelings for you. I've never felt this way toward anybody before. The way I feel about you, Beth…it scares me."

He moved to lift my chin to face him. "I've fallen utterly and deeply in love with you," he said, meeting my eyes. "And the more I tried to stop it, the more I tried to get back to the friendship we had, where we were before, the more those feelings intensified," he said.

"Beth, when I'm with you, I'm more than fine. I'm happy. It's effortless, and I want that back. I want you. I want a chance to work hard to earn you. I want to earn your love. I want to be the man you deserve. I want a chance to give you that movie ending. I want to be your once-upon-a-time, your dream come true, and your happily ever after. Just give me a chance. Have faith in me."

He brushed a tear from my face. It was only then when I realized I had been crying.

"It's like having vanilla ice cream all your life," he began, a dimple emerging. "And being content with vanilla ice cream because that's all you ever knew. Then, someone introduces you to chocolate ice cream and your life is forever changed." He framed my face with his hands. "And you never knew life could be so good. I don't know about you," he said, "but I, for one, cannot live without chocolate ice cream."

I stared into his liquid chestnut eyes. I saw the truth and his sincerity as he'd poured his heart out.

He'd spoken a language I understood. I didn't want to live without chocolate ice cream either.

So, I took a leap of faith.

I lifted my lips to his to answer his silent plea.

And chocolate had never tasted better.

EVERYTHING HAD GONE back to normal. I was terrified to tell my boss that Kent and I had reconciled, especially since Financial State had invested in moving me to California. My job had been my life—that was, until I'd decided that Kent was encompassed in that whole glob of my life. I had been prepared to do long distance until I could figure out what I was going to do with my job.

But when I had called Renee and fearfully delved into all that had happened between Kent and me, she had been more than understanding. That might have been because she was a woman, so she knew these things could happen.

I had offered to move to California for a short period of time until they could find a replacement, but I'd told her that it could never be permanent because my future, my life, and everything in it included Kent. Renee had told me that she'd discuss it with upper management as an option, but in the end, Financial State had offered back my original position in Chicago.

So, every day was routine—wake up, work, dinner, and make out with the hottest husband alive.

He was the one who had suggested we go slow, and I'd agreed. Given that we'd started off as friends and had been thrown into a whole pretend-marriage situation, it only made sense that we started dating as a *real* couple.

When he'd said we should take it slow, I hadn't thought he meant painfully slow, like snail or turtle slow—as in will-this-madness-ever-end slow.

The first few days were fine. I felt like I was in high

school again—going out on dates, making out in the last row of the movie theater, going to second base in the back of his Bentley while parked in an alley, and making it to third base on his couch. But after the fifth date of only making it to third, my insides were about to combust. I really wanted him to take me to home plate, but he would always be the first to stop when I gave him every indication that it was okay to make that home run.

Every night after our date, we'd end up in the same position in the same place—on his couch with barely any clothes on. I knew if we made it to his bedroom, it would be game over for sure, and I would always try to make it to his bedroom. For some reason though, he'd stop before we even got to that point.

While I was only in my bra and skirt and he was shirtless, I pulled his lips back to mine. His masculine scent filled my nose as I tugged on his drawstring pants. I trapped him, wrapping my legs around his waist, as I bit his upper lip ever so slightly. I pushed my pelvis up to meet his hardness, and moved against him until we created this sensation that made it difficult for us to breathe.

His lips trailed kisses from my cheek to my ear until his tongue met that spot on my neck that always drove me mad. My head fell back, and I closed my eyes, enjoying every sensation coursing from where his lips touched to the pit of my stomach to in between my thighs.

My breathing accelerated to match his when I felt his hand inch underneath my skirt before sliding up my thigh. I let my knees fall to the sides to accommodate him, and when he pierced me with his fingers, creating that sensual friction between my legs, a small moan of pleasure escaped my lips.

I lost all control. I lifted my head and attacked his

lips, pushing my tongue to meet his. I dropped my hand and rubbed his hardness against his cotton pants as I heard his labored breathing through his nose. When my hand moved to the waistband of his pants, his kisses and his fingers slowed, just like it had the night before and the night before that and the night before that night.

"No, don't stop," I said against his lips. I moved my hand against his, which was still lodged in me.

His head dropped to the crook of my neck. "What happened to nice and slow?" He exhaled as he tried to control his breathing.

"I don't want nice and slow. I want it hard and fast," I whined as he stopped moving against me.

His fingers moved to my outer thigh, and he hovered above me, using one arm for support. "It's hasn't even been a week since we officially got together."

"So?" I pouted, peering at him through my lashes, all the passion now gone. "Seriously, what's the point? Whether it's one week or one day, it's not like you're robbing me of my virtue. Someone else did that years ago."

The dimple on his cheek emerged as he looked down at me. "You're adorable right now, you know that?"

He kissed the top of my nose, and I pouted like a five-year-old.

"I like how you think I'm cute when I'm going to die of sexual frustration!" I huffed, pulling my eyebrows in. I turned my face to the side and feigned sadness. "It's like you don't even want me as much as I want you," I said softly, hoping he'd feel bad and just take me.

My breath hitched when he lay flush against me and pushed his hardness in between my legs.

"Does this feel like I don't want you?" he whispered before nipping at my chin. He pushed his length even closer to my core and moved a trail of kisses up my neck to below my ear. "I've never wanted anyone so badly," he said softly, his breath tickling my neck. "The first time I make love to you, I'm going to make you come over and over again until you beg me to stop. We're going to make love on every surface of my condo and every time we are alone. You're going to be so sore that you won't be able to walk, yet you'll beg me for more. And you know what? I'll gladly be the one to satisfy your need." His tongue traced a path from the top of my outer ear to the bottom. "And that's why it's worth the wait."

I couldn't move. I held my breath. I couldn't do anything as everything south tingled from anticipation of his promises to come.

He pushed himself off of me, and I tried to trap him again with my legs.

"Don't go," I begged. I gave him the biggest puppy-dog eyes that I swore would work.

"We have work tomorrow, and I don't want you to be tired." He kissed me and pulled me to a sitting position.

For someone who had slept with practically every girl in Chicago, I was surprised by his self-control. During the past week, every time we had found ourselves in the same situation, I'd transformed into a begging, whining little bimbo. I'd practically torn my clothes off, hoping he'd forego the slow and give in to the hard and fast. I'd been staying in his condo but only in the guest bedroom per his insistence. Half the time, I'd been tempted to strip down and surprise him by walking down the hall and slipping right next to him.

"I'm not talking to you," I said, crossing my arms in front of me as he stood. "I want to have hot, passionate sex, so I'm no longer frustrated, and I can finally sleep soundly. Until then, I'm not talking to you."

He moved in front of me, forcing me to drop my crossed arms. I gave in and leaned against his hand caressing the side of my face as our eyes met, his chestnut brown to my emerald green.

"I love you, Bethany Casse," he said, his eyes shining.

The words he'd never spoken to anyone else softened me.

He leaned down to meet my lips and pecked me sweetly. "If you don't talk to me, how will I know what you want for breakfast?"

I kissed him one last time and stood from the couch. "Fine. I'm not talking to you tonight," I said as I stomped toward the guest room. "I want bacon and eggs in the morning. Thank you." I didn't look back because if I saw my beautiful male with his tousled hair and hard, toned abs, I'd lose all self-control and propel myself toward him.

This man is driving me insane, absolutely insane.

I KEYED INTO our condo after work and stepped into darkness. I was about to turn on the lights when I noticed the flicker of candles on the dining room table. I was about to yell out Kent's name, wondering if he was here, when I saw him cooking by the stove.

"Hey," he said, peering back at me. He continued to stir some concoction, its fragrance filtering through the kitchen.

"What are you making?" I dropped my bag on the floor, walked toward him, and hugged his middle as he continued to stir. "What are we celebrating?" I kissed his shoulder.

He angled his head in my direction and continued to stir as a dimple emerged on his cheek.

His eyes moved back to the pot on the stove. "Can't we have a nice candlelit dinner at home just because?"

I angled my head to the side to get a better look at his face. He wouldn't look at me, and I could tell he was being shy for some reason that I couldn't place. My head flipped back to the dining room table where I noticed the light coming from two white tapered candles resting on top of silver holders. A table setting was positioned atop two gold placemats and the glimmer from the light reflected against two wine glasses.

I kissed his shoulder again, and realization slowly set in. Although he couldn't see, a small smile crept up my face.

"So," I used my pointer finger to run a line from his shoulder blade to the inside of his arm, "aren't you the cute one?" I moved to his side and pulled at his belt, tugging him toward me. "I know what you're up to." My hand slipped under his shirt, feeling the firm muscles of his stomach. "You don't have to make me dinner to get laid. All you have to do is ask."

He cast me a look and turned to the stove. "I don't know what you're talking about," he said as a dimple emerged on his cheek.

He averted his eyes, and my insides filled with excitement at him playing cute. As my hands moved to his waistband, he turned to face me.

"Baby, dinner first," he said, dropping the wooden spoon and reaching for my hand to kiss it.

"I'm not hungry." I turned off the stove, pushed him against the counter, and got up on my tiptoes to kiss him. "Dessert first."

He smiled and lowered his head to meet my lips. His hands trailed from my shoulders to my arms before finally resting on my hips. I thought he was going to stop, but instead, he dug his fingers underneath my shirt and into my skin as he pulled me against him.

The kisses started slowly at first until I tilted my chin. He opened me with his tongue and found passage. He lifted me by my bottom, and I wrapped my legs around his waist. Excitement hit me as I felt him aroused, and I fisted his hair as he moved us from the kitchen to the living room and into his bedroom without breaking contact.

He placed me on the bed and looked down at me through hooded eyes. He lifted his shirt above his head and tossed it behind him. I bit my lip in anticipation as he took my face in his hands, cradling my chin. He kissed me tenderly as though I would shatter. I inhaled deeply and took in his masculine scent. Never leaving my lips, I felt his fingers loosening the buttons on my shirt, one by one. I quivered at his touch. When my shirt was off, he unclasped my bra and chucked it behind him. Heat rushed my insides as I felt him on top of me. His hands slowly drifted up my legs and onto my thighs. I lifted my bottom to assist him, and as he started to slip off my skirt, I froze.

"Wait," I said breathlessly, my heart racing in my chest.

He rested his forehead against mine, trying to calm his breathing. "Stop?" Lust filled his eyes. "Baby, I need you. I need in you—now."

"I know," I said. "It's just…I didn't do laundry and…" I was still breathless. I shouldn't have felt embarrassed, but I hadn't been prepared to have our first time be tonight. I wished I'd worn something sexier.

"What?" he asked.

I slipped off my skirt to reveal my flowery grandma panties.

He peered down at the pink-and-green high-waisted underwear and fisted the sides with both of his hands. "Only you can make granny panties look so damn sexy," he said, slipping them off. "I. Don't. Care."

I laughed as his lips connected with mine again. He kissed me until my mouth was raw. His tongue was tasting, flicking, and exploring. I slipped off his pants and gripped his hardness, triggering a switch that seemed to turn up the heat as all his restraint faded. Feeling him at my entrance, I shifted to accommodate him. He cradled my face, and there was a slight tremor in his hands as he rested his forehead against mine.

His eyes filled with such emotion, such intensity. "I love you," he said.

My eyes forced closed, and I bit my lip at his fullness as he rocked into me.

I would have waited forever for this, for him, to feel him inside me. Our connection was beyond physical. It was deeply emotional. I loved him, and now, he was mine, all of him.

As we made love, he whispered how beautiful I was, how good I felt, and how much he loved me, over and over. I watched a look of pleasure pass on his face. When I felt that familiar buildup intensify, the one that only he could give my body, I closed my eyes to enjoy the sensations coursing through me.

His movements increased to a pace that made the tingling at the pit of my stomach spread to my legs. He gripped my thighs hard as he rammed into me again and again until I felt the contractions rise. My toes curled, and convulsions overtook my body. Just when the contractions began to slow, his thrusts became faster and harder, causing the buildup to rise again. Low groans left his mouth as his steady pace intensified. I screamed his name, and he slowed and stilled in me, both of us coming together in ecstasy. I laid on the bed, utterly spent and fully satiated. I couldn't move. My body felt like jelly but in a good, satisfied kind of way. I could lay there forever.

When his breathing slowed, he turned to flip me until I was lying on his stomach. When my heartbeat began to descend to a normal pace, he let out a low laugh.

"This night didn't turn out like I'd planned," he said, running his fingers through my hair. "It was supposed to be romance, candlelight, and dinner first."

I lifted my head to look at him and raised my eyebrows.

"I wanted to give you the movie version."

"Oh," I said, realization setting in. "Well, this is much better than the movie version. If this were the movies, I'd be watching the love story happen on the screen. In this version, the good stuff happens to me." I said, resting my chin on his chest.

He peered down at me and brushed a strand of hair away from my face. "Yeah, this is so much better than the movies."

He kissed me long and hard until I forgot my name, forgot where I was, and even forgot how to breathe.

"Here," he breathed, "I get the girl."

I felt his length harden below me against my stomach. I guessed if this were our movie, part two was going to start real soon.

ONE YEAR LATER...

WARM KISSES WOKE me up from my sleep. I smiled, feeling kisses on my eyes, on my cheeks, on my nose, and eventually my lips.

"Wake up, baby," Kent whispered. "Wake up, beautiful girl."

"No," I said, playing coy and turning over to my other side.

I didn't dare open my eyes as I placed the pillow over my head. My silk nightgown ruffled against the down comforter. Puppy pajamas had been long gone, and had been replaced with silk and lace nightgowns. Kent, being the shopper that he was, had brought home presents almost every day. They had usually consisted of designer clothing or nightwear. Plus, I'd been added as a client on his personal shopper's list. I'd told him that the way to this woman's heart was food, so sometimes, he would bring home dinner instead.

"Baby, don't make me get you up," he said.

I knew he was smiling.

"I want to see you try," I said teasingly as I turned over onto my stomach.

He straddled my back and started poking my sides, left and then right and then left again, tickling me. I bucked him off my back and faced upward.

"Stop, Kent. Don't you start," I said, giving him a playful look.

He continued to tickle my sides.

"Please. Please. Okay. I'm up, I'm up." I cried.

His hands slowly came to a stop, and I gazed up at him, taking in his every feature that I'd memorized over time. His chestnut eyes were full of emotion, and his residual smile faded as he gazed at me intently.

He lowered down on top of me and placed his hands on each side of my face. "God, you're beautiful," he said before kissing me passionately. He slowed his lips to a painful halt and closed his eyes while resting his forehead against mine. "Although I'd love to wake you up in a much more pleasurable way, I have plans for us today. Therefore, we must get up, or I swear, we'll be in bed for the rest of the day.," He opened his eyes with a more serious look now, and the passion was gone.

"There's nothing wrong with that." I smiled and wrapped my legs around him to bring him closer.

When I slowly kissed his neck, he stilled.

"Kent, are you saying no to your wife?" I trailed kisses from his neck back to his lips.

"Baby, when do I ever say no to you?"

He shook his head, disentangled himself from my hold, and pushed himself off the bed. "You are forever going to be my weakness, but I have plans for today. I'm going to take a very cold shower, so I can get ready. Breakfast is right here by the bed." He gave me one last peck on the lips and sauntered toward the bathroom.

The muscles on his back moved with each step he took, and his biceps flexed as he took off his shirt and threw it on the floor before stepping into the bathroom. I was momentarily tempted to jump in the shower with him, but then I smelled the eggs, bacon, and toast beside me. My stomach growled, and food won out. I scarfed down the food and waited for my turn to hop in the shower.

"OKAY, HERE'S THE first surprise for the day. Close your eyes," he said, both dimples appearing.

I squeezed my eyes tightly shut, smiling the cheesiest smile ever. Butterflies were in my stomach as I felt a cold chain being placed around my neck. This wasn't the first time he'd slipped jewelry around my neck, but I got excited every time he did it.

"Open your eyes."

I touched my neck to feel a heart-shaped locket. I looked down, and my hand automatically flew to my mouth in shock.

"Kent, where did you get this?" I whispered. "Pete told me he'd sold it all."

"He did—to me. I picked up all the stuff in Bowlesville when you left me. I needed all the ammunition to win you back. I wasn't going to let you leave me without a fight." He tucked an escaping strand of hair behind my ear. "Picking up Nana's stuff was the first step. Getting my shit together was the second."

He cupped my chin with his palm, brushing his thumb against my lips. "I remembered how you used to look at Brian, how your eyes would fill with admiration. I remembered you telling me once that you wanted your happily ever after, that you wanted it to be with him.

"When I was alone, I would wish that maybe someday, I could live up to those expectations, be that man who deserved you, be the man you'd be proud to have. I would think that maybe you could have that same look in those pretty green eyes just for me. I thought maybe I'd get lucky one day, and at the end of it all, I would be the one to give you that happily ever after ending. I wanted to be your other half, your better half. I wanted to be the man who made you happy.

"Because you believed in me, I took a chance. I took a leap of faith in myself, believing that I could be that guy you deserved. I wanted to be the one you could look at every day, wake up to every morning, and be proud of. That's why I got it together, and I took the job."

A small smile touched his lips. "Who knew that my whole world could be changed by one unbelievably beautiful girl? You're the one girl who occupies my dreams, who lives in my heart, and who owns my very soul. You're that one girl who has changed my everything, everything that I thought was all right to everything that is better. You're the one girl who I'm so in love with that I can't see straight."

He bent down to brush his lips against mine. It was a soft kiss, but nevertheless, it was a kiss that stirred butterflies in the pit of my belly.

He pulled back and brushed his hand against the gold on my neck. "I told Pete not to let you know that it was me. I have the rest of the stuff in our storage."

I opened the locket of Nana and Papa. He had given her the locket on their twenty-fifth anniversary just before he'd passed away. They looked so in love. My chest ached at the memory of them.

"This is the best gift I've ever received," I said, wrapping my arms around him. "Thank you." I kissed him lightly on the lips.

"You're the best gift I've ever received." He placed his arms around my waist. "And there are better things to come."

WHEN I GOT into the car, Kent blindfolded me. I had no clue where we were headed. I was as giddy as a little girl, anticipating what could top Nana's locket.

I knew we reached our destination when the car stopped. When I stepped out of the Bentley, I felt the gravel under my heels and leaned into Kent for support.

"I'm afraid I'll fall," I said, concentrating on walking straight.

"Don't worry. If you fall, I'll always be there to catch you."

I could feel the smile on his face.

I pinched his side. "Just so you know, you've turned into a cornball on me ever since we got together." I laughed.

"You've changed me. What can I say?"

I no longer felt the wind against my short white linen dress, and that was how I knew we'd stepped into someone's house. I heard hushed chatter around me. Kent stopped and released my hand, and a moment later the chatter ceased. I couldn't help my cheeks from hurting from my smile. My heels clicked on the floor and as Kent lead me down more stairs, I felt the warmth of the sun once again and smiled at the anticipation of my surprise.

We stopped, and I felt Kent's hands move me to face him.

He kissed me lightly on the lips and lifted the blindfold from my eyes. "Surprise," he whispered.

My eyes scanned the area, and once again, I was speechless because of this man. Hydrangeas, roses, and lilies filled Kent's parents' backyard. A trail of rose petals created an aisle leading farther down to a twelve-foot arch outlined with pink and white garden roses and green ivy. At the end of the aisle, four wooden chairs were occupied with the people I loved the most in the world. An officiant stood at the center.

When I glanced down, Kent was on bended knee, and the look on his face took my breath away.

"This year has been amazing. You've made me the happiest man, and I never thought I could love anyone as much as I love you." He reached behind and presented me with a bouquet of wildflowers. "Bethany Marie Casse, will you marry me...again?"

I nodded once, tears forming at the corner of my eyes.

He stood, and I wrapped my arms around him. I pressed my lips against his before he handed me the bouquet.

Walking down the aisle, I closed my eyes briefly and smiled. To everyone else, it was a renewal of our vows, but to me, it was my perfect wedding day.

This day, I felt Nana's presence beside me, around me. It was in the chirping of the birds, the scent of the flowers in the air, and the warmth of the sun on my cheeks. I saw the crinkle of her eyes when she smiled and the wisps of gray and white locks on her head. I felt her wrinkled hands upon me where the breeze brushed against my arms. I felt her surround me, and as tears slowly fell down my face, I realized she would be proud of me today—for what I'd become and for what I'd overcome.

Everyone said they married their soul mate. Not only could I say that, but today, I was truly marrying my best friend.

He reached for my hand at the end of the aisle. Seeing the tears under my eyes, he framed my face with his hands and wiped them away. This time, I didn't pull away.

I looked into the eyes of the man that I loved, and I answered his question before he even had a chance to ask. "I'm crying because I'm so very happy."

THE END

Read about Brian's story and find out if he gets his own happily ever after in The Scheme.

Newsletter

JOIN MY NEWSLETTER

IF YOU ENJOYED this story, please sign up for my newsletter. My newsletter subscribers are the first to know about my upcoming releases and always have a chance to receive an ARC (Advance Review Copies) of my book before it goes live. Also, you just never know when some of these characters will stop by.

You can sign up at www.miakayla.blogspot.com.

Thank You

Thank you so much for taking the time to read and review Marry Me for Money. Reviews for an author are so important so please leave an honest review on the site where you purchased your copy.

Let's keep in touch! Here's where I'll be hanging out:

Facebook
Twitter
Goodreads

And read an excerpt of my novel
The Scheme on the next page

The Scheme

Prologue

"WELCOME TO EVANGELINE'S Psychic Readings. Come in young ones." Evangeline's tone was rough, like she was suffering from a sore throat, though her face was serious.

My voice barely squeaked a greeting. "H-hi, I'm Kendall and . . . this is Beth."

The psychic's eyes perused my cousin before intently locking on mine.

Beads of sweat formed on the back of my neck as anxiety rose within me. As I turned back to her, she reached out, took hold of my hand, and flipped it over, surprising me, then she glanced down at my palm.

With a light fingertip, she traced the lines before her knowing eyes met mine again. It was haunting, like she could see into my soul, which sent shivers down my spine. "Hmmm." She reached for my other hand, flipping it over and staring intently as though memorizing every moment in my life through my skin. "Hmmm."

That was all she said before a wicked smile popped up on her face and she turned toward a curtain of beads, which functioned as a door to another room. "Come on back."

I wrapped my arms around my stomach as nervousness bubbled in my chest.

Everyone knew of Evangeline. She was it, the psychic who knew all. People drove from all over the nation to have their fortune told by this one woman. Not to mention I had saved money from my last two birthdays for my turn with her.

She gestured for me to sit on the red cushioned stool in front of the wooden table for two. Well-worn tarot cards were perfectly placed on the circular table.

The build up to this moment was too much to take. I inhaled deeply taking in the scent of the strong incense coming from her candles that lit up the room. I peered back at Beth, who stood by the curtain as I sat down. She wasn't a believer, but I appreciated that she was here for moral support. Though this was about me and my future, I needed her here. I hoped her lack of faith didn't block any truth waiting for me in the stars.

Evangeline patted the top of my hand resting on the table. "Relax, child." Her gray eyes fixed me with a stare. "I know what you came here for." She said it with such certainty that, for the first time in a very long time, hope filled my veins and a lightness spread throughout my limbs. "You want to know what the immediate future holds for your mother."

I released a calming breath at her words, because that

was only one of the reasons I'd come.

"More importantly," she continued, "you want to know your own future and I—" An eerie, knowing grin spread across her face. "—know exactly how it will unfold."

Acknowledgments

AH! IT'S DONE. First and foremost, I'd like to thank my God. I thank him for my eyes for reading, my mind for creating, my hands for typing, and my heart for loving.

I fall in love when I see my children's faces, when my husband holds my hand, and every time my fingers hit the keyboard while I'm writing about people falling in love. I have a super cheesy smile every time I'm writing about these characters, and I'm glad I am finally able to share my stories with readers.

When I started this journey, it was a lonely road at first. I didn't know a single writer, so I joined every writer group out there, trying to connect on a level my friends couldn't understand. When I finally met my first writer friend, Mary, I clung to her in an almost stalker-like fashion, trying to retain as much as I could about the craft and the whole business side of things. She was the first to read my manuscript before it was even in a beta-ready form, and I'll never forget her kindness.

To all the beta readers after that—Jade, Cynthia, Sue and Teri—Thank you for your constructive feedback and your second glances that helped me get this story out to the world.

To Kerianne, Jennifer, Joy and Amanda—Thank you for giving this manuscript one last look before it went to copyediting and formatting.

The writing community is such a welcoming and helpful community.

To all the online communities that I've stalked for knowledge and to the Divas and Divos on RD—It's because of you that I've met some wonderful people—one being, Sera Bright. Even though every writer's journey is his or her own, it's great to have someone who is going through a similar process at the same time, someone to vent and to bond over the same struggles.

I cannot forget the bloggers. Bloggers are the key to readership, and these bloggers have helped me dearly.

To the people I've coined as the Awesome As— Autumn from The Autumn Review and Andrea from The Bookish Babes—Where do I even begin? Thanks for helping me through the whole promoting process, for answering all my questions, and for pimping out my book. Autumn, thanks for reading my story and giving me the feedback needed to take it to the next step. Seriously, both of you have been the greatest.

To my editing team, I stand and applaud you. Because of you, my manuscript is polished and ready for the world to see. Jovana, you are truly a rock star at what you do! You don't miss a single thing with your supersonic eyes. Thank you for having patience with me and for answering every single one of my questions.

To Kayla Robichaux, I thank you. The first time I ever corresponded with Kayla on Facebook, I was freaking out on the train. True story. She added me as a friend, and I totally went crazy writer on her. I think I was suffering my first ever panic attack about the whole book thing. All my friends were nowhere to be found, and my husband was busy with the kids.

I believe the first thing she wrote was, *Team Kent*.

I responded with, *OMG, I'm freaking out here. Did you read it? Is the story okay?*

She calmly said, *I want you to take your earlobes and rub them.*

Even though I was on the train, I did. Ha! I think because it was such a silly move, I ended up laughing. Anyway, thanks, Kayla, for your kind words that day because I needed that boost of confidence at that exact moment to keep me going.

To all you readers, just so you know, Kent and Beth's love scene at the end was not originally in my first version. I added it because Kayla specifically said, *You're leaving your readers hanging. Trust me on this one.*

And I did.

I cannot forget Becky Johnson and her flipping awesome team at Hottree Editing. Thanks for all you do. Your team rocks to the utmost degree. You're just so sweet and thorough. Your team doesn't miss a thing. I think you're one of the very few editors who sends the manuscript for post-beta reads, and let me tell you, I needed those post-beta readers.

Only a writer would be able to understand the insecurities and struggles of the journey of writing. There are very few people in the world who I believe have the kindest of hearts—someone who's not friends with you to get something in return, but someone who wants to help you because she was on a similar journey.

Elisabeth Grace, I heart you in the biggest way. Your books are amazing, but even more than that, you're an amazing person. I hope all good things in life happen to you because I truly believe that good things happen to good people. Just your kind words and your willingness to answer all my many questions are amazing. You're just a great person, who is continuously giving back to this writing community. Thanks for introducing me to the Indie Chicks. You've introduced me to a great group of girls, and for that, I am forever grateful.

I have a great support system behind me. Women bond with other women on a level that men will never understand. Although I have my husband—who is a real Mr. Mom, my rock, and my best friend—he just can't empathize with my womanly issues.

To Nui—Thank you for being the very first one of my friends to read this. Thanks for your feedback, and most of all, thank you for your support. I can always count on you and your positive outlook on every situation. You are the friend who understands my love for food, and I have brought some of that into Beth's story. I can always count on you to help me search for the best brownie ice cream sundae and then be the one to initiate a diet the next day. Ha! I love you, girl.

To Debbie—Words can't explain how much I owe you. I know I'm an *askhole* most of the time, but you should know your advice on business and on life are very important to me. You're a whiz on branding and social media, and I value your advice. Thank you for reading my manuscript, for your feedback, and most of all, for your friendship. I love you in ways no words can express, and I hope to grow very old with you, so we can party like rock stars way into our sixties when our kids are off on their own.

To Melanie—Thanks for your feedback and for reading my book. As I continue on this writing journey, I know you'll be my number one fan. You make me laugh so hard that I'm almost to the point of peeing in my pants as a grown adult. You're the greatest, Mel. Not only are you one of my BFFs, but you are also my BBF (best book friend). You're the friend who took me to Forks to see where Twilight began, and I will never forget that trip—ever. I love how we bond over books and over the hot human men who play our fictional characters on the big screen. My heart will forever belong to Edward Cullen, but today, I'm a Four whore.

And to my husband—I love him, I love him, I love him. He is the epitome of every book boyfriend but in real life. He's my muse when it comes to the sweet stories I write about. This is the man who apologizes by spelling *Sorry* with Kit Kats. He came in and swooped me up, capturing my heart when my heart had been left broken. He's been there ever since, giving me three lovely children and a life truly full of happily ever afters.

I do believe everything happens for a reason. You meet people, and they enter your life at a certain time. When my husband entered mine, I was crying about another man.

He said, "What does he have that I can't give you?"

And the rest is history.

61098508R00215

Made in the USA
Lexington, KY
28 February 2017